BEAU

Dedicated with all the love in the world (as always) to Matthew Waller, Sian Waller and Kirsty Waller, my inspirational children.

BOOK ONE

1952 – 1964 North Cornwall

CHAPTER ONE

July 1952

She wheeled her shiny blue dolls pram across the grass; he watched. His eyes narrowed to slits as he struggled against the brightness of the sun's rays. He followed every movement she made, wondering what it would feel like to touch the long blonde hair that he had sometimes seen in a tight pony tail and at odd times long and flowing, swinging loosely around her shoulders.

That's how he preferred to see her, hair long and free, thistledown soft. He imagined it tumbling gently, lightly, through his fingers as she smiled innocently up into his face, the slow motion effect of his dream adding to his anticipation.

And then he would take her, throw her small immature body down on to the grass; use her. Not love her - no, he didn't want to love her, just hurt her, hurt her, hurt her and hear her scream.

Sometimes, in the dark hours of the night when his brain would search frantically for answers, when he felt almost sane, he would wonder why it had to be a little girl rather than a woman he would find release with.

He knew why it had to be that particular little girl. She was beautiful, the prettiest of all the children who played in the park. Once or twice she had even smiled at him. Those blue innocent eyes had rested on his face, the pretty mouth lifting at the edges - and he knew she was offering herself to him.

She stopped and bent over the pram, laying the hood flat with a gentle push of her hand. Pulling back the covers she lifted out the doll and put it over her shoulder, patting its back and talking to it. Using one hand she carefully placed a small yellow cover over the pram handle, straightened the small sheet inside the pram and began to hum softly.

Then she bent its legs to replace it in the pram in a more upright position, all the time carrying on the one sided conversation. Words drifting on the breeze told him that she had named the doll Patty but then her voice was lost to him as she continued to walk across the grass heading for the thicker undergrowth.

He stood. He knew he would never get a better opportunity.

CHAPTER TWO

Autumn 1952

Words collected, lingered around her; words like uterus, sterility, rape, fading in and out of her consciousness as she slowly began to wake up to a world that, for her, had changed forever. The watchers around her bed saw her occasionally shake her head. They had no idea that the words they were saying were hovering around her like buzzing insects that wouldn't go away.

Her mother's tear-stained, ravaged face was always there at her bedside along with the dozens of teddies and dolls that assorted well wishers had sent. None of them took the pain away. She couldn't understand why her mother was crying - it was *her* tuppence that hurt so much so why did her mother have to cry? Surely her tears were enough?

She wondered what "ruined for life" meant but soon dismissed the thought. There were so many other words. All she really wanted to do, at least for the first four days, was sleep. Sleep obliterated the horror, stopped her smelling the beery breath, the fetid odour of him as he had crushed her young body into the bracken in the woods surrounding the playing fields. Sleep stopped her tasting the rough skin of his hand that reeked of cigarettes, the hand he had held across her mouth as he had pushed some huge part of him into her tuppence. She hadn't been able to cry then; not then.

When her eyes eventually opened and stayed open she realised that everything was white. The walls, glaring in their white brilliance, the nurses in their stiff white aprons and stiffer white caps, the doctors in their white coats; everything was painfully white to her distraught young brain. She hated it. She wanted to go home to her own little flowery bedroom, to the familiarity of the sloping roof, her bed with its bedspread that matched the curtains - she didn't want this awful blankness. They gave in to her every wish except that one, saying she couldn't go home; she had to get better first. She raged inside that they couldn't see that she would get better at home.

She didn't know what they had done to her, just how much of her had had to be removed.

They finally got around to telling her the man had been caught in an empty house.

'Amelia, sweetheart,' Brenda Andrews began, the tremble in her voice telling her husband that what was to come would not be easy. 'The man who hurt you – the police caught him and shot him.'

Jack took hold of his daughter's small hand but she pulled it away from him. He looked towards Brenda and then moved behind her chair.

Amelia stared for a moment at her mother then said 'Shot him?'

'Yes, love, he's dead.'

Brenda sent up a silent prayer to the God she had always believed would keep her daughter safe, asking for forgiveness for the lie. They had talked late into the night about the best way to handle the problem. Treverick pleading guilty and giving a full confession meant Amelia never needed to know what had happened to him.

'Dead like Spot?' she asked.

'Dead like Spot,' Brenda echoed, breathing a sigh of relief that they had explained that they would never see the little dog again.

She stared at a poster fixed to the wall for long

moments and then said,

'Good'. Her eyes closed and she once again slept.

She didn't want her daddy near her in case he wanted to push his

thingy in her just like that man had. She liked the nurses but they quickly had to replace the male doctor with Doctor Jane, as soon as they realised his approach signaled an eruption of tears..

The nurses were the ones who changed her name. Until the assault, she had been Amelia; the nurses called her Amy and she liked it much better.

'Can I always be called Amy, Mummy?' she asked her mother. And so Amy it was.

When Amy left hospital, stitched back together by surgeons skilled in repairing adult women and thankful they didn't normally have to do the same for a child, it seemed that all the nursing staff were on the hospital steps to wave her off. Many were in tears, all aware of what the young body had had so brutally inflicted on it - and just how much of her was no longer there. She would never have a daughter of her own to duplicate her prettiness, never experience the pain and thrill of childbirth.

She had been a good patient, a real hit with the staff with her long blonde hair and eyes that were sometimes blue, sometimes green. As her parents left with her in the taxi, they hoped the mental scars would heal as fast as her body was healing.

'Amy, sweetheart, we think you should go back to school next week.'

Her mother looked tentatively at her unsure how to handle this potential problem. She wasn't the same little girl and they had been warned to expect that but it was still hard not to hold her, cuddle her - and Jack felt it most of all. He wasn't allowed to carry her up to bed at night fireman fashion over his shoulder, read her a story, do any of the things they had done before the attack. Brenda knew he felt shut out completely from their normal life and she didn't know what to do about it.

'Give it time,' the family doctor had said, 'she'll come to accept him again.'

Amy lifted her head from the colouring book and looked at her mother. 'Okay.' No emotion, no disagreement.

Brenda sighed. *Why them? Why Amelia?* Their daughter had always been a free spirit, lively, extrovert - now she was a shell of the little girl she had once been. Amelia would have said, "Aw, Mum, do I have to?" Not, "Okay."

'You feel ready to go back then?'

Amy nodded.

'My tummy doesn't hurt anymore. I suppose I'll be okay.' Her eyes remained fixed on the colouring book, the picture of the parrot completely coloured in black. Brenda leaned over.

'Parrots aren't black, sweetheart. That's ravens and magpies. Look, let me show you, he needs lots of colour.'

'No!' Amy slammed down the black wax crayon. 'Everything's black!' she said angrily, running from the room.

Even the weather was black on Monday morning. Overcast, with no break in the skies. Brenda held firmly on to Amy's hand all the way to school.

The journey seemed shorter than it had in the past. Brenda didn't want to leave Amy. Her footsteps became slower and slower until Amy was pulling her along.

'Now you're sure you feel okay?' she asked several times on the fifteen-minute walk that should have been only ten minutes. Amy looked at her mum without speaking. Of course she would be okay - they were all lady teachers at her school. All except Mr. Mawson, of course, and he didn't count because he was the head teacher. She didn't really have anything to do with him. Ladies didn't stick thingies into tuppences because they didn't have thingies so she would be safe at school. Her mum didn't need to worry at all.

Mr. Mawson, standing in the doorway of his room with his bald head shining in the glare of the overhead electric light, held out his arms.

'Welcome back, Amelia.'

She moved behind her mother, furious that she had brought her to the office instead of taking her to her classroom.

'It's Amy,' she muttered.

He looked at Brenda, his eyebrows raised in query.

'I'm sorry, Mr.Mawson,' she said quietly, feeling quite desperate.

'She...won't tolerate men under any circumstances.' The tears threatened to spill down her cheeks. 'Not even her dad. And she wants to be called Amy from now on, not Amelia.'

'Soon arranged, Amy,' he said cheerfully. 'We're just glad to have you back.' He turned to her mother. 'Are there any special problems we should know about?'

Brenda wanted to scream. She wanted to say yes, the fire in her has died. Instead she said,

'Just don't let her do games or PE for at least six weeks. Her own body will tell her how much running about at playtime she can do.'

He nodded feeling as helpless as Brenda. As soon as

the news of the rape had broken, he had kept in close contact with the family and now felt like a fish gasping for air. Never in his thirty-five years of teaching had he had to deal with such an enormous dilemma. He led the child and the woman from his office and escorted them to Amy's classroom.

Using a repeat action of Henry Mawson's, Claudia Carey held out her arms and Amy ran swiftly to her.

'Aw, Amelia pet, it's good to have you back.' Her soft Teesside accent, mellowed slightly now by the infiltration of a Cornish lilt, was like music to Brenda's ears. She looked at her daughter in Claudia Carey's arms and felt more at ease - she could safely entrust Amy to her until half past three.

'Mrs Carey,' Brenda said quietly, 'it's Amy now, not Amelia.' Claudia Carey lifted her eyes to the woman who was almost exactly the same age yet looked ten years older now and nodded. She tried to smile and wanted to cry.

The boys and girls in the class room sat in silence, watching the scene before them. Most of them knew that a man had attacked Amy but just as Amy couldn't comprehend the word rape, neither could they. They searched for physical evidence of the attack but saw nothing. The bruises to her face, arms and legs had healed, the wounds across her abdomen were almost knit together and no-one would ever see the gashes inside her vagina. She was exactly the same little blonde haired blue-eyed girl they had always known. She didn't look sick, not like their parents had told them she was.

'Amy,' Mrs Carey said, smiling at the little girl who had always been a favourite with her, 'would you like to sit at your desk?'

Amy nodded and moved towards the centre of the room. The children's eyes followed her and she could feel herself going red. Immediately her mind closed down and a mutinous expression crossed her face. Why did they have to look at her? She was no different, only her name had changed. She was still Amelia Rose Andrews and always would be.

She watched her mother and Mrs Carey talking before her mother blew her a kiss and left the room, surreptitiously wiping away a tear.

Brenda felt as though a knife had lodged in her heart as she stumbled away from her only daughter, not seeing the peeling green paint in the corridor or hearing Mr. Mawson's goodbye.

'Right,' Claudia Carey said brightly, 'Now we all want to welcome Amy back to class, don't we children?'

'Yes, Mrs Carey,' they said in unison. She smiled at Amy.

'Amy, the other boys and girls have all made you something.' She clapped her hands. 'Right, everyone take out their cards and hand them to Amy.'

With much clattering of chairs and excited chatter, the children began to leave their desks and move towards Amy. Each one left a card on her desk, welcome back cards they had made as soon as Claudia Carey had learned of the impending return of the little girl. Some children smiled, some stared at her as if she had two heads and some whispered,

'Play with us at playtime?'

Amy suddenly began to feel better as she looked through the cards. It would be good to get back to normal, to play whip and top, hopscotch and sevens again.

Mrs Carey allowed her a few moments to look at her cards, moments in which she too had to mentally adjust. Amy looked the same but she obviously would have changed. She wondered how this would show itself, remembering a child at her previous school who had suffered a severe beating by his father. The man had later died from a brain tumour, which, in retrospect, explained the abnormal behavior but the boy had never recovered mentally from the unprecedented attack. He had become morose, difficult to handle and a bully. She wondered how he was now – he must be thirteen and unless things had changed dramatically he would be a real problem for whichever school he now attended.

The chatter in the classroom subsided instantly as she clapped her hands.

'Right, children, writing books out please,' and she turned to her blackboard to the accompanying sounds of desk lids opening and closing. Amy was back at school.

Playtime was ostensibly the same as always – she remained with the infants on one side of the playground, the juniors congregated on the other, unwilling to mix with "the kids". Occasionally a sibling of one of the infants would wander across but in the main they remained segregated.

Amy stayed by the wall. She had tried playing hopscotch but the jumping had caused her pain. She watched with a degree of surprise as four of the older juniors left the area they normally inhabited and began to infiltrate the infants play area. She felt uneasy, realising they were heading in her direction and began to move slowly along the wall, keeping her back to it, trying to reach the security of the school doors.

One of the boys moved to her right blocking her way into school. The other three ranged themselves around her.

'Okay now, kid?' She recognized Davy Simpson and

flinched. Her mother had told her to have nothing to do with anyone in that family, they weren't very nice. Thugs, she had called them.

She nodded, unable to speak. These were boys and they had thingies. She crossed her arms over her waist afraid that if they hit her it would hurt her scars.

All four of the boys were grinning. She looked around searching for a teacher but saw only the smaller children busy playing with toys or running around. No one was taking any notice of her.

'Tell us what it felt like then, kid.' The speaker this time was Bob Farrow, Davy's constant companion. 'Go on, tell us,' he taunted.

Felt like? What were they talking about? She shivered in spite of the thickness of her coat and pulled her arms tighter round her waist. She wanted her mum, Mrs Carey – anybody, even Mr. Mawson as long as it was an adult.

'Come on,' one of the other boys chimed in, a boy she didn't know. 'Come on,' he repeated, 'had a cock up yer, didn't yer?'

Terror enveloped her as she became aware of two more boys approaching and she sank to the floor. One of the new arrivals grabbed hold of Bob Farrow's hair and threw him to the ground, stamping hard on his hand. Bob let out a yell of shock and pain and tried to get to his feet. John Thornton followed up the hand stamp with a well-aimed foot to Bob's ribcage and the boy, now in considerable pain, rolled over as he attempted to escape from the unexpected assault. Davy, who had been pummeled to the floor by a panting red-faced David Farmer, squashed him.

The first saviour, as Amy now thought of him, turned to the other two boys who were standing mesmerized and held up his hands, his fists clenched.

'Now bugger off,' he said, 'leave the little lass alone, she's gone through enough. An' I'll kill you if I ever see you near her again.' The remaining two boys helped Davy and Bob to stand and rapidly headed back towards the junior area, frequently looking over their shoulders to make sure they weren't being followed.

Amy stared wide-eyed at her two champions. John reached down and took hold of her hand.

'Let me help you up. Are you ok?' She stood and leaned against the wall.

'Yes,' she said, still unable to register what had happened. 'Yes, they didn't touch me.'

'Well, if they bother you again, you tell us.'

She nodded, a worried frown on her face.

'But I can't talk to you. I don't know you and my mum said...'

The taller of the two boys laughed.

'We'll look out for you. My name's John Thornton and this ugly sod is David Farmer. You know us now, so don't forget, if they come near you again, we'll have 'em.' John looked at Amy for a moment as if wondering whether to say anything further or not. 'Look,' he began, 'we... er.... know what happened to you. They're idiots, morons, my mum says, so take no notice. As I said, we'll watch out for you.'

David interrupted.

'Besides,' he grinned at the little girl, 'it gave us a good excuse for bashing them.'

For the rest of the week she was aware of the careful eye kept on her by the two boys. The week after she was conscious of a feeling of disappointment that she didn't see them. It was good that they weren't in school – both had numerous lacerations, black eyes and David had a broken nose.

Davy, Bob, Sam and Stewart had waited patiently until they could take them by surprise and came to understand the true meaning of the proverb they had learnt only that week; revenge is sweet.

Amy began to settle back into school life and the other kids slowly stopped staring at her as if she had two heads. It was tiny Jennifer Wainwright who eventually caused the anger, the tears, the terror.

Jennifer was a pleasant child with a clear melodic voice. At six years of age it seemed as if nature had forgotten to endow her with the necessary hormones for growth, so tiny was she. Everyone, including Amy, liked her and that made it all the more remarkable that she should be the one to open Amy's mind to everything she had suffered.

The whole class was sitting on the floor in the reading corner, listening to the three little pigs. Mrs Carey's voice normally held the attention of the children from beginning to end, grunting squeaking and honking to order but out of the corner of her eye she spotted a movement.

'Jennifer!'

The child looked up guiltily and then a quick smile flashed across her face.

'Sorry, Miss, I was listening, honest.'

'Yes, I realize that Jennifer but what else...yes, Amy?'

'Please, Miss, she was stroking my hair.'

'Stroking your hair? What on earth for?'

Again the smile crossed Jennifer's face.

'Because it's beautiful, isn't it, Miss?'

Beautiful.

The scream seemed to start in Amy's stomach as she

remembered the man hurting her so much she had been unable to cry out – each thrust accompanied by … *'beautiful, beautiful, beautiful'*.

She looked wildly around the classroom then stood and ran, grabbing a pair of scissors from a desk.

For a moment Claudia Carey was immobile, stunned at the speed at which events had got completely out of control.

'Children! Wait here and no talking! I'll just go and find Amy then we'll continue with the story.' She ran from the classroom searching up and down the corridor with her eyes before deciding to head outside. Amy was nowhere in sight and she prayed that she was right in thinking that maybe the child had decided to run home.

The playground was deserted. Rain splattered into the puddles and she shivered as a gust of wind hit her. A door banged and she turned towards the sound. The girls' toilets. She ran, skipping around the ever-deepening patches of water, the heavy rain flattening her hair to her head.

'Amy?' Her voice was soft. 'Amy? Are you in here?' She brushed a raindrop from the end of her nose.

A sob that turned into a hiccup told her that the child was close by and she breathed a sigh of relief.

'Come on, sweetheart, come out and tell me what's wrong.' She tentatively pushed against a door that opened too easily and moved on to the next. The third door remained closed.

'Amy, it's Mrs Carey. Now be a love and let me in so we can talk. Do you want me to send for your mum? Are you hurting somewhere?'

She put her ear to the door and heard muttering.

'Beautiful, ugly, beautiful, ugly, beautiful, ugly' – and then there was a clatter as the small silver scissors fell on to the stone flagged floor.

'Amy?' There was panic in the teacher's voice as her mind visualised the walls and floor splattered with the child's blood. 'What are you doing? Let me in at once...' The door opened abruptly and Amy stood there, tears coursing down her cheeks.

'I'm not beautiful now, am I, Miss?' The long blonde hair lay in swatches all over the floor of the toilet, hacked from her head by the blunt scissors meant only for paper. Tufts stuck up all around her scalp and clumps of hair clung to her wet clothing.

Claudia Carey held out her arms.

'Oh, Amy,' and the little girl moved slowly towards her, tears now flowing unchecked.

'Nobody will put thingies in me now that I'm not beautiful,' she stammered. '*Nobody*!'

She took hold of the teacher's hand and allowed a shattered Claudia Carey to lead her small charge back to the main building.

CHAPTER THREE

Autumn 1954

The man in the grey prison uniform stared morosely into space. Thin almost to the point of emaciation, his clothes hung on him like sacks and his long greasy hair, falling forward to hide a high forehead, added nothing meritorious to his appearance. He had discovered early on in prison life how to make his face a blank, how to hide his thoughts and now it had become a permanent part of him, that vacant staring at the opposite wall.

His bed was hard but he didn't bother moving. The spot six inches away was no more comfortable than where he was sitting now. Occasionally his thoughts turned towards the old red armchair that he had sat in so many times in the empty house, just one piece of furniture in an otherwise bare room.

That chair had been old but wonderfully soft, a haven for nesting mice. He supposed that someone once must have looked at that chair with pride, with its rich red moquette upholstery – beautiful that chair had been, beautiful.

Footsteps moved slowly along the corridor giving advance warning of a meal delivery. He couldn't remember which meal it was. The other prisoners in solitary confinement would receive their food before him; he was in the last cell. Sometimes he regretted being in solitary but mostly he felt comfortable with his own company; he needed the time for formulating plans.

The door opened and a trusty, his red band displayed around his upper arm, moved into the tiny room accompanied by a warder. The warder stood to one side of the door his eyes never leaving Ronald Treverick, as if daring him to make a move.

No words were spoken as the plate containing four slices of bread made into sandwiches was placed on the metal chair. The door clanged shut and the key turned before he made a move towards the food. He felt unusually hungry, eager for the rationed prison fare.

He picked up a sandwich and automatically lifted the top slice. The ball of phlegm lay almost exactly in the middle and he grabbed the plate, hurling it at the opposite wall.

'Fucking Andrews kid,' he screamed. 'One fucking day I'll have the whole bastard family,' and he picked up the metal chair, throwing it to follow the flight path of the plate. 'One fucking day...' he repeated.

The warder and the trusty guard turned and smiled at each other. Another successful mealtime accomplished.

CHAPTER FOUR

Autumn 1954

'But it's not normal, Jack.'

He looked up with an air of resignation from the newspaper he had been trying to read for ten minutes without success and, removing his glasses, calmly surveyed his wife's lined face. She had aged in the two years since Amy had been attacked and every second was etched into her features. She looked ten years older than her true age of thirty.

'Of course it's normal – well, for some children it is. Some children are naturally tidy… we've just been fortunate with Amy. Thank your lucky stars that she does put everything away when she's finished playing with it, it cuts down your work.' He tried to soften his words with a smile but realised the attempt to defend the actions of his daughter sounded aggressive. These days he was always making excuses for Amy, even if only to himself.

What made matters worse was that he knew Brenda was right. Admitting it openly was another thing altogether. Amy's face, a face that so very rarely creased up into a smile, floated through his mind as if some hidden hand was dragging her momentarily across his life. He gave an involuntary shiver.

'But that's just it, Jack, she doesn't play with things – she just tidies up all the time, everything in neat little rows. Even her dressing table set isn't arranged prettily. It's laid out like soldiers along the back of the dressing table. And all I can get out of the doctor is give it time. Give it time, I've given it time.' Her voice rose hysterically. Brenda Andrews felt that she couldn't cope with the rest of her life and she turned her troubled face to her husband.

Jack hurriedly dropped the newspaper and moved to her side. The pain in her voice caused panic inside him. Brenda had always been the rock and he feared for all of them if she gave in.

'Now come on, love, don't let this get you down, not now. We're over the worst, Amy's recovering well, and…'

'Amy is not recovering well,' she retorted angrily, 'there's something very, very wrong with our little girl and only I can see it! You know how she used to love playing with Patty, that little doll – now she won't even look at any of her dolls. She won't get the doll's pram out, won't even look at her bike. It's like she's forgotten how to play, Jack.'

Jack pulled his distraught wife close, kissing the top of her head. 'Brenda, stop it. Amy will be in soon and she won't want to see you upset. Shall we have a cup of tea?'

'That's your answer to everything, isn't it? A cup of tea? No, I don't want a bloody cup of tea, I want a double brandy!'

'You don't drink.' He smiled down into her bloodless face.

'I just started – and don't be so damn calm. I'm frightened, Jack, really frightened.'

The door opened quietly and Amy let herself in.

'Aunt Freda is just locking the car,' she explained.

She moved towards the fire and knelt to warm her hands.

'Well?'

Amy turned to look at her mother.

'Well what? Oh – the swimming? Yes, it was good. I can swim a full length now.'

A curse from outside the door told them Freda

Andrews was about to enter the kitchen and the door burst open with a loud bang.

'Bloody cat,' she complained grumpily. 'Fell over it, soddin' animal.'

Brenda smiled at her sister in law, grateful to her for lightening the tension.

'Well, that's one way of making a grand entrance, Freda. And how's the cat?'

'Dead, I hope,' she said and Amy's eyes widened in horror.

'Aunt Freda!'

'Oh, sorry, pet, I didn't really mean that. Perhaps I just broke its back legs. Or crushed its spine. Here Amy, put these somewhere,' and she handed her niece a towel and swimming costume, both smelling overpoweringly of chlorine.

Brenda wrinkled her nose.

'Disgusting smell, I'll put them to soak. Will you stay for something to eat, Freda? We're having meat and potato pie and there's plenty.'

'No thanks, Brenda, good of you to ask but I must go. Got a game of Bridge tonight.' Her short clipped way of speaking perfectly matched her countryside appearance. Dressed in tweeds with sensible brown brogues encasing her large feet, she looked a true stereotype of landed gentry. In reality she was a doctors receptionist, unmarried, and, as she said, likely to remain that way. Men, she was frequently heard to remark, were alright in their proper place – preferably down a coal mine, never allowed to see the light of day.

She headed for the door and Brenda said a silent prayer for the cat to have disappeared. Moving towards the sink she had a sudden premonition that Freda was hesitating, worried about something, and she paused.

'Er... got a minute, Brenda?'

Brenda turned her head, concerned more by Freda's unaccustomed reluctance to speak bluntly than by her not immediately going out of the door.

'Yes, sure; problem?'

With a swift movement of her head and a glance across at the kneeling Amy, Freda indicated that Brenda should go outside with her. Brenda grabbed hold of a cardigan as protection against the cool of the evening and hurriedly followed the older woman outside.

Standing by the car, again Freda seemed ill at ease.

'What is it, Freda?'

'I, er, oh, hell. Look, I hate to put any more on your shoulders but have you seen Amy's chest?'

'Amy's chest? What are you on about, for goodness sake?'

'Look Brenda I'm only telling you because I love that child dearly and I'm worried. When we came out of the baths we went into separate cubicles and after I'd dried myself I realised I hadn't brought my talc. I wrapped my towel round me and popped my head round the curtain of Amy's cubicle.' She paused while she collected her thoughts, unused to making such long speeches. A long minute passed before she spoke again. Brenda waited patiently knowing that Freda would speak in her own good time and sod the rest of the world.

'She was sitting right in the corner of the cubicle, nothing on her at all, pinching herself on the chest. Oh Bren, the top half of her is black and blue... don't say you haven't seen it!'

Brenda shook her head miserably.

'No, she doesn't allow us near the bathroom now, says she's too grown up.'

'I don't think she even realised I was there. I helped

her to stand and toweled her down because she seemed blank. I dressed her but the funny thing is that when she's got her vest or her swimming costume on you can't see anything. It's as if she knows where to hurt herself without anyone knowing about it. Once I'd dressed her she seemed to snap out of the trance and she just sat quietly waiting for me to get ready. It... scared me, Bren.'

'And it's scared me too,' Brenda said quietly. 'Thanks for telling me. What on earth do I do about this? Where do I turn to for help?' Despair was etched into her voice.

'It's called self-mutilation, Brenda. You have to find somewhere to turn. I'll ring you tomorrow and we can discuss it further.'

Initially Brenda sought the help from school, from Claudia Carey in particular. The teacher, although no longer teaching Amy's class, maintained very close contact with the young child. She was aware of something inherently not right with Amy and hoped to be there when the issue finally surfaced and the volcano erupted.

'Bruises? On her chest?' The look of consternation on her face was unmistakable. 'No, I haven't seen them and I'm sure none of the teaching staff have. It would have been mentioned, you would have been contacted.'

Brenda sighed.

'We just don't know what to do. I'm afraid of approaching her. She closes down if she suspects we're prying. Surely she shouldn't be like that at eight years old?'

'She's not the same as most eight year olds, is she? How many have been through what she's been through? But having said that, I think you've got to pry. In fact I think someone with expertise in the field should do the prying. I don't know what else to suggest.' She shrugged her shoulders miserably.

'What's her behavior like at school? Is there anything you're keeping from us?'

Claudia smiled.

'She's too good. Never have anything to complain about, she sticks by all the rules, answers when she's spoken to but never actually volunteers anything. Sometimes I want to shake her, to bring back Amelia and tell Amy to bugger off!'

'I know exactly what you mean. I'm going to do something about it. I'm going to see our doctor and tell him he's got to refer me somewhere. We can't go on without help.'

The paediatric psychiatrist saw them as a family, as individual parents and then Amy on her own. The little girl puzzled him and he talked at length with her about the pinches, the bruises, asked her why everything had to be in such neat, orderly rows. He didn't really receive adequate answers but he knew she understood what he was saying; she was a good little girl, very sweet. His notes confirmed that opinion and he felt sure given time, Amy would put the rape to the back of her mind and her original personality would resurface. Given time.

Eight visits later he pronounced Amy cured.

'I don't think you have much to worry about, Mr. and Mrs Andrews,' he said. 'Amy has just had to adjust to the turmoil in her life and she's now coping very well. Aren't you, Amy?'

Amy said nothing.

'Now, I don't think I'll need to see you again unless any new problems crop up, so...' and he stood, extending his hand. Jack shook it and they moved towards the door.

'And I might just say that Amy is a very beautiful

little girl, a credit to both of you.'

Amy's spine visibly stiffened and she turned to face the man.

'It's Amelia,' she snarled and ran from the room.

The sun was still high overhead when Amy and her parents returned from the psychiatrist. Brenda felt happier but, if questioned, Jack would have admitted to feeling no easier than before they had taken Amy for counseling.

'Can I go outside, Mummy?'

Brenda nodded and smiled at her daughter. She gave an automatic reaction.

'Don't go too far, sweetheart,'

Amy went into the utility room and looked at the dolls pram that hadn't been out of the house for two years. She walked slowly over to it and pushed down the hood. Her doll, her Patty, was asleep, the tiny eyes closed because of its horizontal position. She picked it up and the eyes opened, bright blue eyes that stared into hers. She held Patty for a moment and then slammed her back down into the pram. Pulling it along by the handle she backed out of the utility room and manoeuvred it through the front door. Leaving it standing on the path she returned to the room to collect the rest of the stuff that she needed.

The sun beat on the back of her head as she walked down the lane nonchalantly pushing the pram with one hand; the other hand was tucked into the pocket of her dungarees, her fingers stroking the box of matches. It was only a five-minute walk to the playing field and she could see across to the playground area where two children sat on the swings. She nodded her head, happy that she was alone. She had known she would be.

She wheeled the pram across the grass retracing her walk of two years earlier and stopped at the spot where he had caught her. She had thought he was nice. He had seemed friendly enough whenever he had spoken to her but that day she sensed he was different. She stood quietly letting the heat of the sun warm her although her body, her mind, felt icily cold as the memories the psychiatrist had regurgitated flooded back.

She felt *his* presence and fear hurtled over her for a second.

'But he's dead,' she whispered. 'Dead, dead, dead.' And slowly some of the fear left her.

She removed the pile of newspapers from underneath Patty and began to roll each individual sheet into loose balls placing them carefully in the bottom of the pram.

When all of them were neatly lined up in straight rows she took out a match and struck it. Her movements were stilted, her mind blanked out to everything but what she was doing. The paper caught immediately and within seconds the pram was fully alight.

She picked Patty up from the ground, stared at her with pure hatred for a moment and threw the tiny doll on to the burning pram.

'You did it, Patty.' She spoke in a low voice, the words directed at the doll. 'If you hadn't wanted me to bring you for a walk he couldn't have done it. You did it! You did it!'

The flames grew higher as the soft-bodied doll ignited and somewhere, a long, long way off she thought she could hear children screaming.

And then there were arms thrown around her, dragging her away from the searing heat.

'Amy, oh Amy, love. What are you doing?'

The child continued to stare into the flames that were starting to die down.

'Leave me alone, Aunty Freda, leave me alone. I'm killing Patty. She's got to die, just like him.'

Freda looked at the conflagration with horror.

'Patty? You mean your little doll? Oh Amy, how could you? Do your mum and dad know you're here?'

'No. Please leave me, Aunty Freda.' Amy's voice was low, speaking with a maturity that far surpassed her years.

'I will not leave you, young lady,' Freda countered, trying to decide what she ought to do next. Amy was obviously a million miles away and intent on revenge in some form or another. She wondered what on earth had happened at that morning's session to provoke such a reaction in her young niece and she flinched at once more being the bearer of bad news for Jack and Brenda.

Taking the child's arm she pulled her away from the flames.

'And I say you're coming with me. Come on, you're frightening those little ones on the swings.'

Suddenly Amy deflated. It was almost a physical action and when Freda attempted to explain it to Brenda and Jack later that night she said it was just as if she had stuck a pin in her and the air had escaped.

Amy nodded.

'Alright, I'll go home now. She's dead. That's all I wanted.' She lowered her head and began the walk back across the playing fields, the face of *him* locked into her mind. And in that moment she somehow knew that it would always be like that – his face there, lurking in a corner of her brain.

Amy's ashen face told Brenda that she was exhausted.

'Come on,' she said gently. 'Let's have you in bed for

an hour. It won't hurt.'

She obeyed, all the fight seemingly knocked out of her. Freda was able to tell the worried parents exactly what had happened.

'I saw her light the match,' she said. 'Even then I didn't really click what was happening. And all the time I was running across that damn field I was shouting her name but she never once turned round. I don't think she even heard me; she was absolutely locked into that fire. She just wanted to kill Patty. That was all I could get out of her.'

'That psychiatrist chap upset her,' Jack said slowly.

'Huh?' Freda looked puzzled.

'Don't get me wrong when I say upset her. I'm blessed if I know how. He actually complimented her, said something about us having a beautiful daughter but she was livid. Snapped his head off, she did. She said she was Amelia, not Amy, so he must really have said the wrong thing. She stormed out of his office and we had to really run to catch up with her. And she never said a word on the way home – must have been planning this, I suppose.'

Brenda, refusing to allow her optimism to be squashed flat, shook her head.

'No, I think she's just tired. We'll see how long she sleeps. You'll see, when she wakes up, she'll be a different girl.'

She didn't wake until long after her parents had gone to bed; Brenda told Jack she knew it was just because of tiredness.

The child certainly wasn't tired at two AM when her eyelids finally fluttered and stayed open. She climbed from her bed and then, in the velvety blackness of the early hours, Amelia carefully arranged all her dolls in a neat and tidy line along her windowsill. She crept downstairs, not wanting to wake her parents, and returned holding the sharp little knife her mother used for peeling potatoes.

Picking each doll up in turn, she hacked at it until all of them were only just recognizable as dolls.

'Beautiful, ugly, beautiful, ugly, beautiful, ugly,' she said, keeping time with each slash of the knife. As the last doll was completely dismembered she sat back, resting on her heels and looking at the damage she had inflicted. Plastic limbs were everywhere, soft-bodied dolls torn apart, their white interiors spewing out like cotton wool entrails; the heads were neatly gathered together and lined up on the windowsill.

'There,' a note of satisfaction crept back into her voice, 'now I'm Amy again.'

The following day Brenda Andrews gathered all the dolls into a pile and burnt them on the bonfire. She could think of nothing to say to Amy and Jack had shrugged his shoulders, afraid to admit his only child, this most precious human being, could be so flawed.

Brenda spoke only one sentence.

'He said she was fine, Jack, he said she was fine.'

CHAPTER FIVE

August 1956

Two days of continuous rain had left the ground with a boggy, springy feel to it. Jack didn't mind in the least – he knew that the weeds grew faster than the plants after summer rain and the damp ground made it easy to uproot them.

His tanned, weathered face smiled in appreciation of what he had. Stonebrook Cottage was enclosed by a large area of land which they had turned into a thriving market garden business. The ground was flat surrounding the cottage and a couple of outbuildings, gradually climbing towards a field owned by a neighbour at the top end of their property. Jack wasn't rich but being comfortable was all that mattered to him – and Brenda and Amy. He made a good, honest living from the land but what Jack regarded as the biggest bonus was that he enjoyed his work and never really thought of it as that; more a paying hobby than employment.

Great Uncle Arnold had left the property and land to Brenda. Their first reaction had been to sell it – Jack had had a good job on the railways and they had just started paying a mortgage on their own little house down in Wadebridge.

Brenda had known nothing of the property until the actual reading of the will because although Uncle Arnold had always said he 'would see her alright' she had assumed she would receive a small behest. The large cottage was a big surprise and immediately they had fallen in love with it, seeing its potential as a family home for the three or four children they planned to have.

Uninhabited for a long time, the cottage had smelt

strongly of damp but after opening all the windows, they had made the plans to put their own tiny home on the market. Situated about two miles outside Padstow they knew it was their idyll. They could see through the damp, through the old fashioned wallpapers and dark brown paint, through the antiquated kitchen. It was close enough to the coast for easy outings yet far enough away from the salt spray that was so troublesome to plants; they said yes to Padstow and no to Wadebridge.

The roses and wisteria climbing around the door and wall hid a multitude of faults but it didn't matter. Jack had taken one look at the land that came with it and decided that this was what he wanted to do; he would grow market produce.

Brenda hadn't taken him seriously at first but then when the jokes about washing mud instead of soot out of his clothes had become more serious, he had known she was giving the idea her full consideration.

Initially, he had tried to hold down his job and work the land in his spare time but when Brenda had become pregnant he had decided to throw in the towel. He had left his job and devoted himself full time to his newly opened business. He loved every minute of it and worked long days constantly planting, replanting, harvesting and delivering. With the advent of the stall at the end of the lane Brenda too was tied up for long stretches at a time during the daylight hours. Their days were busy, full and happy, especially after the birth of Amelia.

Now, Jack looked across at his ten-year-old daughter and sighed. He knew that the psychiatrist had been wrong when he said there was nothing to be concerned about with Amy. She was a constant worry to him.

He kept his thoughts to himself. Brenda had enough to concern herself with without having the burden of his fears. One of the considerations when deciding what to do about the cottage had been the fact that it would be safe for their children, tucked away as it was down a lane – no cars to run up and down, plenty of space for them to play, a playing field at the bottom of the lane... his anger rose like bile in his throat as he thought of the playing field.

And of course there had been no more children. They had reached a point in their lives when a second child was on the cards until that afternoon when their world changed forever. Then, they had both known Amy would always be the only one.

Amy had only ventured back into the garden this year. Right from the start she had been allocated her own little piece of land, about twelve feet square in which, as a three year old child she had grown carrots, beetroot and many flowers. She had loved the speed with which Virginia stock had appeared, the dainty colours of their flowers and the glorious splash of colour created by the calendulas.

She was an enthusiastic little gardener, meticulously cleaning the miniature tools that Jack had fashioned for her, repeating everything her daddy did. She loved working with him and had learnt the names of most of the flowers. They talked, they laughed and the hours he spent with his small daughter passed all too quickly.

Jack gritted his teeth at the thought of what Ronald Treverick had taken from him. He watched the new, more mature Amy bend over and remove a weed. That weed had no place in the well-ordered routine of her little garden. He was almost able to read her mind. She no longer scattered seeds – everything now was in neat orderly rows, each plant having an equal distance between them, the soil crumbled to a fine tilth. Her brain allowed for no disorder and sometimes he could almost hear her tut of disapproval if he planted something where it really shouldn't go. He noticed how she was growing, her own tools now too small in her hand and he resolved to have a look at them.

It was good to see her with the gardening equipment instead of pen and paper and he wondered, not for the first time, why she always refused to let them see her stories and poems, particularly in view of her excellent school reports that praised her creativity in English. He suspected that the darkness in her showed in her writing and sometimes he felt tempted to go into her room and take a look. But he knew if he did that he wouldn't be able to face her – her privacy was sacrosanct.

If only she would talk to him as she had done in times that seemed so long ago. He moved over towards the thick hawthorn hedge and stared in disgust at the invasive bindweed. The flowers were pretty; the stems and roots lethal as they tried to strangle his plants. Amidst muttered curses he began to once more pull out as much of the root as possible, a chore he did regularly with no lasting effect.

Amy turned and looked over towards her father. She could hear the vague grumbles as he talked to himself and she smiled. Sometimes she felt she could almost begin to love him like she used to when they were working like this, but she sensed it was silly to risk letting him know that. He was a man.

Her glance swept around the acre of land, taking in the vegetables, the rose garden her mother tended and the flower garden. The flowers sold really well on her mother's stall positioned at the bottom of the lane leading to the cottage and she wondered if she should ask her dad if she could cut some herself. He didn't usually let anyone touch them but himself, but maybe, just this once...

'Dad?'

Jack almost lost control of the pipe protruding from the left side of his mouth. Intent on vanquishing the bindweed, he was lost in his own world and Amy's voice startled him.

'Sweetheart?'

'Can I cut some flowers to take down to the stall?'

He almost said *no, better not, you might not get the lengths right* and then stopped himself. *What was he thinking?* It was the first time she had made any sort of approach to him with regard to the garden and he was not about to refuse her.

'You surely can, pet. That'll save me a job. Want me to show you what to cut?'

She nodded. He walked to the end of the field where the many different kinds of flowers grew and began to point out the ones she could cut.

'Now,' he said, 'take care to cut the stems as close to the base of the plant as you can, don't cut any that are too small – give them the chance to grow – and make them into bunches of twelve flowers if you think you can do that. If not, just take the whole lot down to mum and she'll bunch them. Give her something to do,' he joked, 'sitting on her backside all day at that stall.'

She didn't smile and Jack groaned inside. He couldn't get through to her at all. 'Okay, sweetheart, think you can manage?'

She nodded, taking the flower cutters from him. Jack didn't make the mistake of staying to watch if she did it correctly; he never doubted for a minute that they would be cut in the proper way, each flower an exact length to match the others.

He picked up his spade and viciously rammed it into

the ground. Perhaps a spot of double digging would help cure the rage he felt inside.

He knew it wouldn't cure it, but it would give him temporary release.

'How's Amy?'

Freda's abrupt tone brought Brenda to her feet. She had been nearly asleep in her deckchair behind the stall, the warm sun working its charm on her and hadn't heard Freda approach.

She rubbed her eyes.

'Oh, hello, Freda. Sorry, didn't hear you. To be perfectly honest, I was just about asleep,' she added with a grin. 'Amy's fine... well, sort of, anyway.'

'More problems?'

Brenda shook her head.

'No, I don't think so. She's just so... oh, I don't know what it is. Uncommunicative. She only speaks to us when we speak to her, never actually volunteers any information and anything about school, I have to drag out of her. We're hoping she'll change when she moves to the big school.'

'What are her chances?'

Her class teacher and her head teacher have virtually told me to get the uniform for Wadebridge Grammar but if she doesn't feel like passing the eleven plus, then she damn well won't. You know Amy; it all depends on how she feels on the day. She's more than capable of sailing through it but will she bother? I try to avoid talking about it, so there's no pressure coming from us. When she goes back to school after this summer holiday, she's in the last year of junior school and that will be pressure enough.'

'And what do you want? Is she likely to be the only one to pass? There's only nine in the class, didn't you say?'

'Only eight now, since the Johnsons moved to Bude. Mr. Mawson says there are only two of them that stand any sort of chance, Amy and Sonia Dawes. But I did hear that Sonia's mum doesn't want her to go to a grammar school, she wants her in the new secondary school. Amy could be on her own.'

'Have you told her that?'

'No, as I said, we daren't say anything at the moment. We'll leave it till nearer the time. Oh, speak of the Devil…'

'Not a devil, Brenda,' Freda said, a slight frown crossing her face, 'not yet anyway.'

They both turned to greet Amy as she wheeled a barrow down the lane, overflowing with flowers. The bundles were compact, precise in length and Brenda smiled with pleasure.

'Well done, love. These look smashing. This could be your job from now on, you know. Has your dad seen them?'

Amy nodded, allowing a small smile to cross her face.

'Hello, Aunty Freda, you look nice. How did you know I'd done them, Mum?'

'Because they're tidier than when your dad does them! I've usually got to rebundle them, bless him.'

'I'll take two bunches,' Freda interrupted. 'They'll look lovely on my little antique table in the hall.' She handed the money over to Brenda and turned to leave. Placing a swift kiss on the top of Amy's head, she muttered,

'Love you, child,' before hurrying away.

'Well!!!'

'Mom! She kissed me!'

'I know, sweetheart. I saw. Our Freda's mellowing in her old age. Come on, let's close down for half an hour and we'll go make your old dad a nice cup of tea.'

'Better make it a brandy – he's swearing something awful at the bindweed that's trying to strangle his cauliflowers.'

Brenda's heart rejoiced at the happy tone in the reply from her daughter.

'That bad is it?' Amy nodded. 'And now he's digging like mad. Have you done something to upset him?' Brenda laughed.

'No, love. It's purely the bindweed. Your dad's cauliflowers are famous round these parts and it's woe betide anybody or anything that tries to damage them.'

She pulled down the awning on the front of the stall and hung up a notice, advising customers that she would be back in thirty minutes.

They walked up the lane arm in arm and Brenda felt uplifted. This was how her daughter should be – maybe she was finally on the mend.

'Mrs Andrews? Helen Dawes here. Sonia's mother.'

'Oh hello, Mrs Dawes.'

She mouthed the words Helen Dawes to Jack and shrugged her shoulders as if to say *I don't know what she wants.*

'Look, I'm sorry to bother you...'

Brenda detected a note of hesitancy in the woman's tone.

'Is something wrong, Mrs Dawes?'

'Well yes, there is actually, but I don't really want to... you know, in view of what Amy's been through... oh, God, I wish I hadn't phoned.'

There was silence for a moment and then Brenda

spoke.

'So what is it? I assume it's something to do with Amy?'

'Yes.'

'And?'

'Well, she's been threatening Sonia.'

'Threatening Sonia?'

Jack looked up catching the drift of the one-sided conversation and moved to stand by his wife. 'What on earth do you mean?'

There was a long pause before Helen Dawes spoke again.

'Apparently Amy doesn't want Sonia at the grammar school. First of all she tried bribing her with money to fail the Eleven Plus and when that didn't work, she tried threats; the usual thing. Hitting her, saying she would break her arm before the exam so she wouldn't be able to do it anyway. I'm so sorry to have to bring this up but Sonia has a nasty bruise at the top of her left arm and she says Amy did it.'

Brenda sat down still clutching the receiver to her ear.

'Mrs Dawes, I'm so sorry, we had no idea... Has the school said anything?'

'No. I don't think anyone's realised what's been happening and it's only because of this bruise that the whole sorry tale has come out. I don't want to have to say anything at school, but...'

'Please don't, Mrs Dawes. We have quite a problem on our hands with Amy and I know it won't help if this becomes public knowledge. Can I ask you to leave it with me? I promise you that nothing else will happen to Sonia and she's not to feel intimidated in any way. Tell her to go ahead and get that scholarship. I'll sort Amy.'

'Well, that's the funny part about it all. We don't actually want Sonia at the grammar school; she'll be going to the secondary modern but Sonia would probably pass if we wanted her to go there. I feel awful having to tell you this but I really couldn't let it go on. Do you understand?'

'Of course I do. And I'm really very, very sorry that you've had this worry. Thank you for ringing – I'll sort it out, I promise.' Brenda replaced the receiver, anger flashing across her face.

'Bren?' Jack looked at his wife, not sure what was wrong but certain that whatever it was involved Amy's behaviour at school.

Brenda took a deep breath.

'You're not going to believe this, Jack.' She explained as fast as she could and then passed a hand wearily across her forehead. 'So what do we do now?'

'We stop pussy-footing around with her for a start. Let's have her in.'

He moved to the door and shouted Amy's name, unable to disguise the anger in his voice.

'Yes?' she said as she entered the kitchen.

Brenda heard the arrogance in her daughter's voice and exploded in sudden fury, sweeping her arm back and cracking her hand across her daughter's face. Amy fell against the table and stared up at her mother, her blue eyes now a definite shade of green and full of tears.

She said nothing, just slowly stood and looked at her parents.

'Sonia Dawes.'

She still said nothing.

'I said Sonia Dawes,' Brenda snapped at her. 'And wipe that expression of your face or so help me, I'll... I'll...'

'What?' The word was said quietly.

Suddenly the anger drained out of Brenda. She pulled a chair out from the table and sat down, her head in her hands.

'Why?'

'Because I don't want her to go to Wadebridge. She's a toad.'

'A toad, is she?' Jack felt he had to step in. 'So you think she's a toad? I wonder just what she thinks you are, young lady. I imagine it's something much stronger than toad. Bully, to start with. Then there's thug, cheat and intimidation's hardly a nice word. Personally I'd rather be thought of as a toad.'

'Is that all?'

'Almost,' Jack said. 'If I ever hear of anything like this again, it won't be your mother who hits you. Just bear that in mind. You will keep as far away from Sonia Dawes as it is possible to be and we shall be having a word with both Mrs Carey and Mr. Mawson to make sure that nothing like this ever happens again. Do you understand?'

'Yes.' She turned and walked out of the door, her cheek glowing fiercely with a vivid handprint.

Jack looked at Brenda and held out his arms.

'Come here,' he whispered, 'let me hold you.' Her shame at this first outpouring of anger against Amy since the attack was total and absolute and she sobbed into her husband's shoulder, grief overwhelming her at last.

*   *   *   *   *

When Amy understood that she was probably the only one who would be going to win a scholarship to Wadebridge Grammar, she decided she would go for it. As her mother had said, it all depended on how Amy felt on the day and on that day Amy felt good.

'You can buy the uniform, Mum,' she said on her arrival home after sitting the exam. 'I'm going to Wadebridge Grammar School.'

What she didn't say was that no one at the grammar school would know her past and that was exactly what Amy wa nted.

CHAPTER SIX

1956-1959

John and David were on the periphery of Amy's world for several years, as her self appointed guardians. For the first two years after the attack she was, at various times, subjected to taunts, cross-examinations and general harassment. It never seemed to mature to anything serious; John and David protected the young girl and eventually all the kids learned to leave her alone.

Sometimes Brenda despaired of her daughter ever learning to trust men again. When she saw the pain on her husband's face every time Amy denied him closeness, she ached for him.

Brenda and Jack dug up a joint strength. At odd times they found themselves considering the possibility of having another baby, partly to give Amy something to focus on and partly to give them some relief from the nightmare that haunted them. But deep down they both knew that it wasn't right to have a baby for those reasons and so the subject was finally dropped from minds and conversation.

*   *   *   *   *

As Amy grew and began to learn about physiology and the basic differences between men and women she finally understood the dreadful tragedy that had befallen her. The pain was now dulled, the mental scars not so traumatic but when other girls giggled about having babies she would walk away and leave behind the subject her mind refused to handle.

"Thingy" became a word relegated to her childhood only to be superseded by penis; she hated it when she heard her peers talk of pricks. Prick was a word for giggling adolescents and Amy had had her adolescence taken away from her. At six years old she had grown up.

She tolerated school. After passing the Eleven Plus examination she put her brain on hold and did the minimum necessary to retain her position at the grammar school. The only compulsory subject she truly enjoyed was English; she had a voracious appetite for all the rules and regulations covering the language. Her writing continued but apart from essays she had to hand in, nobody ever saw any of her work.

Pat Rivers was Amy's best friend. They had been thrown together on the first day of grammar school and had remained together. She hadn't needed to tell Pat about the assault because she had, as expected, been the only one to go to the Wadebridge Grammar School. All her other friends were going on to the new secondary modern school. Pat had only recently moved into the area and Amy closed her mind to the past by making friends with someone who couldn't possibly know about it.

In looks, Pat was a complete opposite to Amy. Short dark hair framed a face that had an almost elfin look with very dainty features, highlighted by dark brown eyes. Around four inches shorter than Amy, she was nevertheless the leader of the duo.

They had many things in common – a love of classical music, a degree of expertise with the flute and a natural ability in English. Together they marched through their first two years, during which Pat never understood Mrs Andrews' reluctance to allow Amy out of her sight.

Amy was thirteen when matters took a turn for the worse. One day Sonia Dawes appeared in her class. The colour drained from Amy's face.

'You ok, Amy?' Pat whispered. Amy nodded, not trusting herself to speak. 'You don't look ok,' Pat persisted.

'Bad head.' Amy hoped Pat wouldn't pry; she needed to work out how to handle the situation.

'What do you think of the new girl?'

This time the whisper drew the attention of Miss Calvert and Amy was thankful that further discussion was out of the question – for the moment.

During the lunch hour she couldn't avoid Pat's comments. The new girl was a topic of discussion amongst everyone in the class.

'The funny thing is,' Pat spoke thoughtfully, 'she seems to know you.'

'We were at junior school together.'

Pat stared at her friend. She sensed a tension in Amy that had been there all morning but didn't know how to react to it.

'But... you haven't even spoken to her...'

'Why should I? She wasn't a friend. I just knew her. I don't know why she had to come here anyway. She didn't want to when we took the Eleven Plus.' She pressed the back of her hand to her forehead and briefly closed her eyes.

'You okay?' There was concern in Pat's voice.

'I've told you, I have a headache.'

'So you say. It appeared at the same time as Sonia did, didn't it? Don't you like her?'

'She's alright. I told you – I never had much to do with her.'

'Well, she's walking this way. Must be going to speak

to you.'

The colour drained from Amy's face and she bent to pick up her satchel.

'I'm going to the sick room, see if I can get an Aspirin.'

'What's up with her?'

Pat looked at Sonia then turned to watch Amy as she ran across the tennis court.

'She's not very well. Headache. Gone to get a tablet.'

'I bet it was because she didn't want to speak to me.'

'Why wouldn't she want to speak to you?' Pat had the feeling she was about to defend her best friend.

A sly, crafty look passed over Sonia's face.

'She knows, she knows. Just tell her I remember, will you? She won't find it quite so easy to frighten me now. I've just spent two years at a lot tougher school than this and I know how to look after myself. You make sure you tell her, okay?'

She turned and walked away from an open-mouthed Pat.

For three weeks Amy managed to avoid being in Sonia's company. She knew it couldn't carry on – Sonia's eyes were constantly on her, a permanent promise of trouble.

It was at the end of a P.E. lesson that Sonia finally broke the tension.

'Had any good fucks lately, slag?' It was said in a whisper, meant only for Amy's ears.

'What?' Amy's eyes widened in horror.

'You heard me. Thought what happened might have given you a taste for it. I suppose friend Patty knows all about it, does she?'

'I…'

Sonia grinned at Amy's discomfiture.

'So that's the score, is it? Nobody here knows? No wonder you didn't want me to pass the exam. Well, well, well. Little Miss Bully – I knew I'd get my own back one day.'

'No!'

'Just watch me… hey, Pat! Come here, I want you!'

Amy stared in mute misery as Pat Rivers walked across the changing room holding a towel around her that was far too small.

'Please…' Amy whispered.

'Hey, Pat – wanna know a secret about little Amy here?'

'Amy? A secret?' Pat grinned. 'Is it sexy?'

Sonia shook her head then looked at a white faced Amy.

'Nope. Not sexy. The secret is that I used to be frightened of her and now I'm not,' and she turned and walked away.

'What is that girl on about?'

Amy shrugged her shoulders.

'Haven't a clue. Forget her. I told you she was a bit peculiar.' But the hatred and fear became even more fixed in Amy's mind.

The school trip to gather species of wild flowers growing in the hills around Polzeath proved uneventful until the skies began to darken. Even dark thundery weather couldn't mar the beauty of this spot. Situated right on the coast with a massive beach stretching a long way beyond the confines of the village, it was the perfect spot for surfing and Amy had always loved coming here with her parents. She would rather not have come on this chillingly atmospheric afternoon.

Amy could see two teachers conferring and knew they were talking about the weather and the imminence of rain. She pulled the hood of her raincoat over her head and began to climb the tricky path leading to the very top of the cliff-side, The stones were loose beneath her feet and it would be more dangerous once the rain started.

'Slow down, Pat' she called and Pat halted momentarily.

'Not likely,' she responded. 'Let's get these flowers gathered and get off the side of this hill. Daft exercise anyway,' she grumbled. 'We're going to get wet through. This biology lesson should have been in the classroom, not on a bloody hillside with fifteen fed up kids.'

As she spoke they felt the first drops followed by a loud shout from one of the teachers.

'Quickly girls and boys! Let's get this over with and back to the coach.'

'*Quickly girls and boys, let's get this over with and back to the coach.*' Amy heard the words mimicked from close behind her and recognized Sonia Dawes' voice

She stiffened and turned her head. The other girl was climbing awkwardly, almost on all fours. Amy laughed softly to herself.

'Well well, the great tough Sonia – can't climb a little hill like this.'

'This is no little hill,' Sonia panted. 'And I've twisted my ankle.' She reached forward with her right hand to grasp at a small outcrop of rock as Amy stepped backwards.

Sonia gave a small cry of pain as she felt her fingers crack under the pressure of Amy's heavy walking shoe.

'Bastard,' she moaned and brought her left foot up to take the strain as she tried to remove her hand from under the shoe. The ankle injury was worse than she thought and wouldn't take the extra pressure applied to it.

Sonia tumbled sideways and down the hill. With a gasp of shock, Amy reached for and caught hold of her arm but Sonia's weight pulled her further down the steep incline towards the rocks on the beach below.

For several long moments everything seemed to stop. Amy looked down into Sonia's terror stricken face and knew that if someone didn't come to take the strain with her, Sonia would crash down on to the rocks to her death.

She sensed rather than saw Pat scrambling back down the path to help and grew aware of the promised torrential downpour. Water splashed on to Sonia's upturned face, a face that suddenly disappeared as Amy carefully, centimeter by centimeter, opened her fingers.

As Sonia's scream began she heard Pat's gasp of shock. For a moment there was stunned silence from the rest of the girls on the cliff side and then everyone began to shout and cry.

Amy slumped perfectly still, the side of her face pressed into the wet grass.

'Amy?' Pat knelt by her, shaking her shoulder. 'Amy?' She lifted her head.

'I couldn't hold on, Pat,' she wept. 'The rain – her arm was just too slippery. I… I tried…'

'Come on.' Pat's voice was gruff. She'd never seen a tear from Amy before, never seen any real emotion at all. 'Come on, we can't do anymore.' She saw the body of Sonia Dawes lying on the rocks at the foot of the cliff and several people running across the sands to her.

A woman reached her first and all the girls paused in their descent to watch. The woman looked upwards towards the party, seeking out an adult figure, and Miss Tomlinson waved a hand. The woman gave a shake of her head and spread her arms wide.

The girl's frightened faces turned to each other knowing what the arm movement had meant. They increased the speed of their downward trek.

Miss Tomlinson shepherded them all on to the coach then left to join her colleague on the beach.

Pat sat beside Amy who was shivering uncontrollably.

'You okay?' she asked.

Amy nodded.

'Will be. It's just shock. I had her, Pat, had hold of her, but...'

'You couldn't have done anymore, Amy,' she said firmly, pushing the vision of opening fingers to the back of her mind. She knew she must have imagined it – distortion caused by the torrential rain. If Amy had done it deliberately, she wouldn't be so upset.

One of the boys looked towards Amy.

'I think she deserves a medal,' he called loudly. 'She almost had Sonia, and none of us did anything at all.'

There was a spontaneous round of applause from everyone and Amy turned her head towards the window.

'Leave it,' she said softly, wiping away a tear. 'I didn't do anything. She still fell.'

'But you tried,' Pat said and placed an arm around her friend's shoulder, drawing her into the warmth of her own body. She knew the violent shivering wasn't caused by the cold.

It seemed a long time later that the two teachers returned to give them the news that they already suspected. The fall had killed Sonia.

They headed back to school and then the coach took each individual pupil home. Amy was the penultimate one to leave the coach and she turned to wave to the last girl left as it drove away.

She walked up the path to her home and allowed a small smile to cross her face.

CHAPTER SEVEN
February 1960

Treverick paused outside the huge wooden gates and looked around him. Nobody to meet him but had he really expected a familiar face? Considering that the only visitor he had seen in eight years had been his brother once, he doubted they even knew he was due for release.

He stuffed the brown paper bag under his arm and set off for the railway station to exchange the ticket they had given him for travel to Leeds for one to Wadebridge. They had advised him against returning to Cornwall. Go north, they had said, put everything behind you and try to do something with your life. He could have told them his intention was to do a lot of things with his life.

As soon as he was seated he began to go over the plans he had spent eight years making. His appearance had to be totally altered; his dark brown hair would become blonde, his thin moustache would go and he would begin wearing glasses.

During his years in that cell he had deliberately lost weight, dropping from an eighteen stone giant to a twelve stone slimmer version of the man who had entered the prison. The important thing to do now was to eat and eat and eat. He had to be so unlike the last picture taken of him that he would be completely unrecognizable.

He doubted that the Andrews kid would remember his face at all but her parents would and he knew that by the time he met them again he had to be a stranger, speak with a changed accent and have a job.

The beatings he had endured, that long night of repeated rape by several inmates, the years of solitary confinement at his own request – all this had to be paid for and the Andrews family was the focus of his anger.

CHAPTER EIGHT

1958-1964

Amy was hailed as a heroine. The headmistress, who was still in shock that a pupil had died while on a school trip, gave her book tokens. The local newspaper made much of her valiant efforts to hold on to the falling child.

Pat still felt uneasy but put it out of her mind – everyone else couldn't be wrong, could they? Surely she hadn't been the only one close enough to see anything...

And so Amy was feted throughout the school; she was happy. Now no one would learn of the rape, no one would be able to taunt her, think of her as someone different to the rest. Yes, she was as happy as she could be, given the fact that she knew she was different, very different.

She never admitted to herself that she had committed murder.

*   *   *   *   *

Brenda had to finally let go of her child when Amy turned fourteen.

'Mom, I'm going to the pictures tonight with Pat.' She eyed her mother as if daring her to say she couldn't go, although she pushed her hair back from her forehead, a mannerism she tended to use when feeling insecure.

'But...'

'Mom, for goodness sake, nothing's going to happen to me. There's very little left that could happen to me,' she added, a touch of normally hidden bitterness in her tone. 'And what's more, I'll be sleeping over at Pat's house - her mom says she'll take us swimming tomorrow morning.'

Brenda looked for help to Jack who shrugged his shoulders. He loved his daughter dearly but he'd been shut out of her life for so long and didn't feel he could interfere now.

Brenda exhaled slowly, looking at the beautiful young woman her daughter had become.

'Yes ok, Amy. Just take care – is it only Pat you're going with?'

'Oh, Mom,' Amy grinned. 'Yes, it's only Pat and if there was a boy I'd tell you. This is 1960 you know – we don't hide things from our parents now.'

'Cheeky monkey,' her mother laughed. 'Go and pack your nightie and a toothbrush then. Got enough money?'

Amy nodded.

'I think so. And I've already packed.' She bent to kiss her mother who was now sitting by Jack on the settee hoping to find solace in his quiet strength. Jack put his hand in his pocket and pulled out a pound note. He handed it to Amy.

'Here,' he said a little gruffly. 'Take this. Don't want you being short of money while you're out. Any trouble and you grab a taxi, you hear?'

Amy stared for a moment at the man who she had forced into playing such a minor part in her life and swiftly placed a kiss on his head, a head now covered by very sparse hair.

'Thanks, Dad, I'll be fine, I promise.'

As she went through the door to walk to the nearby bus stop to catch one to Pat's, a tear rolled down Jack Andrews' cheek. It was the first kiss in eight years from his only child. He felt he had the right to allow a tear to fall.

The girls left the cinema at the end of the film, both drooling over Elvis.

'My word,' Pat sighed. 'That man is wonderful.' She burst into a chorus of *Wooden Heart* and Amy laughed.

'It would almost be worth joining the army,' she joked.

'Wouldn't it just?'

They left the brightness of the foyer and began to walk along the pavement towards the bus stop. Pat felt a hand go round her waist and she turned to see who it was but Amy didn't twist to see who had encircled *her* waist; she swung first and questioned after. Her handbag flew in an arc that terminated on the head of Kevin Morgan, a boy from their school whom Pat had described, at various times, as a wally of the highest order.

'Ouch!' he bellowed and immediately let go of Amy. Pat was struggling to get away from the clutches of Robin Trelawney when their path was blocked by two figures.

'Amy? Having trouble?' John Thornton stared at the girl who, it seemed, had been part of his life forever.

'I think I've handled it,' she said, out of breath and trembling. David moved over to Pat and pushed Robin to one side. The two younger boys walked away grumbling that they were only having a bit of fun.

'Come on,' John said. 'We'll give you a lift.'

'You've got a car?' Amy looked impressed and he laughed.

'Amy, I'm a very junior reporter with the Journal – I can't afford a push bike even! No, young David here has the car.'

David grinned.

'Don't get carried away. It's very old but it will get you home, Amy.'

Pat interrupted, eager to find out how Amy knew these two very good-looking young men.

'Er... Amy's staying with me tonight, she's not going home.'

Amy laughed, recognizing Pat's ploy.

'Pat, can I introduce you to John Thornton and David Farmer? They sort of look after me.'

She didn't want to explain further than that but fortunately Pat was studying David so intensely, it never occurred to her to question Amy.

'Let's go then,' David said, obviously quite taken with Amy's friend who he hadn't met before.

Following Pat's directions they drove down the winding streets into Padstow village and parked looking across the harbour. The moon was low on the horizon, the moonbeam path across the calm waters of the Atlantic Ocean leading in a straight line to the front wheels of the car.

Amy sighed contentedly.

'We could almost walk it to the States, or wherever is at the other end. Isn't it beau... lovely?'

'Come on,' John responded, 'let's take a little walk. Not across the water and definitely not as far as the States! My name's John, not Jesus,' he laughed, aware of a new feeling in the air. 'It's ages since we talked.'

As they strolled around the harbour wall, he mentioned that Pat and David seemed quite taken with each other and Amy looked at him with alarm.

'Don't worry,' he said, placing an arm around her shoulders. 'Not all men are like that brute.'

She found it amazing that he understood her so well. Even her own parents had never fully appreciated the overwhelming fear that all men were animals and yet this boy – no, she corrected herself – this man had the gift of seeing into her mind.

'So, how are things?'

She thought for a moment.

'Okay, I guess. I can't wait to leave school, but apart from that, it's... okay.'

He turned her towards him and the moonlight fell on her dark blonde hair, highlighting it with streaks of silver.

'Only okay? We'll have to do something about that.'

'Nobody can. I just feel different to most people.'

'You don't look any different.'

She shrugged her shoulders.

'I know I don't. But it's here,' She touched her head.

'Oh Amy,' and he pulled her close, nestling her head under his chin. He felt her body stiffen and immediately regretted his action. Then slowly she relaxed, the tension leaving her. Their first kiss was fleeting, a mere touching of lips, chaste, virginal.

It left both of them surprised and yearning for more.

'Come on,' his voice had dropped an octave. 'Let's go back to the car, see what they're up to.'

They held hands on the walk back, reluctant to admit their need to touch each other. Amy felt totally bewildered by her feelings but John was completely and utterly sure of his.

'Can I see you again?'

'Yes.' She whispered.

When they reached the car, Pat had her head on David's shoulder and on the drive home she held his left hand through all the gear changes. They made arrangements to join up for tenpin bowling the following weekend. During that week, Amy kissed her father for the second time in eight years.

*   *   *   *   *

'He's how old?' Brenda looked askance at her daughter. '*Eighteen?*'

Amy smiled, fully aware of what her mother was thinking.

'Yes, he's eighteen but it doesn't seem like we're four years apart. He's always been there, always looked after me...' She continued to dry the cutlery, carefully laying the items in neat orderly piles.

'Looked after you? What do you mean? We've looked after you, my girl, not this John Thornbridge.'

'John Thornton, Mom. And you didn't look after me, at least not at school you didn't. John did. The kids were pretty wicked after it happened, you know, and John and David were always there to help me out.'

'And Pat's going with this David, you say?'

'Yes.' She carefully placed a spoon directly on top of the one below it. 'David works for his dad's publishing company and John's a reporter with the Journal, so they're both very respectable.'

Brenda looked at her daughter for long moments.

'As long as you know what you're doing, Amy. Be careful, love. And what did you mean, the kids were pretty wicked? Why didn't you tell me, or your dad?'

'Didn't need to, I had John and David looking after me.'

'So, when do we get to meet this paragon of virtue?'

'John and David are picking Pat up first then coming here for me. I'll bring him in, if you like.'

Brenda met Jack's eyes and he nodded.

'Yes, I think we would like that. We'd like to know who you're going out with.'

Amy finished the last of the dishes and folded the tea towel meticulously, pressing down on it to seal the creases. Although Brenda had accepted the compulsive tidiness of her daughter she never learned how to ignore it and just for a moment she was tempted to grab the cloth, shake it free of its neatness and hurl it across the room.

To Brenda the week dragged slowly. She worried, fidgeted, walked miles deep in thought and finally gave in to the inevitable. She would be meeting Amy's first boyfriend and she could do nothing to change it.

John Thornton was a complete surprise to the Andrews. Tall, self-assured, he seemed to genuinely care for Amy, promising them he would see that she was home by ten o'clock. His maturity, combined with his blonde good looks won them over instantly and their hearts were considerably lighter as they watched David drive them away.

*   *   *   *   *

Slowly, Brenda and Jack accepted that their daughter had another very important person in her life. As time passed, to Amy it seemed that the sun shone more. She was in love and everything was idyllic. One month later Amy's sixteen year old world collapsed around her.

O level examinations meant her school hours were erratic and Wednesday afternoon found her catching a bus home after lunch. She walked up the lane to find a police car outside the cottage. She quickened her pace, her throat constricting in panic. She began to run.

'Amy!' Her mother's gasp of surprise showed she had not expected her daughter home. Jack stood and moved to her side. He placed an arm around her shoulders and looked at his wife.

'I suppose this takes the decision out of our hands?'

Brenda looked troubled but nodded slowly. Amy swung around and stared at the two police officers.

'What's wrong? Is someone ill?'

Jack left his daughter's side and moved towards the door.

'Thank you, Inspector, we'll handle it now. We'll explain everything – and thank you for keeping us informed. We appreciate it.'

'That's okay, sir. And, as I said, I don't think you've any need to worry.' He touched his cap, nodded briefly at the three members of the Andrews family and walked out of the cottage.

'Mum? Dad?' Amy looked, and felt, bewildered. 'What's going on?'

'Sit down, love. We've something to tell you and it won't be easy to hear. In fact, I don't think we would be telling you if you hadn't come in when you did.'

'I completely forgot you had an exam this morning and would be home early.' Brenda Andrews spoke haltingly, her face haggard. Jack Andrews looked at his daughter and marvelled at her beauty. How could he have produced something as wonderful as she was? He took her hand in his and held it for long moments.

'He's out, Princess.'

Amy jumped at the long forgotten pet name. How many years since he had called her that?

'Out? Am I missing something? Who's out?'

'Ronald Treverick. The animal who attacked you.'

'But…'

He sighed.

'I know. We thought it best to let you think he was

dead. He moved the gun at the last second – the bullet grazed his scalp. Oh, enough to knock him out for a few seconds and long enough for the police to arrive and move in when they heard the shot, but he wasn't dead. He's been in prison for the last eight years. Apparently he had to do extra time because he beat up another inmate. The police were here to tell us he was released yesterday. They don't seem to think we have any need to panic but when he was first imprisoned he blamed us – his twisted mind thought it was our fault he was locked away.'

Amy's face was completely devoid of colour. She stood slowly and then ran into the bathroom, retching. Brenda followed her, trying to hold back the tears. She waited until the spasm was over and then carefully wiped her daughter's mouth.

She pulled her close and kissed the top of her head.

'Don't worry, sweetheart, we'll look after you. From now on Dad will take you to school and collect you at night…'

'No!' Amy screamed the word. 'No! Don't you see, Mum, if we behave like that, like scared rabbits, he'll have won? We carry on just as normal – and don't worry, I'll be extra careful.'

'But you don't even know what he looks like.'

'Then we'll get a picture from the police. Surely they won't deny us that?'

'No, I'm sure they won't but… oh, Amy, I'm so sorry, love.'

'No, Mum, it's him who will be sorry if he ever comes near any one of us,' she said quietly. There was ice in her voice and Brenda shivered. 'Will you get me a photograph of him?'

Brenda nodded and moved towards the lounge.

'I'll ring now,' she said leaving her daughter to adjust

to her new reality.

Amy decided to push thoughts of Treverick to one side. Her exam results were good and her interview at Curran, Trebuthnoe Ltd in Padstow went so well that they rang the following day and offered her the position. Working in a solicitor's office as a junior meant she could inhabit her own world most of the time without having too big a responsibility during working hours.

She was efficient at her job and went to night school and day release for shorthand and typing. Although the partners recognized her value to them as an organizer and frequently spoke about their plans for her future career she knew she wanted nothing more than straightforward clerical work.

She spent a quiet eighteen months not rocking any boats, building a good working relationship with her employers and spending most of her free time with John.

Pat and David grew ever closer and when Pat confessed to her closest friend that she had slept with David, Amy was supportive and understanding. On the inside her stomach churned and she felt sick at the thought of such intimacy.

For her own part she kept John at arm's length and he grew to accept that the love of his life was still damaged, but time would heal her.

He would heal her.

'Marry you? But…'

John took hold of her hand.

'Yes. Marry me. You know, hearts and flowers bit, better or for worse, sickness and in health, forsaking all others. You know the sort of things they say on these occasions.'

Her eyes clouded.

'Don't mock me, John,' she said softly and he suddenly had the feeling that things were going badly wrong.

'Look, forget all I've said and I'll start again.'

They were standing in the kitchen of Amy's home and he led her gently to the kitchen table pushing her down on to a chair. Dropping on to one knee he took hold of her left hand.

'Miss Amelia Rose Andrews, will you do me the honour of becoming my wife? Will you marry me? Please.'

'Why did you call me Amelia?'

He groaned.

'Okay, we'll do it again. Miss Amy Rose...'

She placed a finger on his lips.

'Sssh, idiot. And you know what my answer has to be.'

'Huh? What does that mean? Yes or no? And can I get up now; it's a bit hard on the knees.'

'Of course my answer is no.'

He looked astounded.

'Amy, did you or did you not say you loved me only five minutes ago?'

'Yes, I love you.'

He began to feel angry.

'Then what is it? Is it because you're only seventeen? I'd thought we could get engaged officially on your eighteenth birthday and if you want it that way, we'll wait until you're twenty one before we get married. Just tell me you want me as much as I want you. You know there's never been anyone else for me.'

The anguish showed all too plainly in Amy's face.

'John, tell me in words of one syllable that you will

never want children.'

'I can't. I would love a son one day but, my lovely Amy, that doesn't mean we have to be the natural parents. We will adopt, silly cuckoo. Did you really think I hadn't thought all this through? Come here.' He pulled her close, kissing away the tears spilling down her cheeks.

'Is it yes?'

She nodded, hardly trusting herself to speak.

Jack and Brenda were delighted. The plans for a huge party to celebrate the event took weeks to complete and the Andrews became very close to John's parents as a result. It came as no surprise to them that Lilian and Tad Thornton thought a great deal of their daughter. On a normal day Amy was charm personified. Only Brenda knew just how dark the other side of her lovely offspring was.

CHAPTER NINE
September 1964

'I'm sorry, Jack, Brenda, if I could hold out any hope at all...'

Brenda's ashen face turned towards the specialist.

'What do you mean? Are you trying to say it's inoperable?'

Reginald Smythe nodded slowly, wishing himself for the thousandth time in any other job but this.

'The lumps that we removed from your neck, Jack, were secondary carcinomas.'

Jack's hands shook and he gripped his fingers tightly.

'How long?'

'I can't play God, Jack, but...'

'Isn't that exactly what you're doing?' Brenda screamed. 'Playing God? Deciding what's removable and what isn't. Why can't you try?'

'Mrs Andrews, Brenda...' The man in the grey suit tried to hold her eyes with his. 'You must believe me...'

She stood and staggered towards the door, blind with rage and tears. 'Just don't sit there, you bastard, and tell me my husband's dying...'

Jack's quiet voice cut into the charged atmosphere.

'How long?'

Brenda stared at her husband in horror, unable to comprehend his acceptance of death.

'How long?' He repeated the words.

'Four, maybe six months.'

There was an anguished wail from Brenda followed by the slam of a door. Jack couldn't move, couldn't follow his wife, couldn't comfort her or accept comfort.

'So six months is the outside then?'

Smythe nodded.

'The very outside, Jack. It's well advanced. Did you think this diagnosis might be a possibility?' A long sigh escaped from Jack's lips.

'Yes, I knew. Never mentioned it to Brenda, she's enough on her plate.'

'We can control the pain, Jack. It will be dignified, but… I'm sorry, even if we operated it wouldn't grant you any extensions.'

Jack stood and held out his hand.

'Thanks for being honest, Mr. Smythe. At least I can put my life, or what's left of it, in order. I'll go and find Brenda now. Got to talk, you know.'

He discovered her already sitting in the car, a screwed up handkerchief clutched tightly in her fist. He slid behind the wheel but made no attempt to start the car.

'We have to talk, Bren.'

'Yes.'

'I don't want John and Amy to know. At least, not until…'

'Not until there's no denying it, you mean.' She concluded bitterly. 'Why us, Jack, why us?'

He slid his left arm around her shoulders and pulled her to him.

'Do you love me, Bren?'

'You know I do.' Her head dropped as if her neck could no longer support it.

'Have you always loved me?'

'Always.'

'Then that's enough. You're the only woman I ever wanted and you'll be there with me when things get rough. We have to accept it, love.'

'We don't, Jack. We could get a second opinion.'

'No good, Bren. The cancer has spread through my

body now. Let's make the most of what we have left. I love you, Brenda Andrews and I won't let something like this spoil our last few months together. And I damn well won't let it spoil the kids' engagement do next week.'

'And Freda?'

'We tell her tonight. I don't want her to find out accidentally from my notes at the doctors. Besides, I think she suspects anyway. She's not a fool. No, it's Amy who mustn't know. Not yet.'

The party was a complete success and Brenda, Jack, Amy and John were the last to leave the hall; all the gifts had been loaded into the back of John's car before they could set off for the Andrews cottage. The boot was eventually full and Jack and Brenda safely ensconced on the back seat.

'Well that's it, young Amy,' John remarked with a laugh. 'Time to get you home. Have you had a good day?'

Amy, her eyes shining, kissed him enthusiastically in answer and missed seeing her mother wipe the sweat from the brow of her father, his face ashen as a wave of pain washed over him.

It had been pain that had brought them together twenty-four years earlier and Brenda closed her eyes and moved into memory. It had only been three steps that she had tumbled down thanks to Monty the cat but she had landed awkwardly and finished off a bad day sitting in accident and emergency at the local hospital. She had shared the waiting room with a young man who was also nursing a suspected fracture to his arm and they had begun to talk.

Brenda could still remember the feeling of loss as they moved her into the x-ray and treatment area, leaving Jack in the waiting room. Within ten minutes they were reunited, Jack having persuaded the nurse that they really did want the dividing curtain open so that they could talk.

She smiled to herself as she remembered the conversation, but not the content. That had been irrelevant. They persuaded the nurse who put casts on their arms to give them appointments ten minutes apart at the fracture check up clinic and their love story had started.

It hadn't been easy. She had been seeing Tony Baxter and had to tell him it was over. He hadn't been happy and for some weeks stalked her around town trying to persuade her that Jack was a lowlife, he would treat her like dirt, drop her when he was fed up with her.

Now, she gripped on to Jack's hand as she felt him tense from another pain spasm and turned to him.

'I thought you'd gone to sleep.'

'No, my love,' she said quietly. 'Just remembering, just remembering.'

He smiled at her. 'Me too.'

CHAPTER TEN

Autumn 1964

Just two weeks after Amy and John's engagement party, robbed of his final five months, Jack Andrews died as a direct result of pancreatic cancer.

Amy felt she was quietly going mad. Having shut her father out of her life for so long, she now realised she couldn't handle the guilt. He had been a good man, nothing like the brute who had taken her childhood away from her. She was still struggling with the realisation that ninety nine per cent of the male gender was okay.

She held her mother's hand all the way through the funeral service, both of them relying heavily on John for comfort. The service, the funeral tea and the mourners' departure all passed in a blur.

Finally the three of them were left alone.

'Please,' John pleaded, 'come to our house for a few days. Mom's fixed the spare bedroom ready for you.'

Brenda smiled at the young man she had come to love.

'No thanks, John, really. Your mum's got enough on her plate with the new baby. I promise you, we'll be fine.'

'Liam's a good baby,' he protested. 'And you know she can handle anything. We'd love to have you.'

Brenda shook her head.

'No, we have to be on our own sometime. Everyone's been wonderful but we have to handle things now. I'll ring your mum and dad and thank them later but we're staying in our home.'

Amy chose to say nothing, the numbness refusing to go away. She didn't want anything or anyone around her; she wanted to grieve on her own, in the privacy of her own room. But most of all she wanted her dad back. She wanted to hold him, to try and tell him how she regretted the years gone by since the attack. Her emotions ran the whole gamut - anger, frustration, despair. She wanted to die.

She cursed Ronald Treverick with every fibre of her being. His actions had caused her rejection of all men, including her father. She wanted him to meet the same fate as her father but more painfully; much more painfully.

Lying on her bed, tearless and quiet, her thoughts roamed over the years, always returning to her sixth. She began to pinch the top of her left arm, nipping the soft flesh between her thumb and forefinger, not allowing the pain to register.

Slowly the tears began to fall until finally the nips ceased and a tentative peace washed over her.

She had to wear long sleeves for two weeks until the bruises disappeared.

Nothing helped. She missed the presence of her father dreadfully although she had never taken time to be with him, to talk to him, to allow him to be a dad. Now he wasn't around she felt helpless, rudderless.

The death of Jack Andrews left a big hole in the lives of Brenda and Freda, but especially Amy.

It came as no surprise to Brenda when, six months later, John and Amy asked her permission to marry.

'We know we said we would wait until I was twenty one, Mum,' Amy said, 'but we have the chance of a lovely flat, two bedrooms it's got, and so it seems sensible to get married.'

Brenda looked at the young couple.

'Should sensible come into it?'

John nodded.

'I think so. You know I love Amy, have done since she was six, so you don't need to worry. I'll always look after her and we want to be married.'

'This isn't anything to do with Pat and David having married, is it? You're not just following in their footsteps?'

Amy shook her head.

'No, we're not as stupid as that, Mum.'

Brenda smiled.

'Then of course I'll sign the papers. Did you have a date in mind?'

'September Seventh.'

'Phew! We'd best get cracking then. There's a lot to organise. But you're absolutely sure, aren't you?'

Even as she asked she knew it was a ridiculous question. There was no denying the happiness in their faces, the look in their eyes. She felt misgivings; Amy was too young and John had only just started to climb his particular ladder of success. She wondered what Jack would have said. Suddenly, there was a deep conviction that Jack would have said let them get on with it; they'll sort out any problems later. He had been that sort of man.

'Come on, Mrs Andrews, come with us and let's show you our new home.' John held out his hand to his future mother-in-law and pulled her up from the armchair. 'It's not far, only five minutes away so we're within easy call if you need us.'

'Oh, John, for goodness sake call me Mum, or Ma, or

something, but not Mrs Andrews!'

'Right, Ma,' he grinned, 'and give us a kiss.'

The flat was above a wallpaper shop and boasted a tiny kitchen, a reasonable size lounge, one large bedroom and a much smaller one. The bathroom was so tiny it only just merited the title. The rent was miniscule thanks to the friendship of the owner and John's father. Brenda looked around her and saw furniture that was clearly pre-war and a carpet in the lounge that urgently needed replacing, but nothing seemed to matter..The youngsters, she could see, were ecstatically happy about it.

'It's just a start,' John explained. 'I won't be in this job for ever and besides, David's dad has promised to look at something...' His voice trailed away as if he regretted saying anything.

Amy glanced at him.

'John? What's that?'

He shrugged his shoulders.

'I may as well tell you now. I intended saying nothing until I had something definite to tell you. I've been working on a novel for the past two years. It's finished now, just needs a bit of tidying and Mr. Farmer says he'll have a look at it, tell me where I've gone wrong sort of thing. He... er... looked at the two others I've finished. They weren't any good of course but he's sort of encouraged me...' He looked embarrassed, a flush staining his cheeks.

Brenda's smile extended to her eyes as she tried to choke back the laughter engendered by his discomfort.

'Is it good?' she asked.

Again he shrugged his shoulders.

'Dunno. I've enjoyed writing it. It's a mystery, set in France. Took quite a bit of research but I've done it now for better or worse. I'm giving it to David at the weekend.'

'Does this mean I've to keep on working for a bit then?' Amy laughed. 'Could do,' he grinned back at her. 'But one day…'

They began moving things into the flat immediately and John took the decision to move out of his parent's house and live in the flat until their marriage. Amy was afraid of leaving it empty at night with all their precious engagement presents in it.

She began to unpack a box of items brought from her own bedroom at the cottage and pulled out the photograph of Ronald Treverick. She stared at it for several seconds and shivered. Dark brown hair falling forward on to his forehead gave him an almost rakish air and although the picture didn't show it, the police had told her his eyes were brown. A thin moustache served to emphasise the cruel lips that seemed to mock her. She had studied the photograph so many times that she knew if she ever saw him again she would recognize him immediately.

'Oh yes, Amelia will know you,' she whispered.

They had told her he was twenty-six when he was released, twelve years older than herself and yet he looked younger in the photograph. She hurriedly thrust the picture under the mattress and then began to lay things out in meticulously straight lines. The dressing table set, her beloved collection of frogs, everything had to be straight.

John eyed the frogs with amusement.

'Is this your dowry?'

'I like frogs,' she said defensively.

'Well, I like ice cream but I don't have a collection of cones,' he grinned. She picked up a stuffed frog and threw it at him; in his efforts to avoid it he fell backwards on to the bed and she launched herself towards him, pinning him down with her body. Suddenly he became still, allowing her to hold his wrists. She sensed the change in him and released him but he reached up and pulled her face towards him.

To Amy even his kiss seemed to have changed. What began as a light exploratory movement deepened leaving Amy's senses reeling.

'Amy…' John's voice was guttural. 'God, I want you.'

She hurriedly pulled herself away from him.

'We said we would wait.'

'I know what we said but it's only two months away now. Don't you think…?'

'No!' She was panic stricken. 'No!'

He saw the alarm written all over her face and gently moved away from her.

'Hey, Froggie, come on. It's no big deal. We just got carried away for a moment. Look, tell you what we'll do. Let's arrange these little frogs somewhere and then we'll make a cup of tea.' He stood; moving over towards the dressing table scooped them into a box. 'They could sit on the window sill,' he added. 'They'll look great there.'

He placed them in little groups of two and three and Amy watched in stony silence.

'There,' he said when the box was empty. 'That's another job done. I'll go and make us a drink if you want to open the next box.'

When he returned with the tea tray all the little frogs were back on the dressing table in neat, regimented rows and Amy was smiling.

'Tell me about the book then.' She took a sip of her tea, staring at him, wondering if he had other secrets he was keeping from her.

He shrugged.

'It's just a book. I've been working on it for about two years altogether. No, that's a lie, I suppose. It started in my head when I was at school. I began serious research into it two years ago.'

'And you never said anything?'

'Not deliberate. I did my writing after I left you at night. It just never intruded into our life.' He stared into the flames of the fire. 'It will one day though, Amy. It's what I want to do. The journalism has been good, given me some good characters for the future I can tell you, but all I want to do is write. Novels.'

She turned to him.

'So it's that serious?'

'You bet. And if it doesn't happen with this novel I've lost nothing. It's all experience.'

'Can I read it?'

He looked at her, unsure of her mood. '

Sure. I'll let you have my copy.'

'Why didn't you let me type it up for you?'

'Would you have? I just never thought. I'm so used to doing my own typing at work I did it automatically. Do you want to take the copy with you tonight?'

She nodded.

'Yes. Are you open to criticism?'

He laughed.

'More than open; I'd welcome it.' There was a moment of silence.

'I write,' she said.

'You?' He looked at her, a frown crossing his brow.

'Did you think you'd cornered the market in paper and pens?'

'No, not at all; it just took me by surprise. What do

you write?'

'Short stories, a little bit of poetry.'

'And I never knew.'

'Did I know about your book?' she countered. 'Anyway I've never considered mine for publication, they're for me.'

'Can I see them?'

'No!'

He stared at her, flinching from the anger in her tone.

'Whoa! Don't shout at me. Look, let's drop the subject shall we until we hear from Alistair Farmer. Come on, I'll take you home. I think we both need a good night's sleep.'

'I'm sorry,' she said quietly, taking his hand. John wasn't to know that this was the first and last time he would ever hear Amy Andrews apologise for her actions.

The coffee table was looking good. She had collected pictures of flowers, cherubs and other romantic notions and carefully stuck them to an old coffee table that she had found in a second hand shop. The rubbing down had taken some time and she had been meticulous in her placement of the decoupage. She was about to brush on the final coat of seal when Brenda knocked on the door,

'Can I come in?' she called.

'It's open.' The door opened and Brenda glanced in.

'Aunty Jean has confirmed they're coming and ...Wow!'

'Like it?'

'It's absolutely stunning! I had no idea...'

'I just thought it would look good in the lounge.'

Brenda stared, did a hang-on gesture, then turned and ran down the stairs. She returned with a wooden kitchen chair.

'Can you do the same to this?'

'Sure. Where is it for?'

'For my bedroom; I was going to paint it blue to match the walls but what you've done there is wonderful. I'd actually like blue flowers.'

'No problem, I'll start to rub it down later. You really like this little table then?'

'I love it. And when Freda sees it she'll expect an Amy Thornton original as well.' Amy laughed.

'This could be quite profitable! Perhaps this is my real career move!'

She picked up her brush and began her final layer to finish the table. It would look good in their pretty little flat.

She just hoped John would love it as much as she did. But he would – they were a partnership after all.

CHAPTER ELEVEN

December 1964

He felt the large horn-rimmed glasses suited him, blended extremely well with the blonde streaked hair and gave him a look of intelligence that complemented his fast developing brain power. Running a comb through the fringe that still persisted trying to fall on to his forehead, even after four years of being combed back, he knew that his appearance bore no resemblance to the man who had walked out of prison.

He had been gaunt, dark-haired and moustached. Although he hadn't become totally blonde, the streaks that had been placed all over his head gave an appearance of blondeness without having the problem of dark roots. His glasses did nothing to assist his eyesight – that needed no help. He frequently looked at himself in the mirror, impressed by the change in his face and pleased by the air of gravity the glasses gave him. He regretted he could do nothing about the colour of his eyes but acknowledged that most people trusted anyone with brown eyes for some obscure reason. They might even work for rather than against him.

Those early days after his release seemed so long ago now. A new name had been a first priority along with the removal of the moustache. The hours and hours he had put in at the gym and at home with his own weights had honed his body to a peak of fitness. He had even come to enjoy the gruelling routine he had set himself and now, established in a job he enjoyed, earning more money than he would have thought possible, he knew the time was fast approaching when he could, with confidence in his ability to carry the pretense through, set out to find the Andrews family.

He was ready.

CHAPTER TWELVE

March 1965

'I don't know, Freda. I really don't know what to do.'

'You're absolutely sure they haven't been to bed?'

Brenda nodded.

'Couldn't be more certain. I asked John.'

'Bit of a cheek, what? Didn't he think it was a bit nosy? Bit too much the mother-in-law?'

She shook her head, a worried frown crossing her brow.

'No, I told him it didn't matter one way or the other. I trusted him completely with my daughter, I just needed to know so that I could talk to Amy and be in full possession of the facts.'

'And he told you?'

'What he told me bothered me. He said that Amy insisted they wait until their wedding night and that she hardly even allowed a kiss that was anything other than sisterly.'

'And you obviously think they're going to have problems.'

'I'm sure of it, Freda. She's so... reserved, prudish even. It's not surprising but I feel as though I ought to talk to her, but what do I say? I can hardly suggest to my own daughter that she has a bit of a practice at making love before the wedding night, can I? I thought you might have a bit of advice.'

'Why don't you have a word with Dr. Walters?'

'Because Dr. Walters has never been the slightest bit of help with Amy.' There was acid in her tone. 'He never agreed with me that there was anything wrong. We almost had to bully him into referring us to that psychologist when she was eight, remember?'

'Then I don't know what to say. Bit out of my depth – children and things. Never could quite latch on to the idea of little brats and suchlike. Love her to pieces but…'

Brenda sighed.

'I know and I shouldn't have burdened you with my worries but with Jack gone, I really have nobody to talk to these days.'

'Bren, does Amy still have this compulsion to have everything spick and span?'

'Worse than ever; and if she's got something on her mind she still pinches herself although that, thank goodness, is nothing like as bad as when you caught her doing it. But I think what's worrying me most of all is the possibility that Amy isn't quite right.'

'Not quite right? Don't understand. Mentally you mean? We both know she has her hang-ups about men…'

'No, it's not something you can stick into a compartment and say it's a mental problem. Quite the contrary, really. No it's…down there. I mean, she had a lot of surgery, things stitched back together – what if there's now an abnormality and they can't make love.' Brenda spread her arms as if trying to throw her problems away.

'What did they say at the time? Is that a possibility?'

'I don't know. They said she wouldn't be able to have children and I know John's aware of that but I'm sure he hasn't considered anything else.'

Brenda paused for a moment before continuing. 'She was six years old when she was put back together, Freda. She's not far off nineteen now and she's done a lot of growing. What if something's gone wrong? She's never been examined since.'

'Then it's obvious. Before she marries she has to see a doctor. She must visit a doctor, no question of that.'

Freda stood, agitated, feeling as helpless as she usually felt when confronted with anything regarding Amy.

'Can you see her agreeing?' Brenda was not convinced.

'What if it was a lady doctor? Let me book her in with Dr. Bakewell – a lot of the ladies are asking for her these days.'

'I don't think she would. She never mentions the attack, it's as though she's wiped it all away. That's why I have to tread so carefully.'

Freda moved towards the door.

'Look, I've got to go into work now. If you want me to book her in just ring me. But for goodness sake, talk to her, Bren. Talk to her before it's too late to do anything about it!'

'Hello Brenda. It's Freda. Is Amy home?'

'No Freda, She isn't. She said she wasn't coming home till late. She wanted to go straight to the flat after she'd been to the doctor's. Is it important?'

'She didn't keep her appointment. Is that important?'

'Oh, God, no! Then I wash my hands of it. I've done all I can. If there is something wrong, they'll have to work it out between them.'

'Do you want me to talk to her? Although I don't know how I can get through to her.'

'No, Freda, leave it. We'll just have to keep our fingers crossed that she's okay. It's not just physical though, is it...' her voice trailed miserably away. How she missed Jack, his strength; he would have known what to do.

She replaced the receiver and crossed to the window. The garden, cloaked in summer colours, looked wonderful, and normally she found it a haven of peace. Today it did nothing to help soothe her thoughts. She clenched her fists, hammered them down on to the worktop.

'The bastard,' she hissed, 'the bastard. He killed my Amelia.'

No words ever passed between Brenda and Amy regarding the aborted appointment. Amy dismissed it from her mind and allowed herself to be carried along with the preparations for the wedding.

*   *   *   *   *

On the day of her daughter's marriage to John, Brenda woke Amy with a smile and a cup of tea, determined to forget all her worries on this special day.

'Good morning, sweetheart. It's a beautiful day, not a cloud in the sky.'

Amy struggled up from sleep, tentatively opening one eye.

'Time is it?' she mumbled, and then, as realisation dawned 'Oh God! What time is it?' She sat up in bed both eyes wide open. Brenda laughed.

'Don't panic. It's not nine o'clock yet. You've bags of time. Now get this bit of breakfast down you and I'll go run your bath.'

Amy smiled at her mother as she took the tray and suddenly Brenda knew that everything was going to be all right and that John and Amy would be fine; she could forget all her worries, cancel her doubts. The sun would shine on to them.

'Are you anywhere near ready, Pat – or shall I come up and give you a hand?'

Pat Farmer smiled at her reflection in the mirror.

'You can come up but forget the hands, David Farmer. You come anywhere near me and we'll never get our jobs done.' She leaned forward and applied a small amount of mascara to her lashes. She pressed her lips together to seal her lipstick. Not bad, she thought, not bad at all.

'Happy?' he asked, his slow smile stealing across his face. She turned to see her husband of six months standing in the doorway. 'If you're ready, I ought to be getting you over to Amy's, she probably needs you to fasten buttons and such like.'

'You know I'm happy. If John and Amy are half as happy, they'll do okay.'

'Do you think they will be?'

She paused and looked at him.

'That sounds serious. Don't you think they will be?'

He shrugged his shoulders.

'I...'

'Andrew?'

'Well, you know, with that happening all those years ago, it's bound to have left its mark, isn't it? I don't mean physically, or at least...'

'David! You're waffling!' She stared in surprise at her normally articulate husband. 'What on earth are you talking about?'

The realisation that Pat knew nothing of her best friend's ordeal hit David squarely between the eyes.

'You're not seriously telling me that Amy has never spoken of it?'

She began to feel exasperated.

'David, for heaven's sake, Amy has been my other half for seven or eight years now and I'm about to be her matron of honour – are you telling me there's something she's never told me about?'

He nodded, feeling sick. He'd assumed that Amy would have told Pat.

'So are you ready?' he said a shade too brightly. 'I'll drop you off at Amy's then I'll go straight on to John. I told him I'd be there for about ten o'clock…'

'I'm not moving.'

'What?'

'Not until you tell me what you're talking about. I assume John knows whatever it is, does he?'

Andrew nodded.

'Oh yes, he knows. It's why we've always looked after her. She… she was raped.' He stumbled slightly over the word and Pat's mouth fell open.

'Raped?' It came out as a whisper. 'Amy? Raped?'

'Six years old, Pat. Cutest little kid you could imagine. A guy called Ronald Treverick got hold of her up on the playing fields and tore her apart. That's what I meant when I said I wondered if they could be happy. It's bound to come between them, isn't it?'

She stared at David, horror etched on her face.

'And she's never said a word. All these years…never a word. And I thought we were friends.'

'That's probably why she never said anything. Think about it, Pat, you were the ideal friend for her, somebody who knew nothing about it. With you, she could be natural, not have to pretend that everything was okay. Don't think badly of her over this – especially today.'

'It'll make a difference, David,' Pat said slowly.

She felt as though her brain was stuck in first gear.

She was seeing a frightened face – a face that belonged to Sonia Dawes, hanging over a cliff edge and held by the one girl who would rather she was dead. An image of fingers slowly opening filled her mind and finally she knew she had been right. She also knew she could do nothing about it, that Amy must never learn that her secret had been discovered. Amy had deliberately killed Sonia – she needed help, not recriminations.

'Will you tell her that you know?' David looked closely at his wife, watching conflicting emotions cross her expressive face.

'One day, perhaps.' She paused, "was he caught?'

'Oh yes, straight away. He must have been out of prison for some time now, but I don't think he's come back here. Look, I'm sorry I brought it up, today of all days. Can we forget it and go and enjoy this wedding?'

'Sure.' She smiled up at him, at the man who had recently walked down the aisle with her. 'Let's go and make it a grand day for them, shall we?'

He took her arm and smiled down at her.

'And may I say Mrs Farmer, that you look ravishing? The bride will have to pull her finger out to outshine you today.' He bent and kissed the top of her head. 'And guess what? I love you. Do you think anyone would notice if we were a bit late…?'

'Later, later, Superstud. Come on, let's get on our way.' She pulled him from the bedroom with a laugh.

Pat was quiet on the journey, lost in her thoughts. It was only when David pulled up outside Stonebrook Cottage that she spoke.

'What damage did he do?'

'Huh?'

'The rapist. What damage?'

'I understand she can't have children.'

'Oh, God, no!'

'Hey, come on.' He pulled her to him, holding her tightly. 'John's aware of it all, more so than I am, obviously. But we've talked. They'll adopt.'

'It's not the same.'

'Yes it is. Particularly if they get a tiny baby.'

'No, it's not,' she said stubbornly. 'Don't tell me it's the same, David, because it most definitely isn't.'

David was surprised by the vehemence in her tone.

'Pat, sweetheart, what's wrong?'

'Oh, nothing much,' she said, a touch of sarcasm in her voice. 'But how the Hell do I tell her that I'm pregnant?'

CHAPTER THIRTEEN

June 1965

The man sat towards the back of the church, on the side allocated to the bride's family. No one queried who he was and anyone who happened to notice him just assumed he was a friend.

He turned as the organ swelled with the opening bars of Mendelssohn's Wedding March and stared with awe at the ethereal vision that was Amy. Clouds of billowing whiteness surrounded her and he inhaled deeply.

'Beautiful,' he murmured, 'absolutely…'

CHAPTER FOURTEEN

September 1965

'…beautiful.' John mouthed the word at his new wife and was taken aback by the glacial eyes that stared back at him.

'Mrs Thornton!' the photographer called, trying to organise the boisterous crowd outside the church.

'Yes?' said John's mother and everyone laughed.

'Sorry, love' the young man said with a grin, 'I meant the other one.' Amy felt a blush spread across her face.

'I want you and your husband together and then a group photograph. Okay?'

She nodded and John led her across to the side of the church. They looked into each other's eyes as the photograph was taken and then everyone else gathered around them, pushing smaller ones to the front.

'Now say sausages,' the photographer yelled and was rewarded with a loud shout.

The noise was deafening and no one noticed the man on the back row of the picture, the one with the horn rimmed glasses and blonde hair.

Amy and John led their guests into the marquee, the early September sunshine casting a welcoming glow through the canvas sides. The sun had been in evidence for the entire day and during the service had reflected brightly through the stained glass windows of the church.

Amy's white dress had been a swirling kaleidoscope of rainbow colours; even her cascading blonde hair had picked up the brilliance of the moment.

The seventy or so guests laughed uproariously throughout David's speech then sobered as John began to talk. He kept his speech deliberately short and they all began to realise just how much Jack Andrews was missed on this special day.

Their first dance was to Cilla Black's You're My World, a song that had become special to both of them as they had worked on their flat; the applause at the end of the dance was overwhelming, and John took Amy in his arms and kissed her. He wanted the world to know how much he loved her.

.The next few hours passed in a blur for Amy. She refused drink after drink, afraid of losing control. She was glad when ten o'clock approached and they decided they could leave their reception. As they began to make their way to the door, David and Pat stopped them.

'Hang on a minute, John. Dad wants a word with you before you go.' David's smile spread across his face. John looked over the crowd searching for a wheelchair containing Alistair Farmer. He saw a hand wave and headed for the corner.

'Mr. Farmer? You wanted me, sir?'

The old man nodded without smiling.

'Yes, young man. There's something I want to give you. It's not a wedding present, more of a going away present that I want you to think about when you have a spare moment. But don't you neglect that pretty bride of yours.' The smile finally broke through and he handed John a large envelope, adding 'Have a good holiday.'

John looked at the envelope, unsure what to do next.

'John? Are you going to open it?' Amy was by his side, obviously as puzzled as he was.

John exhaled slowly. He lifted his eyes from the envelope and looked at the older man.

'It's about my book…'

Alistair Farmer nodded.

'A contract. Study it well then come and see me as soon as you get back. I have good feelings about the book, John, very good feelings. I knew three weeks ago that we wanted it but I held back to make your day doubly special. I think your apprenticeship is over.'

Amy and John left the hall, arms wrapped around each other. He clutched on to the envelope as though it contained a million pounds and it was only when they were in their hotel bedroom that he finally opened it.

He grinned, absolutely delighted by the word 'contract' at the top of the first sheet.

'Well, I don't understand a word of it but what a start to married life. I never expected...'

'Well I did and I never doubted your ability.' Amy was firm. 'Don't underestimate yourself, John. I've read it and I know it's good. We'll have to see whether Mr. Farmer recommends the changes that I suggested or whether I was wrong. One day your name will be so well known, we won't be able to go anywhere without being recognized. And then I can stop working,' she added with a grin.

'Dreams, dreams,' he laughed. 'Come here, wife, and kiss me.' He pulled her into his arms and held her close. 'Did I tell you how beautiful you looked today?' he murmured.

He felt her withdraw immediately and a frown crossed his brow.

'Hey! Hey! What's wrong? Did I say something to upset you? You looked absolutely stunning when you walked down that aisle...wonderful. Can't I tell my gorgeous wife just how I felt?'

'I...I'm sorry. It's all so new, isn't it? I mean...oh, you know...'

He laughed.

'Amy, it's me. You don't need to be nervous. I wouldn't hurt you for the world – didn't I just promise to love you till death us do part? I meant it, you know. We are forever,' and he once more tried to kiss her.

'I'll use the bathroom first, shall I?' she whispered, pulling away from him.

He released her and watched her walk to the door to the right of him, bewilderment etched across his face. He cursed their inexperience; hoped their love was strong enough to guide them through the first difficult days of adjustment. He crossed to the drinks trolley and poured two glasses of the champagne provided by the management.

When Amy came out of the bathroom half an hour later the bubbles had disappeared and the drink was lukewarm. Her face was as white as the all-concealing quilted dressing gown that hid her body from his sight and John stared at her; he knew that in some way he was to blame for the terror showing so starkly in her looks and actions.

Brenda Andrews smiled happily at the departing guests. She had had a wonderful time in spite of the aching void where Jack should have been. She felt her loss most when Amy had been standing at the altar – with Jack's brother by her side instead of her father. She had held back the tears then, afraid of spoiling the day but now as she looked out into a starry sky, she felt a deep sense of peace.

'If you're up there, Jack, I'm sure you're feeling so proud right now.' The rustle of leaves and a gentle breeze playing through the treetops rewarded her.

'Brenda? You ready? All the presents are loaded. There's just enough room for you to perch on top,' Billy

Andrews called.

She felt grateful to him for the job he had done giving Amy away and generally standing in for Jack.

She walked across to the over-loaded car and handed Billy a key.

'Do me a favour, Billy. You go on ahead and put the kettle on. I fancy a bit of a walk. It'll only take me ten minutes – that okay with you, Chris?'

Christine, her sister-in-law, was in the front seat of the car with a huge box on her knee and several smaller packages around her feet. She laughed.

'Cheeky so and so,' she said. 'Leaving us to unload this lot! Of course we don't mind. You walk, but take care. It's dark on your lane. I'll make the coffee and we'll have a bit of a nightcap before we turn in, I think,' she added, with a twinkle in her eye.

'You're on,' Brenda laughed. 'See you in a bit.' She turned to begin the short walk home.

Her thoughts flew here, there and everywhere – they were with Amy, with Jack, with John, with the contract; in her mind she was in their tiny flat, she was in her own home.

She soon found herself at the bottom of the lane leading to Stonebrook Cottage.

That was when she thought she heard footsteps and stopped. Turning, she peered into the darkness but could see no one. The sound had stopped.

She told herself not to be such a damn fool but quickened her own stride.

Billy, standing in the open doorway of the cottage was a welcome sight and she ran the last few yards.

'Okay, love?' he asked.

She nodded.

'Yes, fine. Lovely night for walking. I just thought…'

He waited for her to continue.

'Nothing. I'm just being a bit silly. Too much to drink, I expect. Is there coffee on?'

They closed the door behind them as the sound of jogging footsteps disappeared down the lane. The man smiled as he kept up his rhythmic pace.

John came out of the bathroom to see Amy already in bed, the bedclothes pulled right up to her neck.

'I love you, Mrs Thornton,' he said. 'Like the name?'

She nodded, her smile tight.

'Sounds nice. I always said Amelia never went with Andrews.'

'So we're Amelia tonight, are we?' he joked and barely heard the whispered,

'I hope not.'

The sheets were cool as he slid between them and he pulled Amy towards him. There was a token resistance as if she was fighting with herself and he prayed he would have patience.

The white silk pyjamas were excitingly erotic although they had been bought with the opposite idea in mind.

He began to undo the tiny pearl buttons of the jacket and Amy tried desperately to stop the tremble that started in her toes.

He paused.

'Amy, don't be afraid. I won't hurt you, you know that.'

She nodded mutely.

Never in a million years could she have explained to this wonderful man just how bad she was feeling, and for the first time she bitterly regretted not keeping her appointment at the doctors. Suppose there was something wrong? She groaned and John pulled her fiercely to him.

'Oh God, Amy,' he muttered. 'I don't know what to do to help you.'

Seconds passed and she pushed down the bedclothes removing the pyjama trousers. She knelt on the bed and looked down at John.

'I don't know if I can handle it,' she said simply, 'but there's one thing for sure, unless we make love, I'll never know.'

He lifted his arms and unfastened the bottom two buttons. She shrugged the jacket from her shoulders and he looked at the woman before him. Small breasts, a narrow waist flaring gently into rounded hips, he knew he was looking at something so close to perfection that it was almost unreal.

She felt uncomfortable. His gaze was unflinching as his eyes roamed every square inch of her and she shivered. Her nipples became erect under his scrutiny and he reached up and pulled her down.

'Perfect,' he said and for the first time he touched her breasts. The softly yielding flesh under his fingers caused an erection so hard that he felt Amy inhale sharply as he pushed himself against her stomach; he knew that nothing in his life so far had prepared him for this feeling.

He took one of her hands in his, gently guiding it down to touch him.

She stroked him tentatively but then he removed her hand.

'No, don't do that,' he said, his voice thick with emotion.' He rolled over to cover her body and slowly tried to enter her.

She attempted to stifle the scream and it came out as a whimper. He pushed a little harder, somehow sensing that if they didn't make love tonight it would never happen.

She stiffened underneath him and he pushed once more. Seconds later it was over and it was his turn to groan.

'I'm so sorry, sweetheart. I meant it to be so special but I lost control altogether. Come here,' He tried to pull her to him but her look killed any hope of redeeming the situation.

'It…it was horrible,' she said, her voice hoarse with anger. 'Don't touch me again – ever.'

BOOK TWO

1966 –1989 North Cornwall

CHAPTER FIFTEEN

Spring 1966

The scream that drew itself out of Pat Farmer's lungs threw itself into the room on the ragged edges of a long expulsion of air.

'You bastard, you fucking bastard, Farmer!' she shouted.

'She doesn't mean it, David,' the round midwife said, looking at the devastated face of the young man trying to comfort his wife in vain. His curly dark hair was damp with sweat. He had endured every painful contraction along with Pat. 'We're almost there now and this is the most tiring part. She'll have forgotten ninety nine per cent of this by tomorrow morning.'

'I've known her five years, Mrs Kennedy, and I've never heard her say anything stronger than damn.'

Ellie Kennedy laughed.

'Well, if you can't take it, young man, you'd better leave the room. It'll get worse before it gets better.' She turned her attention to the recumbent Pat who was building up to the next contraction. 'Now come on, love. I can see the head. Lots of hair just like daddy but we need to get this little one out. A good push...come on Pat...come on, here it comes. Good girl, now just pant, my love. Don't push again until I say.'

David gripped on to his wife's hand and bent to kiss her forehead.   'Don't you ever come near me again, Farmer,' she growled between clenched teeth. 'This is the most bloody awful day of my life. I'll never forgive you for this, never.'

'Right, Pat, next contraction - just push.'

Pat's yell as her son finally entered the world was one of exultation. When she held him in her arms at last she turned to David with tears of love spilling down her cheeks.

'Hold him?' she asked.

David couldn't speak. He shook his head, afraid even to touch the tiny bundle. Ellie Kennedy lifted the baby out of Pat's arms and placed him in David's.

'There now, don't be silly. He won't break. He's a beauty, does he have a name?'

David finally spoke.

'Richard Alistair Farmer. After both our fathers,' he explained.

'Mmmm,' she said. 'Very grand. R.A.F. Bound to be a pilot.' And so, in the very first few minutes of his life, Richard Alistair Farmer gained a nickname that would never leave him, one he learned to spell before his real name.

*   *   *   *   *

August was a wonderful month for everyone surrounding the baby. At four months of age, he was an entrancing child with a ready smile, able to twist his young parents around all his fingers.

John and Amy became his godparents. Amy struggled with her feelings towards the baby, jealousy often rising to the surface.

In that same month, John and Amy moved out of their tiny flat, taking on what seemed a huge mortgage on a cottage close to Stonebrook Cottage.

'He's a lovely baby, Pat,' Amy said gently, bending

over to stroke the smooth skin of the child's face.

Pat laughed.

'You wouldn't have thought so at three o'clock this morning! Pick him up if you want.'

Startled, Amy shook her head and stepped back from the crib.

'Amy? You okay?'

'I'm fine. Sure. Course, I'm okay.'

'He won't break, you know.'

'No, but the books say don't pick them up all the time, don't they?'

'Listen you, this is my baby and sod what the books say. I pick him up all the time just for the hell of it – I want him to know, to sense, just how much he's loved. Go on, give him a cuddle. He probably won't wake up anyway, considering how little sleep he had last night!'

Still Amy shook her head and slowly Pat began to understand.

'Amy, do you want to talk? What's wrong? Something between you and John? Or is it…the past?'

'You know?'

Pat nodded and watched the colour drain from Amy's face.

'And I suppose David told you, did he?'

'He did, but only by accident. It never occurred to him that you would have kept it from me. He mentioned it on the morning of your wedding…'

'Did he? And what did the great David Farmer surmise? That we wouldn't be able to make love? That I wouldn't want John anywhere near me? Go on, Pat, tell me!'

'Amy, Amy! Come on. Sit down at the table. I invited you over for a coffee and a natter, not World War Three. All David said was that he hoped you would be happy, considering everything that you have gone through.'

Amy placed her head on her arms, unable to speak. Pat felt out of her depth – something was very wrong and until Amy chose to open up, she could do nothing. She placed a cup by her friend.

'Drink that when you're ready.'

It was several minutes before either of them spoke. Amy finally broke the silence.

'I shouldn't have shouted at you. It's not your fault,' she said. 'It's just that…'

'I'm listening and it won't go any further.'

'John and I haven't made love since our wedding night.' She blurted the words out and felt her cheeks suffuse with colour.

'Since…' Pat stared at her friend in horror. 'But that's eleven months.'

Amy said nothing.

'Why, Amy?'

She shook her head mutely.

'I don't know. It was an absolute disaster. It hurt but I don't know whether it hurt because it was the first time or whether it hurt in my head. I still remember it, you know.'

'The wedding night, or…'

'The rape, Pat. It's called rape.'

'Tell me about it.' Pat spoke the words quietly, relieved to see that the tears were slowly stopping. 'Talk to me, I'm here.'

Haltingly and after many gulps of coffee, Amy began to talk of the assault for the first time.

'The pain was unbearable,' she said. 'I suppose the shock of the pain stopped me from screaming or crying – apparently I went into a coma of sorts for four days and they just took everything away. I suppose that's why I can't hold Pilot – that's a different sort of pain.'

She talked and Pat listened, hearing the details for the first time; suddenly aware of just how much David didn't know.

When Amy had finished speaking she seemed to be in shock. Her eyes had taken on a glazed look and bright spots of colour burned in her cheeks.

Pat reached across the kitchen table and took her friend's hand.

'Thank you for trusting me. Now, we have to sort you two out. I can't bear to think of you both being unhappy.'

'We're not unhappy.' The response was a shade too fast. 'Why should we be unhappy? I look after him, especially now I've finished work. His book's due out in another month, we've got our cottage – no, we're not unhappy.'

'But Amy, you can't seriously expect John to go through the rest of his life without sex! One of two things will happen, I promise you. Either he'll leave you and build a new life for himself, or he'll stay with you, make the best of it because he loves you, and have a string of affairs. Which option do you prefer?'

'I think I'd die without him.' Amy shuddered.

'Do you sleep in the same bed?'

Amy nodded and looked down at her hands, restlessly intertwining her fingers.

'We do but I always go to bed before him. He's usually writing until the early hours anyway and then I pretend to be asleep when he does come up.'

'I hate to say this, Amy, but the answer lies in your hands. I'm no psychiatrist, believe me, and maybe that's the sort of help you need, but my inclination is to say seduce him. Give him what for; replace the bad memories of your first encounter with sex with the good memories of your second encounter. But first of all, go see a doctor. Make sure the pain you felt wasn't physical.'

'Seduce him?' Amy looked aghast and Pat doubled up with laughter.

'God, Amy, you're priceless. You know, sexy nighties and such things. Tie him to the bed or something but for God's sake show him you love him instead of just telling him and hoping that will keep him tied to you, because it won't.'

Later that week they went shopping with much giggling from Pat and a peculiar churning of the stomach for Amy. Her quickly arranged visit to Dr. Bakewell had resulted in an internal examination. She was pronounced "fine" and was grateful that the doctor hadn't been censorious.

She bought a black nightie; she wanted a white one but Pat had scoffed.

'You've got to be a femme fatale, not a virgin. Get the black one and knock his eyes out.'

John was surprised at the sumptuous meal, the candles, the wine; he didn't question it, just thanked his beautiful wife with his slow smile then disappeared as normal into his study. Amy felt sick, unsure how to begin the seduction scene.

Taking her courage in both hands, she put her head around the study door.

'Just going for a bath, sweetheart. Anything you want first?'

John glanced up and blinked. He pushed his glasses back on to his head and looked at her. God, how he wanted her.

'No, I'm fine. You go ahead.'

She closed the door quietly, humming softly to herself, trying valiantly to pretend that she wasn't shaking all over.

John smelt the fragrance of her perfume before sensing something was different. Leaving behind thoughts of the Highlands of Scotland, he lifted his head, afraid to turn around, afraid to let his hopes rise. He held his breath and slowly swivelled his chair.

The nightie was sheer, black and all revealing. The small triangle of hair at the junction of her thighs, dark against her white skin, was the focus of his attention at first. Slowly his gaze travelled upwards, taking in every aspect of her body; the already erect nipples, the waist he felt he could span with his hands. He gulped audibly.

'Amy?'

'How important is your writing right at this very minute?' She held out her hands.

'I'll change my job. Become a milkman.'

She smiled slowly, seductively.

'Not necessary, just put it on hold for an hour…or two…or three.'

He felt at a loss not knowing what to say, what to do, afraid that if he walked towards her she would back off saying *fooled you.*

But she didn't. She stood, unmoving, until he slowly lifted her arms, linking her hands behind his neck. He was still unable to accept what was happening. Her words from that September night still seared his brain – *don't touch me again, ever!*

Her kiss began as a light touch then deepened as she thrust her tongue into his mouth. He began to get the message.

At last, his mind echoed, *at last.*

He put his arms around her waist. She felt so fragile, the nightdress silky beneath his fingers. His hands ran lightly over her hips and he became lost in the spiraling vortex created by the fire in her kiss.

'Come to bed, John,' she whispered, 'come to bed with me,'

He couldn't speak. Didn't want to speak. She led him by the hand up the narrow stairs to the large, sparsely furnished room that reflected Amy's character. Turning to him, she beckoned with one finger. He moved as if in a dream resisting the urge to tumble her unceremoniously on to the bed and rip the sexy nightdress from her. He knew that he must not make mistakes this time. From somewhere, he would summon up the experience that he needed but didn't have.

Amy seduced him slowly, carefully, passionately. He required no experience – Amy took over leading him where she wanted him to go and willingly he followed. Eleven months of believing she was cold to the point of frigidity and suddenly she erupted into one vibrating volcano.

They made love through the night until, satiated and utterly spent, John slept. He wrapped his arm around her waist holding her close to him enjoying the new experience of the simple act.

Amy smiled into the darkness. It had been worth the pain, a pain that had lessened the harder John had pushed; now he wouldn't need to look elsewhere for comfort. He was hers.

The other face was something she would have to learn to live with. The face that had been superimposed over John's as he lay across her body at the moment of climax, the face on the photograph given to her by the police. Ronald Treverick ought to rot in Hell she thought before allowing her eyelids to close.

'Help? What sort of help?' Amy looked at her mother in consternation. 'Is something wrong?'

'No, don't worry. It's just that I can't manage the smallholding on my own. I have no intention of asking you and John to work the land for a bit, you're both far too busy with John's new book, so I've decided to take on a man. I can afford it, it's a good little business thanks to your dad and it'll give me a bit more time to watch this new television I've just squandered all that money on.' She smiled at her daughter, a twinkle in her eye.

It had taken John and Amy months to persuade her to have a television. Already, she was remarkably knowledgeable about the characters in Coronation Street.

'Mum, are you sure? You know we'll help wherever we can.'

Brenda laughed.

'John is no gardener, Amy, and you're kept pretty busy editing his writing. I've already placed an advert and I've got a chap coming to see me this afternoon. He rang this morning. Just moved down to Cornwall, he said, from up North, so I'll see if he's suitable. It'll be a load off my mind if he is, I can tell you.'

'Want me there?'

'Well, funnily enough I came to ask you that. If one of you can spare the time…'

'I'll be there,' Amy said firmly. 'Come on. You can take me to that new café down by the harbour for a cheeseburger then we'll go up to the cottage to wait for your man, whoever he is.'

'Cheeseburger? What's a cheeseburger?'

Amy put an arm around her mother's shoulders.

'You, Mrs Andrews, are about to have your taste buds tickled. Tell you what, I'll treat you as it's your first time at having such a gastronomic delight – hang on while I get my coat and bag.'

Brenda watched as Amy left the room and shook her head in wonder at the change in her daughter. Since her wedding she had become more and more morose, unhappy with life but there had been a recent change and now she was blossoming.

Brenda shrugged her shoulders; *oh well, as long as whatever had been bothering her has gone, what did it matter?*

The cloud that had been over her since the age of six was changing from nimbus to cumulus and she knew her Amy was happy at last.

But the darkness was still within Amy – she couldn't shake the image of Ronald Treverick from her mind. How much longer could she stand to have him permanently living with her? No, Amy was not completely happy at last, far from it.

CHAPTER SIXTEEN

Spring 1966

Treverick knew it was time to make his move. A change of direction was needed and handing in his notice was the start. The job had been a good one but it would not have led him to the Andrews family; he had to get a new position and his experience with Taggarts would stand him in good stead.

He fingered the reference from Tony Taggart, a reference given reluctantly since he hadn't wanted to lose a valuable assistant.

'I'm sorry,' he had told the obviously upset man, 'but Mother is ill and I have to go back up North.'

Taggart had said that there would always be a position for him if he ever felt the inclination to return to Cornwall, to come back to Bude.

'Thank you,' he responded, his boyish smile flashing across his face, 'but I can't see that happening. I expect I'll have to take over management of the shop now that Mother isn't well enough to run it herself.'

And now he had to find the job that would lead him directly to Brenda and Amy Andrews.

He regretted missing out on old Jack, but old Jack had left two vulnerable ladies to fend for themselves…

CHAPTER SEVENTEEN

Summer 1966-Summer 1967

Ken Buckingham's short fair hair suited his rounded face giving him an almost boyish appearance despite the fact he admitted he was thirty-five years old. Both Amy and Brenda responded immediately to his ready smile and loved the flat unvarying tone of his Yorkshire accent.

'So, Mr. Buckingham, what experience do you have with medium scale gardening?'

'None, Duck.' He laughed. 'I won't lie to you. But up north we're all gardeners. I had a big garden, grew mainly vegetables, few flowers and had a bit of lawn for the missus that got smaller every year because I needed more for the vegetable plot. Spent most of my time in the garden and that's why I jumped at this chance when I saw your advert.'

'Where are you from, Mr. Buckingham?'

'A place just outside Sheffield, between Sheffield and Rotherham. You'll not have heard of it.' Again the smile appeared.

'So why Cornwall? Why move all this way without any job prospects?'

'Amy!' her mother shrieked.

'I'm running away. Feel free to ask whatever you want, Miss.'

'It's Mrs,' Amy responded, 'Mrs Thornton. So go on then, why Cornwall?'

'I like it,' he said simply. 'I've been here a few times with my brother-in-law. He's a lorry driver and I did some trips with him. I figured if you're going to run away you might as well run away to somewhere that you like.'

Amy nodded approvingly.

'Quite right, but what are you running away from?'

'Amy! That's enough!' Brenda blushed and this time both Amy and Ken laughed.

'Look, I don't want any secrets,' he said. 'I want this job and I'll work hard for you so it's only fair you should know about me. I'm divorced, no little 'uns, so no ties. But the wife – ex, I should say – can't make up her mind whether or not she really wants to be divorced so I've made it up for her and not left a forwarding address. Mind you', he finished with a grin, 'happen that's because I haven't got a forwarding address as yet, nowhere permanent at any rate.'

'Oh?' Brenda felt she ought to join in at this stage.

'Only arrived last night. Booked in at a B&B but I've to look round for something of my own.'

'Can I think about this, Mr. Buckingham? I was actually looking for someone who had worked on a small holding before, but...'

'I can do the job, Mrs Andrews. Shall I call you later?'

She nodded.

'Please. I promise you a firm answer by four o'clock. Oh, and down in Padstow there's Mrs Troon – takes in boarders, excellent place I understand. Here's the address, you'll want somewhere no matter what I decide.' She scribbled on a small piece of paper.

They watched him walk down the lane, his short muscled figure exuding a certain grace.

'Mum, he's just what you want!'

'Is he? He's not done the work before.'

'But he's full of muscles,' Amy protested. 'And you heard him say he loves gardening. That's half the battle.'

'I don't know... there's something about him...'

Brenda sighed.

'Animal magnetism?' Her daughter grinned and once more Brenda was struck by the change in her.

'Well, I'm not looking for animal magnetism in anybody, thank you very much.'

'Don't say you're prejudiced against a Yorkshire accent.'

'No it was quite pleasant to listen to, wasn't it? Oh, I suppose it's just me being silly. It's the thought of somebody else using your dad's tools, doing the work he loved. When he rings, I'll say yes.'

'So when can you start?'

'Yesterday.' The pleasure in Ken Buckingham's voice was undeniable and Brenda found herself smiling into the telephone.

'So will nine o'clock tomorrow morning be okay?'

'You tell me, you're the boss. I can be there earlier if you want. There's a fair bit to do – I had a quick look as I went down the lane yesterday. Oh, by the way, I've taken a room with Mrs Troon, very pleasant it is so I'm nicely settled now. You'll not regret giving me the job, Mrs Andrews...no, you'll not regret it at all.'

And she didn't.

He arrived before eight o'clock, had a cup of tea and then she didn't see him again until lunchtime. He had double-dug a large area of ground ready for the planting of sprouts and had begun work on clearing the dead flowers. Already the land had begun to take on a more business-like appearance and Brenda knew she had made the right decision.

She produced a cup of tea at three o'clock that brought a huge smile to his face.

'Thanks, Mrs Andrews. That cool breeze isn't cool

enough when you're deep digging.' He ran a hand across his brow, removing the sweat and replacing it with a streak of dirt.

'And how's it going,' she asked looking around.

'Very well. Whoever worked for you before knew what he was doing, this ground's been well dug.'

'No one worked for me. My husband worked the land. He died last year,' she said quietly.

'Me and my big mouth.' He dropped his eyes to the ground. 'That's all right Mr. Buckingham, you didn't know.'

'Ken, call me Ken. If we're both suited I intend being here for a long time, so Mr. Buckingham's out. Daft name it is.'

She laughed.

'Ken it is and call me Brenda. If we're going to work together – and we will be, I'm used to doing my fair share of the digging and harvesting.'

'Right then. And I'll tell thee what, Brenda, tha't as good as any Yorkshire lass at mashing tea.'

'Mashing?'

'Aye. It's called a mashing where I come from, but don't worry, you'll get used to translating.'

She took the cup from him and turned to walk away.

'You're okay, Ken, you're okay.' He liked the compliment and the spade suddenly seemed much lighter in his hands.

The telephone was ringing as Brenda re-entered the cottage.

'Mum? It's me. They're here.'

'Who's here?'

'Not who. What. The first copies of John's book.'

Brenda wished she could see John's face. She knew

just how much he had longed for this moment.

'And John? Is he pleased with the look of it?'

'He's just opened a huge bottle of champagne,' she laughed. 'I must go before he sprays everything. We'll bring your copy over tomorrow.'

Brenda smiled into the receiver.

'I'm absolutely delighted for the pair of you. I know how much time you've put into the final draft. Enjoy your evening, Amy – see you tomorrow.'

Her hand remained on the telephone long after she had finished speaking. She sensed a loosening of tension that had been there since her marriage and she wondered what had changed.

Brenda moved into the kitchen to begin the preparation for dinner, looking forward to Freda's company during the normally unbearably long and lonely evening hours.

'Did you know Amy had been for a checkup?'

'Amy? She's not ill, is she?' Brenda looked startled. She pushed back her short brown curls nervously. 'What's wrong?'

'No. I had a quick peek at her notes before filing them. She just came for an internal examination. It said everything was fine.'

Brenda stared at Freda.

'But... I don't understand. Why would she suddenly need a check up now? She wouldn't go before she was married.' And then the cogs began to turn in her brain. 'Freda, you don't think...'

'Think? I try very hard not to think where Amy's concerned because if I did I'd worry myself into an early grave,' the older woman said gruffly.

'But they've been married eleven months. Surely they

haven't only just started making love…'

'Looks like it.'

'What sort of a mother am I, Freda?' she said slowly.

'A darn good one,' was the sharp retort. 'You've brought up that child under extremely difficult circumstances and she's a real beauty.'

'I should have seen something was wrong; she's my daughter for God's sake! John's a son to me, not a son-in-law, and he must have been hurting so much. Why didn't I see it?'

'You probably did. I did but didn't want to see it. Anyway, no point worrying about it, it's their life.'

Brenda stared at Freda.

'I don't think we need to worry now. There's a change in Amy, a sort of lightening. She's suddenly started laughing. I noticed it first with Ken yesterday and couldn't believe it.'

'Ken?'

'Ken Buckingham. I hired him yesterday to work the market garden. If you'd arrived five minutes earlier you'd have met him. He's a real work-horse. I'm hoping it's going to be okay.'

Freda stared closely at her sister-in-law.

'Have you checked him out?'

'Checked him out? No, not really. He's just moved here from Yorkshire – running away from an ex wife who can't make up her mind whether or not she wants to be ex, so he says.'

'So he says.'

Brenda laughed.

'Don't be so suspicious. I like him, he's got quite a sense of humour and that very flat Yorkshire accent – I think he's okay. You're so against men you can't trust any of them!'

'Quite right!'

'No, it's not right. I had a wonderful husband in your brother and you know it. I couldn't have wished for better.'

'Jack...' Freda said quietly. 'Yes Jack was different. I miss him you know.'

Brenda reached across the table to touch her hand. 'I know. He never talked a lot but always listened and now I find myself talking, expecting him to be there, to listen and just nod in that way he did, wobbling his pipe up and down. I don't cry though. I wouldn't have wanted him to linger, not in the pain that would have followed if that embolism hadn't released him first.'

Freda nodded.

'And he wouldn't have wanted us to be wittering on like this either. Now, shall we have a game of cards?'

Then the distant sound of a car engine brought a smile to Brenda's face.

'That sounds like John and Amy. They must have decided to come over tonight instead of tomorrow. Could be four handed cards.'

John had autographed the books and he handed them over to Brenda and Freda with a diffident air.

'Don't be so self-effacing, young man,' Freda chided. 'This is no mean feat, having a book published. We're very proud of you and I can't wait to read this. Is it sexy?'

'Aunt Freda!'

'Oh, Amy, don't be such a prude. If there isn't a bit of sex in it, it can't be very true to life.'

'It's true to life. And I don't think Amy was being a prude, she just didn't expect you of all people to come out with it!' John grinned.

He thought back to their love-making, to the uninhibited wildness that was in Amy and he felt warmth begin to spread through his body. There was nothing prudish in their shared passion.

He wasn't unduly worried that last night she had turned away from him as soon as he had slid into bed – she had acknowledged that sex could be wonderful and he felt sure things would be okay between them.

Casually he took hold of his wife's hand and raised it to his lips, an action that didn't go unnoticed by Brenda and she hid a smile of satisfaction as she touched the front cover of John's book.

'Many congratulations, John,' she said softly. 'As Freda said, we're very proud of you.'

'Not all my work, Ma. Amy did some of it and she's done even more on the new book.'

'And how long before that goes to Farmers?'

'Another week at the outside. Then,' he added wryly, 'the real work starts.'

Brenda took the book to bed with her and read far into the night. She tried to be objective but felt a growing sense of excitement as the words tumbled from the pages. Her son-in-law was definitely not a run of the mill author – he had a wonderful far-reaching talent and it was with reluctance that she had to put down the book and sleep. S he would never be up in time for Ken's arrival.

Treverick glanced at his watch as he saw her bedroom light extinguish. Half past three? Maybe she was entertaining a gentleman friend… he jogged to the telephone box and dialed her number, a smile crossing his face. He could just imagine her annoyance at being interrupted – he waited.

'Hello?' he heard before quietly replacing the receiver. Half an hour later he rang again and then silently headed home, smiling all the way.

CHAPTER EIGHTEEN

January 1969

John stared with wonder at the face and figure of David's new secretary. Her long dark brown hair echoed the beautiful brown eyes she turned towards him. She was tall and slender, and with long tapering fingers that emphasised the sheer femininity of her. The slight blush on her cheeks was pure English rose.

'Dawn, get these contracts sent off will you?' he heard David say from a distance. The woman smiled and took the documents.

'Right away,'

Her voice, just as he had known it would, fitted the rest of her with warm, sensual perfection.

'She's an excellent typist, too,' David said drily, following the direction of John's look. 'She's off limits - you're married.

Now, the figures for *Grave Matters* are in and they're through the roof. You're number three in the best sellers list and we couldn't ask for more. 1969 is definitely your year.'

John grinned.

'And I've got some more news for you. If I can find a secretary within the next couple of weeks, you'll have *The Son* finished by November.'

'A secretary? But I thought Amy did all your typing.' David frowned. 'She did for *Rest in Pieces* and *Grave Matters* but as you know she edits my work as well and I don't think it's fair to put everything on her. I can well afford a secretary so we're going to advertise. Wouldn't mind one like your Miss...?'

'Mrs Dawn Lynch and believe me you don't get many like her.'

'I just bet you don't,' he said to himself. Standing, he reached across the desk and ruffled David's hair. 'I am only joking you know. Amy's the only woman in my life and always will be.'

David nodded and smiled but he knew without having to have it spelt out that his long-time friend was half serious.

'Whatever you say, John, whatever you say – just leave Dawn alone. By the way, is it still okay for you and Amy to come over on Saturday?'

John nodded.

'Definitely. And don't put Pilot to bed before we get there. Give us a little bit of playtime with him, for goodness sake. We don't see nearly enough of him.'

'It's time you had one of your own. Have you...?'

A shrug of John's shoulders spoke volumes.

'It's been tentatively discussed but...oh, you know Amy. She's frightened of committing herself to the idea of adoption. Sometimes I think we should never – oh, forget it. I'm just feeling a bit down.'

'Want to talk?'

John shook his head.

'Nothing much to say. You know how much I love Amy but I don't think she really loves me. I don't think she can love. I think Treverick killed something inside her...I know, I know. It's hardly surprising but there are times when I feel so damn lonely, so...' He turned to leave David's office. 'Take no notice, David. I'm talking out of my arse.'

'If you are, it's the first time ever, mate.' David spoke

quietly, trying to suppress the worry he felt for John. 'I'm always here – don't forget that.'

John gave himself a mental shake-up and forced a laugh.

'See you Saturday. And remember to keep Pilot up.'

He left David's office feeling angry at how much of himself he had revealed. He was almost through the outer door of the office suite when he heard Dawn Lynch call him.

He turned with a smile – her voice putting a silly grin across his face.

'Yes?'

'Would you mind…?' and she waved a copy of *Grave Matters* at him. 'I have all three of your books but this is the only one I have with me.'

He took the book from her and wrote his name on the flyleaf.

'Okay?' he asked with a smile.

She nodded, no trace of shyness or embarrassment in her manner. 'Thank you. I'll treasure it.'

'Ah', he responded with a twinkle in his eye. 'But have you read it?'

'As soon as it was released. I was a fan long before I came to work for Farmers. And I won't insult you by pretending I wanted your autograph for my son or my mother!'

'Have you got one?'

'What?'

'A son.'

'Oh, I see. No as a matter of fact I haven't – I do have a mother, though,' she laughed.

'And a husband?'

'No, no husband.'

'I'm sorry. I thought David said…'

'Mrs. Yes he did. I'm divorced. No husband, no children.'

The slight tone of bitterness in her speech was apparent but John wisely refrained from continuing. Instead he smiled at her, lightening the mood.

'Congratulations! An emancipated lady. And what does a feminist do in Padstow when she's not working for David?'

'I don't live in Padstow for a start. I live in Rock. I prefer the other side of the estuary to this side. And I do very little really. I read a lot, enjoy the theatre, have a sizable record collection – I keep myself busy.'

'So, can I tempt you into taking a trip to the theatre with me?'

Her laughter was infectious – her put down was excellently accomplished.

'And will Mrs Thornton need a ticket as well?'

He paused for a moment.

'You're right, of course. Forgive me, Dawn, it was unthinkable that I should ask you.' His words sounded stilted even to him.

'That's okay. Don't let it bother you.'

He gathered up the items he had placed on her desk and walked to the door. Turning he looked at her for a moment.

'See you around – it was good talking to you.'

'And you,' she said softly, 'and you.'

CHAPTER NINETEEN

January 1969

Treverick was happy with his new job. He was starting at the bottom but that didn't worry him in the slightest – his newfound confidence in his abilities ensured a quick climb up the proverbial ladder.

It was harder now to keep a watch on the two Andrews women; it had been necessary to move to London. When he had applied for the new position he had discovered the drawback that he would be away from Cornwall, but London wasn't that far away and acquiring a car had made life a whole lot easier.

He guessed it would take anything as long as ten years before he could capitalise but he knew one day he would be rewarded for his patience.

He had completed two thirds of his project; his appearance was now so completely unlike the younger Ronald Treverick as to be entirely unrecognisable and this job was a way to get to the Andrews family easily and smoothly.

If Treverick permitted himself the occasional small smile of pleasure, it was to be understood.

The girl lying below him on the bed saw one of his rare smiles and assumed it was for her. She guessed the smile meant he was enjoying the sex but inwardly she wondered. If he never climaxed surely that meant he wasn't getting any satisfaction?

She moaned and thrust with her hips; Treverick looked down into her face with its flushed cheeks and closed eyes.

No, not beautiful, but she'd do for the time being.

CHAPTER TWENTY

Spring 1969

The Farmer residence was impressive. A large, six-bedroomed house set in extensive gardens, its walls covered with Ivy and Virginia Creeper, it exuded an air of welcoming tranquility. Pat loved it, loved the security it afforded after a childhood of tension and unhappiness.

And she thoroughly enjoyed entertaining. Having Amy and John over for the day gave her a great deal of pleasure and she appreciated just how much John loved playtime with her young son. Sometimes she wondered about Amy, about how she felt towards the bundle of mischief hell bent on having the time of his life no matter who was there to join in with him – Amy was a very difficult person to understand.

She opened her mouth to remonstrate with the child – he was getting a little too loud – but John shook his head slightly and smiled at her as if to say leave him, he's fine.

Pilot grinned up at John and then began to rain blows on his face.

'I'm a boxer,' he shouted then giggled as John placed a fist against his snub nose.

'I'm a better boxer,' his Godfather declared, 'and if you don't behave I'll prove it! I can beat any four year old on this earth!'

'Sorry, John,' Pat said. 'That's David's fault - we're working our way through all the sports to see which Pilot excels at. So far it's tiddley winks.'

'Tiddley winks, huh? Fancy taking me on, Champ? Used to be pretty nifty at that myself…' and the little boy took hold of his hand as they walked together across the lawn.

'He's lovely, Pat,' Amy said, trying to squash the emotions that threatened to rise to the surface every time she saw Pilot.

'Have you done anything yet about adoption?' Pat as usual went straight to the heart of the matter. Only her appearance had changed in the eight years since they had left school. Her face had lost the elfin look, become more rounded, prettier, and she had put on a little weight following Pilot's birth.

'I can't...'

'But John would love a child. And so would you.'

'Would I? I had a hell of a childhood – why would I inflict that on some other poor child?'

Pat stared at her in amazement.

'But your childhood was so...extraordinary as to be almost unbelievable, Amy. How many children experience something like that? It wouldn't be the same for your child.'

Amy looked across the expanse of green lawn obstinately putting her thoughts on hold. Who could say for definite that there wouldn't be another Ronald Treverick out there, waiting for her child?

'Let's change the subject, Pat.'

Pat shrugged.

'You can't keep changing it forever. At least promise me you'll think about it. John needs a child.'

She didn't add what she was thinking – that maybe John needed a wife as well. She could see lines of tension that had appeared on his face and she wondered just how far Amy's sexual revolution had taken her. She was only guessing but it wasn't difficult to figure out that their relationship had taken a nose-dive.

'Come on,' she said, standing and placing cups on the tray. 'Let's go in. It looks as though we're going to have to drag David off that phone.'

'Don't say a word to John, will you?' There was pleading in Amy's voice. 'He's in the middle of a book and can do without any hassle...'

Pat looked at her friend.

'I won't say anything but I think you should. Take a close look at him, Amy, a really close look.'

Dawn was on the telephone when John entered the reception area and she looked up, greeting him with a smile. She liked the tall young man very much and was all too aware of the physical attraction. Forbidden territory.

She held up a finger and mouthed one minute. In return he blew her a kiss. She felt herself begin to blush and turned her back on him as she continued her conversation.

'Okay, Mr. Matthews, I'll make sure it's in the post to you tonight. Bye.' She replaced the receiver.

'And will you?'

'What?'

'Make sure it's in the post. Whatever it is he wants.'

She laughed.

'Of course – I never make promises I can't keep.'

'Never?' He raised one eyebrow and again she felt the blush start. He was blatantly flirting and she should have known how to handle it – would have known how to handle it if he hadn't been so good-looking and pleasant with it.

She tried to be firm, to put him in his place.

'No, never,'

'But you're divorced...'

'I didn't break the promises, he did.'

John managed to look contrite.

'I'm sorry. That's unforgivable, prying into your private life. Apology accepted?'

She smiled.

'Of course. And you can pry all you like because I'm not telling you anything else. My marriage is over, wiped out and dismissed from my mind.'

'Dawn, come for a drink with me?'

She shook her head, troubled by the response surging through her. She would love to be in the company of this man but…

'No thanks, John. You're married.'

'Dawn…'

'No, John. Drop it. And just how long do you think my job would last if Mr. Farmer found out?'

'Oh, David's a man of the world…'

'Is he indeed? Why would I need to be a man of the world?' David's deep voice cut into their conversation and for a moment there was silence.

John was the first to break it.

'We were discussing part of the plot of this damned novel. I've hit a bit of a writer's block and I was considering sticking in a raunchy sex scene. Dawn said she didn't think you'd appreciate it at that particular point but I think she's wrong…' John was aware he was waffling and was angry with his friend for causing his defensive attitude.

'If in doubt, stick in a sex scene'. David paused and rubbed his chin. 'Sounds like a good enough rule to me and there's no getting away from it, it sells books. So did you want me, John, or has Dawn been able to help?'

'Didn't particularly want anyone, just happened to be in the neighbourhood and I thought I'd call in. But a coffee sounds like a good idea.'

'Well, I've got a meeting but Dawn will look after you. Are we still on for golf on Saturday?'

'Sure. Dawn – milk, no sugar.'

She smiled at him.

'Milk, no sugar. David, do you have time for one?'

He shook his head.

'No thanks. I'm meeting Jack Brammah in an hour and I'm already late setting off.' He crossed to the exit door. 'Be good you two, and I'll see you Saturday, John.'

Dawn left the reception area and moved into the cubbyhole they used for making drinks. Her hands were trembling and she clenched her fists tightly. Off limits her brain kept repeating, off limits.

But he wasn't; he was standing by her in a space hardly big enough to accommodate one person, never mind two.

'Dawn,' he said softly, and she turned. Too close. Too damned close.

'Please, John…' She knew the words were ineffectual.

He bent and placed a gentle kiss on her lips. For a moment she froze and then pushed past him.

'I think you'd better make the coffee.' Her words were tremulous. 'I've some typing to do for when David gets back…'

She looked towards the office door as it opened. David looked around it.

'Forgot this, John… Oh, where is he?'

'He's making the coffee. I want to get these letters done for you.'

John came out of the small room, a half smile on his face.

'David? Thought you'd gone.'

'I had but I remembered you saying you wanted a

secretary. Done anything about it yet?'

John shook his head.

'Well, this is the name of a girl who came along for interview for Dawn's job. I think she'll suit you. Why not go along and see her? Name is Linda Chambers. Right, I'm off.'

The door closed and Dawn turned to John.

'And I think you should go, John,' she said, her voice low. 'No,' she held up a hand as he moved towards her. 'Please don't come near. I would be stupid to encourage you, I'm no marriage wrecker.'

'Marriage? What marriage?' He laughed bitterly before hanging his head. 'I'm sorry, Dawn. I shouldn't involve you. God, all I ever do is apologise to you. I'm not apologising for the kiss, though. You're right, I should go. I'll see you soon, and on a strictly professional basis, I promise you.'

It was as he was going down to street level that Dawn finally admitted to herself that she wanted him. But there was no chance in the world that she would ever give in to that need. He was a married man.

Linda Chambers hated her new job. She would have really enjoyed the one at Farmers but had to settle for routine employment in an estate agency and she most definitely did not like the work.

She jumped off the bus and held out a hand, surprised to feel raindrops in spite of the sunshine. She pulled up the collar of her jacket and quickened her footsteps as she crossed the square to her parent's home; she was disconcerted to find the door already open and her mother waiting for her.

'There's a man here to see you,' she whispered.

'A man? Don't tell me – it's Cliff Richard.'

'Huh, you should be so lucky, my girl. No, but he looks nice. Something about a job, he says.'

'A job?' Just for a moment her heart lifted – could it be someone from Farmers? Her mind cast itself back to the interior of the publishing company offices, to the book covers showcased on the walls, the lovely stained wood paneling, the huge display given over to that biggy author of theirs, John Thornton…

'Hello, I'm John Thornton.'

She put her hand to her mouth to stifle the small shriek.

'Are you all right?' John watched with consternation as colour flooded her face.

'You took me by surprise,' she laughed shakily. 'I had just been picturing that display they have in Farmers of an author called John Thornton and then you said you're called John Thornton. Just took my breath for a minute.'

He laughed. He liked this girl.

'I'm not just *called* John Thornton, that really is me. I wrote those books, which is how I came to have your name. David Farmer passed it on to me because I'm looking for a secretary, but your mother said you have a job.'

'You mean you want me to work for you?' Her eyes widened when he nodded. 'Then I most certainly don't have a job, Mr. Thornton. Mum was mistaken. And so are Ellis and Gould.'

'The estate agents?'

She nodded.

'Ex-employers. And I don't think they'll give me a reference because I'm about to walk out on them. I can start anytime, Mr. Thornton.'

He felt a lightening of his spirit – maybe he and Amy would get on better if they didn't work so closely together. This girl could take away a lot of the pressure on his wife.

'Then let's see... today's Thursday, so shall we say next Monday if you're absolutely sure you won't have to serve a period of notice? And shall we say your present salary plus £5 a week?'

'I don't ever have to do anything I don't want to do, Mr. Thornton,' she said, her eyes dancing with excitement. 'And the wage is fine. This is even better than working for Farmers, and I really wanted that job!'

He handed her his card.

'This is where we'll be working. Now, the way that I work is a bit complicated and you could end up typing, re-typing and re-re-typing but basically I hand write the initial draft. I try to do at least 1500 words a day. The following day I edit it, make any alterations I want and that's the stage it's passed over to you. You just keep typing then until we get the polished draft for submission to Farmers. I'm not the sort of author who just bangs away at it until he has the novel down on paper before he edits it – I like to edit it as I go along. You'll soon get used to the way I work, I'm sure.' He stood to leave.

'Thanks, Mr. Thornton. Can I offer you a cup of tea or something?'

John declined with a smile.

'No thanks, Linda, your mother saw to that. Very nice lady – makes excellent scones.'

'I'll bring some for our tea break,' Linda promised. 'So, I'll see you Monday. Nine o'clock okay, or do you want me earlier?'

'Nine is good, Linda,' he laughed. 'And if I'm not up, ring the bell until someone answers!'

'You've hired a secretary without consulting me?'

Amy's eyes filled with tears. At one time John talked everything over with her.

'Yes. But it's for a reason. I think it's time we did something about adopting a baby,' he said gently. 'You won't have time to do any of my work with a little one to look after.'

'But I'm not ready! We've only been married four years.'

'I'm ready, Amy. Pilot's a cute little thing and I love him dearly, but he's not ours. And we have so much to offer a child – financial security, a lovely home, and we're still young.'

Stop it, stop it, her mind screamed. *Don't ask this of me. Change the subject, must change the subject.*

Once again Amy used sex for her own ends. John put the adoption plans on hold as he reveled in his wife's attentions – with the occasional superimposing of a face over hers, a face that belonged to Dawn Lynch.

Linda Chambers arrived early but John was already in his study trying to make sense of a particularly difficult place in the novel. He was just deciding it was divine retribution for the way he had tried to con David into believing he had a problem with the plot, when the doorbell pealed.

He glanced at the clock and grinned. Fifteen minutes early – that he liked.

'Hi,' he said. 'Come in and I'll show you where everything is.'

He gave her a guided tour of the downstairs, terminating in the study.

'And this is where the real work is done. I've arranged for a desk and a new typewriter to be delivered tomorrow and they promised faithfully it would be here before lunchtime.'

'Which suppliers?'

'Dodd's in Padstow.'

'Right.' She picked up the telephone, rifled through the directory and dialed. 'Dodd's? You're making a delivery to Mr. John Thornton tomorrow but we need it now. How quickly can you get it here, please?'

There was silence for a moment.

'I see. No, don't worry about it. We'll cancel the order and go somewhere else. I expect the Typewriter Company can accommodate us... oh, I see, so you can get the van here within half an hour? That will be fine. Thank you.' She replaced the receiver.

John stared in amazement.

'I think you've just earned your first week's salary, Linda!'

'They tried to waffle saying it would be here by four o'clock tomorrow. My mum says it's always best to check up on delivery times.'

'Then I owe your mum. So, your first job is to make coffee, I think. There's very little you can do until that typewriter gets here. I'll see if Amy wants a drink.'

'Amy?'

'Oh, sorry. My wife. She gets up around 9.30, usually. I'll go and find her.'

Linda wandered around the study looking at the hundreds of books lining the walls. The copies of Francophile, Rest in Pieces and Grave Matters had a small shelf all to themselves.

She had spent the weekend reading his books and knew she was going to working alongside a writer of considerable expertise in spite of his youth. How old was he? Twenty six? Twenty seven? With three books behind him and a fourth one well on the way to completion, it was pretty impressive. And she knew her mum would think it was wonderful. Funny how he hadn't mentioned a wife until now, though.

'Hello.'

Linda turned round and her first impression of her employer's wife was of a beautiful fawn, a golden haired Bambi.

'Hello,' she said. 'I'm Linda Chambers.'

'I know. John told me.' There was frostiness in Amy's voice that she didn't bother to disguise. Okay, so this Linda was no raving beauty but she definitely had a certain charm. She'd have to keep a close watch on this young secretary.

'Have you two met?' John stood behind his wife in the doorway of the study, his hands resting on her shoulders.

Amy nodded.

'Yes, and I think Linda was just going to make some coffee.'

All three turned their heads at the sound of the doorbell. Linda checked her watch.

'Ten minutes,' she said with a grin. 'Not bad, I suppose.'

John stared at her.

'You don't think that's Dodd's, do you?'

'I'll answer the door, shall I, so we can find out?'

'And I'll make the coffee, I suppose,' Amy said coldly. Somehow she felt she'd just lost the first round.

In the kitchen she took out three beakers and spooned coffee into them. She stood them in a neat row, meticulously regimented, and switched on the kettle. Amy didn't feel the little nips on her arm, unaware she was hurting herself. She felt inner rage that John had invited another woman into her home, a young woman who had the potential to be a rival.

She carried the coffees though to find John and Linda rearranging the study to accommodate the extra desk.

'It was Dodd's, Amy.'

'Fancy that,' she said drily, not really understanding John's surprised attitude. Hadn't Dodd's promised a morning delivery? 'Here's the coffee – I'll be upstairs if you want me.'

But already John and Linda were bent over the typewriter, with Linda showing her employer the intricacies of the machine.

The disquiet in Amy continued all day, even after she watched Linda leave for the night. And then she knew just what she had to do – the one thing that would tie John to her for infinity.

'John,' she said to him as she lay in his arms that night, 'tomorrow we'll see what we have to do to adopt a child.'

CHAPTER TWENTY-ONE

Spring 1969

'You know, Brenda, I've been thinking.'

Brenda looked at the man sitting across the kitchen table from her and smiled. She had never regretted for one minute giving him the job three years earlier; she had come to recognize his particular talents and skills and to give them the appreciation they merited.

'Serious thinking, or just thinking?'

'Serious thinking. I know I don't speak much about my life up north – it's all in the past – but I had a cheque last week. Oh, not an enormous one but my ex wife has finally realised I'm not going back and the cheque was for my share of the little house we had.'

Brenda lifted her cup and drank from it. Remaining silent seemed to be the order of the day – Ken wanted to talk.

He shuffled uncomfortably in his chair. He'd spent most of the previous evening wondering how to conduct this conversation, to show her the benefits in their true light and now he felt like a silly young boy who couldn't string a sentence together.

'You see, the thing is I've watched you in that greenhouse. You're a marvel with our seedlings... I think we can capitalise on that. Expand the business. And if you'll let me, I'd like to buy into it.'

For a long time Brenda didn't speak, just stared at him. She could tangibly feel the tension in him and wondered just how long he'd been bottling up his thoughts and dreams. She smiled.

'What would we need? Be more specific, Ken. What

sort of increase in business are you proposing?'

'Something more than just a market garden. A garden centre. We would need two large greenhouses to start with and naturally we'd need to buy quite a large amount of stock – and set on a youngster to help…'

'Whoa!' She held up a hand, laughing. 'Slow down, Ken. I think it's a wonderful idea but where are you planning to site this garden centre? You know the extent of our land and every inch is utilized.'

He grinned.

'That field at the back. It belongs to Mrs Troon's brother and he'll rent it to us.'

'But he farms it.'

'Not anymore. Him and the widow Troon are going to live in Spain. His son's moving into the farmhouse but he's something big like a solicitor and doesn't want the land. I took the old man for a drink, mentioned we might be interested and he jumped at the chance.'

Her brain was whirling.

'Can we do it, Ken? It'll take a fair bit of money.'

'I have ten thousand pounds. I've got a bit more but I've to find somewhere else to live.'

'Somewhere else to live?'

'Mmm. Not happy about it but with Mrs Troon deciding to pack it in for the Costa del Sol, we've all to be out in a month. I thought I'd try and find a cottage to rent a bit nearer to here.'

'Ken, let me think this through. When does Joe Williams want an answer about the land?'

'I told him we'd let him know by the end of the week.'

'Fine. The main thing that puts me off is am I a bit old to be expanding the business? I'm forty five now; can I keep up the hard work?'

He laughed.

'Brenda, I'm no spring chicken but I'm prepared to sink everything I have into this. We've nobody else to worry about, what's to stop us? And,' he paused, and she watched as a blush began to creep up his face, 'you certainly don't look forty-five. You're very pretty...' His words died away as it occurred to him that he had overstepped the boundaries of their working relationship.

Her eyes twinkled.

'Ken Buckingham, I do believe you're flirting; pretty indeed. Amy's pretty – and she gets her looks from her dad, not me.'

'So,' he said in his slow Yorkshire way, 'if I'm flirting, will you go for a drink with me? Tonight?'

For a moment she was at a loss for words. Knowing Ken as she did she recognised how much courage it had taken for him to ask her and she had to be so careful how she declined.

But she didn't decline.

'That would be lovely. And we can perhaps thrash this idea of yours about a bit.'

He pushed his chair away from the table.

'I'll go and clear a few weeds then. Eight o'clock be okay? I'll pick you up in the van.'

He had bought the van two weeks earlier to help with the work-load. She now realised it had been bought with the expansion of her business in mind.

'That'll be fine,' she smiled. 'I'll be ready.'

To her surprise she enjoyed the evening very much. She got on with Ken, liked his quiet nature and had grown fond of his quirky Yorkshire sayings.

The pub he had chosen was out in the countryside, small and comfortable. She ordered a fruit juice. He laughed and ordered a pint. She noticed, without passing any comment, that the pint was shandy and she gave him full marks for consideration – it was a long drive home.

He produced a file that contained several sheets of handwritten notes, diagrams drawn to scale and costs he had already investigated. She looked at him with new respect.

'Well, Ken,' she said softly, 'you've stunned me. I always knew you were a hard worker but it never occurred to me that you could plan something like this. You know what I'm going to say, of course; we'll do it if you think it's viable.'

He laughed.

'God bless you, Brenda Andrews. I'm not sure what viable means – we don't use posh words in Yorkshire but I am sure we can make this work. I'll be late in tomorrow, got to go and see about the field. We mustn't waste any time.'

'There's something else I'd like you to think about.' She reached across and touched his hand. He stared at it for a moment then met her gaze. 'Your accommodation problem,' she said.

'Oh that. Look, if I've to buy a tent I'll have something by the end of the week,' he said with a smile. 'Don't worry about that, that's the least of my worries.'

'Then move into Stonebrook.'

He looked startled.

'What? What would people say? I can't do that.'

'What do people say about Mrs Troon?'

'Well, nothing I suppose, but that's different. She takes in lodgers…'

'But that's what I'd be doing, taking in a lodger.'

'Brenda,' and this time he reached across to take hold of her hand, 'that's very good of you but I've no intention of compromising you like that. There's a world of difference between you and Mrs Troon. She's about seventy years old for a start and you're a very classy lady. People would talk.'

'No they wouldn't. And to be perfectly honest Ken, I really don't care. There is a large spare bedroom, we'll share costs and I'll do the cooking. Take it or leave it, Mr. Buckingham, but you won't get a better offer anywhere else in Cornwall.'

'Too right I won't,' he said with a grin.

'And there is something else – I'd feel a bit more secure with a man about the place. I won't lie to you – I'm not making this offer just to help you out.'

'But what will John and Amy say? And Freda?'

'Aaagh!' She pretended to scream and one or two people turned round to look at them. 'I've told you, they can take it or leave it. I don't care either way. It's my life, my decision. Now do we have a deal, or have I got to buy a big dog?'

He gave a brief pause.

'We have a deal,' he said. 'I'll need to move before the end of the week.'

'Tomorrow?'

'Tomorrow.'

Ken Buckingham had never been upstairs in Stonebrook Cottage until that night. He was pleased by the size of the room.

'This is twice as big as my place at Mrs Troon's.' He looked around appreciatively.

'Do you like it?'

'It's great. I still feel a bit worried about what the neighbours will say, though.'

'Ken – what neighbours?'

'Well, I know you're a bit isolated, but you know

what I mean.'

'Stop worrying. If anybody becomes obnoxious I'll tell them we're married,' she said with a grin and then burst into laughter as she saw his face suffuse with colour.

'Ken Buckingham, you're priceless.'

Some time after midnight she walked down the garden path with him to the van.

'Thank you for a lovely evening, Ken, and I'm so glad we've sorted things out. Forget the garden tomorrow; sort out the details about the field and move your things in. We'll have a day off, I think.'

'We'll see,' he said. Brenda knew there was no way he would take the entire day off.

He moved towards the driver door and then stopped, looking around him.

'What's the matter?'

'Did you hear that? Something…somebody moved.'

Brenda shivered. The feeling of being watched flooded back.

'No, no. I didn't hear anything. It's probably a fox or a rabbit.'

He climbed into the van, wound down the window and closed the door.

'I enjoyed tonight, Brenda. Perhaps we could do it again sometime.'

'I'd like that,' she said putting her head through the open window and placing a swift kiss on his cheek.

'See you tomorrow, Ken.' She laughed inwardly at his stunned expression then watched as he drove down the lane.

'The devil's in you tonight, Brenda Andrews,' she murmured to herself. 'Poor man, he won't know what to make of you.' She walked back up the path listening for sounds of movement. Hearing nothing, she locked the door behind her and breathed a sigh of relief.

Ronald Treverick watched all the lights go off in the cottage and smiled.

'So what do you think?' Brenda changed the telephone receiver to the other ear leaving her right hand free to scribble down something; another question to toss around with Ken.

There was a long pause.

'Freda? I said what do you think.'

'I know what you said. I'm just trying to work out what I think. And I think you're doing the right thing. I think.'

There was hesitancy in Freda's voice and it troubled Brenda.

'But you're not sure?'

'Look, Bren, you know me and my attitude towards men. I feel we can manage perfectly well without them but that's personal, isn't it? You, you're different. You need a man...'

'Freda! He's a lodger for heaven's sake!'

'For now.'

'But...'

'Bren, Ken Buckingham thinks the sun shines out of your backside and you know it. And,' she said with a little chuckle, 'I reckon you've got more than a soft spot for him. Don't let your memories of Jack hold you back. I knew my brother very well and he was the most unselfish person I ever met. He'd have wanted you to move on as long as it made you happy.'

Brenda knew it was useless to protest further; Freda wouldn't have it that there was no romantic connection;

she'd just have to show her.

'So you think it's okay for Ken to move in?'

'It doesn't matter what anyone thinks, does it? You've already decided. Have you spoken to Amy?'

'Yes, but she's so wrapped up in the adoption proceedings that I don't think she was really listening.'

'Oh.'

'Something wrong?'

'No...no. They're still going through with the adoption then?'

'They've put the papers in applying for a child, yes.'

'Think they'll be successful?'

'I'm sure they will. They've everything going for them, haven't they? Financially they're fine, they have a lovely home, John has a secure future...'

'And the poor child will have to live without any sort of mother love,' Freda said drily.

'No!' Brenda was stunned.

'Bren, you know Amy is incapable of normal love. She needs psychiatric help, always has. Ever since...'

'They'll be all right.' There was stubbornness in Brenda's voice.

'Yes, they'll be all right,' Freda said with a sigh. 'Look love, I've got to go to work. Good luck with Ken and the new business. I'm pleased for you, really I am.'

Brenda replaced the receiver thoughtfully. Sometimes she dreaded talking to Freda – she made her think too much.

CHAPTER TWENTY-TWO

Spring 1969

Dawn found John waiting near her bus stop in his unpretentious green car. The passenger door opened as she approached and she felt a brief hesitation before climbing in.

'Want a lift?' He smiled at her.

'You don't go my way.'

'I go any way you want me to go.'

'John…'

'Please, Dawn, I'm only joking, honestly.'

'So why are you here?'

He shrugged his shoulders.

'To see you. I like you. Look, you can throw all the clichés you like at me – married man, you don't want to get involved, once bitten twice shy – but the simple fact is I like you. I can see no reason why I can't be in your company. Can you?'

'No, not if you put it like that.' Her voice wobbled.

'You still sound troubled.' He dropped the car into top gear as they hit the long stretch of road outside Padstow. It was a warm evening and he leaned forward and moved the heater control lever, pushing it to cold.

'I am troubled. Don't ask me to explain why. You know why.'

She stared out of the passenger window wondering what on earth had possessed her to get into the car. This man was dangerous. He came with complications she would rather manage without. She was starting to enjoy the advantages of being single and didn't want involvement with anyone, even the charming John Thornton.

The scenery rolled by, the high Cornish roadside almost completely obliterating the view. Ragged Robin and wild cornflowers swept past in a blur of colour.

'You did say you lived in Rock?'

She nodded.

'Directly opposite the ferry berth; that's why I don't take my car to work. I virtually fall straight out of bed and onto the ferry. When I get to Padstow it's only a few minutes walk to the office. It was really silly of me to accept a lift home, it's taken you miles out of your way and my journey home really couldn't be easier.'

'It's worth it, and it's what I want to do,' he said simply. They remained silent as they began to drop down the steep lane into Rock. The little village was busy with tourists wanting to catch the ferry to Padstow and he slowed the car to a crawl.

'Over there,' she said. 'That small apartment block with the car park.'

He pulled on the handbrake and she moved to open the passenger door.

'I could use a coffee.'

She paused.

'I need my head examining. One coffee, John, and then it's goodnight.'

He followed her across the car park, drinking in the slim figure, the long dark hair that swung as she walked, the legs accentuated by her high heels – and he gave a small sigh of pleasure. It was just like watching Amy's slow saunter… he shook his head and banished his wife from his mind.

Dawn unlocked the front door and he followed her

down the entrance hall. She stood by a small doorway painted a soft grey and began to remove her coat.

As he placed his hands on her shoulders preventing her from moving, the air crackled with tension. She stood perfectly still. The silence between them was interrupted by the loud tick of a nearby clock; slowly his arms encircled her from behind and he began to carefully unbutton her coat. He slipped it from her and turned her round to face him.

Placing a finger under her chin, he lifted her head and bent to kiss her. As the kiss deepened she began to sway.

He released her and gave a shaky laugh.

'Should I apologise?' he whispered. 'I don't want to…'

She shook her head, not trusting herself to answer the way she felt she should.

'Dawn…'

Pulling away from him, she moved into the kitchen.

'Coffee, we said. Keep away from me, John.'

'We have to talk.'

'No we don't have to talk,' she retorted angrily. 'Okay, so now you know how to manipulate me, you know how I feel, but by God, I can still say no, John Thornton.'

'Do you want to say no?'

'Yes…no… I don't know! Just leave me alone and don't kiss me again.' She banged the kettle down on to the work surface and took two mugs from a cupboard, her fingers trembling. She stared at her white walls, the pretty yellow gingham curtains, the gleaming fitments – anything other than look at the man standing close to her.

He moved behind her and kissed the back of her neck. John sensed a momentary panic and was on the point of releasing her when he felt her acceptance; she capitulated and leaned back into the kiss, closing her eyes.

'John, don't...' she moaned softly and he cupped her breasts with his hands. They were soft and full and womanly. Slowly teasing the nipples he continued to place tiny kisses around her neck, unsure whether he was going too far but unable to stop.

Her hands came up and covered his, encouraging him. Slowly he unbuttoned the thin silk blouse and touched her warm flesh. She gave a long low moan and turned round to face him.

'Don't do this unless you're serious, John. Don't play with me. I've fought this for many weeks now and you damn well know it.' Her words were ragged, the high colour in her cheeks showed her emotion.

'I'm not playing,' he said and pulled her close to him.

He cupped her bottom in his hands and pressed the lower part of her body into his. She responded with a small cry of part panic part pleasure, and pulled his head down to hers. Her lips parted allowing his tongue to enter her mouth.

The blouse fell to the floor without assistance and she felt him unhook her bra.

'Take me,' she whispered between kisses, accepting now that this was going to happen.

Nothing could have stopped it, not the unknown Mrs Thornton, not her own conscience and not the possibility of losing her job.

She was naked when he carried her through to the bedroom. Placing her on the bed he looked at her and marveled – not so much at the beauty of her body but at the fact that it was there for him to see.

What was happening was a shock – he had genuinely wanted to talk to her and the situation had escalated beyond return. He rejoiced as the barriers between them tumbled to the ground.

John didn't remember taking off his own clothes but he could recall with clarity every movement, every sigh, every kiss over the next hour.

As he entered Dawn for the first time, he felt his own climax begin immediately and groaned.

'God, I'm sorry,' he began. She silenced him placing her finger against his lips.

'There's no greater compliment,' she said quietly and thrust her hips towards him. His response was immediate and she felt his tumescence increase before he called out her name.

'Now, John, now,' she cried as he ejaculated.

They lay quietly side by side, his hands running over her body. Their closeness after the sex came as a shock to him.

'There's something I have to tell you,' he began, but she stopped him.

'You don't have to tell me anything.'

'Oh, I do. I have to explain why I made such a complete hash of it...'

'Look, I said it's the greatest compliment you could have paid me, and I meant it.' She lifted her hand and stroked his cheek.

'Dawn, I've got to tell you. I've never made love to anyone other than my wife. We've been married just over four years and that's the sixth time I've ever made love.'

'The sixth time? I don't think I understand...'

'I can't spell it out any clearer than that. Amy doesn't like sex. She has a problem with it. That's why I couldn't control myself.'

'Why don't you walk away from it?' She looked puzzled. 'You don't have to tolerate it. Believe me, I know.'

'There's more to it than that. There are things in Amy's past… well, let's just say there's no way I can ever leave her. In a way I suppose I still love her. I'm not making excuses for being here with you. I'm not going to lie and say my wife doesn't understand me or any other crap like that. I'm here with you because I think this is good for us. I like you – a lot. And if you don't want this to happen again, I'll understand. I won't like it, but I'll understand.'

She took his hand and placed it on her breast.

'Shut up,' she whispered, 'and make love to me again. Stop when I start to scream, okay?'

'It doesn't stop here?'

'It doesn't stop here,' she confirmed, 'but I might have to think about going on the pill!'

CHAPTER TWENTY-THREE

Summer – Winter 1969

At first, the garden centre occupied every minute of every day for both Brenda and Ken. Two huge glass houses mushroomed out of the ground and daily trucks rolled up with supplies to stock inside the building and out.

They created a herb garden. Ken said it was the stoniest ground he'd ever come across and he had lived near some of the biggest stones God ever made. She loved it when he spoke of Yorkshire. He had pride in his home county and the surrounding hills of Derbyshire and she told him he should go home to visit whenever he wanted – he hadn't taken a holiday since starting at Stonebrook.

'Nay, lass,' he would say, 'we've plenty of work here a-while.'

But eventually the heavy workload began to lessen, particularly after the employment of a young boy fresh from school.

Malcolm had been frank with them when he applied for the position.

'Can't do sums. Never wanted to do sums. But I can make plants grow. Ask my dad.'

They had been so impressed with his willingness and enthusiasm that they had asked his dad. One glance at the Winterton family allotment convinced them.

Brenda found she could delegate any job in the nursery to him and it would be done with flair and without argument.

One day he came to her clutching a shrub that on

closer inspection proved to be a Hebe. The label said Midsummer Beauty but that was hardly a fitting description.

'Can I take it home, Mrs Andrews?'

'Take it home? But it's almost dead!'

'No it's not. I've got some stuff…'

She laughed at his eager expression.

'Do what you want with it, Malcolm. But for goodness sake get it out of here. It'll put our customers off!'

He proudly returned with the shrub six weeks later in full flower and supremely healthy.

Brenda stared at it.

'Are you sure this is the same one? You haven't been out and bought another one, have you?'

The hurt expression on his face told her it was and she felt suitably chastised.

'Well, it's not for sale. I want you to plant it at the entrance – in fact there's a small patch of land just outside the gate that I want you to have. Take what you need from the stock, let me know what you're using and build us a welcome garden.' She pushed her fingers into the compost, withdrew them and crumbled the earth.

'What is this?'

'I make it…'

'Make it? With what?'

'Oh, this and that. I sell it to the other men.'

She looked bewildered.

'Other men? What other men?'

'On the allotments. I don't sell it to my dad though.'

'You sell compost to experienced gardeners?'

'Not to my dad,' he repeated.

'Well, I should think not!' Her laughter was infectious and he grinned at her, not sure why she should think it so funny. The other allotment holders wanted it, he had it, and so he sold it.

'It's good stuff.'

'I can see it is. And is this the magic ingredient that's saved our Hebe?'

He shook his head.

'Not on its own. I make my own fertilizer.'

'And do you sell that?' she asked.

'Not to my dad.'

'Look, we need to talk, with Ken. Go and find him, will you, Malcolm? I think he's down in the cottage garden.'

It turned out Malcolm would call the shots. Yes, he would make as much compost as they wanted and yes, they could pay him an extra £10 per week but no, he wouldn't give them the secret. He wanted sole control of the compost heap and he wanted every bit of recyclable material that Ken and Brenda used in the home.

And he wanted a hut... with a lock.

The hut became known as Malcolm's Place and neither Brenda nor Ken dared enter without permission.

He began production of his fertilizer immediately – he said it needed five and a half weeks to brew before being bottled. He spoke of nettles and took two comfrey plants from stock that he said were adequate.

On the day the hut was erected, he turned up for work on a bicycle that was in a state of disrepair but none the less strong enough to pull the box on wheels he had attached to the back. He was very proud of it.

'Made this last night,' he said. 'Bought the bike for a quid and made the trolley. It's for collecting stuff.'

'Stuff?'

'For the compost.'

Brenda looked at the contraption with interest. The

brakes were so worn as to be dangerous; the back mudguard was tied on with green garden twine and although it had two lights, neither worked.

'So it's a company vehicle, then?'

He gave one of his rare laughs.

'Suppose so. It gets me here quicker than the bus does anyway.' She didn't doubt it, with virtually non-existent brakes.

That week Brenda put a bonus payment in his pay packet.

'For the company vehicle,' she explained with a wink.

Ken was happy at Stonebrook. He tried not to worry about the love he felt for Brenda; she was an independent lady who didn't need the encumbrance of a man in her life.

He was too much of a Yorkshireman to say it, but when they sat together at night watching television he felt a sense of peace and happiness that had never existed during his marriage.

And so it fell to Brenda to make the first move.

'Ken, are you happy here?'

'How long have I lived here?'

'Nearly six months.'

'It's flown. I'm happy.'

She liked his Yorkshire stoicism.

She had seen him looking at her with adoration and that look had given her confidence.

'And do you think we made the right decision?'

'Brenda, I've told you I'm happy here with you, love this cottage, and feel settled here.'

'I meant the right decision about the business.'

'Oh, er yes, we made the right decision. It's paying, we're getting more visitors than soft Mick since we started advertising, so we were right.'

'So everything's okay? And who's soft Mick?'

'Nobody you'd know. Brenda, you trying to say something? Ask something?'

'Yes.'

'Oh.' He felt intrigued and reached over turning off the news on the television. She stood and came to sit by him on the settee. He blushed.

'Would you like to kiss me?' she asked.

His blush deepened.

'Kiss you?' He knew he sounded stupid.

'Here,' she touched her lips with a finger and he saw the sparkle in her eyes.

'How did you know?' he asked quietly.

'Know what?'

'How I feel about you.'

'You looked at me.'

'I tried to hide it, you know.'

'For goodness sake, Ken Buckingham, I know you're a foreigner but they still kiss up in Yorkshire, don't they?'

So they did. Successfully, solidly and with more passion than she had been expecting.

'I love you, you know,' Ken said, as he pulled out a cigarette and lit it.

She nodded.

'I know. And I'm a bit stunned that I love you. When Jack died I felt… bereft. I didn't think it possible that there would ever be another man in my life, but here you are. I'll always love Jack, but you've crept up on me, Ken Buckingham.'

'And where do we go from here?'

She looked at him, at the firelight flickering on his face, at the love in his eyes.

'Bed?' she said simply.

It was Malcolm who unwittingly let their secret out. Amy met him as she walked up the lane and asked the whereabouts of her mother.

He looked around.

'I'm not sure. Last time I saw them they were heading for the top greenhouse. They'll be together, anyway,' he finished with a grin. Sometimes he could do sums – like adding two and two together.

'What do you mean?'

'They're always together now. 'Bout time as well.'

Amy stared at him for a moment then stormed into the cottage.

'Mother, are you in here?'

Brenda looked over the banister and waved at her daughter.

'Up here, Amy - won't be a minute. Put the kettle on and we'll have a cup of tea.'

'Don't bother. I'm not staying. I just want to know if what Malcolm is hinting at is true.'

Brenda went cold. Damn Malcolm – she'd wanted to tell Amy herself. She wished now she'd not delayed imparting the news as she walked slowly downstairs.

'What are you on about?'

'You and Ken. Malcolm seems to think there's something between you.'

'And what if there is? Don't you want me to be happy?' Brenda placed a hand on Amy's shoulder.

'Mother, you can't! Dad's only been dead –'

'Nearly four years, Amy. Life doesn't stop.'

'But he's not right for you,' she wailed.

'He's absolutely right for me. Just as your dad was. Loving Ken – '

'Loving Ken!' Amy spat the words. Two bright

spots of colour glowed angrily on her cheeks.

'Yes. Loving Ken doesn't stop me loving Jack. I'm only forty-five, Amy, not ninety. I still need the companionship of a man...'

'Sex, you mean.' Her tone was vitriolic.

'That as well, but Ken is good for me in every way.'

'I just bet he is,' and she turned and stormed out of the cottage unable to bear her mother's company a minute longer.

Malcolm watched her go and knew without having to do any sums that he shouldn't have said a word, not one word.

Amy stopped halfway down the lane and then cut across the field towards the glass houses. She spotted Ken inside and went in, carefully closing the door behind her.

'Amy? Can I help? Your mum's down in the cottage.'

'Well, I don't really know,' she said softly, moving closer to him. He looked at her for a moment wondering what was on her mind. He didn't trust Amy, never had done, and he sensed she was up to no good.

She pressed herself against him and linked her arms around his neck. Forcing his head down she pressed her lips to his, pushing her tongue deep into his mouth. He staggered away from her, still feeling the outline of her breasts against his chest. A huge surge of anger overwhelmed him as well as the sexual response she had intended.

'What the -?'

'I just thought I'd show you that you're anybody's, Ken. You enjoyed that, didn't you? Do you want me to lie down? I'm sure you'd enjoy that too. I'll do it if that's what it takes to get you out of my mother's life.' She started to pull up her skirt and he stared mesmerized as she revealed her long legs. Slowly she rubbed the palm of her hand along her thigh, bringing her hand round and in between her legs.

'Here, Ken, you do it. You touch me,' she said softly.

He deliberately turned his back to her, trying hard to hold his temper in check.

'Bugger off, Amy. You may be beautiful but your mother is worth twenty of you. Straighten yourself, girl, and get out of here.'

He didn't anticipate the fingernails. They raked down the back of his neck and he felt sick with the stinging pain.

'Don't call me beautiful,' she panted. 'Don't ever call me beautiful!' She turned and ran from the greenhouse.

Standing in the back bedroom window, Brenda watched the drama playing out before her; saw Amy run down the field and back onto the lane. She knew what Amy had tried to do and it made her feel drained and miserable.

Ken gave her only the sketchiest of detail because he had to have the scratches bathed.

'Forget it, Brenda, she's just a mixed up kid,' he said and kissed her.

'I love you.'

'And I love you, even if you do have a crazy daughter,' he said with a brave attempt at laughter. But he couldn't help wonder if she really would have had sex with him on the floor of the glass house... would she really have gone that far to get him out of her mother's life?

CHAPTER TWENTY-FOUR

Autumn 1969

Carefully, meticulously, Amy dusted along the mantelpiece, her mind in turmoil. She didn't know where to turn; suddenly her life was undergoing great change and she was out of her depth. The cocoon she had so carefully built around herself was crumbling; her self-imposed security dissipating.

The problem – and she knew it was most definitely a problem – concerning her was John's withdrawal. Slowly, inexorably, he was moving away from her, away from their relationship. Yet in many ways he was still the same man she married.

She couldn't figure out what was wrong. There had been no evidence of another woman, but...

She paused, the can of spray polish held aloft, and then moved across the room to stare out of the French windows at the neatly trimmed lawn. She shivered. *Was it possible? Could John really be involved with someone else? A secretary perhaps? A young secretary called Linda?* A surge of anger threatened to overwhelm her and she banged a fist against the door frame.

John was hers and she would not lose him to anyone – not to a floozy of a secretary, not to a baby, not to anyone.

The baby. Inwardly she groaned and began to pace backwards and forwards. She had concealed her true feeling from everyone. To others, their lives would be fulfilled; she would become the woman Treverick had tried but failed to destroy.

Treverick. Again she paused and moved towards the window. The weather outside was cool yet she burned with intensity. Treverick was haunting her...

She was still afraid of him and remembered telling John how she felt. What had he said? *'Forget him, Amy. He can't hurt you anymore. You're an adult now, not a child. You could fight back, and you have me, don't you?'*

There had been impatience in his tone and she had vowed never to bring up the subject again.

Would there be a Treverick waiting in the wings for her baby? The baby, sex still unknown, was weeks away from arriving in their home. Perhaps already born, just not allocated yet.

And only she knew the real reason for wanting this baby – to tie John to her that he would never be able to fall into some other woman's arms.

She knew John wanted a baby for all the right reasons but she just wanted another possession, one to add to her list; John, her mother, Freda and a baby.

Did she possess her mother? The great Brenda Andrews slumming it in bed with a younger man; a man who was threatening to take the place of her father. *How could she?*

Amy gave an anguished cry as shame flooded her. Her behavior in the glass house had been so uncharacteristic and yet it had happened. Exposed herself, blatantly offered herself to him, and for nothing. They were still together and she might be about to lose her mother.

Freda had been no help; she had made it perfectly clear that she approved wholeheartedly of the liaison and welcomed Ken Buckingham as a replacement for Jack Andrews.

Amy opened the French windows and allowed the cool air to bathe her hot face. She had problems. She would resolve them all.

She would start with John... and Linda.

CHAPTER TWENTY-FIVE

Spring 1970

Lauren came into their lives in late February, 1970. She was just six weeks old and totally captivating. They were told very little about her background – her birth mother had not wanted her and the father had abandoned his responsibilities.

To Amy, she represented perfection; she was kept spotlessly clean and fed at precise times. She was a showcase baby. Her sheets and blankets were meticulously wrapped around her – Amy's compulsive tidiness undiminished.

Lauren's finalized adoption was to happen in June and would coincide with the publication of John's fourth novel, *The Son*, and they decided to throw a party to celebrate both events.

Amy chewed the end of her pencil as she stared at the list. She was tired; Lauren had been troublesome all day and she was finding it hard to concentrate.

'Do we have to invite Ken Buckingham?'

'Naturally, he's your mother's partner.' John was looking out of the window watching the grey skies turn darker. They were in for a good old storm.

'He's more than her partner...'

'That's what I meant,' John responded drily, turning his head to look at his wife. 'Stop knocking him, Amy. He's a decent chap and she's lucky to have found him. Just as lucky as she was to find your dad all those years ago.'

'Criticising me again, John?' Amy was close to tears; it was all too much for her.

No matter how hard she tried, Lauren remained like a doll to her, not a child to cherish and because she did nothing purely out of love for the little girl, everything became harder.

He stifled a sigh. Every day now they bordered on an argument and he recognised that it wasn't always Amy's fault. His deepening relationship with Dawn was to blame for his intolerance. He wanted to be with Dawn more and more, the only thing drawing him back to his home was the baby, not his wife.

'No,' he said. 'I'm not criticising you. You liked Ken before he became such a big part of your mother's life and I fail to see why that should change. He's still the same man.'

'But Dad...'

'But Dad, nothing. Your dad would have welcomed Ken, would have wanted someone to look after Brenda and if you'll only stop being so self-centred and melodramatic about it, you'd see that for yourself.'

She flinched, recognizing something new in John. He was no longer easily manipulated.

'Don't shout at me, John. You're probably right – perhaps we should have them over for dinner one night before the party, build some bridges.'

The rain began to patter on the windowpane.

'Perhaps we should... if they'll come. Personally, I wouldn't blame them if they never wanted to set eyes on you again.'

He returned to chapter three of *Blood Red* and switched off from his wife. It was a difficult part of the book and required all his concentration – let Amy cope with the party arrangements. And let the damn rain come down. It matched his mood.

'John – can I talk to you?'

'Sure, Linda. A problem?'

She shrugged her shoulders.

'Sort of. Can I have a general job description?'

He laughed aloud.

'Job description? For this job? It's just to type, re-type, and re-type the re-type I suppose.'

'So it's not to babysit and make party arrangements?'

The laughter died in him.

'No, it's not. What do you mean, babysit? I wasn't aware we had asked you to look after Lauren.'

'No, you haven't. It's Mrs Thornton.' Linda couldn't bring herself to use Amy's Christian name. 'Whenever you go out, she treats me like a housekeeper.'

John looked at her and tried to disguise his guilt. He had been going out more, generally at four o'clock so that he could meet Dawn as she stepped off the ferry.

'Explain.'

'Well, Mrs Thornton brings Lauren in here as soon as you go – oh, she's always got a good reason and she really is a good baby, but it does tend to stop me working.'

'What sort of reason?'

'It varies. She wants a bath, or she needs to go to the shops, anything really. I do hate telling you this but I don't want you thinking I'm not doing what I'm paid to do.'

'Leave it with me, Linda. I'll talk to Amy. She probably doesn't realise...' He knew he was lying to himself. Amy realised perfectly well.

Amy denied it and accused Linda of lying.

'Why on earth would I want to leave Lauren with her? Our baby is very precious, John, she's mine, not

Linda's, and I want her with me.'

'I'm only repeating Linda's complaint, Amy,' John said mildly. 'Don't go off the deep end.' He waved a piece of paper at his wife; a list of people they had decided to invite to the celebration. 'And if you want to send invitations out to this party, don't expect Linda to do it. I employ her to type my books, not arrange your social life.'

The words sounded harsher than he intended and guilt washed over him again. Would he have been so nasty to Dawn?

He looked down into the baby's crib and smiled.

'You're right. She is precious.' He reached out and stroked a finger across Lauren's cheek; the baby snuffled in her sleep.

'Don't wake her,' Amy said quickly. 'She'll want feeding if you do.' She tried to quash the feeling of jealousy that erupted when she saw the love John felt for his tiny daughter.

'I thought you liked feeding her.'

'I do, it's just that I wanted to go up to Mum's house, take the invitation, and I can feed her there.'

'Oh, you're going out.' He felt a surge of excitement. He had told Dawn he wouldn't be able to see her but if Amy was going out...

'Yes. Will you come with me? You've not stopped today; you must have done more than usual – unless you and that girl haven't really been working.'

'Amy...'

'Well, she is attractive.'

'Not to me.'

'Oh, come on, John. When was the last time you tried to make love to me?'

'When was the last time you allowed me to make

love to you, Amy? Go on, answer me that.' He felt his temper begin to rise. It subsided when he saw the tears in her eyes.

'You know I have problems,' she began and he put his arms around her shoulders.

'I'm sorry,' he said and once more the guilt settled around him like a cloak. 'Come on, I'll walk up to Stonebrook with you.' He squashed the image of Dawn's face from his mind. 'Perhaps later...'

She smiled and gently kissed his cheek.

'Mmmm,' she said, 'perhaps later.'

'Does this mean she's accepted me?'

Ken and Brenda stood at the gate of Stonebrook and watched as Amy with John pushing the high-wheeled pram, made their way back down the lane. The evening was fine but there was a chill in the air and the young couple walked quickly, pausing at the bottom of the lane to turn and wave.

Brenda shrugged her shoulders.

'I don't know. I'm just so glad they came. Lauren is my grandchild, you know. But I fear for her, Ken, I fear for her.'

'Who? Amy?'

She shook her head.

'No. Little Lauren. I fear for her. Ken, there's something I must tell you before we're married...'

'Married? Is this a proposal, Brenda?'

She clapped a hand to her mouth.

'Oh God! A Freudian slip I think.'

'Meaning you want to marry me?'

'You big wassock, Ken Buckingham. Of course I want to marry you.'

'Wassock? Wassock? Where've you learnt Yorkshire

rubbish like that?'

'So?' She grinned at him.

'As you've proposed to me, does this mean you buy me the engagement ring?'

'Oh no, you don't. You're not getting out of buying me the biggest diamond in Padstow... I might have proposed but you can dig deep into that pocket.' She paused. 'Can I take it the answer's yes?'

He nodded and took her face in his hands.

'The answer's yes. Brenda Andrews, you're beautiful, beautiful, beautiful,' he bent and kissed her.

'Feel any better about Ken?'

John sat on the edge of the bed and removed his trousers. Amy had been quiet ever since their return from Stonebrook. He was curious about her reaction now the news of the relationship had settled and she had met them as a couple.

She took off her bra and, unusually, turned round to face him. He felt his erection begin against his will and his eyes lingered on her breasts. Absolute perfection.

She cupped them with her hands and stroked the nipples with her thumbs.

'Forget Ken,' she said throatily. 'Make love to me, John.'

He groaned softly and reached across to pull her down on to the bed.

She was, as usual, superb. And clinical.

'You have someone else,' she said as they lay back to back. John's heart skipped a beat.

'Someone else?'

'Yes. Someone who's teaching you how to make love, how to control yourself. I'm not stupid. And what's more I know who it is.'

'You're being silly, Amy. I...'

'No excuses, John. Finish it, or else.'

'Or else what?' He played along.

'Or else you'll never see Lauren again.'

'And that's what she said,' he finished with a sigh. 'She was quite adamant that she knew who it was. She can be very vindictive. I thought I ought to warn you. If we carry on seeing each other, she could do anything.'

Dawn smiled at him.

'I think you're over-reacting.' She stroked his stomach and he gave a small sigh of pleasure. 'Do you want to put a stop to what we have?'

'Quite the opposite. If I was to say I was thinking of leaving Amy, what would you say?'

Her laughter pealed around the bedroom.

'What would I say? I'd say you're talking through your proverbial hat. You'll never leave Amy – I don't know what happened in her past but it's tied you so firmly to her that you'll be there until the day you die. However, my delicious John, all that is irrelevant. I want to keep my independence. I'm committed to you and there will be no other man, but I won't live with you.'

He was silent for a long time.

'John? You still with me?'

'Yes.'

'Have I upset you?'

'Yes.'

'Do you love me?'

'Yes.'

'Then respect my wishes,' she said.

Amy's confidence in her ability to dispose of rivals to John's affection was astounding. She didn't mention the subject to him again and put it on a back burner. She had the party to organise and that had to come first. After that…

And then of course, there was this damn dinner.

'Egg mayonnaise for starter?'

'Whatever. Keep it simple. You've still got Lauren to look after.' John spoke without looking up. She placed a tick by egg mayonnaise and moved on to the main course.

'Do you think steak?'

'Sure. Everybody likes steak.'

'What if he doesn't?'

'He will.' John finally looked up.

'But he might not. I mean, what do we really know about him? He says he's from Yorkshire, but is he?'

John burst out laughing. '

'You've heard his accent for heaven's sake! He's definitely from Yorkshire.'

'Och aye! And are you absolutely sure?' Amy responded in a pure Scottish accent.

He laughed again.

'Point taken – so you can change your accent. But he even looks like a Yorkshireman – stocky, fair hair, craggy features…'

'Just like Ronald Treverick would look now,' she said quietly.

'Oh, Amy, you can't be serious!'

'Never more so.'

'Look, go and get that photograph, then we'll see. I don't remember that picture looking anything like Ken, not even in a vague sort of way.'

'Not much point, is there? He obviously won't look like that now. The first thing he would do is change his appearance – no, John, he'll not look the same as he did all those years ago. We'd never recognise him now.'

He stood and pulled her into his arms.

'Hey, come on. You're getting yourself into a real state. Ken Buckingham is not Ronald Treverick, believe me. He's much too nice a chap. Besides, Treverick won't want to go back to prison again. He'll never come near you. Now let's sit down and finish this menu off. Accept it Amy, he's clearly in love with your mum, just as she is with him. We were talking steak, weren't we? Well, let's consider jacket potatoes, maybe with peas and carrots? And what about one of your famous trifles for dessert?'

That night Amy dreamed of Ronald Treverick and woke screaming in the early hours of the morning. It was the first dream of many, every one of them ending in violence.

CHAPTER TWENTY-SIX

April - June 1970

'Was the steak all right for you, Ron?' she had asked. Amy passed off her slip of the tongue with laughter.

Brenda had stared.

'Ron? Did you say Ron? Look young lady, if this feller's going to be your stepfather, you'd better get used to his name. Ken, Ken, Ken. Think you can remember that?'

Amy laughed again.

'Memory must be going. Did I really say Ron? Can't think why.'

But John knew it was a test. If Ken had responded...
But he hadn't.

John was angry with Amy for carrying on with the idea that Ken Buckingham was Ronald Treverick out to wreak revenge – or to repeat the crime. But he accepted that what Amy had gone through had left her vulnerable. He stifled any recriminations. He'd let it drop, provided she did.

The meal was a success. Brenda proudly showed off her engagement ring without attempting to hide that her wedding ring had moved to the third finger on her right hand. Amy's congratulations had been stilted; John's warm and meaningful. They had toasted Brenda and Ken with champagne and kept the conversation light.

Amy never asked if they had set a date for the wedding.

It was only as they said their goodbyes that Ken spoke directly to Amy.

'The wedding will be in four weeks time at the

Registry Office. We'd like you to be there but it will be a very quiet affair. Freda is one witness and we'd like John to be the other, if he agrees.'

Amy nodded.

'I'm sure he will.' There was no warmth in her voice.

'I love her very much, you know. I won't hurt her, always take care of her – do you deny her right to some happiness?'

'Of course not.'

He looked at her for a long moment.

'Then accept me. I'm a very lucky man. Your mother is beautiful inside and out. Beautiful, Amy. You are only blessed with looks.' He turned and walked to where John and Brenda were standing.

He didn't see the anger and fear on his future stepdaughter's face.

Ken and Brenda walked home slowly, arm in arm, pausing occasionally to enjoy the warm evening air of early June.

'Bren, when you proposed you were about to tell me something. In fact, isn't that how you proposed?'

Brenda hesitated momentarily, and then nodded.

'Mmm. And I know I've got to tell you because Amy is my daughter and I want you to understand why she is as she is. Although God only knows how you'll understand – I can't, and I'm her mother.'

'Freda understands her.'

She turned to look at him, eyes wide.

'How do you know that?'

'There's something about Freda. She's got nous.'

Brenda laughed.

'God, I love you. Nous, indeed. But I think you're probably right. She's always seemed to know what was

going on in Amy's head. But I'll start at the beginning…'
She grabbed his arm tightly for a second, her face vacant,
her eyes searching his and recalling the pain of years gone
by. 'When Amy was little, six years old, she was raped. An
eighteen year old called Ronald Treverick attacked and
raped her.'

There was absolute silence until Ken exhaled.

'Dear Gods,' he said softly. 'That poor child… how
you must have all suffered. So that's why they can't have
children?'

She nodded

'Yes, he tore her apart. They had to remove virtually
everything. It was a bad time – still is.''I don't know what
to say. It explains a lot, doesn't it? She's frightened of
men. She thinks I won't be any good for you because of
that animal.' He held her close. 'Thanks for telling me.
This will make things easier; help me understand why
she's being so bloody awful to me. And it will help me be
more tolerant towards her.'

'She'll come round,' Brenda whispered into the cool
fabric of his shirt, 'I'm sure she will.'

'The party,' Amy said woodenly, still recoiling from
everything Ken Buckingham had said to her. 'We'll set it
for the 21st June and make it a triple celebration.
Publication of *The Son*, Lauren's adoption will be finalized
by then and Ken and Brenda's wedding.'

She never called her mother anything but Brenda
from that day on.

*　　*　　*　　*　　*

Freda couldn't ever remember wanting to cry tears of
happiness so much. She wasn't a crying person – quite

the opposite. She'd cried when they had said Amy would recover, she'd cried when Jack had died and she'd cried two days ago at Ken and Brenda's wedding. She sat quietly on a garden seat and pulled her straw hat over her face, ostensibly to shield her eyes from the sun but really because she enjoyed observing people without them knowing. Looking around at all the people assembled on the green lawns at John and Amy's cottage, she wanted to cry again. And she didn't really know why.

'Silly old fool,' she muttered to herself, 'nothing to sniff about.'

But she felt happy. She'd suffered alongside her sister-in-law after Jack's death. Looking at Brenda now, those black days seemed long ago. In Ken, she had found another soul mate – two in a lifetime, an incredibly lucky woman.

She had never regretted being single, at least, not until today. Brenda glowed and Ken looked as though he'd won the lottery.

So many people she knew were all there smiling, sharing in the pleasures of the family. They'd participated in the hard times and now had taken time out from their own lives to join in a celebration, to join in welcoming two new members into the family, baby Lauren, now officially adopted, and Ken Buckingham.

Amy looked spectacular in a peach trouser suit, her long blonde hair loose and flowing. If she hadn't known she was twenty-four, Freda would have put her at eighteen years old. Pat looked far more mature in a turquoise dress that ended just above the knee. The two of them were engrossed in whatever they were discussing.

The noise of the party, inconsequential snippets of conversation, clinking of glasses, laughter; all of this washed over Freda as her eyes began to close 'Miss

Andrews?'

Freda was interrupted from her slumber but smiled at the young girl.

'Linda – good to see you. Are you enjoying the party?'

'I would be if…' Her voice trailed away. Linda stared across the lawn towards her employer's wife. Freda patted the chair next to her.

'Sit down, young lady, and tell me what's wrong.'

Linda continued to watch Amy and sat by Freda's side.

'I don't know what's wrong.' She shook her head as she spoke. 'Mrs Thornton's so against me and I've no idea why. I've worked here for nearly a year now. She only speaks to me in a decent way when John's around. When he's not there, well…'

'Linda, you're very young. Has it not occurred to you that you're a pretty girl? Amy is lacking in confidence…'

Linda snorted.

'No, seriously, she is,' continued Freda. 'There are things that make her different to other women. I suspect she sees you as a rival.'

'But that's ridiculous!' The protest came too readily.

'Ridiculous, is it? I think you have a soft spot for your employer – am I right?'

Linda stared into space for a moment.

'I know.' Freda patted her hand. 'Amy's sensed that. Oh, I know John would never stray, he loves Amy far too much, but my niece is too insecure to see that.'

Linda looked at the older woman, a frown on her face.

'Then what do I do?'

'Put up and shut up if you want to carry on working

here. Sorry to be so brutal – my nature, you know. Amy won't change. Don't see why you should, so…'

Linda continued to look across at Amy, still deep in conversation with Pat.

'I hope Mrs Thornton does change,' she said slowly, 'but she won't.'

Freda was intrigued by the note of sadness in Linda's voice.

'Why do you say that?'

'It's Lauren.'

Freda paid special attention.

'Lauren? Something wrong? Tell me, girl, don't hide it.'

'There's nothing to hide, but that's just it. I don't think she loves that little girl. She keeps her clean and well-fed but she doesn't play with her, cuddle her… nothing.' She turned swiftly and spoke with vehemence. 'She doesn't love the baby.'

Freda wanted to believe it was the fanciful imagination of a young girl in love with her employer, but in the depth of a velvety black night, she lay tossing and turning, unable to sleep for thinking about what Linda had said.

Could Amy really be that unfeeling? She thought back to the time when young Amy had burnt the doll and pram. It had been horrific and she had talked through many long hours with Brenda about the lack of emotion in the youngster.

She obviously hadn't improved with age.

And yet the baby appeared contented enough, was beautifully attired and well fed.

Freda rolled out of bed cursing the extra weight she was carrying and the arthritis that was slowly stiffening all her joints.

'Cup of tea,' she muttered and headed downstairs.

Freda recalled that at the party Amy hadn't once looked at Linda; it was as if the young girl didn't exist to her. At the end of the party when everyone was making plans to go home, Linda had approached Freda again.

'I've decided what to do,' she had said quietly. 'I'm going to look for another job, starting tomorrow.'

She had gone before Freda could persuade her to change her mind.

She sighed as she switched on the kettle in the sterile, cold kitchen.

'Damn and blast you, Amy!'

She hit her fist hard on to the work surface, a huge surge of anger washing through her. Then she crumpled. It wasn't Amy she should be railing against - it was Ronald Treverick. He was the cause of all their problems.

Amy had been a perfectly normal happy child until 1952. In the long grass at the edge of the playing fields, something inside her mind as well as her body had been destroyed forever.

The cup of tea didn't help and at seven o'clock, with the sun already hot, she went for a walk. It was inevitable that she would find her way to Stonebrook.

Ken was already up in the glass house, Brenda tidying away the breakfast dishes.

'I don't want to do this to you.'

Brenda looked closely at her sister-in-law. She seemed more brusque than usual – a sign that she was deeply troubled.

'Don't want to do what?'

'Burden you when you've just got married.'

'Burden me? Do I need Ken here?'

Freda shook her head.

'Think not. Women's talk. Young Amy.'

She sat down and told Brenda of her conversation with Linda.

'I'm sure she's wrong. Amy loves that baby...'

'Does she? Or is she going through the motions? Has she fooled everybody yet again, just like she's done for the past eighteen years or so?'

'She couldn't fool John, could she? Not with something as important as this,' Brenda said quietly. 'Perhaps Linda has some ulterior motive for saying these things, you know. Amy loves that baby and she takes such good care of her. She's fine, Freda. Lauren is the one thing that will bring Amy back to us, I'm sure of it.

CHAPTER TWENTY-SEVEN
July 1970

June had been a hot month and the July heat showed no sign of lessening.

Pat's invitation to Amy to spend the day with her and Pilot had received a lukewarm response. But, in spite of Amy's growing obsession with getting rid of Linda Chambers, she was enjoying the day out.

'Do you know the biggest advantage with adoption?' Pat said thoughtfully.

'No, but you'll no doubt enlighten me,' Amy replied with a smile.

'You stay slim.' She patted her hips. 'I didn't lose it after I had Pilot.'

'No sympathy. Go on a diet.'

Pat looked across the lawn towards Pilot and Lauren.

'Can't. Wouldn't be much good anyway now. I'm er... expecting another baby.'

There was a lengthy silence from Amy before Pat spoke again.

'Amy? Did you hear what I said?'

'I heard. Why? Why do you need two children?'

Pat laughed self-consciously.

'I don't need two children. I want two children. Different thing altogether. In fact, I'd like more – possibly four.'

'Oh.'

'Aren't you even a little bit pleased for me?'

Pat now felt angry. She hadn't relished the idea of telling Amy but it had been worse than she thought. Amy seemed dead inside. Her long blonde hair stirred slightly in the breeze as she leaned forward to look at Pat.

'Are you pleased?'

'Of course I am. We have planned this child.'

'Then I'm pleased for you. When's it due?'

Pat breathed a sigh of relief. At last, a normal question.

'Around Christmas. Hopefully just before Father Christmas comes. You'll be able to enjoy that, this year.'

'I always enjoy Christmas.'

'But it's different when you have a child. Completely different. Christmas really is nothing to do with adults, you don't realise that until you have a baby.' She paused for a moment. 'Are you enjoying Lauren?'

'She's got some lovely clothes.' Amy nodded.

'That wasn't what I meant. Dolls have lovely clothes – are you enjoying play times and such?'

'Play times? Sure. Shall we take these dishes in?'

She stood and began to stack the tray with the crockery they had used for lunch, her movements hurried and efficient.

Pat looked at her for a moment and then called Pilot over.

She hugged him, hoping Amy was taking note; Amy turned away and began to walk towards the kitchen door.

'Listen, sweetheart,' Pat said to her son. 'If baby Lauren wakes up, will you come and get Aunty Amy?'

The little boy nodded and ran back over to where he had his fort on the lawn. She'd been asleep ever since she'd arrived – boring. He wanted her to wake, and then perhaps she could play. He threw himself back into his game and promptly forgot the grown-ups.

Pat washed while Amy dried. The kitchen window overlooked part of the garden where Pilot was playing and where the pram stood in the shade cast by a large tree.

Amy watched Pilot stand and walk over to the pram then look at the baby before speaking to her. Amy continued to carefully wipe the plate she was holding, meticulously polishing it until it shone, her eyes never leaving the lawn.

Pilot reached into the pram and tugged at the baby. He struggled and managed to get her to a sitting position. She held out her chubby arms to him, one hand waving a pink dummy.

Amy carefully placed the plate neatly on the pile of other plates and picked up a fork. She rubbed it until it shone.

Pilot placed his arms around Lauren and tried to pull her, but her baby harness held her firmly in place. He let go of the child and bent inside the pram to undo the restraining hooks.

The fork was carefully placed in the cutlery drawer and she tidied the others already in there, aware of Pat on the other side of the large kitchen who was cleaning the work surfaces.

Amy's eyes never left the pram and Pilot.

The boy reached into the pram and lifted the little girl. She waved her arms once more and he lost his grip, dropping her on to the grass.

Amy continued to dry the cutlery. She didn't react until Lauren's yell of pain and shock ripped through the air.

'Pilot's just dropped Lauren on the ground.'

The words were quietly spoken. At first they didn't register with Pat. Amy carefully folded the tea towel and moved towards the kitchen door but Pat was there first and running across the grass before Amy had even left the kitchen.

Pilot was standing a small distance away from the

baby, sobbing hysterically.

'I didn't want to hurt her, mummy,' he was saying through his tears. 'Wanted to play. Mummy – I wanted to play!' His voice rose as he tried to explain but Pat pushed him to one side. The baby came first.

By the time Amy had walked across the lawn, Pat had turned Lauren so that she was lying on her back, still screaming and in obvious pain. She took a blanket from the pram.

'She's hurting somewhere,' she said frantically. 'I'll deal with Pilot later – we have to get her to hospital. Here, wrap her tightly in this so that the arm moves as little as possible. I'll go and get my car. You can hold her on your knee. She turned to her son, 'Pilot, you're in big, big trouble. You're coming with us now, but I'll sort you out later.'

'No, please,' Amy said, still not bending down to her daughter. 'He only wanted to play with her, I'm sure. He didn't realise he couldn't hold her. He did try…'

'You mean you watched this happening?' Pat was incredulous. 'You saw what he was doing and didn't say anything? Just carried on wiping the bloody dishes?'

'I didn't think he would drop her.' Amy shrugged her shoulders.

In that instant Pat decided her son would only receive a mild telling off – this could have been prevented.

'Wrap Lauren up, for heaven's sake, Amy, and give her a cuddle. I'll get the car.'

John was distraught at the sight of the tiny plaster cast on Lauren's arm. He'd had a hell of a day – first there had been Linda's letter of resignation on his desk, then David had rung to discuss his new book and mentioned that he and Dawn had to go away to Edinburgh overnight. Now this.

He had risked ringing Dawn at the office to find out if she was going with David.

'I didn't know how to contact you – yes, it's something that's cropped up with Jean McBlair. Her agent's proving difficult. I'm so sorry; we'll have to put off that meal until tomorrow night.'

'I needed you tonight, needed to talk to you. Linda's handed in her notice, won't say why, and now I can't see you.' He groaned.

'Can't be helped,' she said. 'I'll see you tomorrow. Want a tip about Linda? Ask Amy if she knows any reason why she would want to leave.'

'What do you mean?'

'I don't know. Just a hunch. Look, I've got to go. Got loads to do before we leave for Edinburgh. I'll see you tomorrow. Love you.'

'Love you, too much,' he said and smiled into the receiver before replacing it on the rest.

He was thoughtful as he walked back down the stairs and into his study. How on earth could Amy have anything to do with Linda leaving? The girl had been upset when he had tried to discover the reason for giving her unexpected and sudden notice. In spite of the offer of a significant pay rise, she had refused to change her mind.

He opened the door of the study and stood watching Linda for a moment. She continued to type, fully aware of his presence.

'Is it Amy?'

Linda looked up at the unexpected question. She felt her cheeks suffuse with colour and knew denial was useless. The expression on her face said it all. She didn't need to speak.

'Linda, is Amy the problem? Is that why you want to leave?'

'I don't want to leave,' she said quietly. 'I don't have a choice in the matter. Just forget it, John, and let me go.'

She returned to her typing. John looked at her for several long moments before turning and leaving the room.

Amy was sitting in the garden, the pram some distance away. Occasionally a tiny arm covered in a cast could be seen over the edge of the pram. She was enjoying the late afternoon sun waiting for the minutes to pass and for Linda to go home. Then she could feel more at ease. She hated having the girl in the house, hated...

'Amy. A word please.'

She very rarely heard anger in John's tone and turned in surprise.

'Good grief, you sound out of sorts.'

'That's one way of putting it. Another way is bloody furious. Why is Linda leaving?'

'Linda? Leaving? When did this happen?'

'She handed in her notice this morning and I know you're involved somehow. Amy, for God's sake – she's a good secretary and I don't want to lose her. What have you said?'

Amy's face was all innocence.

'Said? Nothing as far as I know.'

So Linda had kept quiet about their conversation – John obviously didn't know that she had asked the young secretary if she was having an affair with her boss.

The scene was imprinted in her mind – Linda's chalk white face, then the burning cheeks as she had vehemently denied the accusation.

'No!' she had cried. 'No, don't ever think that!'

But Amy did think it. John had changed. It had to be another woman. The only other woman in John's life was Linda, as far as she was aware.

For the first time, faced with an irate husband, she began to wonder if she had been right. Maybe he had met someone else... the girl had been pretty convincing. But it was irrelevant now; Linda was going and good riddance.

'John, I don't know what you're on about. Granted, I've never really got on with her and maybe that's her reason, but I can't think of anything else. I've just never found her to be a particularly friendly person. I don't think she likes me very much, so handing her notice in is probably for the best.'

John sat on the garden seat, holding his head in his hands. Sometimes he found it very hard to understand his wife.

'You make life so difficult, Amy... Look, it seems that I can't change Linda's mind, she's already found a new job, so to save this happening again, I suggest you choose our new employee. Will you see to it tomorrow? And, Amy,' he said as he stood and began to walk away, 'try and get one we will both like, huh?'

'Sarcasm isn't necessary, John,' she said stiffly. 'I'll get on to the employment bureau tomorrow. You'll have your new secretary by next Monday.'

CHAPTER TWENTY-EIGHT

September 1970

Treverick was happy. He was in the right position, at the right time and his plan was moving along smoothly.

One day the Andrews family would realise their worst nightmares. All the years they had spent hoping he wouldn't return would count for nothing. Nothing.

She'd got a baby now. He hadn't allowed for that but it made no difference. It was a girl baby.

That bore thinking about…

CHAPTER TWENTY-NINE

September 1970

Linda avoided Amy all week. John was aware of the undercurrents between the two women. As much as he hated to lose Linda, he realised that it was probably better she left if there was no hope of amicability between secretary and wife.

Amy interviewed four applicants for the position and John left her to get on with it. He knew she wouldn't tolerate anyone who was incapable of doing the work. He hoped she wouldn't choose someone who had a face like the back end of a bus but suspected she might. Still, if she could type and correct his spelling mistakes…

Linda placed the cover on the typewriter and sighed. She was walking out on a very enjoyable job. And she was walking out on the best employer she'd ever have.

No use denying it any longer, she was going to miss him.

But it had been out of the question that she should stay. Amy had made life so difficult ever since the first day. Now Linda was admitting defeat.

She stood and walked over to the window, wondering where John was. Only two minutes to her normal home time. The study door opened and she caught the familiar smell of aftershave.

'Linda,' he said, 'Are you absolutely sure?'

She nodded. 'It's time to move on.'

'Then here.' He handed her an envelope and she lifted an eyebrow in query.

'It's a reference, your wages and a bonus. And if ever

you need help, anything… you know where I am. I just hope you know what you're doing.'

She smiled but the smile didn't reach her eyes.

'I do, John. And thanks for this.' She patted the envelope. Moving towards the door she turned. 'Let's not beat about the bush any longer. Mrs Thornton thought we were having an affair and that's why I'm going. A word of warning, John, and believe me I'm not being clever, or nasty, or anything when I say this … be careful what time you go out in the afternoon. Vary your times. She'll soon realise that my leaving doesn't change things and when she finds out who the real mistress is, well… hell hath no fury, you know.'

'You know?'

Linda dropped her eyes.

'I know. And now I'm going. Take care, John. Remember what I've said,' and she brushed a swift kiss against his cheek. 'I won't say goodbye to your wife.'

John could only stare at her.

As she reached the front door she paused.

'She's a very lucky lady, John. And I don't mean Mrs Thornton.'

'Your new secretary starts Monday morning.'

John lifted his head from the book and looked over at his wife.

'Oh…er…good. Okay, I take it?'

'Fine. Comes with excellent references and has very good speeds. Did Linda say anything before she left?'

'She did, but nothing that would interest you.'

Amy felt tears prickle her eyes. She used to enjoy their evenings watching television or listening to the radio but she couldn't cope with this new John. He'd always been so considerate, so loving, there for her whenever she needed him but now all he seemed to do was snap at her. She hoped things would change for the better once he got over Linda.

'I spoke with Pat today.'

'Oh?' He didn't bother to lift his head to look at her.

'She's fine. Not being sick or anything with this baby.'

'Getting at something, Amy?' He still didn't lift his head.

'No – should I be?'

'Thought you might be hankering after a second child yourself.'

She looked alarmed.

'No – oh no! I was just making conversation...'

'Good,' he said shortly, 'because it's completely out of the question. I won't consider a second child until you start being a mother to the first one.'

Rain coming down in torrents, a girl falling part way down a cliff side and clutching at something, anything, an open hand of another girl. The second girl slowly opening her fingers, letting the first girl go, sliding slowly at first then gathering speed as gravity pulled her towards the bottom of the cliff; a broken body smashed to pieces on the rocks at the edge of the beach.

Pat screamed and sat up in bed. Sweat beaded her forehead and she screamed again.

'Pat! My God, what's wrong? Is it...?'

She turned to David for comfort.

'No, everything's okay. Just a dream, a nightmare.' Tears ran down her cheeks and when he switched on the bedside lamp he realised the extent of her terror.

'Come here,' he said and pulled her close. 'Want to tell me about it?'

She shook her head.

'No. It's over now. Just one of those silly dreams, being chased, that sort of thing. Turn out the light and hold me, I'll be fine.'

But she wasn't fine and she couldn't get back to sleep. She didn't know why she couldn't tell David about what had happened all those years ago – maybe because he would want to take it further, tell John or something like that. It had to be kept away from her husband.

David's small snores further prevented her from sleeping and in the end she gave up, creeping downstairs for a cup of tea.

The nightmare had evoked old memories and she knew without a doubt that what she had thought she had seen had actually taken place. Amy had deliberately opened her fingers and let Sonia go. There was a cold, cruel streak in her friend. Amy needed professional help but what could she do about it?

She wished the adoption agency had said no; Amy Thornton wasn't fit to have a baby and Pat feared for Lauren.

With the rising of the mid-July sun she wandered out into the garden pulling her cardigan around her against the early morning chill. She walked to the summerhouse and went inside. The seats were comfortable and she curled up on a sun lounger, her thoughts muddled.

Could she perhaps talk to Brenda? She had to tell someone; a child's future well-being was at stake. And then it suddenly hit her that it wasn't Lauren's physical well-being that was the problem, it was her mental state.

She was one of Amy's possessions, kept scrupulously clean and tidy, presented for viewing at every opportunity to be admired and then filed back into the appropriate drawer ready for her next outing. Her mind would become scarred, perhaps irrevocably.

Pat shuddered at the thought. Childhood shouldn't be like that, it should be fun and laughter with a lot of Ken Buckingham's muck thrown in for good measure. She felt helpless, particularly when she recalled a conversation she had with John. He admitted nothing came before his writing. It was out of his control, his pen was his life. He couldn't help Lauren, that much she knew. He would be a good father but from a distance.

By ten o'clock that morning she was in Brenda Buckingham's kitchen at Stonebrook drinking a very welcome cup of tea as she fought the nausea of early pregnancy. With her heart in her mouth, she started to talk.

And Brenda listened.

Brenda didn't accompany Ken when he left for three days to go travelling around the West Country, his new venture bubbling in his brain.

He picked up a contract at the first hotel he visited; it was a very good Monday for Ken Buckingham.

For Brenda, it was not so good. She had to face the possibility that her daughter was a murderer.

CHAPTER THIRTY

October 1970

Amy checked through the spy hole then opened the cottage door with a smile fixed on her face.

'Welcome,' she said. 'If you follow me, I'll take you to meet my husband.'

The study door was open and John looked up expectantly. His own smile froze on his face before he recovered sufficiently to hold out a hand.

'John,' Amy said, grinning triumphantly, 'this is Mark Carter.'

Carter's short, stocky figure paused momentarily in the doorway. He could tell that this extremely attractive woman had forgotten to mention to her husband that his new secretary was a man.

Mark strode forward and clasped hold of the proffered hand.

'Mr Thornton, it's good to meet you. I've long been an admirer.'

'Please –' John vaguely waved a hand, furious with Amy for the subterfuge. It didn't matter that his new employee was a man, it did matter that she had hidden it from him.

'It's John. We'll be working closely together.'

'I'll leave you to get on with it.' Amy closed the door as she left the study. Her sense of satisfaction knew no bounds.

John looked at his new employee with interest. Around five feet nine inches tall and well built, he was smartly dressed in a pale blue shirt and navy pin stripe suit – with a horrendous eye-catching tie. It added colour to his staid appearance. His glasses afforded him a serious air but on that first morning John came to appreciate his subtle sense of humour. By lunchtime he was reluctantly beginning to admit to himself that Amy had chosen well.

At lunchtime he also decided to do away with the title 'secretary' – he now had a personal assistant.

Mark was good; a fast typist, an excellent telephone manner and, to John's amusement, he had an intimate knowledge of every character in all of John's earlier books.

'Adam Clarkson,' he said slowly, chewing on the end of a pencil.

John looked up and waited for him to go on.

'Adam Clarkson,' he repeated. 'He's almost exactly like Alan Chivers in Rest In Pieces. Even got the same initials.'

John was intrigued.

'Go on.'

Mark had the grace to look a little uncomfortable. After one day in the job, he was already picking at the author's work.

'Well, as I said, their names are too similar, they both have grey eyes that change to blue in sunlight, both have short blonde hair. One has a wife called Carole; the other has a girlfriend called Catherine. They both live in penthouse apartments, both rolling in money. Both drive Lamborghinis. Thing is, anybody who is a fan will spot it straight away.'

'And I didn't.' John stared at him thoughtfully. 'You've already earned this month's salary. It's going to need a major re-write. Damn, anything like that slows down the momentum but I couldn't carry on knowing that that part's wrong. Still, I'll make a start tonight...'

'Can I suggest something?'

'As long as it's not along the lines of scrapping the book altogether.'

'Hardly. I know I've only seen a small part of it but it's superb. No, I was going to say that if you tell me the changes you want to make to his appearance and life style, I'll go through it and alter everything. All you need to do then is okay the changes and you won't have lost the pace.'

'Think you can?'

'I'm sure I can – I won't actually be doing anything except substituting brown for grey, little things like that. You've already done all the work.'

'Well, I'm glad you've picked up on it before I go any deeper into the book. It's funny – I'm so careful not to get characters with any similarities within the novel but it never occurred to me that characters in separate novels shouldn't have similarities either. My problem is that I never read a book after it's written – it goes on the shelf and off we move on to another. I forget who is in what. These two men play the same sort of anchor role in the novels. I suppose that's why they ended up with similar characteristics. Thanks, Mark.'

'No problem, boss.'

John soon learnt that the phrase *no problem, boss* was a stock answer from Mark that was always meant.

Amy smiled all day long and even gave her tiny daughter five minutes of her time before putting her back into her pram with a pink dummy.

CHAPTER THIRTY-ONE

October 1970

That bleak, cold Monday in October was a memorable day for Ronald Treverick. It was a new branch in his working life and one more step closer to the Andrews family. He was slowly, carefully getting within striking distance of Amy.

And Amy's baby.

CHAPTER THIRTY TWO

November 1970

'I want to take you out. Buy you something.'

Dawn laughed.

'Got anywhere special in mind?'

'As a matter of fact, Cleverclogs, I have. Do you think you can persuade David to let you have a couple of days off? I thought we could go up to London, take in a show and stay overnight.'

'David won't need to be persuaded. But how can you get away?'

'I'll tell Amy it's a book signing. She hates them, all the hanging around. Besides, now that we've got Lauren, she'll have to stay at home.'

'Doesn't sound chauvinistic, John Thornton?' she rebuked. 'Little wife staying at home...'

'Wasn't meant to. So? Can we go?'

'If you can get away with it, I definitely can. And surely no one will see us together in London!' She laughed. 'We'll be so anonymous, we'll be invisible.'

'I feel like a beached whale.'

David looked up from the newspaper to smile at his wife.

'You're beautiful.'

'So is a beached whale to another beached whale but that doesn't mean I have to enjoy looking like one.'

He folded the paper and dropped it into the magazine rack.

'Now tell me what's wrong. I'd say come and sit on my knee and tell me what's wrong but you're so much like a beached whale...'

She threw a cushion at his head.

'I hate you.'

'No, you don't. Would you love me just a little bit more if I treated you to a couple of days in London?'

Pat's eyes sparkled.

'I'd love you a hell of a lot. I'll ask Mum and Dad if they'll have Pilot. When can we go?'

'Whoa, whoa! We have to go mid-week. I like my weekends with Pilot. Besides, Dawn's booked a two-day holiday next week and it's easier if I take the same days off. She wants to go and see her mum.' He paused for a moment. 'Why not ask Amy and John if they'll have Pilot for us?'

'No!' Her reply was too fast.

'But they think the world of him and we've never asked them to look after him.'

'I'd rather not, David. Mum loves having him, you know she does.'

David shrugged his shoulders.

'Whatever you say.'

'And don't think you can bring any work for one of the London publishers. You tell everyone at that office that we're going to the Cotswolds or they'll have you running errands all over the place.'

He laughed.

'Okay, I give in. The only people who will know where we are will be our parents. Promise.'

She smiled and patted her bump.

'Good. Mother and baby whale feel quite happy now.'

John booked them into the Royal Garden Hotel. Dawn stared around their suite then sank onto the bed.

'This is wonderful,' she sighed. 'When you said a

couple of days in London I didn't expect this!'

'Only the best for my princess.' He lay by her side then reached across and kissed the tip of her nose. 'I love you, Dawn'

'And I love you,' she laughed, 'but please don't spoil things. Let's not mention sharing lives, setting up home together or anything like that while we're here.'

Just lately John seemed to bring up the subject every time he saw her and yet she knew if she ever agreed he would not be able to walk out on Amy and Lauren.

He kicked off his shoes and placed his hands behind his head.

'What do you want to do, Dawn?'

'Harrods,' she said promptly.

'You know what I mean.'

'Leave it, John.' There was a warning note in her voice.

'No, I'm not pushing for anything. Answer me honestly, where do we go after this?'

She thought for a long time and John was just beginning to think she wouldn't answer when she spoke.

'I see us carrying on exactly like this until the day we die. I don't want any more from you than that. I've had a taste of a man permanently in my life and it's not what I want. I'll always be your other woman, John. That's enough. Give me whatever time you can without rocking the boat at home. I would never take you away from your Lauren permanently.'

'So you don't want a child?'

The question was so sudden, so unexpected that it took her breath away. It was as if he had read her mind.

'What made you ask that?'

'Most women wouldn't settle for what you say you're prepared to put up with. I wondered if a child is likely to figure in your life.'

'Ask me in another year,' she said enigmatically. 'Now come on, let's go shopping. I want a new dress for tonight's outing.'

Pat eased her bulk down into the armchair and kicked off her shoes. David bent and kissed the top of her head.

'Okay?'

'Tired. It's a long drive and I don't feel very comfortable. I think I'll have an hour's nap, if that's okay by you.'

'It's your break, sweetheart. You do whatever you want and perhaps later we can go shopping. I think you deserve something special.'

'For putting up with you?' She grinned.

'Just for being you. I bless the day I met you – you know that, don't you?'

'Hey! Why so serious? I know you love me.'

'It's just that sometimes I get so wrapped up in work I forget to let you know how much you mean to me. I'll go down to the foyer and have a mooch around. Never stopped at the Hilton before. And while I'm down there I'll see if they can help us get tickets for a show. Anything special you'd like to see?'

'Well, I know this sounds silly with all the musicals that are around at the moment, but I'd really like to see the Mousetrap.'

'Your wish is my command,' he said with a small bow. 'Now go to sleep and I'll see you in an hour.'

He closed the door softly behind him. Pat walked over to the bed. She didn't bother to undress, just put her head on the pillow and drifted away.

The baby moved several times but she didn't notice. She dreamed that the newcomer would be a little girl and that the midwife was Amy Thornton. As Amy pulled the baby out of her she grasped it by the head and gave a sharp twist. The baby gave one cry and died, her neck broken.

Bathed in sweat Pat woke with a small gasp of protest. She looked at the clock realizing that she had only been asleep for about ten minutes. She stood no further chance of any rest.

She walked over to the large window and looked down on the metropolis bustling many floors below her. Amy was haunting her.

She was in the bath when David returned, proudly carrying two tickets for The Mousetrap.

'Okay?' he asked smiling at her huge stomach.

'Mmmm,' she said. 'Fine. No problems at all.'

Dawn had never had a dress that cost £250 before. She had also never owned shoes costing £100, or six sets of matching lingerie. When John had said he wanted to buy her something she had imagined a gold bracelet or a watch.

She took the cream stockings and dress out of the hotel wardrobe for the fifth time and held it against her.

'But do you really like it?' she asked.

'I like it,' John said with a smile. 'I love you. Can I tell you again how much pleasure you've given me today? And after we've fed on the best that this hotel has to offer and been to the theatre I'm going to bring you back here, take you to bed and make love to you all night long.'

'All night long?' She looked at him, her eyes dancing.

'All night long.' He was emphatic. 'I'm going to start at your toes, then up to your knees, then your inner thighs are going to be so delicious, then…'

'Whoa!' she called, laughing. 'Before we get to the next bit I think you should know something. Contraception's off the menu.'

There was silence for a moment.

'But…I haven't brought…'

'Doesn't matter. I stopped taking the pill a month ago. My choice.'

'I don't understand. You said ask me in another year or so.'

'I know. Hopefully in another year I'll either be having a baby or already have one. Ask me in another year if a baby is on the cards.'

'Shouldn't we have discussed this?' He sounded pompous.

'No. I'm ready for a baby in my life. If it hadn't been you it would have been someone else. I won't ask for support, I won't ask for involvement with this child. Given a choice I'd choose you for its daddy because I desperately love you, but if that doesn't suit…'

'It suits all right.' He said with a growl. 'God, you're the most dogmatic, stubborn female I've ever met in my life. Do you have to be so independent?'

'Yes, I do.' She turned and hung the dress in the wardrobe. 'Now, John bloody Thornton, take off your clothes and get in that bed. We've still an hour before we need to get ready. Let's make a baby.'

It was during the interval that David spotted John. His blonde hair and height made him stand out in a crowd. Not expecting to bump into anyone who knew him John had taken no steps to hide.

'Isn't that John?' he said, nudging his wife. She looked in the direction of his pointed finger.

'Yes, but that's not Amy. She's got dark hair.'

John lifted his head from Dawn and his eyes locked on to David's face. He blanched and gave a half wave.

Dawn, standing facing him and with her back to the Farmers, glanced up at him.

'You look positively ill,' she said with a smile. 'Too much sex can turn you grey, you know.'

'Dawn...' he faltered, 'there's something you should know. Standing about ten yards away is someone we both know quite well.'

She stiffened and didn't turn.

'Do you want to tell me who it is or shall we play a little guessing game?' she asked with a shaky laugh.

'I'll give you a clue. He's spending a couple of days in the Cotswolds. Oh God, they're coming over.'

'Can you hide me under your jacket?'

'No.'

'Then it's face the music time.'

She turned round and smiled at the Farmers; there was an audible gasp from Pat.

David's smile became fixed.

'Dawn! But...'

'My mother's fine, David,' she said with a grin that she didn't feel like displaying. 'How's the Cotswolds?'

He said nothing for a moment then roared with laughter.

'Touché!' He turned and looked at his lifelong friend. 'Although your mother doesn't look too well from where I'm standing. Sit down over here John. Pat, come on, you look as if you could do with a sit down as well.'

He took charge, feeling a sort of hysteria bubbling inside him. He didn't know what to say and wanted to get John on his own. The theatre foyer was hardly the right place to do that.

Whisky for the men and Martinis for the ladies calmed the situation and they agreed to meet up for coffee after the performance. Neither John nor Dawn remembered much about the rest of the play.

CHAPTER THIRTY-THREE
November 1970

He closed the room door behind him and pulled Dawn into the shelter of his arms.

'How do you feel?'

'Oh, John,' she sighed. 'It's not my problem really, is it? It's yours. Pat is Amy's closest friend. She's bound to tell her.'

He shook his head.

'I don't think so. As we left the restaurant she pulled me back. She asked if you keep me sane. When I said yes she smiled and said "well that's all right then '. So I don't think we need to worry about Amy finding out, not from Pat anyway. No, it's David who's prudish. I'll have to talk to him of course, explain how much we mean to each other. But he could go either way.'

'Well, I guess I've lost my job. That was always the risk I suppose. It's a shame because I like working at Farmers.'

'Whatever happens, you won't suffer financially I promise. But let's not jump the gun. In fact, let's go to bed, forget the rest of the world and screw each other silly.' He bent, picked her up and threw her on the bed.

'What's this?'

'My notice.'

David stared at Dawn, taking in the unusually sombre outfit she was wearing; it made her face look even paler.

'Why?'

'Because…well you know why. We work closely and

something like this will come between us. And I can't give John up, not for you, nor Amy, not for anybody.'

'Not even for Lauren?' he asked.

'Yes, for Lauren.' She said it without even having to think about it.

'That's the Dawn I've grown to admire over the past eighteen months or so. I don't want to lose you so take this back,' and he handed her the letter. 'However, as you say we do have a close working relationship. If you are open and honest perhaps we can face it then put it to one side. How long has it been going on?'

She shrugged her shoulders as she sat in the chair opposite her employer.

'About a year and three quarters. I should make one thing clear though – I have no intention of taking him away from Amy. Even if he left her I won't let him move in with me. I'm his bit on the side, David, and that's how it will stay.'

David smiled.

'I saw how protective John was towards you – he's fully committed to you. Don't forget I've known him all my life. I think I understand him better than anyone.'

'I think you misunderstood me. I'm fully committed to him. I just refuse to have a man in my life full time. The only time I have spent a full night with him was in London – he's never stayed over at my flat.'

David paused for a moment.

'Tell me something, Dawn. Have you ever met Amy?'

'No, I think it's better that way.'

'Then let me tell you a bit about her –'

She held up a hand.

'No! I know there is something in her past that ties John to her but that's all he's ever said. I don't want to know if John can't tell me himself. Don't burden me with any more guilt than I already have, David.'

'I can tell you what she's like though. She's beautiful. Long blonde hair. The sweetest face since Helen of Troy. Style. Figure that belongs on Venus de Milo.'

'Then why…?' Dawn looked bewildered.

'Why does John want you? Because beneath this perfect beautiful exterior is a mind that is warped and twisted.'

'Don't exaggerate, that kind of stuff belongs in books.' She let out a dry disbelieving laugh but her hands clenched.

'It's not her fault. Please don't run away with the idea that she controls this attitude. She doesn't. I can't say much more without revealing her problem but I wish to God John and I had never met her. Although,' he said with a smile, 'just to lighten the atmosphere, if I hadn't known Amy as a child I wouldn't have met Pat. There's a plus side to everything if you look hard enough.'

'Can there be a plus side to my staying on here? If my private life will cause you difficulties, or you can't accept this relationship between John and me, then it's better that I go now. I don't want our working partnership to deteriorate because…'

'It will only deteriorate if you cause him any grief. He's my best friend, Dawn. We've always looked out for each other and I'm looking out for him now. Word of advice though, don't ever let Amy find out. She'll kill you.'

Dawn laughed.

'She can try.'

'She'll succeed.'

Ken was immersed in facts and figures when Brenda

walked into the lounge. He looked up from his notes and smiled.

'I can put this away if you want to watch television. Want me to wipe the pots?'

She loved the way he always said wipe the pots and not dry the dishes but that night she didn't want him to perform either the Yorkshire or the Cornish version. She shook her head.

'No, they're done. I hope you don't mind but I've asked Freda round for a drink. I need to talk. Will you walk her home afterwards?'

'Sure, no problem. You look harassed. There's been something on your mind for some time. Is that why Freda's coming round?'

'Yes. She's so full of common sense – like you in a lot of ways. I think I need my imagination slapping down.'

She sank into the old armchair. In this worn grey chair she could relax, curl up with her legs underneath her and meditate on pleasant thoughts – and unpleasant ones.

She stared into the fire, her mind in turmoil. Every word of the conversation with Pat Farmer was etched into her brain and she knew she'd kept those words to herself for far too long. She needed someone to tell her that Pat was wrong.

'She actually saw this happen?'

Brenda nodded miserably.

'She was as close as I am to you. She says she saw Amy's fingers open and let the poor girl fall to her death.'

'And why has she suddenly decided to tell you? I thought she was supposedly Amy's best friend.'

'She's worried. About Lauren.'

Freda gave a small cry of surprise. Ken watched her

closely.

'Something wrong, Freda?' he asked.

'I don't know. Another person said the same thing. Nothing to worry about I'm sure.'

'Somebody else has expressed concern about Lauren? Who?' Brenda was beginning to think she was going insane.

'That young secretary of John's. Linda. She didn't say anything so awful as ill treatment... no she was bothered that the baby isn't loved, at least not by Amy. She seemed to think she's a showpiece.'

'That's almost exactly Pat's words,' Brenda said slowly. 'She told me about the Sonia Dawes incident along with one or two other things that have bothered her over the years. She needed to drive home just how unbalanced Amy is. And how clever she is at concealing it. We had no idea did we?'

'I did,' Ken said, his face colouring up. 'I knew she was disturbed that day in the glass house. She wanted me to make love to her, no to fuck her, on the floor. And she wanted me to do it right there knowing you would see it happening. Oh, I knew all right but then when you explained what had happened to her Bren, it seemed to make sense.'

'So what do we do?' Brenda's face was devoid of colour.

Freda stood and moved towards the kitchen window. Both Brenda and Ken followed her movements, waiting for her to speak. She stared for a moment at the pathway leading to the garden gate, her thoughts in turmoil.

'I don't know what we do,' she said quietly. 'I really don't know.'

'Then it's up to us to think of something, Ken. I'm going to take more of a back seat in the business, spend time with Amy and Lauren, try and teach her how to love this little girl, because if I don't that baby is going to have a miserable life.'

Ken reached across and touched his wife's hand.

'I'm sure you're right, duck. Let's have her to stay here, give Amy a break. We can make her a bedroom; decorate Amy's old room for her.'

'Ken Buckingham, you're wonderful.'

'No, I'm not but I'll need Freda to work in the fields if I'm losing you.'

Freda ignored the joke.

'Right, I'll be off. Er… any help, Bren, you know where I am.'

'It's helped just talking about it. Thanks for listening.'

'I'll walk you home, Freda. Don't worry; we'll have Lauren more. Amy's baby will be quite safe here.'

CHAPTER THIRTY-FOUR
December 1970

'It needs a new carpet.'

Ken laughed as she stood hands on hips staring at the newly decorated bedroom. Mickey Mouse was running riot along one wall.

Bending, Ken began to pull the carpet away from the skirting board. 'And to think I took all that care not to catch the carpet with the paintbrush. Why didn't you say at the beginning you wanted a new one?'

'It didn't look shabby until we decorated. Let's take it up.'

Fifteen minutes later they surveyed the bare floor, coffee cups held in their hands.

'Needs a bloody good clean.'

Brenda nodded. 'I'll sweep and mop it. Looks like a loose floor board over there near the skirting board. Want to fix it before I mop?'

'I'll fetch my tools.' He put the cup on the floor and went downstairs.

When he returned Brenda was sitting on the floor in the middle of the dust, the floorboard pushed to one side. In the revealed hole he could see bundles of papers. She was holding a sheet of white foolscap in her hand, scanning the words.

'What...?'

She looked up to face him.

'Amy's,' she swallowed, 'Amy's stories.'

Freda was almost afraid to open the pink cardboard folder. She had seen the distress in Brenda and had tried to refuse the papers.

'Please, Freda,' Brenda begged. 'Read them and tell me she's not completely insane.'

Sure that she would need the comfort. Brenda lit a cigarette, her first for three weeks. There were some twenty stories in all, ranging in length from a thousand words to nine thousand six hundred and eighty two. Each one had a meticulous word count typed in at the end.

And each one dealt with the subject of rape from the victim's point of view with the exception of two. One portrayed a bungling police officer who didn't believe a victim and the other, a far more horrific story, was from a rapist's viewpoint.

Freda didn't go to bed that night. It would have been a pointless exercise. There was no way she would have slept.

The stories had proved what she had known for many years. She understood Brenda's distress. Brenda had always looked on the bright side, but after reading the stories she could no longer deny the enormity of the damage done by Treverick.

And she also knew without a doubt that John had to see these stories.

Brenda had been reluctant to give the stories to John. Freda said it was only fair; he should know just how deeply her past still affected her. And just how wrong the paediatric psychiatrist had been.

'But even if he knows, can he really help? It's professional help she needs...'

'Brenda, that young woman is in a dreadful state but what I find most disturbing is that she fools everybody. Oh, I know Pat was concerned and so was Linda, but we would have swanned along pretending everything was okay, wouldn't we? It's only these stories that have showed us just what is below the surface, below that beautiful exterior.'

'Oh, I don't know, Freda. It's like peeking into her life, the part that she wants to keep private. She would be furious if she knew we had read them, wouldn't she? Even if John reads them, what can he do?'

'They have a young daughter and Amy is going to be the one to bring her up. John works far too hard to have time for his daughter so she will be most influenced by her mother. Is that what you want? A warped, dangerous mind bringing up your granddaughter?'

Brenda felt and looked as miserable as she had ever been in her life.

'Okay, I know you're right. But just what can John do? Answer me that one, Miss Logical.'

'He'll think of something. He's got to.'

Mark Carter saw very little of John that Wednesday. It had been a peculiar day.

Carrying little Lauren, Amy had been standing in the hallway when he had arrived at nine o'clock. He couldn't remember seeing her holding the child before and he tried hard to hide his surprise.

'Morning, Mrs Thornton. Everything okay?'

She had looked at him for a moment trying to work out if he was being sarcastic, before deciding he wasn't.

'I'm fine. Just waiting for Brenda to call for me, we're going shopping. She wants Lauren to stay for a couple of days. They've decorated my old bedroom and she wants to get some nursery furniture for it, so I'm going with her.'

'That's nice. She's a lovely lady, your mother. It'll give you and John a bit of a break as well. I'm sure you'll welcome that.'

'Have you got children, Mark?'

He shook his head. 'No, I'm not married.'

'Then you're hardly qualified to judge whether we need a break or not,' she said icily and turned to walk into the lounge with Lauren. He stared at the closed door for a moment before touching his burning cheek. She certainly knew how to put someone down. Luckily, if that was how she wanted to play it, he didn't need to have anything to do with her.

He walked into the study and removed the cover of his typewriter. The French windows were open and he crossed to look outside. John was in the garden staring at the herbaceous border, clearly lost in thought.

'Morning, boss,' Mark called and John turned and waved.

The room was warm even with the windows open and Mark eased his bright yellow tie slightly as he bent to look at John's list of things for him to do. He pushed his glasses further up his nose, aware of how much his eyesight was changing since starting to wear them.

The list was short but comprehensive and Mark went to the filing cabinet to take out the relevant paperwork. He heard a car horn beep, and then the front door open and close.

Amy had gone, and suddenly the air felt lighter.

John was surprised to see Freda. He couldn't ever remember her calling before working hours and he led her into the lounge.

'We'll leave Mark struggling with my hand writing,' he said with a grin. 'To what do I owe this pleasure?'

'Straight to the point as ever,' she quipped in return, feeling sick.

'Then I must have caught it from you,' he returned with a laugh. 'Can I get you a coffee? Tea?'

'Not just yet. I need to talk to you.'

'Sounds serious,' he said, a frown crossing his face. He pushed his blonde hair back with one hand and sat down opposite her. 'I presume that means it's something to do with Amy? That's why Brenda has taken her out, so that you could come here?'

'That's very astute, young man. It's also correct.' She bent down and reached into the bag she had brought with her. She handed a battered pink cardboard folder to him.

'Brenda found these.'

As he began to lift the flap, she stopped him.

'No, leave it until later and don't read them in front of Amy. First I must tell you what they are.'

'They're Amy's stories, aren't they?' Suddenly he felt cold.

'Brenda found them hidden under a loose floorboard. We've both read them and they show a very disturbed mind, John.'

'But she wrote these eight or ten years ago, Freda.'

'One of them is dated eight months ago. I suspect she started writing it around the time you had Lauren, or just after. It's about a sexual assault on a young baby by its father.'

John stared at the folder in his hands. He wanted to throw it into the fire but he knew that he couldn't. Not yet.

'Has she any idea that you've found these?'

'No, she probably thinks they're unobtainable now. She won't be able to take up the carpet without it being obvious.'

'Have I got to read them?'

'Oh yes, without a doubt. You must, John. Don't

bury your head in the sand. I'm not saying you can help Amy; if she won't help herself, there's not much you can do. What Brenda and I want is for you to be aware of this. You have a young daughter. Think about that, John, before you throw those straight into the fire.'

He looked up guiltily.

'No,' she said with a smile. 'I didn't read your mind. It was my initial reaction too. But I did read them. And you must do the same in order to understand Amy. Then you'll know what you're really up against.'

She stood and picked up her bag.

'Forget the coffee – I've given you enough to think about. If you want to talk when you've read them, you know where I am.'

She walked from the room leaving a bewildered man to stare morosely into the flames, the pink folder bent over in hands that trembled.

CHAPTER THIRTY-FIVE
December 1970

'Get your friggin' hands off me, David Farmer!!'

'Friggin' hands? Pat, I thought you promised to be a lady this time,' he grinned into the sweat-streaked face of his wife.

'This time, this time,' she muttered through clenched teeth, 'there'll never be another time.'

'But,' he said, holding her tightly as another wave of pain began to take over, 'I thought we'd arranged to have four?'

She sank her teeth sharply into his chest and he yelled.

'You... you bloody vampire!'

The midwife hid her smile as she listened to the exchange between the expecting parents, knowing that in five minutes everything would be joy, tears and laughter.

'Don't you swear at me, David,' Pat warned. 'Oh, God, no...' Her long low moan rose as the contraction began to take hold. 'David,' she screamed. 'Tell them that they're hurting me. Tell them!'

'Hush, Babe,' David said, holding tightly in spite of the bite she had inflicted. He'd have to take the chance she wouldn't do it again. 'We're nearly there.'

And suddenly the head was through.

'Pant now, Pat.' The midwife began to check the baby's neck for obstruction and then leaned over to feel at Pat's stomach. 'Right, lovey, with this next contraction we want this baby out. It's a hairy little thing so let's have the rest of it to look at. There, it's starting. Now come on, push...'

Pat took a deep breath and almost before she had started, it was over.

'It's a girl,' David yelled. 'God, Pat, we've done it, we've got our daughter!'

'I don't care if it's a monkey,' she said. 'I'm knackered.'

'You're such a lady, sweetheart,' David said leaning over to kiss her. 'I love you.'

Pat watched as the baby was handed to a nurse and taken over to one side to be checked.

'Is she okay?'

'She's fine for a monkey,' came the cheerful response. 'Now relax while we get this placenta out of the way. She's beautiful – I'd guess about eight and a half pounds. Do we have a name?'

'Bryony Leigh.'

'Bryony. That's lovely. A very pretty name for a very pretty baby.'

The nurse brought the now quiet baby across to Pat and placed her in her arms.

'Bryony,' she said. 'This is your mummy. She swears a lot and bites people but apart from that, she's fine.'

He read the stories and was unable to dismiss them from his mind. In spite of what Freda had said he had thrown them on to the fire after reading them, before scrambling madly to retrieve them.

They had to be kept – from a writer's point of view they were technically brilliant. He knew that if David ever got hold of them he would want to meet the author.

What hurt John the most was that he couldn't discuss them with Amy.

He knew what the stories meant; what he didn't know was how to handle the situation.

He had been staring into the fire, turning the dark

implications in the stories over in his mind when she appeared holding a small table. With only a few days to go to Christmas he guessed it was a gift for someone.

'Look,' she said. 'Do you like it?'

The table was no more than two feet high with a drawer that had an ornate brass handle.

It looked exquisite. The top of the table was inlaid with flowers and the wood had a wonderful gleam. He reached out a hand to touch it.

'That's beautiful,' he watched her face harden unaccountably.

'Do you think Brenda and Ken will like it? It's their Christmas present.'

'They'll love it. I'll not ask what it cost,' He looked into the unexpectedly animated face of his wife. Could this really be the same person who had written such horror?

'I have every intention of telling you, skinflint,' she chided gently. 'It's cost me just over £5. I bought the table from a market stall in Padstow, stripped it, made a collage with dried flowers on top and then varnished it.'

'But…'

'I know,' she grinned. 'You thought you had a dumb blonde for a wife.'

'No, I didn't,' he said, not altogether sure he was telling the truth. 'What I actually think is that you seem to be wasting your life. The only thing you do is care for Lauren.'

'Well, now you know differently. This isn't the only piece I've done. I've commandeered that old shed down the garden to work in. The chemicals I use can be a bit overpowering. My biggest problem is I have no electricity so I've rung someone up. He's coming tomorrow to put me into the twentieth century.'

'I can't believe this. It's tremendous.' He lifted the table and turned to inspect the back. 'It's a real work of art. Take you long?'

'About a month. That's what's going to make them exclusive.'

He took his eyes away from the table and looked at her.

'You want to do this for a living?'

'Not exactly a living; I don't need money, do I? I don't know why I'm doing it. I suppose it's because I get a real kick out of seeing the finished object. I've completed about half a dozen but this is the best. And I'm starting to get specific orders – the collaged flowers are sort of becoming a trademark.' She shrugged her shoulders diffidently.

'You're putting yourself down,' John said slowly. 'You have a talent that is…well, I can't think of words to describe this.' He gently touched the table top. 'Go for it, Amy. Can you cope with this and Lauren?'

She stood and moved towards the door, carrying the table carefully.

'Amy? Can you manage both?' he repeated.

'Well, if I can't, I'll get a nanny,' she said without looking at him and went through into the hall.

CHAPTER THIRTY-SIX
Summer 1972

David pulled the framed photograph towards him and smiled. He had brought into the office that morning and every time he looked at it, delight lit up his face.

Pilot had just turned seven and Bryony was eighteen months old. She was almost a mirror image of Pat as was obvious from the photograph. They had the same hair, same smile and same-coloured eyes. He loved them all so much. And he wanted to spend more time with them.

It was three years since she had started working for him and for the past week he had been considering cutting back his hours and giving Dawn more responsibility. He hoped she would agree. She had been taking on more of the work lately and was proving to be worth every penny of her salary.

His idea was to promote her to do more of his work and get an assistant for her, someone not too junior. He hesitated momentarily before pressing the bell and summoning her into his office.

Since their talk about John two years earlier, they hadn't mentioned the subject but David knew that they were still together. He looked up as she walked through the door.

'Come in, Dawn. You don't need your notepad; I want to talk to you.'

'Oh dear,' she quipped. 'Am I fired?'

'You will be if you don't pour us both a cup of coffee. It's ten minutes since I last had one.' David was known for his coffee consumption.

She carried the drinks across to his desk and sat facing him.

'So, what's wrong?'

'Nothing at all. In fact, things couldn't be better.' He pushed the photograph across the polished surface of the desk. 'Like it?'

'It's terrific. They've all got their heads.'

'That's because Dad took it and not me. Don't digress. The point I'm trying to make, if you'll cut the sarcasm, is that I think they're terrific and I want to spend more time with them.'

Dawn raised the coffee cup to her lips and put it down without taking a sip. Her stomach churned at the smell.

'How would you feel about promotion?'

At first his words didn't register; she was too busy fighting the nausea. When she did take in what he was saying, she didn't know how to answer.

'Promotion?' She sat back in her chair trying to focus her concentration, knowing time had run out. 'David, it would be pointless. I'm expecting a baby.'

He was silent for a long time, his eyes never leaving her face.

'Do I say congratulations?'

'I hope so. I think it's a pretty impressive achievement.' Her tone was as flat as his.

'Does John know?'

She shook her head.

'Not yet. I wouldn't have told you if you hadn't sprung this on me. And it would be unfair of me to accept such a good offer knowing it couldn't last. I only found out yesterday and I haven't seen John yet.'

She felt defensive and she was angry. The censorious note in David's voice was riling her. She took a deep breath.

'This baby is planned, you know, David. I'm not a

silly kid in a no win situation. It won't have to change our relationship…'

'If you believe that, Dawn, then you don't know John as well as you think you do. And have you considered Amy in all of this? You're going to tear him in two; he'll want to be with both of you more than ever now.'

She stood and walked towards the door, her back stiff with resentment. Pausing in the doorway, she looked at him for a moment.

'David, we've been friends for too long to fall out over this; irrespective of that, I will say what I feel. This is my life and it really doesn't matter whether John wants to be with both of us or not, because he can't have me. This is my baby, my body, my pregnancy and my decision. I take it I don't need to ask you to keep quiet until I've spoken to him?'

He shook his head and sighed.

'Of course I won't say anything. Dawn – be careful. Independence is a wonderful thing but do you know how expensive a baby is?'

'It won't be a problem.' She smiled across the room. 'John and I aren't stupid. We know what this child means and all royalties from the new book are for our baby. I guarantee you this, David, with this news under his belt; John will write his best book ever.'

David finally smiled.

'I don't doubt it, Dawn; I don't doubt it for one minute.'

'I think I love you more at this minute than I've ever loved anyone or anything in my entire life.' John pulled Dawn close to him and held her, rubbing his face into the top of her head.

'You're pleased, then?' She raised her head.

'Pleased would be an understatement. I feel as though I'm the only one who's ever done it, super-stud Thornton, no less.'

'Oh, no,' she said gravely. 'I'm sure it must have been done before. I've seen the odd child or two down in Padstow, so somebody must be doing it somewhere.'

'You're an idiot. So – when do you finish work?' He laughed.

'What?' She pulled away from him slightly. 'Finish work? My God, not for ages yet, I'm only ten weeks, you know. I'll work until about eight months provided everything's ok.'

'You don't need to work.'

'I do. Subject closed, John. I'll work for as long as I can.' Once again she had a defensive feeling and didn't like it. Why wouldn't people let her make her own decisions without trying to influence?

'But…'

'John, just drop it right now. Let's talk about other things – like decorating the nursery, buying new furniture, kitting this baby out head to toe.'

He looked at her for a long moment.

'So I'm to be allowed some share in it then?'

She nodded, trying to stop a smile that threatened to cross her face. 'Sure – I never said I wouldn't let you support us. I just don't want you to leave Amy and Lauren. I'm no good as a wife, John, but I'm bloody good as a mistress.'

He felt bewildered. This woman had taken over his life; she would only allow him into hers on her terms.

'Dawn – what will the baby be called?'

'My God, I haven't thought about names yet! Have you? Do you have a preference for one?'

'I didn't mean that. I meant what surname will he or she have.'

'With your permission I'd like Thornton. But if you feel that it will ever make life difficult for you, then we'll keep it at Lynch.'

'It's Thornton,' he said. 'His voice had a rough edge to it. Hang the consequences. This little one will know me as its father.'

'If we call it Thornton,' she said slowly, 'one day the whole world might know you are its father.'

*　　*　　*　　*　　*

John lifted his head and smiled at the sight of his wife.

'You look terrific, Mrs Thornton. Going somewhere?'

'Yes I am. I intended to go on my own but I think maybe I would feel happier if you came with me. Can you spare an hour?'

He looked at his watch – 11.32 am.

'Mark, what time is David coming?'

Mark opened his diary to check, even though he knew.

'Not until three o'clock, boss.'

John stood and moved around his desk.

'Then I have an hour. Is it important?'

'I think so. I've decided the shed is far too small. I'm going to look at a shop that's just become available. Prime site in Padstow, and the back would convert into a workshop. I just think a male presence will have more effect than if I turn up on my own. And I value your opinion. Do you mind?'

'Not at all. Is Lauren…?'

'With Brenda,' she replied. 'She's staying overnight.'

John pushed back the feeling of relief. He'd talked long and hard with Brenda and Ken and they had all decided it would be for the best if Lauren spent a lot of time with her grandparents. Collectively, they decided not to tackle Amy about her problems. In spite of everything, they all concluded she had a right to her hang-ups.

They left the study and Mark sat back from his typewriter, loosening the tartan tie he had carefully knotted that morning. He disliked his employer's wife and had little respect for her – he didn't like women who had children they completely ignored. But when she looked as lovely as she looked today…

He grinned and felt his penis harden, pushing against the zip of his trousers.

'Down, boy, down,' he muttered and bent over his typewriter. His fingers flew over the keys before he sat back to read what he had typed. *Jack took out his knife and held it loosely balanced in his fingers, watching the erotic movements of a fly as it crossed the window pane.*

Erotic movements of a fly? Mark picked up John's handwritten notes, scanned them carefully and laughed. John's word was *erratic not erotic.* He knew exactly why he had transcribed erotic – damn Amy Thornton and her smart little rump. He loosened the tartan tie a little further and began to retype the page.

The shop was double-fronted and had previously been used as a bakery.

'Look,' she said enthusiastically, standing on the pavement in front of the shop. 'It's perfect. A coat of paint will transform it. I want it to look really classy and up market. My furniture is expensive and this shop front has to reflect that.'

John stared at his wife, curiosity etched into his face.

'Expensive? You never said…'

'You never asked,' she countered, her eyes fixed firmly above the plate glass window.

'Okay, I'm asking now. You're sure you're doing well enough to be able to afford something like this?' On the way down to Padstow in the car he had asked about finances and she'd laughed and said he didn't need to worry because she had made enough money to set up a shop. There would be no need to tap into the family finances to fund the venture.

'Yesterday I sold a table. That table had been commissioned. I bought it for £23. I sold it for £350. I make a profit. Now stop being an old woman and let's go inside and speak to that young man. I want this shop up and running within the next two months.'

At one o'clock that day, Dawn went down to sit on the harbour wall to eat her lunch. She finished most of it, fed the seagulls with the last of her sandwiches before heading back to the office, deep in thought about what she and David had been discussing before lunch. Someone would need to be trained to take over her job when the time came.

She reached the shop door as John and Amy came out.

'Dawn!' John's shock left him no choice but to introduce the women.

'Amy… this is Dawn Lynch, David's personal assistant. Dawn, I'd like you to meet Amy, my wife.'

Dawn fixed a smile on to her face and held out a hand.

'Mrs Thornton, it's good to meet you. I hear a lot about you.' She felt her cheeks flush.

Amy looked at the other woman.

'That's funny. John's never mentioned you.' Her tone was cold.

'That's probably because the only words we ever exchange are "hello" and "I'll see if Mr. Farmer is in." Half of the time he doesn't even remember my name, usually refers to me as 'erm'.'

'Well, it's been nice meeting you, Miss Lynch.' Amy began to brush past Dawn.

'It's Mrs actually. Divorced. Footloose and fancy free. Goodbye, Mrs Thornton. Goodbye, John.' As she passed John, she winked. He felt bubbles of laughter begin to erupt in his throat. God how he loved her, this woman who was the only person ever to have bested Amy Thornton.

Padstow Harbour is made up of a long row of shops, leading to the steps at the end where tourists and locals alike catch the ferry to Rock. Amy's shop was almost central along the parade and stood out significantly following the refurbishment work she had authorized to be done.

She called the shop Optimum. The exterior was painted in French Navy with the shop name lettered in gold. Precariously balancing on a ladder,

she carefully stuck dried flowers in a circle to create the letter O.

The effect was stunning and on opening day she felt a justifiable pride in her achievement. She invited all her past customers to a wine and cheese evening at the shop and gave them open invitations to attend with guests.

Ken, Brenda and Freda all arrived together. Freda was staggered by the sumptuous surroundings, the elegance of the fittings and by the furniture already on display. Amy had closed off the workroom area but when Brenda asked to see it, she relented.

It was exactly as Brenda had imagined it would be. Meticulously appointed with gleaming shelves and cupboards, every tool, every bottle of chemical, every piece of furniture undergoing transformation lined up in neat rows; it resembled a chemist's shop.

'It's beautiful, Amy, absolutely beautiful.' She felt her daughter stiffen. 'You've certainly hidden this talent well. Many congratulations on the opening of your shop, love. You've worked hard for it.'

'It's not beautiful, Brenda. Not that. It's functional, practical, whatever else you can think of, but it's not beautiful.' She turned and walked towards the door, holding it open for her mother to pass. Locking the door carefully behind her she fixed a smile on her face and turned to mix with the other guests.

'I've been thinking…'

David looked up. Dawn's pregnancy hadn't reached the stage where she was blooming. Today she looked sallow. He stood and moved around his desk.

'You look awful,' he said.

'Spoken like a man who knows about this sort of thing,' she countered. 'And I feel bloody awful. Just don't offer me a cup of coffee or I swear I'll throw up all over this new, very expensive carpet.'

He laughed. 'For heaven's sake come and sit down before you fall down. Tell me what you've been thinking about?'

'Linda Chambers. She's good and since she worked for John she understands the author's side of the publishing business. I think she'd make a good replacement.'

'Know where she is now?'

She shook her head. 'No, but we have her address on file. I could pay her a visit and get her to come in for an interview.'

'I trust your judgment implicitly, Dawn. You interview her and if she wants the job make her an offer. John was satisfied with her work, I presume?'

'More than satisfied. He was sad when she left but she didn't get on with Amy.'

'Then find her. The sooner we get her the better and you can start to take things a bit easier.'

'I'm okay. I'm almost over the worst part. A couple more weeks and it will have passed. Your carpet will be safe until we get near the end – and I'll try not to let my waters break on it.'

He watched as she left the office. He was going to miss Dawn Lynch. John was a lucky man. He hoped it stayed that way because if Amy ever found out... it just didn't bear thinking about.

CHAPTER THIRTY-SEVEN

November 1972

Linda paused before climbing the stairs to the offices of Farmers publishing house. The past week during which she had served her notice had gone by quickly and even though it was a cold, rainy Monday, the weather did nothing to dampen her spirits.

Dawn Lynch seemed very nice, very capable and she prayed she could match up to her. She hadn't hesitated when Dawn had said

'Would you like a job at Frederick's?'

She entered the reception area to find Dawn already there.

'Hi,' she said with a smile. 'Nice and early. That's good because judging by the sheaf of notes Mr. Frederick's has left, we've a busy few hours.'

Linda was feeling better than she had since leaving John's employment.

Dawn had explained that she was pregnant and that Linda would be working with her for four months while Dawn took steps back. After that she would be on her own, provided she and David Farmer were happy with that arrangement.

'Is this your first baby?'

'Yes, and if this sickness happens every time you get pregnant, it'll be the last. I can't drink anything but water and the thought of cooking makes my stomach somersault. Don't get pregnant, Linda. The hormones go into overdrive.'

'Not likely,' Linda laughed. 'I haven't found anybody good enough yet. Perhaps working here I'll get to meet a rich author, unmarried, who'll whisk me away to his desert island.'

'Don't think we've got any of those on our books.'

'So what about your husband? Is he pleased?'

'No husband. Or at least, not a current one.'

'Oh…' Linda looked flustered. 'I'm sorry… I didn't mean to pry.'

Dawn laughed at the crestfallen younger woman.

'No worries, Linda. I chose to have a baby. I didn't need or want a husband. End of story.'

Linda stared at her for a moment.

'I think that's pretty brave if you don't mind me saying so, Dawn.'

'So do I. Maybe I wouldn't have been so brave if I'd known that morning sickness lasted all day and all night. Now, let's put this pregnancy on a back burner and I'll get you started on transcribing this tape.'

She was immersed in the tape when the office door opened.

'You've just made my day, Linda. Settling in okay?' John's face creased with delight.

She nodded, feeling stupid. She had known she would see him again – had to, considering he was Frederick's top selling author; she just hadn't reckoned on it being on her first day.

John moved behind Dawn's desk, ostensibly to give her a document. It was only because she had to move slightly to one side to get an extra sheet of letter heading that she saw John's hand close over Dawn's.

She knew at once who the father of Dawn's baby was. What had she said to John on the day she had left? *'She's a lucky lady.'*

Dawn Lynch, as far as Linda Chambers was concerned, was the luckiest and most envied lady in the kingdom.

But she couldn't help the little hint of malice that invaded her thoughts – what a smack in the eye it would be for toffee-nosed Amy Thornton.

Brenda blessed the day that Amy opened her shop. She persuaded her daughter there was no need to employ a nanny for Lauren; she would have her during Amy's working day. She'd considered offering to have the child full time but thought better of it; John would miss Lauren, even if Amy didn't.

The little girl had opened up in the presence of her grandparents. Ken doted on her, working in the tiny patch of ground he had given her, just as Jack had with Amy. She used the same tools that her mummy had all those years ago.

At two and a half, she captured everyone's hearts. Even Freda gruffly admitted she'd never met a more charming child.

One warm July afternoon Freda, Brenda and Lauren were sitting in the small back garden of the cottage enjoying the drone of the bees in the lavatera growing by the back door and drinking homemade lemonade. The peace was shattered by shouts coming from the market garden, adjoining the cottage. Brenda knew it was either Malcolm or Ken. They employed extra staff during the summer, leaving Ken and Malcolm free to concentrate on growing the produce they sold.

Both Brenda and Freda stood and looked at each other.

'You go,' Freda urged. 'I'll watch Lauren. See what's wrong. Bren – don't rush, it's probably nothing.' Then they both heard Malcolm's frenzied calling for help. 'Right, I'll go and get somebody from the centre – you go and see what's wrong. Hurry up, he needs help.'

Malcolm was fine but furiously trying to lift the large water butt that they had erected. It had been a wet May and June and the container was full. 'Malcolm,' she called. 'Slow down. You'll have a heart attack! We can fill it again.'

Malcolm turned at the sound of her voice.

'Brenda… for God's sake… Ken's under it.'

The following quarter of an hour was a blur.

They managed to lift the water butt with the help of two customers and watched as the ambulance men lifted Ken on to the stretcher. He was conscious throughout, reassuring Brenda that he was okay. She saw the state of his legs and knew he wasn't.

'Go in the ambulance with him. I'll see to Lauren and make sure she gets home to John.' Freda was as strong as ever, seeking to comfort her sister-in-law. She had also seen Ken's legs.

She rang John immediately but Mark informed her that everyone else was out.

'He's had to go to see David and he said he would call round at the stationers for some supplies we need. Would you like me to try and contact him?'

'No, we'll be fine. Just ask him to ring Stonebrook when he gets back,' she said, looking at her delightful great-niece. She felt quite disgruntled when less than half an hour later the telephone rang and John announced he was home. She quickly explained the situation and he said he would collect his daughter.

'No,' Freda responded. 'I'll walk down with her. Be sorry to hand her back.'

John laughed.

'Well, well. Is this a new Freda? Soft spot for a little one, is there?'

'Don't be stupid, John Thornton. You have a writer's imagination. I'll see you in fifteen minutes.'

She put down the receiver, her smile belying the sharpness of her words.

Both Ken's legs were badly broken. Brenda stared at his face, peaceful now after the initial pain following the accident. His eyes were closed and he was breathing quietly. She held on to his hand, willing him on.

It was horrifying – all the mechanical hospital equipment sticking out of him. Now that he was asleep, she could relax.

She recalled words like physiotherapy, pins and extended treatment. What she remembered most of all was the reassurance that they would do everything in their power to ensure that one day he would walk again. She thanked God that it was not his head that had taken the weight of the water butt.

'We'll study the x-rays today and first thing in the morning we'll have him in theatre and sort those legs out. In the meantime we're going to induce sleep so he doesn't feel the pain. Try not to worry, Mrs Buckingham.'

The surgeon smiled at her and she was reassured by his optimism. She prayed he was right and that nothing awful showed up when he had to study the pictures of the crushed and shattered bones.

She settled down still clutching a totally unresponsive hand and prepared for a long wait. Tomorrow would be a very difficult day and she needed to prepare herself.

'I'm going to take Lauren for a walk through the bottom woods, take her mind off what's happened to her granddad.'

'No problem, boss,' Mark said looking up to grin at

his employer. 'I'll repel all boarders while you're away.'

'I'm going – see you in about an hour. Oh – and would you mind trying the shop for me? I've tried to contact Amy to tell her about Ken but the line's been out of order. If you manage to get through, tell her what's happened, we don't know anything yet but tell her I've got Lauren and everything's okay here.'

'No problem, boss,' Mark said, once more tugging nervously at his crimson and yellow silk tie. He didn't relish the thought of ringing Amy – he never knew how she would react but he knew how he responded to her – with impure thoughts.

Lauren held John's hand all the way down to the bottom wood and he wondered why they had never done this before.

'Lauren like trees,' she announced solemnly.

'And daddy likes trees too, pet. Look, this big one is an oak tree. It's very old. Can you see how big it is?'

She stared at it for a long time.

'Big tree,' she said finally, obviously impressed. 'Cat?'

She was pointing into the leafy branches and John craned his neck to see what she was peering at.

'No, Lauren, that's a squirrel. See! See him running?'

'Lauren want kirrel.'

'Well, Lauren can't have a squirrel,' he teased. 'They live in woods, not houses. But maybe if we talk to Mummy, we could have a dog. Shall we ask her?'

Lauren smiled nodding her head, her blonde hair fluttering in the warm breeze. This was a new experience for her, walking with daddy, and she was enjoying it. She ran ahead a short way and stopped when she heard John shout.

'Not too far, Lauren, you'll get lost. Want to go to the pond? See the ducks?' He cursed the fact that he hadn't brought any bread to feed. Lauren would still enjoy seeing the swans and moorhens.

She stopped and waited for him to catch up to her then held his hand.

'Lauren like ducks,' she said solemnly, nodding her head.

'As well as trees? And kirrels?' He smiled at his daughter.

She was a serious little mite and how he loved her. He picked her up and carried her the few yards down to the pond; the banking sloped steeply and he wanted to avoid another accident.

Kneeling, he held her hand.

'Look, Lauren, that's a swan, that big white bird. Isn't he beautiful?'

'Oooooh,' she said with a long drawn out breath. 'Swan.' She was entranced as the swan sailed gracefully towards them.

'That's right, sweetheart, but we mustn't get too near it. Swans can peck and hurt little ones. Come on, let's go a bit further. There's some moorhens over the other side.'

Afterwards he couldn't really remember what happened. One minute she was holding his hand and the next she was in the water. It wasn't deep at the edges but the shock and the coldness made her cry. He dragged her out and held her tightly.

'Hush, baby,' he soothed. 'Daddy will take you home and clean you up.' He didn't add *before Mummy gets there* but he felt it.

Mark raised his eyebrows in query.

'Bath?' he asked.

'Good idea. Think you can run it for me while I undress her?'

'No problem, boss,' he said disappearing into the bathroom.

John quickly stripped the wet clothes off his daughter and wrapped her in a warm towel taken from the airing cupboard. She snuggled inside it smiling at her daddy. He gathered her into his arms and carried her to the bathroom.

'I contacted Mrs Thornton – she said she'd probably go straight to the hospital but would ring you just before she closed the shop.' Mark looked up, speaking as he turned off the taps. 'There, young Lauren, I think that bath is fit for a princess.'

She giggled. She liked Mark, he had funny ties.

He stood in the doorway and watched as John removed the little girl's towel. She was extremely muddy and her blonde hair hung limply, darkened by the pond water.

He shook his head. Amy would not be amused.

'Give me a shout if you need anything else,' he said closing the bathroom door.

John glanced at his watch as he took it off. Four thirty – half an hour or so before Amy would ring, plenty of time to clean Lauren up and dress her in fresh clothes. He dipped a hand into the water and, satisfied it wasn't too hot, lowered Lauren into it.

The plastic ducks and the submarine didn't stand a chance against the carefully aimed sponges, but the frog took evasive action. Its back legs moved as the clockwork mechanism forced it through the bubbles; Lauren shrieked with laughter. Soon John wondered who was wetter.

The bathroom resembled a war zone and he knew he would have to change his jeans. They'd been wet enough when he'd got back from the walk but that was chickenfeed compared to this. Lauren picked up a dripping sponge and pretended to aim it at duck. He wasn't fooled and didn't move as it came flying towards him, hitting him fair and square on the chin.

'Enough, enough, young vandal,' he called out amidst gales of laughter from his daughter. He hadn't had this much fun in years and he began to realise just what he had been missing, thanks to Amy. 'Let's get you washed down and then we must get you out of there.' Obligingly she stood for him. He soaped her legs, running his hands up and down with the sponge when the bathroom door opened.

'What are you doing?' Her tone was icy.

'Amy! I thought Mark said…'

'That I wasn't coming home? Obviously. So I'll ask again, what are you doing? Why is my daughter in the bath at this time in the afternoon?'

'What are you inferring, Amy?' John felt cold.

'I want to know why your hands were around my daughter's naked legs and why you were so blatantly enjoying it.'

'You are a stupid woman.' He spoke quietly, knowing how dangerously close he was to losing his temper. 'I am bathing Lauren because she fell into the pond. If you'd like to go into her bedroom, you'll see a pile of extremely muddy clothing – including her knickers. I am washing and playing with her, something alien to you. The pond is full of very cold, very dirty water in case you didn't know. Now – spell it out in words of one syllable just what you thought I was doing with *our* daughter.'

'It's irrelevant what I was thinking – it's what I'm seeing that bothers me. It's a good job I closed the shop early and decided to change before going to the hospital.'

John slowly stood and walked over to his wife.

'You bitch,' he said calmly before hitting her once across the face. 'You finish bathing Lauren. I'm going out. But think on this, Amy. One of us is perverted and it isn't me.'

Dawn had never seen John so distressed. He arrived unexpectedly – they had no plans to meet that night – and she knew without being told that something serious had happened. Her first thought was that he had left Amy.

'But I hit her, Dawn,' he groaned. 'I hit Amy.'

Dawn held him knowing he needed sympathy. She tried desperately to stifle the feeling of revulsion at his uncharacteristic act.

'It's understandable,' she whispered. 'Not excusable, but understandable.'

He sounded broken.

'I can hardly believe I did it – and in front of Lauren which makes it ten times worse. I've never lifted a finger to her before.'

'Go home, John,' she said gently. 'Go home and mend things.'

'No, not yet.' He shook his head. 'I need some time... I need to think.'

'Then think in the lounge,' she said with a smile. They hadn't progressed beyond the hallway. 'Brandy?'

'Thanks. I really need it.'

CHAPTER THIRTY-EIGHT

November 1972

One brandy led to another and in the end Dawn left him asleep on the big sofa, covered him with a blanket and went to bed.

He was still asleep when she went into work the following morning. She had set herself the task of sorting out her filing system in order to leave everything as tidy as possible for when Linda finally took over. She was immersed in reading and packing away out of date documentation.

The telephone call came as a surprise.

'Hello. Is Mr. Farmer there?'

She didn't recognise the voice.

'No, I'm sorry; he won't be in until later. Can I ask who's calling please? Maybe I can help. I'm Mr. Farmer's personal assistant.'

'Not really.'

Dawn had a vague feeling she knew the caller.

'I'm trying to contact my husband. Is that Miss Lurch?'

'Mrs Lynch,' Dawn responded drily, now aware of the caller's identity. 'Who's calling please?' she repeated.

'Mrs Thornton. Is my husband due to see David, do you know?'

'No, he's not in the diary.' She was angry with this woman who had upset John so badly. 'As I said, David isn't available and I really don't know what time he will be in. Can I get him to ring you?'

'No.' Amy was short and to the point. 'If my husband calls in, will you ask him to ring me? I'm not going into the shop today.' She hung up.

Dawn looked at the silent receiver and swore under her breath.

'Bitch. A please wouldn't have been out of order.'

'Pardon?' Linda looked up, a frown of concentration on her face.

'Oh, nothing. Just thinking aloud.'

'So, who's the bitch?'

'Three guesses,' she said lightly.

'I only know one bitch. It has to be Amy Thornton.' Dawn didn't reply but was unable to hide her smile. 'So I'm right. Shall I put a note on David's desk to say that she called?'

Dawn shook her head.

'Not necessary. She wasn't actually looking for David. She wanted John.'

'Has he seen sense and left her? The plot thickens...'

'That's enough, young lady,' Dawn chided. 'It's not for us to speculate.'

Linda looked at Dawn for several moments.

'So where is he then?'

'Would you believe me if I said I didn't know?'

Linda shook her head. 'Nope.'

'Then don't make me lie to you. Now get on with that tape, Miss Nosey-Parker, and let both of us have nothing more to do with Mrs Thornton.'

'I'll second that,' Linda replied.

John returned home to find Amy unresponsive. He said nothing of his whereabouts the previous night. He walked straight into the study and wished Mark good morning.

Mark looked up in surprise.

'It's one o'clock.'

'I know. Can you be a little quieter please if you insist on being censorious? And your tie's hurting my eyes.'

'No problem, boss,' Mark laughed, beginning to remove the tie.

'For goodness sake, leave the damn thing on. You wouldn't be the same without your ties.'

'If I'd known you were planning on having a massive hangover, I'd have worn something a little more subdued.'

'Like funeral black?' John moved across to the window and stared across the expanse of lawn. 'I suppose I'd better go and explain,' he sighed.

'Mrs Thornton's in the lounge with Lauren.'

'I know. I saw her as I came in. None of this is going to get any easier so I'd better make my peace.'

'The red mark's gone off her cheek…'

'Oh?'

'The mark that happened when she walked into the bathroom door.'

John looked at his assistant.

'She told you?'

'She didn't have to – both of you were pretty fired up. I…er…made a point of playing with Lauren for a bit, she was a tad upset.'

'Thanks, Mark.' John touched his shoulder. 'I think I regret Lauren being there more than I regret hitting Amy. I'll make it up to them.'

With a heavy heart he left the study and walked into the lounge. He stood in the doorway and look at his wife.

She raised her head from the book she had been studying and waited, unsure whether to speak or not. His absence had frightened her almost as much as the lack of communication.

The sun streamed through the window creating a

golden halo around Amy's blonde hair. God, she was beautiful but… he knew nothing could kill the love he had for her since they were children.

'Amy.' He felt his vocal chords tighten. She stood and moved across to him. He wrapped his arms around her and felt her shudder with sobs.

'God, Amy, I'm so sorry.' He kissed the top of her head and she clung tightly to him.

'Don't do it again, John, please.' Her voice was muffled as she pressed her face into his shirt.

'I'll never lift a finger to you, Amy, I promise,' he whispered, his lips still pressed into her hair.

'I didn't mean that. I meant don't ever leave me, not even for just one night. I don't think I could stand it again.'

'I won't leave you, Amy. You and Lauren are my life.' The pause was only noticeable to him.

'I hate falling out with you. Kiss me.' He bent his head. 'And then you can tell me where you spent the night,' she said in the split second before their lips met.

She didn't know whether to believe him or not. He said he had driven for miles and eventually pulled up at a bed and breakfast. He hadn't a clue what it was called but it was just outside Bude. No, he didn't keep the receipt and yes he did pay in cash.

She brought him a cup of coffee and two painkillers, outwardly calm, inwardly seething. *Where had he been?* Not at David and Pat's home and definitely not at Stonebrook.

'Why don't you go to bed for an hour? Your B and B was definitely serving alcohol. You look dreadful.'

'Too much brandy, I think.' He couldn't understand why she was being so considerate, why she hadn't asked more searching questions. Had she really been so afraid that he wouldn't come home at all?

He walked towards the hallway.

'Perhaps an hour in bed will make me feel a bit more like John Thornton and less like Methuselah.'

She waited ten minutes before going to see Mark. His face remained expressionless as she perched herself on the edge of his desk, revealing a lot of thigh in the mini skirt she wore.

'Mrs Thornton? Where's John? Is he okay? I thought he looked a bit under the weather...' His tug on his tie revealed more about him than any words could have done. He was nervous and it showed, wishing desperately that she would stick to routine and not bother with him.

She smiled.

'John's gone to bed for an hour and Lauren's having her afternoon nap. Have you got five minutes to spare?'

'Sure. Something you wanted doing?'

'No.' She waved a hand in the air, the movement emphasising the curve of her breasts against the silk blouse. He swallowed audibly and looked down at his typewriter. 'No, I just thought it would be nice to get to know each other a bit better.'

Know in the biblical sense? The thought flashed across his mind and he touched his tie again.

'You've worked here for ages now and I know very little about you other than the things John tells me.'

He laughed, his nervousness still showing. *What the hell did she want?* 'I hope it's all good.'

'Oh, it is. He thinks very highly of you... and so do I.'

What was she getting at? Mark's eyes kept straying to her legs, to the deep pink painted fingernails lying along the thigh. Just for a moment he imagined the long slender fingers running along the length of his spine and his penis responded traitorously. What was worse was that he knew she was fully cognisant of everything going through his mind.

She leaned over the desk slightly, her nipples now outlined by the tightness of the fabric, only inches away from his hands, his mouth. Her lips were slightly open and he could almost taste the sweetness of her breath.

He pushed his chair away from the desk and, turning his back to her, walked towards the filing cabinet.

'So was there something you want me to do for you?'

She laughed throatily.

'Don't make me answer that, Mark.'

Motionless he stood with his hand half way to the drawer. The air felt heavy around him, he couldn't move. There was no denying the sexuality she was imparting and he hadn't a clue how to handle it. His penis throbbed and he couldn't think with any clarity. He didn't hear the rustle of her blouse as she moved from the desk towards him.

Her perfume told him just how close she was. Her fingers said it more explicitly.

The fingernails that had held his attention a short time earlier now travelled the length of his spine and he slumped forward on to the filing cabinet. Dear God, he didn't stand a cat in hell's chance of saying no. She moved to face him and linked her arms around the back of his neck.

'You're a very desirable man, Mark,' she whispered softly.

'Mrs Thornton...' he began shakily. 'I...'

'It's Amy. Say it Mark, say it.'

'Amy...'

'That's good. It's the sexiest sound in the world

hearing your name spoken by the man you want.' She pulled his head down to meet hers.

His initial reaction was that he was drowning. He clung to her, tasted her as she slipped her tongue into his mouth, allowed his tongue to respond. His hands touched the breasts he had dreamed of, pulling at the buttons that held the flimsy blouse together.

Slowly they sank to the floor still lost in the kiss; Amy feverishly tugged the zip on his trousers and took his penis in her hands. He pulled off her blouse and unhooked her bra.

He broke away from her lips to look at her as she slowly opened her legs.

'Do you want me?' she asked.

'Dear God…do I want you? I've wanted you since the first time I saw you…'

'I know.' She stroked the long fingernails along her inner thigh and he groaned. His eyes roamed back to her breasts. He couldn't believe his luck. She was his for the taking, this beautiful woman… his. He bent to kiss her but she put up a hand.

'Where was John last night, Mark?' she said softly.

'John?' he was puzzled. 'Last night? I haven't a clue; we haven't talked much today. I doubt he'll tell me.'

He bent his head once more and she rolled away from him. Standing, she looked down at him, her breasts unfettered. She picked up the bra and blouse and slung them over her shoulder.

'When you find out where he was,' she said coldly, 'come and see me and maybe we'll carry on. Until then, pull up your trousers, you look ridiculous.'

For long moments after the study door closed he lay there, unable to believe recent events. *How could he have been so stupid?* He'd jeopardised his job, admitted how he felt about his employer's wife and almost betrayed his employer. The intention had been there. He had betrayed John, whether they made love or not.

He straightened his clothes and sank down at his desk, his head in his hands. He couldn't face John, not today.

He scribbled a note to say he'd developed a raging toothache and had managed to get a dental appointment. Then he left the house as quickly as he could.

Amy watched him drive away, a small smile on her face. That little episode had brightened the afternoon – he was a well built young man and although the object of the exercise had been to find out John's whereabouts the previous night, she had enjoyed herself. She touched her breasts, remembering the feel of his hands on her; it felt good, exciting. In some ways it had been a shame to stop...

Mark drove home feeling increasingly angry with himself. In spite of the degradation he had almost seen Amy naked. No matter what he still wanted her.

One day he would... he stopped a smile that threatened to cross his face and instead hit his hand hard on the steering wheel. Damn that woman, damn her to hell and back for making him feel like this.

He rubbed his hand against the front of his trousers in a vague attempt at easing the ache – but he knew the ache would always be there. He wanted her, no matter what.

CHAPTER THIRTY-NINE

January-February 1973

Linda found the work much more complex after Dawn's departure. It had been quite a shock when the woman had turned up after an ante-natal appointment and calmly announced that she was leaving early.

High blood pressure, nausea and extreme tiredness meant the consultant was unequivocal in his decision – finish work or risk losing the baby.

'Frederick's Publishers. Linda Chambers speaking. How may I help you?' She had adopted her own version of an American greeting, smiling as she spoke

'Linda Chambers?' There was a moment of silence and Linda knew she was speaking to Amy. 'I see. My husband is on his way to see Mr. Farmer. Tell him to ring me.'

The receiver was replaced and Linda held it away from her. What had she done to upset the woman now? She looked up to see John framed in the doorway, his hand raised in salute.

'Hi. Everything ok?'

She shrugged her shoulders. 'Your wife was on the phone – briefly.'

'Oh… did she know it was you?'

Linda nodded.

'She was a bit short with me.'

'You haven't done anything,' he interrupted.

'I'll ring David and let him know you're here. Do you want to ring Mrs Thornton first?' She pushed the telephone across to him.

He shook his head.

'No, I'll ring her from David's office. Just buzz him, will you?'

David acknowledged him with a smile. He had put his plans for semi-retirement on hold but refused to work anymore than forty hours a week. He was into the third hour of his day and already looking forward to going home.

John placed his briefcase on the desk and opened it. He took out a hefty pile of paper and laid it in front of David.

'Is this...?' David's surprise showed.

'Blood Red.'

'But I'd no idea it was so near completion.'

'There'll be another one next month.'

David stared at him.

'Do you want to tell me something?'

'*Blood Red* is to be published in my name. It has to be that way because Amy knows the title. The one I will be delivering in a month is written by someone called Callum Brennan. It's called *In Praise*.'

'Callum Brennan? Am I missing something?'

'Callum was my great grandfather's name and Brennan was his wife's maiden name. Simple really.'

'Oh, dead simple. I suppose there's a good reason for using a pseudonym? You do realise that your books sell in advance because they know they're getting quality from John Thornton? How do I sell this if I can't use your name?'

'The readers are still getting the quality,' John said mildly. 'That hasn't changed. You'll have to launch this as the first book by a new writer – and I promise you I will deliver others. I've been working on two books at the same time. As far as Amy is concerned there is no gap in my publication schedule. All royalties from this and subsequent Callum Brennan books are to go directly to Dawn. I have to provide for her, our future and our child. Will you do it?'

There was a long silence before David spoke.

'You're not only my top selling author, you're my closest friend. You will lose money on the Brennan book; you know that, don't you?'

'Of course I do. But the next one will be an earner.'

'And you can keep producing two books every two years? With the amount of research you undertake? And what happens when someone recognises that Callum Brennan is John Thornton?'

'How can anyone possibly do that? Even my dedication is *To my love and her child...* nobody could glean anything from that.'

'Let me tell you something, pal. Two or three years ago Paul McCartney said something about the Beatles going out on the road as a band called something like Randy and the Rockets. The idea was to wear masks and things to disguise themselves so they could have a rave up like in the old days. The chap interviewing them pointed out that the exercise would be a bit pointless, their voices would be recognised. What I'm trying to say is that your voice, your writing voice, is unique, John. Anybody who really knows your books and who reads Callum Brennan will recognise that the writing resembles yours.' He paused for a moment and reached for his coffee. Sipping it slowly he added 'and a second book would confirm it.'

'I can lie.'

'For how long? Get real, John. We're talking literary critics here, not John Doe from down the road. These chaps can read a paragraph and make a bloody accurate guess as to the author. But, if you're prepared to try, I'll do what you want. I'll promote Callum whatsisname in exactly the same way that I launched you with your first book. After that it's in the lap of the gods as to who believes you! And just where does Mark stand in all of this? He typed it so won't he wonder what's happened to it?'

'Mark's been told the minimum. He knows I'm using a pseudonym and he's to forget I wrote the book. He's probably adding two and two together but he won't say anything, especially not to Amy. I don't think they get on. Thanks for agreeing to do this. Dawn and I have discussed it and we feel it's the safest way of keeping things from Amy. If I started paying out regular amounts from my bank account I think Amy might notice.'

'You do make life difficult, John. Why couldn't you have believed what you promised in church and stuck to one woman –'

John stood and banged his fist down on the desk.

'You bloody well know why, David. I married a cold-hearted, cold-blooded woman who doesn't care two hoots about anything or anybody. She's devious, conniving, manipulative...'

'Then why the hell don't you divorce her?'

'Because,' John closed his eyes, 'because... I still love her.'

At first Dawn tried to ignore the back-ache. She had been told that the baby was a good size. The lack of a view of her feet confirmed that. She had carried the baby to the front and presumed the aching pain in her back was a result of that. She sat down, rubbing the lump gently.

'Come on, baby,' she said softly. 'Settle down. We've three more weeks to go and I don't want three weeks of back ache.'

She shuffled in the chair to make herself more comfortable but two minutes later stood again, unable to bear the ache in a sitting position.

She wandered over to the window wishing John was with her. She knew he would massage her back. She smiled at the thought of what his back massages usually led to and then gripped tightly on to the window sill as a wave of pain washed over her.

'Dear sweet Jesus,' she gasped. She reached behind her for the telephone and dialed her doctor, hoping against hope that the surgery was open.

It wasn't but a doctor was there and she spoke about the back ache and pain, which was met with laughter.

'Listen, Dawn,' Dr. Carrian said. 'Have you ever heard of labour?'

'Labour? But…'

'But you thought it started with waters breaking, contractions and general discomfort? Forget it. It starts in a different way with everybody. I suspect your labour is beginning. If it's any consolation it's the worst way to start, the most uncomfortable, but by this time tomorrow you should have a baby. Now, take a couple of painkillers, they might just take the edge off. Do you need an ambulance or do you have transport?'

'I need an ambulance.' She laughed nervously. 'Best not drive myself.'

'How long has the back ache been going on?'

'Since last night. I've hardly slept with it. I'm still three weeks away from my due date you know.'

'Doesn't mean a thing,' the doctor cheerily replied. 'Not a damn thing. They come when they decide and there's not a great deal you can do about it. I'll ring the hospital and tell them you're on the way and I'll order the ambulance. If you've had back ache that long I don't think we should delay!'

She replaced the receiver and stared at the telephone. How could she contact John? They had decided that in two weeks time he would start laying the idea of a possible trip to promote his book – one that could happen at a moment's notice. They hadn't counted on the baby coming early.

She knew he wanted to be there for the baby's birth and now she couldn't reach him. She daren't ring him at home...

David. She'd ring David and zap him with the problem.

'Hi, it's Dawn.'

'Hey, supermum, how's it going?'

'It's going,' she paused. 'I'm in labour and I'm early. I don't know how to get in touch with John. I know it's an awful cheek considering you've never approved but can you ring him and tell him I'm going straight to the hospital? There's an ambulance coming any minute to get me. Please, David...'

David hesitated, but only briefly.

'I'll do what I can, Dawn. Now take things as easy as you can and good luck. When it's all over, get John to ring me, will you?'

He kept his finger on the receiver rest for several seconds wishing Dawn hadn't asked him to do this. He didn't want to get involved. He didn't want to be a part of something that was going to cause grief for all concerned.

Matters were worse when Amy answered.

'No sorry, David, he isn't here. He and Mark have gone out somewhere. They didn't tell me what they were doing, just said they'd be a couple of hours. Can I leave a message for John?'

'No, just ask him to ring me. It's only a query on the

book, nothing urgent.'

It was only as he replaced the receiver that he realised she might put non urgent on the note she left for him. Heaven only knew when John might get around to calling.

He picked up his jacket and went into the reception area.

'Just going out, Linda. Er... if John calls in tell him I need to speak to him as a matter of urgency.'

'It's Dawn, isn't it?' She looked anxious. 'Oh, don't worry I guessed a long time ago. Is the baby coming?'

He nodded.

'And I can't get in touch with John. He's not at home. I thought I'd nip down to the car park in Padstow, see if I can see his car. Thank God we don't live in a big city; I wouldn't know where to start. Look, give Dawn a ring and tell her I'm having trouble locating him but I'll find him somehow.'

Linda allowed the phone to ring for a long time into an empty lounge – Dawn was already on her way to hospital.

'It's a good job you came in when you did, Mrs Lynch,' the midwife said cheerfully. 'You're already six centimetres dilated. You shouldn't be too long.'

Dawn bit her lip as another contraction began its steady build. *John, where are you?* Her mind screamed. *I need you, I need you, damn it!*

'Is somebody going to be with you, lovey?'

'I hope so,' she muttered through clenched teeth. 'I've left messages for him.'

'Well, let's hope he gets here in time. You're well on your way now.'

She was only vaguely aware of what was happening

around her; the contractions were increasing in length and intensity. She had to focus and shut out the world.

As John walked through the Labour Suite door she was busy being sick.

'There, there, dear,' he heard the midwife say. 'Most of our mums are sick just before delivery. It's a good sign.'

He moved her head gently on to the pillow and she smiled weakly up at him.

'I hate you, John Thornton.'

'I know,' he said bending to kiss her forehead. 'It's a good job I've enough love for the two of us. Has it been awful?'

'Piece of cake,' she responded. 'Rock cake.'

He held on to her hand and watched her face change as the pain began again. He was concentrating so hard on holding her and talking her through it that he didn't really notice instructions being given to her.

'It's a boy!' the midwife called out.

They cried together.

'God, Dawn, if I'd been another twenty minutes I'd have missed this.' There was awe, wonder, love and pain in his voice.

He stared down at the child wrapped in a blue blanket and didn't try to stop the flow of tears.

'He's perfect, Dawn. Perfect.'

'What did you expect?' she responded, smiling. 'He looks like you.'

He pulled the blanket to one side and stared down at the child.

'He doesn't, he looks more like Alfred Hitchcock.'

'You wait,' she said with a laugh. 'Believe me, he looks like you. So – decision time. We have to decide between the three names we picked.'

'Adam, Joshua and David.' He moved the blanket and looked closely at his son smiling. 'Thank goodness we didn't include Alfred in that list. I think he looks like a Joshua. What do you think?'

'Joshua John Thornton. I like it.' Suddenly her face changed. 'Now go and ring David – and thank him for finding you. Where does Amy think you are?'

'With David making some changes to the book. It's Mark who's bewildered. He was with me when David finally found us and I drove like a madman to get Mark back to his own car at the office. I had to do a pretty sharp turn around to get here. Like something out of keystone cops. I just hope he didn't click on to what was happening.'

'And,' she said smugly, 'wasn't it smart of me to do all this during the day? You can now go home to Amy and she'll be none the wiser.'

She felt him stiffen.

'How do you think I can go home to Amy and not be changed by today? You're asking the impossible, Dawn. I need to be with you.'

'And I know differently. I know you still love Amy and you're devoted to Lauren. You're one of those unfortunate men who can love two women at once. I accept that – and I think you must, or you'll tear yourself in two.'

'Well, I can't normally see any parents resemblance in newborn babies,' Pat said, staring down at the little one, 'but he is definitely John Thornton's.'

Dawn, still apprehensive at the unexpected visit, nodded.

'I know. I'm wondering if I'm right in agreeing to call him Thornton. What if it causes problems later.'

Pat turned away from the baby and looked at Dawn.

'I think this young man is going to cause problems anyway. Affairs have a strange way of being discovered, sooner or later. Amy will be a mighty adversary – make no mistake about that. I don't think calling him Lynch will make a scrap of difference. And let's be practical, Dawn.'

'What do you mean?'

'Eventually John will quit this earthly life –' she held up a hand as if to stop Dawn from interrupting. 'And when he does he's going to be a very, very rich man. With Thornton on the birth certificate he has as much of a claim to his father's estate as Lauren. You have to think of his future, Dawn. He didn't ask to be born.'

Dawn's smile was crooked. She was unsure how to respond to Pat. 'His middle name is John.'

'My word, you really do believe in playing with fire. For heaven's sake don't announce his birth in the local paper! I'm not sure I could lie to Amy – we've been best friends for too long.'

Dawn raised her head to look at her visitor.

'Why did you come, Pat?'

Pat shrugged her shoulders.

'Don't ask me. David thinks I've gone to the cinema to escape being with the kids for a couple of hours. I just felt I had to see you. You see, Amy is my closest friend, has been since we were eleven, but I know things about her... anyway, what I'm really trying to say is that I don't approve of John playing around but I don't disapprove either. If things had been different, I would have put you down as John's ideal match.'

'But that still doesn't explain why you came to see me.'

Pat grinned.

'There's a baby. I love babies. And in six months or so I'll be back in here.'

'Congratulations... have you told Amy?'

A cloud passed over Pat's face.

'That's been the most difficult part of each pregnancy. The rape robbed her of everything you know.'

Dawn felt a shiver run through her. *Rape?*

Pat continued to speak unaware that she was imparting new information to Dawn.

'When I found out about Amy's past I made a point of pulling back copies of the newspapers that were around at the time; I needed to know details so that I didn't put my foot in it. Treverick was an out and out bastard. He tore her apart...' her voice trailed away and suddenly she understood the reason for the stunned expression on Dawn's face. 'You didn't know, did you?'

'I never wanted to know but to be honest I didn't think it was anything like that. I'm still not sure I want to know but now I have to, don't I? So sit here, Pat.' She patted the armchair by the bed. 'Talk to me. Tell me everything I should have asked at the beginning.'

CHAPTER FORTY

February 1974

1974 started very well for John. He was thirty-two years old with more money than he could ever have dreamed of and the two women in his life both loved him as much as he loved them.

He had long since learned to accept the fact that he did love them both and once that had sunk in he found Dawn's reluctance to have him move in understandable.

The icing on the cake was that he had two children. Lauren at four years old was a treasure. He knew it was thanks to Brenda and Ken's influence and he blessed them for it.

Amy's business had taken off in a big way. She now employed two assistants in the shop and several outworkers. This left her with little time for her daughter but fortunately there were other people willing to step in.

Josh, nearly thirteen months old, was getting into more mischief than John would have thought possible and he worshipped him. Even he could now see the strong resemblance to himself; it was impossible to deny.

The blonde hair, blue eyes, high forehead and dimpled chin were all there – along with the height. The little boy was tall for his age and growing rapidly.

As John looked out of the window at the ever-deepening snow he reflected how well life was treating him. With the growth of Amy's business she had channeled her energies and now was no longer being so vindictive.

She hadn't been looking forward to the birth of Pat's

second son, Daniel, but at nine months he was a little charmer and of all the children in their lives she seemed to take to him the most. Certainly more than Lauren.

John reached into his back pocket and pulled out the letter that had arrived that morning.

Normally Mark would have seen it first and they would have discussed the implications but Mark was taking a few days holiday. John was grateful for that; he didn't want to discuss it with anyone yet.

It was from the BBC, signed by someone called Brian Lazenby. He was a producer who wanted to make a series of programmes about writers. He asked that John contact him so that a meeting could be arranged.

Although he knew the publicity would be invaluable he was reluctant to go on television.

'Not go on television? You must be crazy. Of course you'll do it!' He imagined David's reaction.

He watched as Ken, Brenda and Lauren walked up the snow covered driveway, Ken's limp still noticeable after months of treatment. Lauren saw him looking and waved. He heard stomping and laughter as all three came through into the lounge, hatless, coatless and shoeless.

'Daddy!' Lauren flung herself into his arms rubbing her wet hair into his face.

'Stop it, brat. You're wet,' and he tried to hold her away from him. She giggled and pushed even harder.

'Coffee? Tea?' He looked at Brenda and Ken, taking in their bedraggled state.

Brenda nodded enthusiastically.

'Yes please. Hot, strong and wet.'

'Whisky,' Ken growled. 'These two women are wearing me out. I swear I won't be half as tired when I get back to working in the garden again.'

John laughed and went to get Brenda's tea.

'Help yourself to the whisky, Ken,' he called.

He made tea and carried the tray into the lounge before turning to Ken. 'So when will that be?'

'What?'

'Work. When can you start again?'

'The doctor says that all things being equal I can start doing light work towards the end of March.'

'And it will only be light work,' Brenda intervened. 'We've had a rough time and I don't intend on letting him over do it.'

'Oh, stop fussing, lass.' Ken shook his head. 'The truth is, John, I can't wait to get back to work. Malcolm's been a godsend but until this accident I've never been out of work. He's matured, has young Malcolm, and I know that when I do start back it'll be different. He's been used to being boss. The sooner I get back, the better.' He sipped at the whisky and moved across to the window. Brenda's eyes never left him.

'You're so stubborn, Ken Buckingham. The doctor said March at the earliest so don't go thinking I'll let you go back if you're not fit.'

'And I second that,' John said. 'You're still favouring that right leg, Ken. You'd be crackers to put yourself back for the sake of an extra month.'

Ken turned round.

'You're ganging up on me! We didn't come here to talk about that or for me to be bullied by my nearest and dearest. I'll be fit, I promise.'

'And here I am thinking maybe my daughter wanted to see her old dad...' He laughed and swung Lauren round. She squealed and kicked out her legs.

'Put me down, daddy. Put me down. Listen to Nanny Brenda and Gramps Ken.'

He put her down and turned to them.

'Something wrong?'

'Nothing at all.' Brenda smiled. 'No, it's just that we're going up to the Peak District for a couple of weeks – Ken's old haunts and he wants me to see them. We'd like to take Lauren if that's okay with you and Amy?'

'When?'

'First two weeks in March.'

'I'll check with Amy but it sounds fine. Would you like to go, Lauren?'

The little girl nodded enthusiastically.

'Gramps told me about things.' She looked questioningly at Ken. 'Frog rock?'

He laughed.

'Toad's Mouth, pet. It's a rock, John, perfectly balanced, and it looks just like a toad. Quite famous it is. I said I'd take her to see it.'

John lifted Lauren on to his knee and held her close.

'Well, I'll miss you, sweetheart, but you'll have a great time. I've got to tell you something though – it's a foreign country. You'll need to learn the language. Gramps Ken will teach you,' and he winked at Ken.

'Don't listen to him, Lauren. Yorkshire's not the foreign country, Cornwall is. There's nowt up wit' way I speak, is there sitthee?'

'Nay, duck,' Lauren replied and all four dissolved into peals of laughter.

Mark was clearly impressed.

'I have the first few days holiday since starting here and something like this arrives in the post. Why didn't you ring me at home?'

'I thought a lady might answer.' John's tone was dry and he tried hard not to smile.

'Depends what time the phone call would have

been,' Mark answered with a grin.

Mark's private life was definitely that. He'd only once mentioned anything about seeing Greta, a librarian he had come to know through collecting books for John.

'Are you serious?'

'Could be... we had a good holiday anyway.' He didn't add that as they had made love the face superimposed on Greta's body had been that of Amy Thornton. 'But enough of that. What are you going to do about this?' He waved the letter in the air.

'Nothing yet. I wanted to talk to you and David. I know what David will say, he's all for publicity, but this is going to open me up. Know what I mean?'

'Your life will no longer be restricted to the blurb on the back cover. People will know you intimately. From the way this reads the entire half hour will be devoted to you. That's a lot of private life airing. Can you handle it? If you can't I suggest you don't mention this to David. For what it's worth though, I say go for it.'

'Why?'

'You're an interesting man. You're young, extremely successful, got a nice family, and you've got me!'

John threw a well-aimed paper-clip.

'I shan't even mention you. I've got to let my public think I do all the work. In any case I can't have the viewers dazzled by your ties.'

'Nothing wrong with my ties. It's just jealousy on your part. So – how do we reply to this?'

John walked across to the window and looked out at the snow covered garden. The big snowman in the middle of the lawn seemed to be winking at him. He made a decision that was to bring major change to his life without giving it further thought.

'We ring David.'

John and Amy took to Brian Lazenby immediately. He was about five feet ten inches tall, stocky with brown-blonde hair. A ready smile enhanced a rounded face and the dark rimmed glasses lent him an air of maturity.

His brown eyes flashed warmth as he turned to Amy.

'I'm absolutely delighted to meet you both. I've been a fan for so long.'

John laughed.

'I bet you've said the same thing to all the authors in the series.'

'Not likely. There's one thing you'll learn about me, John. I speak the truth. I don't read a lot, don't have the time, but I would stand in a queue for one of your books. I wouldn't pick up a romance, sci-fi, or supernatural. The first programme in the series is with an author who writes for Mills and Boon. A lovely lady but it's hard to raise the enthusiasm. I've had to read a couple of her books obviously, to get the feel of the programme, but that genre is not my choice. You have a devious mind, John Thornton, and I want to see where the ideas come from.'

'So where do you want to start?'

Brian smiled.

'I have to go into Padstow and book into my hotel. I wanted to meet you so I came straight here but if you'll give me an hour to get myself sorted, I'll be back out here notebooks at the ready.'

'You're staying in Padstow? But surely you'd be better staying here?' John turned to look at Amy. It was the first time she had opened her mouth apart from saying hello. He never suspected she was about to make the offer of accommodation.

'Mrs Thornton, I wouldn't presume...'

'It's Amy,' she said quickly. 'And you're not

presuming, I'm inviting you. Carol Jacks is our housekeeper. She will be delighted to have a guest. She normally only has the three of us to look after,' she added.

'You've made my day, Amy. I'll cancel the hotel and take you up on the offer. It'll take about a week to follow your husband around and sort out the way the programme should be filmed. Then I'll go back to London, organise the crew, and we'll be back to do the actual filming. The series is going out in August.'

'Then come with me and I'll introduce you to our staff.' John stood and waved his arm around. 'While you're here, treat this as your home. This is the lounge, no television in here. Strictly music and books. We have a separate room where we watch television.'

He gave Brian a tour of the house, showing him to his bedroom before

leading him downstairs into the room where he spent so many hours of his day.

'Brian, I'd like you to meet Mark Carter. He's been with me for – oh, I don't know. It seems like half my lifetime. But don't let him tell you he writes 90% of my books, it's just not true. He's a pathological liar. Mark, Brian Lazenby.'

The two men shook hands and John was once more struck by their similar appearance. Thank God Brian didn't wear designer silk ties.

'Hi, Brian, I write 90% of his books.' Mark winked.

'I believe it,' Brian replied.

For the first time in their history John invited Mark over for a drink.

'Bring Greta.'

'Thanks. She'd like to meet Brian. He is quite well-known, you know.'

'Is he?'

'You mean you didn't know? He's been on the scene for a couple of years now and if you look through the Radio Times you'll see him mentioned frequently. There's an article on him in this week's issue. I'll bring it in. I know you're too tight-fisted to buy it.' He grinned at his employer. 'Apparently he's taken a bit of a sabbatical to do this series. He's not doing any other work for six months. Says because of his love of books it's something he's long wanted to do.'

'That's funny – he said he didn't read much. Only my novels. And that means he's only read six books. Did he strike you as a liar?'

'Not at all. Perhaps it's just waffle on the part of whoever wrote the article. They couldn't really put that he wanted to make a whole series on the strength of his admiration for just one author, could they?'

'No,' John said thoughtfully. 'You're probably right. Perhaps we'll know him a little better after tonight.'

In the end it proved to be quite a party. Ken, Brenda, Pat and David joined them with Freda an accidental guest. She had gone for a walk and called in to see John and Amy. It was soon obvious that she was getting on well with Brian.

'Fascinating woman,' he said later to John, as they were busy dispensing drinks. 'Is she always so blunt?'

'No, sometimes she doesn't call a spade a spade, she calls it a JCB. Freda is the backbone of this family, I can tell you. My own parents left Cornwall just after Amy and I married, so we see very little of them. Thankfully I married into a family who completely adopted me. But Freda is the one we all turn to if we have a problem.'

Brian looked around at the assembled company.

Ken, Brenda, Amy, Pat, David, Mark and Greta – they didn't look as if they could rustle up a problem between them.

'I've never met a more stable set of people. You're all very friendly. And Lauren's a treasure. I must confess I pictured she'd look like you, but she has Amy's characteristics; the long blonde hair, the wonderful eyes. A beautiful child.'

'You knew we had a child before you came here then?'

Just for a moment Brian looked off guard.

'It's my job to know a bit about you although I must confess that all I know about you is from book covers. You're a very private person, John. You do understand that it will change after this programme, don't you? Everyone will want to know you; your life won't be the same. I don't want you to have false illusions.'

'No false illusions, I promise you. Both David and Mark say it's time I came out of the garret and admitted I am a writer. Okay, everybody.' He clapped his hands to attract their attention. 'Carol's left us a buffet in the dining room. I gave her the night off because I didn't want her to think I always mixed with a set of drunken louts. Once that lot is eaten if you want anything else go raid the kitchen.'

There were several jeers and catcalls but they all stood as one to sample the delicacies made by the housekeeper.

'Is Carol looking for a new job?' David asked, his mouth accommodating a prawn vol-au-vent.

'Definitely not,' John retorted. 'If she is, I'll give her the worst reference ever.'

'Then I'll have to marry her.'

'Oh no you don't, David Farmer.' Pat was swift with

her reply. 'I'll ask her for her recipes.'

The evening passed quickly and when John finally locked the doors after midnight, he moved into his study.

'Be up in ten minutes, Amy,' he called. There was no reply. She was obviously already sleeping.

He sat for a moment in the leather armchair he called his deep thought area and stared at the flames now almost dead in the hearth. The lamp cast a warm glow but the room was cooling rapidly. His eyes strayed to the shelf of books he had written and he stood and walked across to them.

He stroked the covers, smooth in their newness. He had never read any of his books – he knew the characters and plots so well he never felt the urge to read the finished product. Both Amy and Lauren had their own copies of his books; Amy's well read and Lauren's still in pristine condition. He hoped one day she would want to read them.

This set was for Josh. His will already made provision for the little boy and in it he had specifically stated which of his possessions were to go to him. He wondered at times if the secret would remain a secret until his death but he knew that the reading of his will would bring everything out into the open, and rightly so. He didn't want Josh living his life unable to acknowledge his father.

He took down the books and looked at them. It was only when he turned over the copy of *Blood Red* that he realised the author note on the back of this latest book was exactly the same as on Francophile, his first novel.

Jenny's child, his newest book, was almost ready for David – perhaps they should think about updating the author notes, particularly in view of the upcoming television programme. People would know more about him then anyway.

It was only as he was climbing the stairs he realised that the author notes did not state that he had a daughter.

CHAPTER FORTY-ONE

March 1974

It was time to take stock, to make sure he was on the right track. Appearance completely changed, lifestyle changed, knowledgeable, reworked background and identity; everything was good to go for the next phase.

Amy was still beautiful. She had been beautiful as a child and remained so. Her daughter Lauren was also beautiful, almost a mirror image of her mother. But he no longer wanted to fuck children; he had moved on so Lauren would have to wait until he decided she was mature enough. Then, and only then, would he enjoy her as he intended to enjoy her mother again.

He stared at the photograph of the family, of the group that had gathered on the night they had all met at John and Amy's home; even Lauren was included. John had given them all prints of the snap and he treasured it now. It meant he could focus on her, on Amy.

He had tasted her sweetness long before John and he intended to have her again. But he would give her time to be with John before he got rid of him.

This next phase was now firmly entrenched in his mind. He would allow John to live until he was fifty and then he would dispose of him. It would be an accident. And then he would have Amy again.

And Lauren.

CHAPTER FORTY-TWO

March 1974

'Right, thanks, I think we've done enough for today.' Brian closed the notebook, and put it into his briefcase.

'Is it any good?' John was enjoying having the producer around the place - he has a strong sense of humour and he would be sorry to see him leave.

'Well, I feel as if I've known you for a lot longer that four days, so I guess that means we've come up with the goods. How do you feel about it? You don't think you're showing too much?'

John shook his head.

'No, you've treated me gently so far. But let's face it, Brian; I've had a singularly uninspiring life, haven't I.'

'Cushioned is the word you really want. I suspect there might be a couple of skeletons lurking there somewhere, they just haven't come out yet.'

John felt uncomfortable. *Back off, back off.*

'So, off the record, notebook put away, no tape recorder, who's Callum Brennan?'

There was silence from John, not because he didn't want to answer but because he didn't know how to. What had David said about knowing the Beatles' voices?

'Aha! A skeleton!'

'Not at all.' John knew he had to recover, and fast. 'I don't know Callum Brennan. Who is he?'

'He's another author from the Frederick's stable. And if you'd said as much, I might have believed he was just another author, but now I know I'm right. Why did you use a pseudonym? It's obvious to any fan that you wrote *In Praise*.'

'It's nothing to do with me.' John knew he was fighting a losing battle. 'I don't know him, but I've read the book and I would certainly like to meet him. There is a superficial resemblance to the way that I write...'

'Cut the crap, John. You must have your reasons for not wanting to be linked with CB, so we'll leave it at that. But don't run away with the idea that I'm the only one who will notice.'

John shook his head as if to dismiss the subject and watched as Brian picked up the briefcase.

'So can I go back to *Jenny's Child* now?'

'Thank goodness for that,' Mark's dry voice came from the background. 'I thought it was only me doing any work around here.'

Brian laughed.

'Don't worry Mark. I'll make sure everybody knows who the brains behind this outfit is. Your coffee's superb.'

'Up yours, Lazenby,' he grinned. 'You want coffee, you make your own - you're part of this family.'

Dawn missed John more than she cared to admit to herself. They had agreed, in a flush of optimism, that while Brian Lazenby was there they shouldn't meet. In spite of having a mini-John in the shape of Josh, she felt bereft.

She knew it made no sense to risk seeing him – an investigative producer like Brian Lazenby would soon have latched on to that side of John's life – and while it wouldn't have been made public knowledge, it would have meant a stranger knew of their relationship.

The weather was too cold and miserable to spend much time out of doors, and she longed for the summer when they would really be able to appreciate the incomparable Cornish beaches. So they stayed in the flat, drawing pictures, reading books, watching silly television programmes that had Josh squealing with delight.

They waited for the following Monday when John would return to see them.

'Have you enjoyed your stay with us?' Amy looked questioningly at Brian.

'Do I need to answer that? I can't ever remember enjoying an assignment more. John is an interesting man, and with Mark they make a brilliant team. But I rather suspect you have more to do with his success than is immediately obvious. Am I right?'

'No, I don't think so. Optimum keeps me out of the way, so I suppose my absence gives him the freedom to put in whatever hours he needs, but no, I don't think I'm particularly a help to him. I'm just not a hindrance.'

'Optimum? I'm missing something here…' He looked at her for a moment. 'I've committed an unforgivable sin. I've assumed that as you've been here all week you don't work. I'm wrong…'

She grinned at him, feeling relaxed in his company.

'You're wrong, but it really is irrelevant. You're doing a programme on John, not his family.'

'His family is John. So come on, Amy Thornton, spill the beans. What is Optimum?'

'A shop.'

'Selling what?'

She stood and moved across to a large roll top writing desk. Pressed flowers had been inlaid across the top, and it gleamed with the patina of old age.

'Come and look at this,' she said.

'I don't need to – I've looked at it many times already,' he laughed. 'Did that come from your shop?'

'Sort of. I buy old furniture – this piece cost me £20 – and then I work on them. The pressed flowers are my trade-mark. In the shop this would sell for a lot more. A tremendous amount of work goes into each and every item. They carry very high price tags. I took this week off partly because I was ready for a holiday and partly because I was interested in what you did.'

He stood by her side, his hand resting lightly on the writing desk.

'Was it worth it?'

She moved away from him, aware of his closeness and disturbed by it. 'Yes, I've thoroughly enjoyed watching you. How long have you been in television?'

'Oh, a few years now. It's only recently that I've realised I've finally got where I wanted to be when I joined the BBC. It's been hard work.'

'I can imagine.' She smiled at him, 'we'll be sorry to see you go. Will you stay here when you come back to do the filming?'

'If you'll have me. Thanks very much. And quite apart from this programme, I'd like to keep in touch.'

'We'd be delighted,' she said simply. 'You're welcome here anytime Brian.'

Their reunion was passionate and all-consuming. John had said goodbye to Brian in the morning and by two o'clock was in Dawn's arms, with Josh asleep in the next bedroom.

'If you only knew,' he said softly, 'if you only knew just how much I've missed you…'

'I do.' She reached up and stroked his hair. 'Oh, my love, it's been a very long week.'

She rested her head against his chest, and he bent to kiss her hair.

'Is everything okay? Josh?'

'We've been fine; just wish this whole project was finished. So come on, tell me all about it.'

She moved away from him and he followed her into the lounge.

'He's a nice chap. We got on very well – he's staying with us when they come back to do the actual filming. He wants to get that in the bag as soon as possible. I think that will take about a week, and then it's over.'

'Good,' she said. 'Let's go to bed.'

He didn't argue.

When Lauren left for Yorkshire and her promised visit to Derbyshire's Peak District, she was on a high. She had experienced the unique world of television first hand and had loved every minute of the attention given to her.

Uncle Brian had gone to a great deal of trouble to explain everything to her, even though a lot of it was beyond her comprehension. And he had given her two ten pound notes to spend on her holidays – said it was her wages for all the hard work she had put in.

It seemed as though the house was always full now – such a contrast with normal. Even Mummy had taken another week off work. Everyone in the house had been on television at some point, even Grandma Brenda and Gramps Ken.

'Are we nearly there, Gramps?'

'We're about five miles outside Padstow,' he smiled 'so I guess you could say we're nearly there.'

Brenda turned around in her seat to smile at her granddaughter.   'If you close your eyes and go to sleep, I'm sure we'll be there when you wake up.'

'Okay,' she said, and snuggled under the blanket. Within five minutes she was fast asleep.

'Clever idea travelling this early in a morning,' Brenda said. 'With a bit of luck she'll sleep most of the way. So… let's talk. What was bothering you last night? You were the quietest person at the party.'

The party, held at John and Amy's house, had been to celebrate the last of the filming. There had been about thirty people there and Ken had hoped Brenda hadn't noticed his mood.

'Oh, you know.'

'No, I don't know. What was wrong? Your leg?'

He shook his head.

'No, I don't get pain in it now, just stiffness. I'll be fine for the end of March…'

'Ken Buckingham, you're changing the subject. Somebody or something made you feel out of sorts. What was it?

'There was tension.' He sighed. 'Tension?'

'Uh-huh. In Amy. She either doesn't like that Lazenby chap, or she likes him too much.'

Malcolm let himself into Stonebrook, and gave a cursory glance around the hallway before going into the kitchen. He switched on the kettle before heading for the stairs. He'd promised he would check everything every day – Brenda kept muttering about leaks in the cold weather, and not going on holiday unless someone looked in every day to make sure their furniture wasn't floating away. He smiled at the thought of her worried face as she had handed him the list of instructions.

'Get on with you,' he had said. 'Everything will be safe, and I've got the address of the hotel so I can contact you anytime.'

He looked in all three bedrooms, and began to descend the stairs. He paused as he saw the front door at the end of the hall begin to open. A wave of cold air blew in and his heart sank as he realized it was Amy closing the door behind her. She turned and saw him standing halfway down the stairs.

'Oh, it's you,' she said icily. 'I wondered why the door was unlocked. What are you doing here?'

He continued to descend the stairs, angry with himself at the surge of irritation that had passed over him.

'I'm doing what Brenda asked me to do – check the cottage every day.'

'Mrs Buckingham, not Brenda. And in future I'll check it.'

'Then it'll be checked twice,' he said, and pushed past her into the kitchen.

'What are you doing now?'

'It's my tea-break,' he said. 'Don't cheek your elders,' his mum had always said, but he wanted to do more than cheek this toffee-nosed bitch.

'You can have your tea-break with the others from now on.'

'No I can't,' he said. 'I've had my tea-break in this kitchen every day since I started here. I'm not changing just because you say so.'

He pulled the boiled kettle towards him, and reached for a mug. She stormed into the kitchen and knocked the mug out of his hand. It smashed on the tiled kitchen floor.

He stared down at the mess for a moment, and then moved towards the broom cupboard. Without speaking he began to sweep up the shards then he tipped them into the waste bin.

Amy stared angrily at him and turned to go upstairs.

He reached for another mug, and made himself the promised cup of tea. His hand shook with the force of his fury, but his mind kept counting to ten over and over again. His mum said it worked and so it must do - but he still wanted to smash her beautiful face.

It was only when he sat down at the kitchen table that he heard the sounds from overhead. It sounded like furniture being moved, and he waited.

She came back downstairs as he was rinsing out the mug. He turned to look at her as she stood framed in the kitchen doorway. Her face was a mask of pure venom. She was distraught about something, so angry that she could hardly speak.

'I'll check the cottage in future,' she hissed.

'And I'll follow my instructions and do it too,' he said quietly, 'so it should be pretty safe, don't you think?'

She stared back at him.

'You'll pay for this,' she snarled and backed out into the hall.

'And don't worry,' he called after her, a smile on his face when he realised he had scored points, 'I'll replace the mug you broke.'

He heard the front door slam, and then her car engine churn into life. Pulling the gingham kitchen curtain to one side he watched her departure, wheels squealing as she let out the clutch too fast.

'Sod off,' he said to himself, and then went quickly upstairs to see if he could find out just what she had been doing.

He went into Lauren's room first – the noises indicated that was where she had been.

The furniture had been moved so that she could pull back the carpet. It was now lying loose on the grippers.

He fixed the carpet firmly into position, as tight as it had been before. If she tried to pull it back, she would know that he knew what she had been up to – further points scored.

Much as she had loved her holiday, Brenda was glad to be returning to normality. She had enjoyed the big city shopping that Sheffield had offered, had reveled in the beauty of the Derbyshire countryside, and had taken a real liking to Ken's family, small though it was.

But she missed Cornwall, missed her life on the smallholding and missed running their business.

Now they were almost home, and she snuggled into her seat with a small sigh of contentment.

Ken knew what she was thinking. He reached across to squeeze her hand.

'It's home to me as well, now,' he said. 'I always thought of Yorkshire as my home but it isn't. It's Cornwall, and I can't wait to get back. My leg feels great, I feel great, and it's a new growing season. What more could we want?'

'What more indeed,' Brenda said smiling at him in the darkness.

Thirty more minutes and they would be at Stonebrook, the warmth of the new central heating system welcoming them home. She hoped Malcolm had remembered their instructions about switching it on. Dear Malcolm, what a gentle lad, a treasure. She knew there would have been no hiccups – not with him to look after things.

CHAPTER FORTY-THREE

Summer 1984

They had decided shortly after Josh's fourth birthday to find a new home for Dawn and her son, somewhere not too close to schools that Lauren, Pilot, Bryony, Daniel or Rhys, Pat's youngest child, would attend.

Both John and Dawn knew with a degree of fatality that one day their relationship would become public knowledge.

So now she and Josh lived in Delabole, a few miles further up the coast. They enjoyed a large cottage with a glorious garden that gave her pleasure in tending.

At eleven years of age – eleven going on twelve he insisted, Josh was tall, muscular, and as blonde as ever.

He never queried his mother's strange relationship with his father. Dawn had explained some years earlier that John was his daddy, but it wasn't possible for him to live with them. He had accepted that with equanimity.

He looked forward to John's visits, but John sometimes felt that it wouldn't really matter to Josh if he never saw him again – he was his mother's child. Understandably.

Lauren too had grown up remarkably well under the influence of her grandparents but it grieved John that Amy had so little to do with her; he knew it wasn't the fault of his child.

Thirty two years after her rape, the hauntingly beautiful thirty eight year old Amy had never recovered; it seemed the scars would remain forever.

She persisted in keeping the entire world at arm's

length, and John knew that she waited for Treverick's reappearance in her life.

Lauren had been six years old when John had written her a story about a lizard, an iguana named Iggy. She had demanded more and eventually there had been fifteen of them. Iggy was a prolific adventurer, never went anywhere without his pure silk ties which his front feet frequently ripped to shreds; it was only when he was putting the latest one into the ring-binder that he realized he had just written his first children's book.

'Do you know I took three thousand pounds worth of orders in an hour today?'

John laughed and handed her a sherry.

'You shouldn't be so damned good. Have you finished the coat stand yet?'

'Not quite. It's taken a bit longer getting the right flowers. I had to use all the blue ones because of Brian's colour scheme, but another week and it should be ready.'

'You get on okay with Brian, don't you?'

'If I didn't he wouldn't still be on the open door list after all this time. I consider him to be a good friend – don't you?' She raised her eyes to meet his and sipped at the sherry.

'A very good friend. It's just that you don't make friends easily – you never cease to surprise me, Amy'

'Even after all these years?'

He bent to kiss her and she turned slightly so that his lips brushed her cheek.

'I've got something to show you,' he said and handed her the file of short stories.

'Carol says dinner will be at eight o'clock, so you've time for a quick scan through them.'

She pulled her legs up underneath her and opened the folder.

There was absolute silence for almost an hour. John felt uncomfortable watching her, sure that she hated them. Her reading wasn't accompanied by a smile, never mind the great guffaws of laughter that had come from Mark.

Suddenly she closed the folder.

'Short stories,' she said.

'Brian said...'

'And has Brian said anything about my stories? The stories that I wrote, that were personal, that were for my eyes only? I know you've seen them John – and probably Brenda, Ken and Freda too. Tell me – have you shown them to Brian?' Her voice rose hysterically as she hurled accusations at him.

'Amy –'

'Don't bother to deny anything, John. Your face says it all. Is that why Lauren spends most of her time at Stonebrook? So that my twisted and warped mind won't influence her?'

'You know that's not true, it's because you're so busy at Optimum –' The words sounded false and banal.

'So where are they?'

'In the loft. Slightly charred.' He'd never felt so miserable in all his life. 'I tried to burn them, but I couldn't.'

'I want them.'

'How did you know? I don't understand.'

'I went to get them when Ken and Brenda took Lauren to Yorkshire. I took up the carpet, and they'd gone.' Her tone was icy. 'I think I've waited long enough to have my property returned to me.' She threw the folder containing the Iggy stories on to the floor. 'And as far as they're concerned, the stories just about match your mental age.'

He avoided looking at her, her anger marring the perfection of her beauty.

'They don't match up to the quality of yours, that's for sure. I'm not patronizing you. Your writing is excellent – it's the content that bothered me… us. We worry about you, Amy, can't you see that?'

'No, I can't. You seem incapable of accepting the fact that *He* is always with me in here.' She tapped her head. 'And one day he'll be back. Not just for me, but for Lauren as well.'

'No!' He reached for her to stem the distress.

'Get away from me. And I want those stories returned – now.'

The next day twin beds arrived at the cottage and John understood that his marriage had finally crumbled.

CHAPTER FORTY-FOUR

October 1984

Iggy Iguana had been an instant and huge success, and now, some eight years on, long after Lauren had outgrown the stories, the BBC were negotiating with David.

He wished he could tell Josh, but both he and Dawn knew it wasn't possible, not yet. As far as Josh was concerned, his father was a salesman.

He walked towards the door, rubbing at his chest and promised himself that he would cut down on coffee; just lately it seemed that every time he had a cup, it gave him heartburn. He tried the door before hunting for his key, but he wasn't really surprised that it was locked. His was the only car parked on the drive.

What did surprise him was a note propped on the work surface in the kitchen.

Gone to an auction this evening in Bristol. Staying overnight at Grand if you need to contact me. Back tomorrow midday. Amy

He read the note twice, still rubbing his chest, and then went in search of some Rennies. He rang Dawn and told her was coming to spend the night.

'Why?'

'What do you mean why? Don't you want me to stay the night?'

'You know I do, but how come?'

'Amy's away overnight in Bristol, and Lauren's staying with Ken and Brenda for the night.'

'And guess what Josh is doing?'

'What?'

'Staying at Michael Palmer's. They're watching a video tonight. I dread to think what, in view of their reading tastes.'

'I'll be there in an hour. Just going to have some milk. Touch of heartburn.'

'Shall I cook, or shall we have a salad?'

'The way I feel right now I don't want anything. God, I hate being middle-aged. See you soon.' He replaced the receiver, bit into the tablet and then pulled a face at the chalky taste.

By the time he reached Dawn's cottage, he felt much better. He parked the BMW round the back and tried to make-believe he was really coming home to his loved one and not just playing at it.

It almost worked.

'I can hardly believe this is happening.'

John stroked her left breast and kissed her.

'Does that convince you?'

Dawn laughed.

'Idiot. You know what I mean. In the last fifteen years I think we must have spent all of ten nights together.' She reached across to the bedside table for her glass of champagne. 'Tell you what, John, I could get used to it.' She raised her glass. 'And to this.'

'If you say so, it can be changed. I'll leave Amy...'

'No! Look, we've been over and over this. I don't want you to leave her. Lauren is far too important to you. Josh has grown up having one and a half parents, Lauren has always had two.'

'Why are we discussing this?' He nibbled gently at her ear. 'We should be making love.'

'Again?' She laughed softly. 'I'm so glad I met you John.' She took another sip of the champagne. 'And this, and the bouquet of flowers, was a lovely touch. Quite the romantic, aren't you?'

He smiled at her.

'We try, we try. Any Rennies in that drawer?'

'Oh, very romantic.' She pulled open the drawer and handed him a pack.

'Are you okay?'

'Fine. It's either the pizza I had at lunchtime, or too many cups of coffee.'

'I can think of a cure.'

'Can you?'

'Mmmm.' She kissed his neck, and ran her fingers down his chest.

'You're curing me, you're curing me. Just don't stop, Doctor Lynch. Bugger the Hippocratic Oath.' Then he rolled onto his side. 'I love you,' he breathed, and stroked her breast again.

Sighing, she gave in to feelings he aroused in her, and opened her legs. His hands began to stroke her inner thighs, and his kiss deepened, each exploring the other's mouth with their tongues.

John broke away from the kiss to pull the sheet away from Dawn.

'I love to look at you.' He bent his head, and his tongue began to travel the length of her body.

She moved on to her back.

'Take me,' she whispered.

He moved on top and began to enter her. Sliding her arms around his buttocks, she pulled him firmly in.

Suddenly he fell on to her, and gasped.

'John? John?'

Moaning, he clutched at the centre of his chest.

'Dawn. Something wrong…' He rolled to one side, his face grey with pain. She stretched an arm out to touch him and realised there was nothing she could do. He needed professional help, and he needed it fast.

She reached across for the telephone, struggling to pull her legs from underneath him. He was only forty-two; he couldn't be having a heart attack. There had been no earlier indications. Then she remembered the heartburn that he had blamed on the pizza and coffee.

She glanced across at him as she dialed the emergency services, seeing the tell-tale signs of sweat on his forehead. His eyes were beginning to roll and he was struggling to hold on to his arm.

'Here, let me rub it for you,' she offered, knowing his left arm was hurting badly.

She was hardly dressed by the time the ambulance arrived and she followed in her car, running a comb through her hair as she pulled onto the main road.

Driving to the hospital she daren't let her mind dwell on possible complications. The paramedics had stabilized him. He had looked dreadful, his colour non-existent.

She knew she was travelling too close to the ambulance but she didn't want to be more than a few feet from the vehicle carrying him.

When they arrived at the hospital, she was taken to a small room and told someone would be in to talk to her as soon as they knew anything.

It was three o'clock in the morning before someone said he would live. 'It was a bad attack, Mrs Thornton, and he'll be in hospital for some time. He's sleeping now so why don't you go home and get some rest yourself. You look worn out.'

Dawn didn't try to stop the tears of relief.

'I'm not Mrs Thornton. I'm Mrs Lynch. Tomorrow Mrs Thornton will be here and she must not know about

me. I'm not going home until I've sorted something out.'
Dawn dried her eyes. 'Have you ever heard of a novelist,
an author by the name of John Thornton?'

The sister's eyes widened.

'You mean…?'

'Exactly. If the press pick up on this… we've
managed to avoid scandal for fifteen years. We have a
child, so please forget I was ever here. I'm going to ring a
friend who I'm sure will say John was with him when he
had the heart attack.' She sounded calmer than she felt.

'Would you like to see him?'

'Thanks. It could be some time before I see him
again.'

'What time is it?'

Pat peered at the bedside clock. She had to look
twice, blinking to focus her eyes. 'Phone's ringing,' she
said. '3.18 am.'

'Are you answering it?'

'No,' she said and pulled the sheet over her head.

He reached out for the receiver.

'David?' Is that you?'

'Dawn?'

'Yes – listen. I'm at the hospital. It's John, he's in
intensive care. He's had a heart attack.'

David sat up in bed, now fully awake. Pat was already
getting out of the other side. Hearing Dawn's name, she
knew that something was wrong.

'I'll be there in twenty minutes. And don't worry,
we'll sort it out.'

He put down the receiver and looked across at Pat.

'Where's Amy?'

'I don't know. What's wrong?'

'John's had a heart attack, a bad one, and for some reason he was with Dawn. Look, you go back to bed and I'll go and see what's happened. I don't understand why he was with Dawn – we'll probably have to alibi him. How does that grab you?'

'You know it doesn't, but we'll do what's necessary. It's difficult liking both Amy and Dawn. But go on; see if you can help poor Dawn. She must be nearly out of her mind.'

He nodded, struggling into jeans.

'She sounded it.'

Kissing Pat, he left the house and headed for the hospital, his thoughts in turmoil.

How could someone as young as John have a heart attack? It made him question his own mortality – they had been born within a month of each other.

Dawn came straight into his arms and he held her.

'Dawn, look at me.' She raised tearful eyes. 'Where's Amy?'

'As far as I can remember, she's in Bristol. She's staying overnight but I don't know where. I am pretty sure she's coming home tomorrow, though. David, he was with me – in bed.'

'I'm not going to make any corny remarks, don't worry. So what do you want me to do? Say he came over to us for a drink and had the attack at our place?'

She nodded.

'Amy will have enough on her plate, without finding out John's had a mistress for most of their married life.'

'And what about Lauren? Do you know where she is?'

'Brenda and Ken's. My God, I never even gave her a thought! And Josh…complicated, isn't it?' She gave a watery smile. 'The awful thing is, David, when I leave here tonight I don't know when I'll see him again.'

'We'll find a way,' he promised. 'Have you been in to see him?'

'Yes, he looks a lot better than he did a few hours ago.'

'Right – I suggest you go home now. I'm going to ring Brenda and she can make the decision how and when to tell Lauren. But it's likely that they'll come straight here. Have you got your car?'

'Yes, I didn't come in the ambulance. I… I guessed I'd have to make my own way home.'

David's heart lurched as he watched Dawn walk out of the hospital. That woman totally and honestly loved John but because of misguided loyalties they were denied the right to share their lives.

The ward sister took him to John's bedside and left him for a minute. 'He's sleeping,' she whispered, 'and he's in no pain. Will you be contacting his wife?'

'You know the problem?'

'And no-one else needs to know.' She nodded. 'The day staff will presume he was brought in by his wife, I don't think questions will be asked. I understand you're telling Mrs Thornton he had the attack at your home?'

'I'm just going to ring his in-laws – his daughter is staying with them.'

'I think they should come.'

'But I thought…' David raised his eyebrows.

'That he was out of danger? He's stable. Heart attacks are very unpredictable. The first few hours after an attack as bad as this one are always the worst – but, the consolation is that he's responded well to the treatment. Fortunately he's kept himself in good shape.'

David briefly touched John's hand before going to find a telephone.

Initially, Ken had been against waking Lauren. They had a lengthy discussion about it but Brenda clinched it.

'And what if John dies? What if she never sees her dad alive again? Could you live with yourself, Ken?'

Consequently it was almost half past five when they woke Lauren. She listened carefully to what they were telling her and then quietly put on her jeans and top.

She told herself it wasn't necessary to panic, Dad was in good hands at the hospital. Thank goodness he had been over at Uncle David's and not at home on his own.

In the car she cried.

'Tell me he's okay. Tell me he won't be dead when we get there,' she sobbed.

Brenda, sharing the back seat, put an arm round her.

'Hush baby, of course he'll be okay. Uncle David said he was stabilized in intensive care. He'll be monitored all the time; they won't let anything happen to him.'

'And what about Mum? Didn't she leave a phone number?'

'Probably with your dad but not with us. She'll be home in a few hours and we'll be there to meet her. Now come on, your dad won't want to see you like this. We have to look as though we're not worried at all.'

They were allowed in to see him briefly. John lay surrounded by tubes, drip feeds and monitors bleeping quietly into the night.

Lauren willed her own life into him.

'Live, Dad,' she prayed. 'Live, and I promise I'll be there more for you.'

Brenda felt sick as she stared at the man she loved as

a son. He'd stuck with a difficult marriage, never had much of a life with Amy and now he was reduced to this at such a young age.

Ken merely stared and wondered. Where had John been when the attack had happened? With David and Pat or at that smart cottage in Delabole where he'd seen the BMW parked on several occasions? While the cat's away...

He volunteered to go and wait for Amy's return leaving Brenda and Lauren to try and get some more sleep at home.

Brenda had given him specific instructions about what to say, about breaking it gently to Amy.

'Kid gloves, I promise you... and I'll tell Mark as well. He'll be shocked – he knows John better than anybody.'

Mark was devastated at the news.

'Intensive care? Was he on his own?'

Ken shook his head.

'No, he was at David's, thank God. I don't like to think what would have happened if he hadn't got help quickly. It was a bad one.'

'So you're waiting here for Amy?'

'Yes. We thought it the right thing to do. I've just seen her note but I don't think I should ring the Grand. I don't want her to drive down here worrying about John.'

Mark wondered if she would worry about John and he moved around to the computer.

'It's a good job I've a fair bit of work to do but if I know John, he'll carry on writing even in the hospital.'

They looked at each other as the sound of gravel crunching on the driveway indicated a vehicle had pulled up.

'Amy?' Ken raised his eyebrows in query.

Mark nodded.

'Sounds like her car. Want me to make myself scarce?'

'No, I'll take her into the lounge.'

They met in the hall and Amy didn't bother to disguise her dislike of him.

'Ken – something wrong?'

'Come in here, Amy.' He held open the door leading into the lounge and she went by, a puzzled expression on her face,

'Is it Lauren? Has she had an accident?'

'No. Lauren's fine. Now sit down.'

'Oh for God's sake, stop it Ken. I'm not a silly little woman who falls to pieces. What's wrong?'

'It's John. He's in hospital. In intensive care. He was at David's last night and suffered a bad heart attack. I'll run you to the hospital if you want.'

'Heart attack? John?' She stared at him. 'That's right. Brenda thought it would be better if you didn't drive, so I'm ready when you are.'

'What time's visiting hours?'

'On normal wards, it's seven until nine at night but John's in intensive care. We can go now.'

'Well, thanks for telling me.' She took off her jacket and dropped it onto a chair. 'I'll go tonight. Now, if you'll excuse me, Ken, I've got work to do.'

As Ken walked towards his car he found himself wishing John had been at that cottage in Delabole, with whoever she was.

CHAPTER FORTY-FIVE

October 1984

He slept through most of the first day and his first conscious impression of having a visitor was when he opened his eyes and saw Amy.

'Amy?'

'Hi…' She leaned across the bed and placed a kiss on his brow.

'Did one of your characters need to have a heart attack?'

'What?'

She smiled.

'Write about what you know – rule number one.'

'This might go into a book. I take it I'm still alive?'

'You've scared everybody else to death. But yes you're still alive. It's a good job you went over to David's or I might not have been able to visit you at all, other than in a funeral parlour.'

'David's?' He looked puzzled, his brain not properly in gear.

'I thought you were at David's house last night?'

'Oh, God, yes. Was it only last night?' His mind cleared abruptly and he saw a brief vision of Dawn's horrified face as she dialed for the ambulance. She must have orchestrated a cover up.

'You're right, I did.' He spoke slowly, wondering just what she had been told. 'I fancied a bit of company and I wasn't feeling brilliant. I can't remember much beyond that. Except it hurt.'

She took his hand and squeezed it sympathetically.

'You really did frighten me, you know.' Her voice was soft.

'Have they told you anything?'

She shook her head.

'Not yet other than they're pretty sure you'll survive.' Grinning, she added 'you'd better survive, you're halfway through a book and we'd like to know what ending you've got planned.'

'Me too,' he said.

'I'm not staying long – there's quite a queue of people waiting to see you and I think a certain daughter of ours is nearly tearing her hair out with worry.'

She bent to kiss him once more and moved to the doorway.

'I'll try and get in to see you tomorrow, John.'

It was only as she left the room that her words permeated his brain. *Try and get in?*

Lauren was tearful and clinging.

'Hey,' he said into her hair that was threatening to choke him. 'I'm not going to die. Your old dad's a fighter.'

'But you're not old,' she wailed. 'Other people's dads don't have heart attacks at your age.'

'Yes they do, honey, and we have to learn to live with it. But don't worry, I intend doing everything they tell me.'

Ken held tightly to Brenda – he knew without having to be told that she was very close to tears.

'So, you'll not be helping me in the fields in my old age,' he said with a smile.

'Not for a couple of weeks…'

'Dad!'

Brenda moved to take the young girl in her arms.

'Come on, Lauren, I think we should go now. We'll be back tomorrow but I think your dad needs his rest right now.' She turned to face John. 'And as for you, you lie there and do nothing. No pen, no paper, no Dictaphone. And no telephone. Mark's looking after things at home so you don't need to fret.' Her voice dropped slightly. 'We love you very much, you know, so just take care.'

'I promise,' he said, his eyes already closing.

It was five days before David managed to smuggle in Dawn and Josh.

'Well,' she said after the longest kiss she had ever known, 'I thought you were supposed to be at death's door!'

'I was.' He grinned. 'It didn't open.' He turned to his son. 'Good to see you, Josh.'

'Dad – did we cause it?'

'What?'

'The heart attack. We saw you that day, didn't we? Was that what made you ill?'

'Don't ever think that, Josh. All the signs were there – I just didn't recognise them. I'll know next time, though.' He sounded rueful.

'Next time?' Dawn looked startled.

'Hey, stop panicking. I could be seventy-five before I have another one. And if things do get worse there's always treatments like coronary artery bypass.'

'You've talked about it then?' Her eyes clouded over as she struggled to come to terms with what she was hearing.

'No, just listened. There's others in here with the same sort of thing. But I'll be fine, honestly. A couple more days and I'll be home. Did you do something with the BMW?'

David laughed. 'Don't talk about it. Amy rang and said she was going to ask Mark to run her over to our house to collect it. I flapped, I can tell you. I got straight on the phone to Dawn who scooted over with it. Pat then took her back home. Amy and Dawn missed each other by oh... all of thirty seconds I would say.'

Moving around the room, David took Josh by the arm. 'Come on, Tiger, let's go down and see if we can find a coffee bar. See you at the car in fifteen minutes, Dawn?'

'Fifteen minutes.' She nodded.

They waited until David and Josh had left the corridor before turning to each other.

'God, I was...'

'Dawn, I...'

They laughed. There were tears in Dawn's eyes as she folded herself against him.

'I was going to say how much I've missed you and how damn worried I've been. You've never been ill before... I couldn't believe it was happening at first. David's been a rock. He's telephoned every day with news but it's not been easy, John. Being the mistress isn't much fun when it's a situation like this.'

He held her close to him and kissed the top of her head. 'And the ironic thing is that you love me. Amy doesn't feel anything for anybody. The strain's showing with Ken, Brenda and Lauren, but Amy...'

'And it's showing here,' Dawn said softly. 'I couldn't live without you, John. Wouldn't even want to try.'

CHAPTER FORTY-SIX

May 1989

John's enforced idleness following his heart attack had reflected on Mark. There was no longer the daily rush to complete a section of work; although John still wrote every day, the number of words was greatly reduced.

Amy's attitude towards Mark had soon reverted to normal and she now left him to take care of himself. Mark left nothing to chance and five years on was still carefully monitoring everything that John did.

'It's nearly two o'clock, boss. Go for your walk.'

It had become a standing joke between them that John's daily car drive was his walk. John told him that the reason he went out in the car was to go to a different beauty spot every day and then walk. In reality the car took him to Delabole.

'Nearly finished, Mark.'

'No, not nearly finished. Finished.' He was firm as he took the pencil out of John's hand and John looked at him.

'One of these days I'm going to take one of those expensive silk ties and pull it very tight. Probably on a day when you wear that purple yellow and red one.'

Mark laughed.

'Greta would help you. She hates that one as well. I personally think it all adds to the image – suave, debonair, a certain flair for fashion…'

'Is that what you think?' John raised his eyebrows in query. 'And just when are you going to make an honest woman of Greta? It's time we had a wedding round here.'

Mark blushed.

'It won't be me who provides the wedding. Greta and I are ok.'

'What do you mean it won't be you who provides the wedding? Is there something I'm missing?'

'Well, I don't like gossiping, as you know, but Lauren seems pretty keen on Pilot.'

John laughed, the relief obvious on his face.

'Phew... for a minute you had me going there. No, Pilot's just one of the crowd she knocks around with. There are always other people about when she sees him. Besides, she's too young to have a serious boyfriend.'

'Spoken like a true father, John. I think I ought to point out that Lauren will be twenty in November. Didn't you marry Mrs Thornton when she was only eighteen?'

'Yes, but...'

'But me no buts, John Thornton. Greta and I went to the sports centre last week. Pilot was there. So was Lauren. No friends, just the two of them and obviously in love.'

John pushed his chair away from the desk. He remained silent for a moment and then smiled.

'Well, I don't want anyone taking my daughter away from me but I must say if it's got to be anybody, I'd like it to be Pilot. Wonder if Amy knows.'

Mark refrained from saying he doubted it.

'Don't say anything to Lauren, boss. She'll know it's because I've told you. Let them come to you in their own time. Now, are you going out or not? I've work to do even if you haven't.'

'I'm going, I'm going.' He stood and moved towards the door then turned. 'You're sure -?'

'I'm sure I saw them together, yes. Go away, John and take things easy. Got your tablets?'

John patted his jacket pocket.

'As always. Wouldn't dare go without them. I'd never forgive myself if I died because I hadn't got them with me. I'd miss your nagging.'

Mark threw a paper clip.

'Out! I'll see you tomorrow morning.'

'We'll have to tell them sometime.' Pilot smiled into Lauren's beautifully anxious face and then pulled her close.

'It's not "them" collectively that bothers me. It's Mum. Why can't we just carry on as we are?'

'Because you nearly had kittens when we saw Mark and Greta last week. If it were out in the open that we're closer than friends, it would take away all that hassle. We don't need to tell them everything…'

She giggled.

'I should hope not. I can see it now – oh, dad, just thought I ought to tell you, I've lost my virginity…to Pilot. He'd string you up.'

'Regret it?' He tilted her face to his and kissed the tip of her nose.

'Not for one minute. I love you.'

'And I love you, so let's tell them.'

The sigh was long and drawn out.

'Whatever you say. What shall we tell them?'

He pulled her closer and they began to walk down to the harbour wall. 'How about – we're engaged?'

'But we're not.'

'We could be.'

She didn't reply for a long time. Reaching the wall she sat down and stared out across the harbour, the last of the daylight slowly disappearing with the screech of the seagulls.

'Well?'

'Is this a proposal?'

He dropped to one knee and held her hand loosely.

'Lauren Thornton, will you do me the honour of becoming my wife? Please?'

Again the giggle prompted by excitement.

'Be serious, Pilot. Are you really proposing?'

'I don't get down on one knee to just anybody, you know. Of course I'm proposing.'

'I don't know what to say. I've never been proposed to before.'

'I should hope not. So do I get an answer or are you going to prevaricate all night?'

'Don't use big words at me. Can I think about it?'

'No.'

'Then I suppose I'll have to say yes.' She turned to him. 'Yes, yes, yes! Although, goodness knows what they'll say. I don't want to get married though.'

'But you've just said…'

'I know what I've said. Mum and Dad are married and from what I've seen I don't want that, not for a long time anyway.'

He took hold of her hands.

'But my mum and dad are married and for them it's totally worked. It all depends on what you're like as a person. Your Mum –'

'Do you know,' she said, 'I used to think it was Dad's fault. I used to think he worked such long hours that they grew apart. But that's not it. Mum's got no idea how to make a marriage work.'

'We have but I'll give you whatever time you need. You're not your mum, Lauren. You're Brenda's product really and look at her and Ken. Tomorrow we'll go shopping for a ring and then we'll tell them.'

'We'll tell Brenda and Ken first – I owe them that.

And we'll start looking for a place to live.'

'But you said...' he looked bewildered. Her grin was wicked.

'I said I wouldn't get married. I didn't say I wouldn't move in with you.'

He groaned in mock horror.

'I think I've just changed my mind about all this.'

Amy felt a calming relief at the news. At last this child would be off her hands. And at least they knew Pilot, knew she wouldn't be forever running back home – he would take care of her. With a good job at Farmers and the subsequent heir to the business, she needn't worry about Lauren.

She was surprised by how well John had taken the news – almost as if he had known. She raised the glass of champagne.

'To both of you! Many congratulations. We're delighted.'

'And I endorse every word.' John was all smiles. 'We'll have David and Pat and the rest of your crew over for a meal this weekend, sort of make it official. I presume they know?'

'Not yet.' Pilot shook his head. 'We're going over later to tell them.'

Amy stood and walked across the room to kill the strident ringing of the telephone. She said hello and then said she would take it in the hall. Minutes later she returned.

'That was Brian. He was ringing to see if he could come down for the weekend. I said he could. Looks like we are going to be having a party anyway. I'll ring the caterers tomorrow and see what they can do. I'm not landing Carol with this, as good as she is. And really she should be invited as a guest, not a housekeeper. I've a couple of pieces of furniture to deliver tomorrow and one to pick up, so I'll finish earlier than usual and put my organising head on.'

John watched his wife in amazement. She hadn't been as voluble as this in years. It couldn't be that she was glad to be free of Lauren?

They waved the young couple off and returned to the lounge.

'Are you really pleased?' he asked quietly.

'Of course. A little surprised – she's certainly kept this from us. But we've always liked Pilot. I wonder when they slept together...'

'But...'

'Now, John, please don't be naïve. Nobody gets engaged these days without having slept together first. I just hope she's using contraception. Perhaps I should talk with her.'

He refrained from saying it would be a first if she did.

She was cruising slowly along one of the small side lanes in Delabole when she saw his car. The new white Ferrari was parked half in the driveway and half on the pavement.

Slowing to a crawl, Amy wound down the window of the transit van. A woman ran down the drive and jumped in the car that was blocking his entry. Amy heard her call out.

'Sorry, didn't think you'd be here yet – I'll move mine round the back.' She watched the Ferrari follow the Astra around the cottage.

She knew the woman. She scanned her memories but couldn't come up with an identity... but she did know that woman.

Driving slowly past the cottage she picked out the name half hidden by a rambling rose that festooned the wall – Mayflower Cottage. *Why was John visiting someone in Delabole – someone he'd never mentioned?*

She pulled the transit into the side of the road and sat for a minute, her head in her hands.

Who was that woman? And where the bloody hell was this cottage she was meant to be looking for, anyway? She glanced at the address on the piece of paper – pick up a writing desk at Rosemary Cottage, Delabole. First things first, she had to find Rosemary Cottage and then she could decide what to do about John. And that woman.

She drove into the centre of Delabole looking for a newsagent.

The old lady appeared from out of the back of the shop, her face wreathed in smiles.

'Hello, my love, and what can I do for you? Lovely weather for the time of year, isn't it?'

'Yes, lovely,' Amy replied vacantly, her mind on the woman who lived in Mayflower Cottage. 'Erm, can you help me? Do you know where Rosemary Cottage is?'

'Well, bless you, of course I do. Old Mr. Dobbs.'

'That's right.'

'It's just round the corner. Go out of here, turn left by the post box, down the road about a hundred yards and it's on your right.'

'Thanks very much. Er… I've also got something to pick up at Mayflower Cottage –'

'Oh, that's Dawn. Dawn Lynch. Now if you want to know where that is, ask that young man across the road. He'll probably take you himself. That's young Josh, her son.'

Amy looked across to where the old woman was

pointing and saw three young men in their late teens, standing by an old mini.

She walked out of the shop, her mind turning. Dawn Lynch, she knew that name. Crossing towards the group of three, she suddenly stopped.

She didn't have to go up to them and ask which one was Josh. There was no mistaking her husband's son.

CHAPTER FORTY-SEVEN

June 1989

The house was crowded. Amy was quiet and in control. Her plans had been carefully laid and she intended on seeing John's world crumble by the end of the evening.

She had gone to a great deal of trouble to organise the party and had invited everyone they knew. A marquee was erected in the large back garden and even the weather stayed fine. Lauren looked supremely happy and Pilot carried an air of pride that nobody could mistake.

'It looks wonderful, sweetheart,' John whispered as she hurried past carrying a tray loaded with drinks.

Brenda, at sixty-five, looked ten years younger and Ken's eyes were fixed on her. They had supplied all the flowers for the house and marquee and everywhere looked spectacular. The fragrance was breathtaking, perfectly complimenting the warmth of the late September evening.

And yet Brenda felt uneasy. She took Freda to one side but before she could say anything, Freda spoke.

'There's something wrong.'

'What do you mean?'

'It's Amy. Has she said anything?'

'No, not a thing. Why do you think something's wrong?'

'Don't know.' Freda ran a hand through her grey hair. 'It's that smile – as though there's something going on in her mind that has her scoring points. I just hope it's not against Lauren.'

Brenda nodded.

'I'd just said as much to Ken but he laughed. Does it make you uneasy?'

'Sure does. Behind that beautiful façade is one hell of a woman and I have to admit I don't trust her an inch. I love her to pieces. And if I could get my hands on Treverick...'

'Please... he's been on my mind such a lot lately. He'll be what, fifty-five now? I'm surprised he hasn't reoffended since he came out of prison. When they told us he'd been released, the police inferred he would be back behind bars in no time. Once a rapist always a rapist. Thankfully, he's never been back to this area. At least, as far as we know.'

'As far as we know.' Freda said. 'Just look around this room – I bet there are half a dozen men here who we know very little about. Tell you what, Bren – I shan't write Treverick off until the day I hear he is dead.'

'Have you ever considered he might be dead?'

'No,' she said slowly. 'Don't ask me to explain but I know he's not. We wouldn't be that lucky. Besides, the police would have informed us.'

'Don't forget,' she whispered. 'Nine o'clock in my bedroom.'

John turned to look at Amy and grinned.

'Best offer I've had all night.'

'Just don't forget. Dead on nine o'clock. The cake is too big for me to carry down on my own. Don't let me down, John.'

'Have I ever let you down before, my love?'

'I don't know. Have you?'

The emerald green silk of her dress swished as she turned and walked away from him.

'Mark, can I have a word?'

Mark turned, surprised to hear Amy's voice and excused himself from Greta.

'Back in a minute,' he whispered. 'Grab another champagne when one passes, okay?'

She winked and blew him a kiss.

He followed the green dress as Amy made her way to the garden. He felt his hands twitch as he imagined the body beneath the smooth silk. It wouldn't do at all to torment himself, tonight of all nights. Not filled with champagne anyway.

'Mark,' she said, turning to face him. 'I need you.'

Inwardly he groaned and hoped that his thoughts didn't show on his face. He tugged on the pale blue and peach tie.

'I've laid a surprise on, but I can't do it on my own. It's a surprise for John. Can you escape at about ten to nine and go up to my bedroom? I'll tell you what we're going to do when you get there.' She looked at his expression and laughed. 'Nothing raunchy, I promise you. I need you to carry something.'

'Do I get a clue?'

'Certainly not. Just bring those chunky arms and I'll do the rest.'

He had a feeling she was flirting with him and he tried to squash his panic.

'You know, Mark,' she said in a gentle voice. 'You've worked for John for a long time now and we've never said thank you. For what it's worth, I think you do a great job. And I know you keep an eye on him for me.' She reached up and planted a kiss that was half on his cheek and half on his lips. 'Thank you from me anyway. So, you'll come at ten to nine?'

He nodded. Whatever she had planned, he would do

without question.

He ached for her.

At 8.45 pm Amy went upstairs. The party had grown noisy with laughter and loud music. Nobody noticed her disappearance except Mark Carter who swallowed nervously.

She slipped into the pink and grey bedroom and closed the curtains. She pressed the pink velvet against her cheek before walking back to the door. Turning the key in the lock she shrugged the low cut dress from her shoulders.

It fell to the floor in a shimmering cascade of silk and she bent to pick it up before carrying it to the side of the bed and dropping it once more on the floor. It was all about staging; she wanted John to think they hadn't been able to control themselves.

The mirror revealed a perfect body. Unmarred by the travails of giving birth, her breasts and stomach could have belonged to a twenty-three year old rather than a woman in her forties. She reached up and loosened the clip holding her hair high and allowed it to fall in golden-blonde waves around her shoulders.

Hearing the tap on the door, she turned and crossed the room.

'Yes?' She kept her voice low.

'It's Mark, Mrs Thornton.'

She opened the door, staying behind it.

'Come in, Mark,' she said throatily. 'Call me Amy.'

His penis began to harden as she spoke. He remembered the tone from years earlier when they had almost made love on the office floor and he knew he was lost.

As she moved from behind the door he caught her

reflection in a mirror and he groaned.

Softly closing the door she came into his arms.

'This time, Mark,' she whispered, her lips soft against his ear. 'This time, we don't stop. I've waited too long for this and I want you. Now Lauren is leaving, I can have my own happiness.'

He wished he hadn't had so much champagne.

'But... where's John?' His brain felt woolly, his speech uncoordinated.

'John's downstairs with his guests and I've locked the door.' She began to loosen his tie. Stroking his bulging penis through his trousers, she began to lower the zip. Sinking to her knees, she took him into her mouth.

'Stop!' he spluttered. 'If you don't...'

'Then take off your clothes.' She crossed the room, his eyes never leaving her. Lying on the bed she rolled on to her back. 'Come on, Mark, I'm waiting. I've waited too long.'

His clothes joined hers and he lowered himself on to the bed. Tentatively he began to stroke her. Greta was banished from his mind for ever. Amy's skin was baby smooth and he counted to ten in his mind. He wanted to take his time.

She opened her legs a little wider.

'Amy...' His voice was guttural. 'Amy, I can't believe this –'

'Believe it, Mark. Take me, take me now.'

He lay on top of her and she removed his glasses, placing them on the bedside table. The digital clock read 9.01.

'Now, fuck me,' she commanded and pulled him into her

'Amy, you're beautiful,' he murmured as he thrust in and out, neither noticing her hardening expression nor the click as the bedroom door opened.

John stopped on the threshold of the bedroom and was instantly sober. And murderous. A wave of grief overwhelmed him but the sound that came from the back of his throat was sub-human.

And Mark heard it.

He rolled off Amy and tried to grab the bed cover, ineffectually.

Amy gave a deep laugh.

'Hi, John. Fancy seeing you here. You might have knocked.'

'Amy?' He felt dazed, as though the walls were closing in on him. 'But...'

'But what, John?' Her voice was sugary sweet. 'You want to know why? Try Dawn Lynch. And try your son.'

The pain hit him and his legs buckled. He clawed at his chest and then at his throat, fighting for air. He was on the floor before either Mark or Amy could move.

'Tablets,' he gasped losing consciousness.

Mark turned to look at Amy as she rolled away from him and off the bed.

'Get his tablets, Amy!' he shouted. 'Quick, Amy, they'll be in his coat pocket.'

John was curled on the floor in a foetal position when Amy reached him.

'Hang on, boss, we're getting the pills!' Mark shouted as he struggled to disentangle himself from the bed and get to John.

Amy looked at John for some time then reached into his coat pocket. She palmed the small bottle of tablets and slid them under the bed.

Agitated, she tried to shake her husband.

'John!' she said with just the right note of urgency. 'Where are your tablets?' There was no response as she feverishly went through all of his pockets. 'They're not here, Mark! Check his bedroom.'

Mark stood and looked around wildly for his clothes. He was all too aware of the naked figure of Amy within reach of him.

Then Freda handed him his trousers. He looked at her with utter shock. 'I've told Brenda to ring for an ambulance,' she said icily. 'I imagine about half the people at the party will be in this room in about thirty seconds. I suggest the pair of you get some clothes on.' She looked down with disdain at his shrunken penis. 'She must have been desperate. Now get out of my way while I help John.'

She didn't notice any movement from Amy as she frantically searched for a pulse.

Standing, Freda straightened to her full height and walked across to Amy. Pulling her arm back to its full extent and with all her strength she hit Amy across the face.

'You bitch,' she hissed'. 'You did this. You used Mark.'

She turned to the stricken man still trying to get dressed.

'He's dead, Mark. I hope you never sleep again.'

CHAPTER FORTY-EIGHT
Autumn 1989

Dawn couldn't rest, couldn't concentrate on anything. She glanced at the clock and stood.

'I'm going to bed,' she announced.

Josh moved away from the window. He had been looking out at the garden for more than five minutes without actually seeing it.

'It's only nine o'clock. Are you okay?'

'Fine. I'm tired, that's all.'

'I'll lock up,' he said and smiled at her. 'You look a bit peaky. Want me to bring a cup of tea up?'

She smiled and kissed his cheek.

'That would be nice.' It was as she was climbing the stairs that she began to retch and only just made it to the bathroom before vomiting harshly.

She leaned with her head against the hand basin, feeling too weak to stand. What was wrong with her? All day she had felt out of sorts and Josh was the same.

'Mum?' Josh stood in the doorway, concern clouding his face. 'You all right?'

'I hope so now. I've been sick. Think I'll just crawl into bed for the night. Perhaps I'd better not have that tea, love, just water.'

'That's okay,' he said. 'Don't worry. I'll stay downstairs for a bit until you're asleep then I'll lock up. Give me a shout if you need anything.'

She smiled and went to her room.

Downstairs was eerily quiet. Josh didn't want the television on, didn't feel like listening to music and didn't feel like reading. He paced the lounge, listening for any sound from upstairs; he went to the bottom of the stairs twice just to make sure she wasn't calling him.

At ten o'clock he decided enough was enough and switched off the lounge light. He went through to the kitchen and locked and bolted the back door. As he turned off the kitchen light he saw the headlights of a car sweep into the driveway. He waited and dread settled over him like a cloak. He recognised David's dark green Volvo.

Josh didn't want to open the door. He was sliding back the bolt when David knocked using the brass lion's head.

'David?'

'Josh.' David's bulk moved into the kitchen and without speaking he pulled Josh towards him.

'It's Dad,' Josh said, his face smothered in David's jacket.

'Where's your mum?'

'In bed. What's wrong? He's ill again, isn't he?'

'Go and get your mum, Josh.'

'David?' Dawn came into the kitchen tying the belt of her housecoat. She looked wan.

He held his arm out and she moved towards him.

'It's John. What's wrong?'

Her anxious face searched his. He couldn't speak. Didn't know how to tell her.

'Dad's dead, isn't he?' Josh spoke quietly, realising David couldn't bring himself to tell them.

He nodded and sank on to a kitchen stool. His legs wouldn't support him any longer.

Dawn stared at him.

'Dead? But... he'd been so well. How can he be dead?'

'Details later, Dawn.' David spoke wearily. 'He died just after nine o'clock...'

Dawn sat down at the table and stared.

'I know,' she said blankly. 'I felt him leave.'

Josh gave a low moan and sank to his knees.

'Josh, sweetheart.' Dawn knelt by her son and cradled his head against her bosom.

'He would have come here to live, Mum.' The boy was crying.

David stood.

'I'll get you a drink, Dawn.'

She nodded, still holding Josh.

'And one for Josh, I think he needs it.' She bent to kiss his head. 'Come on, love, come into the lounge. We need time to make sense of this.'

'Sense,' his bottom lip quivered. 'How can it make sense? My dad's dead. That'll never make sense.'

BOOK THREE

1989 – 1992 North Cornwall

CHAPTER FORTY-NINE

July 1989

'You can't go to the funeral.' David's voice was low and distraught.

In the two days since John's death, he had only been in contact with her by telephone. Delivering this news had to be done face to face.

She smiled gently and touched his hand.

'Stop worrying, David. I realise I can't go. It would upset too many people. There isn't only Amy to think about.'

'Can I sit down?'

'Of course you can. Come through to the lounge. I need to talk to you.'

He took off his jacket and sunk into a large armchair. She handed him a glass of brandy and he smiled gratefully at her.

'Right, David. Tell me about it now. I need to know he didn't suffer.'

He shook his head.

'He didn't suffer – physically he didn't suffer. Mentally he must have suffered – because of what he saw.'

'What he saw? I don't follow…'

'He walked into Amy's bedroom and found Amy having sex with Mark.'

'Mark? And Amy?' She found it hard to believe what she was hearing.

'And don't jump to any conclusions. Talk to Mark. He came in to see me this morning at the office. If Mark's telling the truth – and I have no reason on earth to doubt him – Amy set up the whole thing. Oh, not to kill John, of course. She wanted him to catch them. Apparently she'd found out about you.'

Dawn rubbed a hand wearily across her forehead.

'We'd no idea…'

'I know. Mark said that as John walked into the bedroom he started to ask her why. Amy then said something about Dawn Lynch and Thornton junior. Then John collapsed. It was over in seconds. We had no chance of reviving him. Freda and Brenda were halfway up the stairs when they heard the noise. Freda was first on the scene. She sent Brenda to phone for an ambulance and then tried to help John but it was all over. Mark said she hit Amy hard across the face – the bruise backs up his story.'

Tears filled Dawn's eyes as she looked at David.

'What a bloody mess. Not only is John dead but his name's going to be dragged through the mud because of me.'

'You're wrong. Only Mark, Amy and I know what happened. As far as the police are concerned, it's death by natural causes, brought on by finding his wife in bed with another man. We can't hide that part but we can hide you.'

'And Lauren? How is she? I've never met her but I regret that.'

'She moved out straight away. She's living with us at the moment. It's only a matter of time before she and Pilot find a home and move in together. She's in a terrible state, crying all the time.'

Dawn stood and moved across to the window.

'I could kill her. I could kill Amy Thornton. She's taken away my reason for living, David. I gave her John for all these years – he would have moved here at the drop of a hat, you know.' She continued to stare out of the window at the raindrops trickling down the windowpane. 'I wouldn't let him. I lied for twenty years. I told him I didn't want a man permanently in my life. That wasn't true, David. I would have taken him in a heartbeat if I hadn't known that he still cared for Amy and loved Lauren to pieces. And now she's taken him from me. I don't know how to carry on.'

She dropped her head and leaned against the window. It felt cold against her skin.

David moved behind her and put his arms around her.

'Come here,' he said. 'I think you need a hug.'

'Yes,' she said and folded herself against his body.

'Me too,' David said. 'Me too.'

The following day David took Dawn to the Chapel of Rest. Josh hadn't wanted to go. He wanted to remember his father as he had always been, full of life.

She said her goodbyes quietly and with dignity.

Amy wanted to bury herself in bed and never surface again. It wasn't only John she had lost, it seemed to be everybody.

She had never given much thought to death. Even after his first heart attack, it had never occurred to her that his death might be premature. She had taken it for granted that he would always be there.

Now she couldn't stand the loneliness. Only five minutes ago she had rung Brenda who had been curt to the point of rudeness.

'I can't talk to you, not yet,' she said and replaced the receiver.

She sat at John's desk and ran her hand along the

surface. In this room she felt closer to him. After Friday he would be gone forever and all she would have left would be this room.

It seemed even emptier without Mark. He had showed up briefly to empty his desk and hadn't spoken to her until he was leaving through the front door.

'I'm going to see David now,' he had said. 'Someone has to know the truth. My key is on the desk.'

With a finality that jarred her, he had closed the door.

She sank her head on to her arms, smelling the lavender in the polish that Carol always used.

'Hi.'

She lifted her head and blinked her eyes to clear the tears.

'Brian.' The word sounded flat on her lips and she tried to smile.

He crossed the room, pulled her gently to her feet and held her close.

'Had enough?'

She nodded.

'Everybody against you?'

Again she nodded.

'Is that because you're a bit of a cow?'

This time she had to smile.

He tilted her head and looked at her.

'That's better. And for what it's worth, I do understand. You found out about John and his lady friend, didn't you?'

'You knew?'

'Guessed. It was only because you tied yourself to that shop and your work that you missed it. So how did you find out?'

'I saw his car at her house and when I found out her

name it all fell together.' She paused for a moment. 'And then I saw his son. He's John's double.'

'And so you took your revenge?'

'I took my revenge. Back-fired a bit, didn't it? Now everybody thinks I'm the wicked witch of the west for seducing Mark. But Mark could have said no.'

'Nobody in their right mind would have said no, sweet one. Especially Mark – you chose well when you picked him to help, however unwittingly he did it. He's been in love with you for years.'

'Don't tell me that – I've enough on my conscience.' She moved away from him and sat down at the desk again.

'There is something puzzling me though – why didn't you give John his tablets? I'm not saying they would have saved him, I think it was over much too quick for them to have any effect... I just wondered why you didn't try.'

'I couldn't find them. I searched his pockets –'

'They were in his pocket, Amy.'

'No – '

'Yes, my lovely Amy. I found them in the bathroom ten minutes or so before you went to your bedroom. I took them to him and he put them in his jacket pocket. I know the tablets were in his pocket, Amy. I didn't see them when we all piled in to try and help. Wonder what happened to them?' He turned and walked out of the study, gently closing the door behind him.

Friday was cold, bleak and rainy. It brought with it a peculiar clinging grey mist and by the time Amy climbed into the first funeral car she was soaked.

Lauren, dressed in black, had barely spoken to her mother and insisted that Pilot sat between them in the car.

David had aged. He couldn't believe that just a few days ago his closest friend was alive and well. He was struggling with coming to terms with the reality of the situation. Pat wasn't a great deal of help. She was sure that Amy had killed and got away with it. Again. And Amy was like a sister.

The church was filled with mourners and Amy stared around in disbelief. She hadn't thought beyond immediate family and friends and was shocked at the numbers standing in the pews. Their eyes followed the coffin down the aisle.

Press and television cameras huddled around in the church grounds.

The vicar spoke of the great loss to the literary world, the great loss to his family, the great loss to his friends; she heard it all and registered nothing.

She couldn't cry. Lauren wept during the whole service. Ken, in his role of supporting the widow, could do little other than give Brenda a shoulder to lean against.

Brenda was unable to cry. She had shed all her tears at Stonebrook. The funeral was a goodbye to the public face of John.

It was only when David read a piece from one of John's books that Amy allowed tears to trickle down her cheeks. It was a short paragraph, just a few sentences. It showed a perception of death.

David looked around at the congregation.

'When John brought *The Son* into my office, almost apologetically, he said it was different. He was right. It had much more depth to it than his previous novels and I considered it to be a superb piece of fiction. It was shortlisted for the Booker prize and although it didn't win, it did more to establish John as a writer of importance than any of his other books.' He paused for a moment to collect his thoughts. 'The paragraph I have just read stood out. John and I discussed it, not as a literary piece of work but as a concept. I know John believed wholeheartedly in what he had written.' He paused again, his eyes sweeping the faces in front of him. 'I'm sure that wherever he is, it is a place made all the better by his presence.'

He moved back to his seat beside Pat, gently touching the coffin as he passed it. Pat squeezed his hand and smiled at him through tears.

'Beautiful,' she whispered.

It was three days after the funeral when Ken told Brenda about the cottage in Delabole. He ached for Brenda; her suffering was too much.

She hadn't only lost John; she had lost Amy too. Ken couldn't help but think there was more to it than Amy taking Mark to bed. Nobody in their right mind would go to bed with someone in the middle of a party. Especially when that party was to celebrate the engagement of the daughter...no, he knew there was more to it. Amy must have engineered her own discovery.

Ken had gone to David, told him what he knew. David had cried like a baby.

Ken waited twenty-four hours before deciding to tell Brenda that John had had a double life.

Brenda listened dry-eyed.

When he had finished speaking, he sat back and waited for something to happen. Her reaction surprised him.

'Poor Amy.'

'What?'

'Poor Amy. She didn't know how to handle it. Have

I let her down so much that she couldn't come and talk to me? She found out that John had someone else and all she could think of was revenge. Which brings us back to Treverick again, doesn't it? I'm sure she never thought for a minute that it would cause a second heart attack… she just probably wanted to give him a taste of his own medicine.'

'Does it change your feelings towards John?' Ken reached out for his wife's hands.

'Not in the slightest. I don't think we know the half of it. I should imagine John had precious little in the way of love from Amy. That is why he turned to the other woman. I'm surprised he managed to cover it up for so long. I always used to worry that he had a soft spot for Linda Chambers… seems silly now in view of this, doesn't it?'

'So what now?'

'Now I go and make my peace with Amy. John Thornton was my son, not my son-in-law. Tell you what, Ken; I'm glad his family has gone back up to Scotland not knowing any of this.'

'Good thing he didn't leave anything in his will to Dawn and Joshua. That would have blown it wide open!'

'I didn't think of that.' Brenda bit her bottom lip pensively. 'I wonder why? He obviously loved them very much.'

She sighed.

'It's such a mess isn't it? I'm going over to Amy's. Would you mind if I went alone?'

'Not at all, duck,' he said, kissing the top of her head. 'Go and do some fence mending.'

He watched her walk down the lane, the arthritis pain now becoming noticeable.

Going back into the lounge he picked up a

photograph of Amy and stared at it for a while before replacing it on the shelf.

'Bitch.' he said and limped across the hallway and into the kitchen.

Dawn heard the knock at the kitchen door and assumed it was Gary.

'Josh,' she called as she passed the bottom of the stairs. 'Are you ready?'

'One minute, Mum.'

Even his voice, now fully mature, was like John's.

She opened the door forcing a smile. Since that unforgettable night every smile was forced.

The smile disappeared fast.

'Oh.'

Amy's own smile was glacial.

'I've brought you something. Actually it's not for you; it's for that son of yours.' She handed the Tesco carrier bag to a stunned Dawn.

It took her a moment or two to recover before she stepped back. 'Please – come in.'

'Thank you.' She inclined her head as though she was bestowing a great favour. Dawn's instinct was to smash her teeth into the back of her throat. Amy's glance around the kitchen was full of scorn.

'So this is where he spent his time, is it?'

'Yes it is.' Dawn didn't have the energy to lose her temper. Besides she'd had more of John than his wife had – clinging to that would get her through.

Amy walked through into the lounge.

'Have you looked in the bag?'

Dawn opened it and glanced inside.

'Josh's books.'

'He left me a letter. His will didn't mention either of

you, so you missed out there. The letter asked me to make sure I handed these books over to Joshua Lynch.'

'His name isn't Joshua Lynch, Mrs Thornton. He said Joshua Thornton.'

Amy shrugged.

'Whatever. Anyway, I'm here to do what he wanted. I swept them off the shelf and put them in that bag. I want nothing more to do with them. Is he here?'

'Josh? Yes, he's getting ready to go out.'

'Is he really John's son? You went with my husband so I presume you put it about a bit.'

'I don't have to answer that. If you met Josh, then you'd know.'

'I've already…' Amy paused afraid of saying too much. Dawn let it slide but made a mental note; so Amy had seen Josh. No wonder she had been upset enough to stage that fiasco at the party.

'And I certainly don't put it about, as you so delicately put it. The way I understand it, that's your way of handling things.' Dawn's voice now matched Amy's coldness.

'Unlike my husband I have never been to bed with any other partner – until the party. And I think that was justified.'

Dawn found it hard to believe what she was hearing.

'Justified? You killed John! How can you justify that? You took away our children's father for the sake of an over-dramatic bit of play-acting. You didn't want Mark, you just wanted to make John suffer.'

'And it worked.' Amy's voice held a note of triumph. 'You see, Ms. Lynch, in spite of this affair, he still loved me.'

'I know,' Dawn saw the insecurity in Amy. 'You and Lauren meant a lot to him and I couldn't take him away from that.' She paused gathering her defenses. 'Every time he asked to move in here, I said no.'

Amy stared at her for a long time and then left the room.

'Wish your son happy reading, won't you?'

CHAPTER FIFTY

August 1989

Things had changed. Treverick could hardly believe his luck.

He hadn't intended John to live past the age of fifty but to die by natural causes before then was a bonus to be pounced upon.

The whole family had been gutted by it. He was now so close within their circle that he shared their distress. On the surface.

The only drawback had been the defection of Lauren. It would have been easier if she had remained at home, but so be it. She would keep for later.

And so the die was finally cast. The culmination of his campaign could now begin.

New clothes – he would buy some new clothes bought specially to impress. And get his hair looked at – it needed a cut and perhaps re-streaking.

He switched on the television to watch a wildlife programme – he would make his starting point, her interests. She liked wildlife programmes; he would like wildlife programmes. And she would like him.

He would make her like him.

CHAPTER FIFTY-ONE

March – August 1991

'I'm leaving.'

'Leaving?' David smiled at her. Dawn hadn't changed at all in the past twenty years – still the same smile, the same glint in her eyes. A touch of grey in her naturally brown hair but that added to the effect of maturity without aging her. It was good to see her back in his office.

'Josh and I are selling up and going to live in the States.'

'You're running away.' His tone was flat.

'Maybe. But why not? Everywhere I go, everything I do – it all reminds me of John and it's not getting any easier.'

'But it's been less than two years, Give it time.'

'There'll never be enough time. You won't talk me out of this. We have a buyer for the cottage who's willing to pay what I've asked for it. And you know John made sure we have more than enough money for the rest of our lives.'

'You'll always have the income from John's Callum books –'

'That's what I want to talk to you about. From now on I want that put into a special fund for Josh. He can have it when he's twenty five, or earlier if I should die before then.'

'Heaven forbid.'

'We would have said that about John, wouldn't we? Having someone close die so young, brings it home. Didn't you find that?'

'I updated my will within a fortnight of his passing. I still think you're making a big mistake though.'

She shook her head.

'I need a fresh start. And there's nothing here for Josh.'

'I told you if he needs a job...'

She laughed.

'I know and it's good of you but Josh only inherited his father's looks, not his gift with words. Josh is more scientifically minded. No, we're going and that's the end of it. Besides I think I need to escape from Amy.'

'Amy?' David raised his eyebrows in surprise.

'She calls in to see me and it's beginning to wear me down.'

'Why haven't you mentioned this before?'

'Because it's nothing to worry about and I can handle it; I just would prefer she didn't.'

'Start at the beginning.' He sighed.

'There's nothing much to tell. She's called a dozen or more times since John died. It's weird – there's so much hostility when she's there and yet it's as if she can't stay away. I'm only just beginning to realise how much she loved him. Perhaps she's trying to understand our relationship and why it lasted so long. I don't know. She stays for about an hour and then goes. She really hates me but she needs to be close to John. She knows Mayflower Cottage was a huge part of his life.'

'How does Josh feel about this?'

She shrugged her shoulders.

'Most of the time, I don't tell him. He calls her Witch Amy. Normally he's out, either at work or with his friends.' She stood and walked over to the coffee machine. 'Coffee?'

He nodded.

'But the old Dawn wouldn't have stood for it. Why don't you just tell her to get lost?'

'Well… I know you won't believe this but I feel sorry for her. Lauren will never be close to her again. I hear Brenda and Ken are now talking to her but she really is pretty much on her own. Does she have any friends?'

'Not many. There's Pat and myself and Brian Lazenby, that television chap, and Mark.'

'Mark? I thought he'd disappeared.'

'He took a break but he's been back for the last six months. He went to see Amy and she actually apologised to him. He goes to see her occasionally. I don't suppose he'll ever really get over her. He'll always be there for her, I'm sure. It's changed him though – he dresses smarter and he's lost a bit of weight. Always liked Mark though and never blamed him for what happened.'

'She never mentions him. She's spoken about Brian a couple of times and I rather got the impression that he's been good for her.'

David nodded.

'He has. I just can't understand why she comes to see you. Perhaps if I had a word with her?'

Dawn held up a hand.

'No, don't. It will all be irrelevant soon anyway. We leave April 1st.'

'Hope that date's not significant,' he answered with a grin that exaggerated the lines on his face.

'All Fools Day… it made me smile as well. It's only three weeks away, so hopefully I won't see her again.'

David walked around his desk and placed a hand on her shoulder. 'You will come and see me before you go? I'll need you to sign some papers Er… does Amy know you've sold the cottage?'

'Shouldn't think so. It was never advertised. I've sold

it to a friend of a friend. Why?'

He ran his hand through his thinning hair.

'So she won't know you're planning to leave?'

Dawn looked puzzled.

'No. Come on David, what's the problem?'

'Don't tell her, Dawn. Just don't tell Amy that you're leaving.'

'David,' she said slowly. 'You're starting to frighten me.'

'Good. Better frightened and alive than brave and dead.'

She stood and picked up her bag.

'Now you're being silly. Can you have the papers ready by the 28th?'

'Certainly. Bring Josh in with you. And remember what I said. Don't let Amy know you're leaving.'

It didn't take David long to recount Dawn's visit.

'So Amy has been stalking her.'

Pat looked sick.

'Did you say anything about Amy?'

'Not in detail. It's difficult isn't it? How can I say my wife believes Amy has murdered in the past? How can I say that, without us looking complete idiots?'

'You have to say something. Amy hates Dawn— I know that because she's told me. What she hasn't said is that she has been seeing her. She's never once mentioned that. Don't you find that a bit scary?'

He nodded.

'I've told Dawn not to mention that she's leaving. We've no proof that Amy killed Sonia Dawes out of spite…'

'She killed John as well. Don't forget that.'

'Not in the eyes of the law.'

'Huh. The law.' Her tone was contemptuous. 'What's the law got to do with it? I know what I know and I'm worried for Dawn. I'd ask them both to come and stay here...'

'No. We can't do that. If Amy goes to see her, she'll find an empty cottage. You can't hide her away every time Amy comes round. She'll soon add two and two together.' He paused for a moment. 'What are we doing, Pat?'

'What do you mean?'

'We're saying that Amy is likely to murder Dawn. Are we crazy or what?'

'Perfectly sane,' was Pat's response. 'I'm surprised she's let it drift along as long as this.'

Amy laughed at him.

'You want to do what?'

'Take you to the cinema. Isn't that what one generally does on a first date?'

'Brian, forgive me for appearing stupid but I don't know what you're talking about.'

He held up a finger.

'Hang on a minute.' He left the lounge returning moments later with a single red rose. Presenting it to her, he smiled. 'I would like to take you out. Is that so presumptive?' He lit a cigarette, puffing nervously at it as he waited for her response.

Amy found herself giggling.

'Not at all. And this is lovely.' She waved the rose around. 'But I don't want to date anybody. I'm too old for that sort of thing.'

'I'm not. And it's been over eighteen months, so I thought...'

She stared at him for a long time.

'Are you serious? You want to date me?' She sounded incredulous.

'Amy – for goodness sake. I'm not asking you to go to bed with me. I've asked you to go to the cinema. Not only do I want to see this particular film, I want to see it with you.'

'Okay.'

'You mean...'

'I mean okay, it's a date.'

'A proper date? Did I get it right?'

She laughed.

'You got it right. It'll cost you dinner before the film though – you might be behaving like a teenager but I'm a bit wiser. Dinner and a film.'

'Done. Want the rest of them now?'

'What?' She looked mystified.

'The rest of the bouquet's in the hall.' He left stubbing out the cigarette in an ashtray. He returned moments later with twenty-three roses.

'They're lovely,' she said, her eyes shining. She stood and kissed his cheek. 'Thank you.'

He placed his hands on her shoulders.

'It's my pleasure,' he said and softly kissed her lips. 'You deserve them.'

Dawn cried most of the way to Heathrow. Her brave words about a new start in the States now seemed like a dream. She was leaving so much behind – memories, friends, Cornwall.

David had been wonderful; he had sorted out last minute problems and was now driving them to the airport.

Pat's tears hadn't helped. She was convinced she'd never see Dawn and Josh again even though Dawn insisted they would come back sometimes. They also would expect visitors from England.

The hardest part had been leaving Mayflower Cottage. John had loved the home he had bought for them and when she had turned the key in the lock for the last time, she had been unable to speak.

It was only as they neared Heathrow and she sensed the excitement building in Josh that she knew she had made the right decision.

She climbed the airliner steps and tapped Josh on the back. Together they turned and waved towards the observation platform. They could see several hands waving but couldn't pick out David from the rest of the tiny figures.

Suddenly it didn't matter. A new life, a new home and shared memories of a love that had lasted half a lifetime.

Amy was happy. For the first time since John's death she thought she could see a glimmer of light at the end of the tunnel.

Brian had taken her out several times. They seemed to be getting on as close friends. She was no longer just John's wife; she was Amy.

He arrived on her doorstep every weekend carrying a gift – she smiled at the memory of the little Pen Delphin rabbit he had presented to her last week. The kiss that followed was something to be relished.

She knew she was starting to soften, starting to forget Treverick because John was no longer there to remind her.

As she raised her hand to knock on the cottage door,

it occurred to her that she didn't really need this anymore. She didn't need to feel close to John anymore. In mid-movement she made the decision not to force herself on Dawn any more. She would live with her memories and look to the future.

The lion's head knocker had changed into an anchor.

The man who answered the door smiled at the beautiful woman standing on his doorstep.

'Hello,' he said. 'Can I help you?'

'Is Mrs Lynch in?' Amy knew what the answer would be. She could see half of the kitchen and it was no longer Dawn's kitchen.

'Mrs Lynch? Are you a friend of hers?'

Even now, when it didn't matter one way or the other, Amy couldn't answer that question.

'Acquaintance.'

'Oh, that explains why you don't know. Mrs Lynch has left.'

For a long moment Amy stared at the man.

'Left? Has she left a forwarding address?'

'She wants all mail forwarding to a Mr. David Farmer.'

'Oh – I know David. I'll get the address from him.'

She made a hurried departure, snagging her tights on a holly bush as she climbed into the car. Angry, she dropped into reverse and backed out of the drive.

The journey to Pat and David's seemed to take forever and she cursed them every step of the way. She couldn't rationalise her feelings; it was nothing to her if Dawn Lynch moved house. But it hurt that Pat hadn't told her.

And now the decision not to see Dawn again had been taken out of her hands. She hit the steering wheel with the heel of her hand in frustration as she turned into

Pat's driveway.

Pat watched from the window as Amy climbed out of her car. She knew what was coming.

'Hi, Amy.'

'Don't you hi Amy me,' she snarled. 'Where's Dawn Lynch?'

'Dawn Lynch? What's it to you?'

'Oh, come on, Pat. Don't play games with me. You know I've been going to see her – she must have told you.'

'I found out three weeks ago,' Pat said. 'She'd already made her plans by then and sold the cottage. I didn't think it concerned anybody but her. If she'd wanted you to know, she would have told you.'

'Does this mean you won't give me her new address?'

'Why do you want it?'

Amy visibly crumpled.

'I don't know,' she sobbed. 'I really don't know. It was the cottage, not her. I needed to feel close to John, and now she's sold it. I would have bought it, Pat. John's soul is there, not at my place. I could feel him there.'

Pat put her arm around her friend and led her into the house.

'So you don't really need to know where she is then.'

Amy shook her head.

'No, I suppose not. It upsets me that she never said a word about any of this.'

'Well, to be perfectly truthful, Amy, I don't have an address, not yet.'

'What do you mean?'

'She's gone to live in America. She said she would write as soon as she found something. Until then she could be anywhere.'

Amy's eyes widened.

'America? But why America? When that old chap said she'd moved I assumed he meant to Wadebridge, or Padstow, somewhere like that.'

'She felt both she and Josh needed to make a new start.'

'I can't believe she didn't tell me. What did she think I would do? Try and stop her?'

'I don't think anyone's ever managed to stop Dawn Lynch doing exactly what she wanted. No, I really don't know why she didn't tell you. But why are we talking on the doorstep? Are you coming in?'

Amy turned and walked back to her car.

'No… no, I'm going home.' She climbed in the driver's seat and then lowered the passenger window to speak to Pat. 'By the way,' she called. 'I've finally decided what to do with John's Ferrari. Do you think Pilot and Lauren would like it?'

'I'm sure they would!' Pat gasped. 'They're coming over for dinner later – why don't you join us and give it to them then?'

'Do you mind if Brian comes?'

'Not at all. You two an item?'

Amy laughed.

'You sound definitely juvenile. Bye.' She raised the window, slipped into first gear and drove away leaving Pat to stare thoughtfully after her.

She hadn't answered. But the faint tinge of a blush in her cheeks had said it all.

Brian found Amy in the study reading through one of John's manuscripts.

'What's that?''

She looked up and smiled. She was enjoying having

him around.

'It's *Spider Web*, John's incomplete book.'

'Is it good?'

'What do you think? Did he ever write a bad one?'

'No – it was a stupid question, I suppose. It's a pity we'll never know the twist at the end of it. That was always John's strength, his twist endings.' He put out his cigarette in the ashtray he was carrying.

'But I do know it,' she said softly.

'You've found a synopsis?'

She shook her head.

'No, John never used one. He always said it was a complete waste of time writing one because he never stuck to the planned story line. He always let the story develop in its own way. No, it's not a synopsis, it's me.'

'Am I being thick? I don't understand.' Brian looked at her, aware of her excitement. He wanted to kiss her quite desperately.

'It's me. The ending is in me. I'm going to take up John's pen and see where it leads me. I'm going to finish this book, take it to David and see what happens.'

CHAPTER FIFTY-TWO

November 1991

'Amy? Can you come into the office sometime this week?'

Amy smiled down the line at David's voice.

'Yes – have you read it?'

'I have and we need to talk. But not on the telephone. When can you come in?'

'Not today. I'm going to Optimum this afternoon. I'm there for the full day on Thursday. Is Wednesday any good?'

'Two o'clock?'

'Fine. See you then. Erm… how's Lauren?'

'You haven't seen them?' There was surprise in David's voice.

'Not since they said they didn't want the Ferrari. My daughter doesn't like me very much.'

'Oh, I'm sure she does…'

'Don't talk platitudes, David. You've never been very good at that. So how is she?'

'She's fine; no problems. What will you do with the car?'

'It's done. I sold it. Didn't get what it was worth, of course, which was why I wanted to give it to them. I presume Lauren thought I was trying to buy my way back into their lives.'

David felt uncomfortable. Amy had virtually repeated word for word everything that Lauren had said.

'You are in her life, Amy, whatever she may think. You brought her up.'

Amy gave a brittle laugh.

'Did I? I seem to remember John and Brenda

organising things so that I had very little to do with Lauren. Still, it's all in the past. She's turned out to be a daughter I'm proud of. Anyway, I'll see you Wednesday.'

She replaced the receiver thoughtfully. He hadn't said a word about whether he liked it or not and she ran a hand through her hair with a gesture of frustration.

Damn him.

She pulled a sheet of paper towards her. She had been running a plotline through her head for some time and she began to make further notes on the main character, expanding him. He was already very real to her.

She wanted to write. Finishing John's book had showed her that. The one thing they hadn't taught her was how to use a computer and she stared at it with distaste.

She, like her late husband, preferred the feel of a pencil in her hand. She recognised that if she did write a novel under her own steam she would have to have it typed. Unless...

She picked up the receiver again and dialed Mark's number.

'Hi.'

'Amy?' She heard a note in his voice that was part panic and part joy.

'Listen, I've had a thought. Are you still not working?'

'No. John's bequest gave me a breathing space. I'll have to give it serious thought soon, though. Why? Do you know of something?'

'Mmmm. Would you like to work for me?'

There was a long, drawn out silence.

'Mark? You still there?'

'I'm still here.' He sounded guarded. 'What do you mean? I'd be absolutely no good at sticking flowers on furniture!'

Her laughter was infectious.

'I didn't think for one minute that you would be! No, I've finished *Spider Web*.'

'Finished it? Did you know the ending?'

'Did you?' She was intrigued.

'Yes. John was near enough to the end of it to have worked it out. We usually discussed from about half way through.'

'Well, I didn't know it, so I created my own ending. David's got it now and as of yet I don't know what he thinks. I'm seeing him in a couple of days. But that's irrelevant really. I have an idea bubbling away for a novel, a different type. More of a saga. And just like John, I feel happier using a pencil. If you want the job, it's yours.'

'Can I think about it?'

'Mark, don't be scared. I think we have a reasonable relationship now and I know I'll be able to work with you.'

'You're right. When do you want me to start?'

'Tomorrow?'

'Fine, I'll be there at nine o'clock, Amy – I'll look forward to it.'

She felt restless. Brian had returned to London that afternoon and she missed him. She even missed the smell of cigarette smoke around the place. She knew that she was falling in love and she felt a sense of shock. This love was different. She wanted to be with him, to hold him, to share secrets with him; she had no idea if he felt the same.

A sudden whim made her get into the car and drive into Padstow. She parked on the road and walked along to sit on the harbour wall. The moon was bright, exactly the same as when she and John had first started seeing each other in their teens. She remembered how they had joked about it being a straight path of moonbeams to the United States – funny how it had been Dawn in the end who had taken the moonbeam path.

She pictured John and found that his image came swiftly to mind. What was difficult was remembering how he felt, the essence of him. And sitting on that harbour wall at eleven o'clock at night, completely and utterly alone, she wondered whether it had ever been love. She wiped away a tear from her cheek and stood up.

She had to talk to Brian.

'Brian? It's me.'

'Hello you.' She could hear the fuzziness of sleep in his voice. 'Shouldn't you be in bed?'

'No. I need to talk. I've been out, down into Padstow, and I've been thinking. About you. About us.'

There was a long silence.

'Oh?' She heard the sound of his lighter as he lit a cigarette.

'Don't just say oh! You're not making this easy.'

'If you're going to say you think we should end our relationship, I don't want to make it easy.' He sighed.

She laughed, her mind feeling free.

'No, quite the opposite. I think I'm about to bare my soul, so will you wake up?'

'I'm awake, I'm awake! Is something wrong, Amy?' She could hear the concern in his voice and loved him for it.

'Yes. Something is wrong. I think I'm about to declare my undying love.'

Again there was a long silence. She panicked.

'Brian?'

'I'm here, Amy. Just say it. Just say I love you.'

'I love you.'

He whistled down the line.

'Phew – I thought you couldn't do that. I honestly thought that you wouldn't be able to say that.'

'Can you say it?'

'Sweetheart, I can shout it from the rooftops!' he laughed. 'Amy Thornton, I love you!'

'Then why haven't you told me before, you moron? Why make me wait?'

'I had to wait for you. I had to make sure you could put John to one side. I don't expect to take his place, I expect you to love me for what I am, for who I am, not because John is no longer there. I think now that you're ready.'

'I'm ready.' She was aware of what she was being coerced into admitting. 'But there's a lot about me that you don't know.' She felt nervous and moved her frog collection on a table nearby into regimented lines.

She talked quickly and jerkily.

'My past is complex. When I see you, I'll tell you. I have to tell you, so that you'll understand. I have to tell you everything.'

'Hey, hey! Don't frighten me. And whatever it is, it won't matter. I haven't just fallen in love with you, you know. I never imagined myself being able to tell you. Look, I can't get to you until the weekend because we've got a hectic week – I'm off to Scotland tomorrow. We'll do all the talking we need when I get there. Are you all right?'

'I'm fine. I love you so much. You've been good for me. I just hope you'll still feel the same after this weekend.'

'I promise you I will. Now sleep well, sweetheart. I'm so glad you rang, it was worth waking up for.' He blew a kiss down the line.

'Love you,' she said and replaced the receiver. She stood for a long time just looking at the handset. Before she moved away, all the little frogs had been put back into their random positions.

'I saw Amy last night.'

Ken looked up in surprise.

'Where?' Amy very rarely went anywhere after dark.

Malcolm pushed the fork into the ground before speaking again. 'Sitting on the harbour wall.'

Ken was intrigued now.

'Doing what?'

'Just sitting.' He levered the fork and bent to pick out the potatoes. 'She was there for quite a long time.'

'Did she say anything?'

'She didn't see me. I went down to do a spot of fishing off the end of the harbour – I reckon she was there for about half an hour. I was pretty close to her but she couldn't see me round the concrete post.' He straightened and moved on to the next plant. 'I'm pretty sure she was crying though.'

And am I supposed to feel sorry for her? Ken thought angrily.

The most evil woman he'd ever met in his life was sitting crying on a harbour wall and he was supposed to do something about it?

'I'd better tell Brenda,' he said.

'Of course I'm all right, Brenda.' Amy smiled at her mother. 'Couldn't be better actually. Why?'

'Oh, you know…' Brenda felt uncomfortable. 'Just worried, that's all. Me being a silly old woman, I expect.'

She picked up her cup of coffee and sipped it. The

kitchen of Amy's home had undertaken a transformation in recent months. She viewed the oak cupboards with something bordering on envy.

'I love this kitchen,' she said and smiled at her daughter as she skillfully changed the subject.

'I'm having the entire place done. Sort of 'out with the old' type of thing.'

Brenda stared at her, suddenly aware of the difference. Amy actually looked happy.

'Why?' The question was blunt and Brenda knew it.

'Because things are happening in my life and I feel as if I want to go forward.'

'What things?'

'Brian. We... care for each other. And other things – I've almost sold the business.'

Brenda stared at Amy.

'I don't believe it! You've lived for that business...'

'Not any more. It's time to get out. I was doing very little of the work anyway so I've sold it on the understanding that the Amy Thornton of Optimum name is kept.' She laughed. 'The buyer, a nice chap from Derby, didn't object.'

'So what will you do with your time now?' Brenda felt a little dazed. This was a new Amy.

'Write.'

'Write?' She felt a cold shudder run through her remembering the contents of Amy's early stories.

'John didn't have a monopoly on pen and ink, you know.' Amy realised she sounded harsh and softened her words. 'I've just finished off John's last novel. David has it and he wants to see me tomorrow. I'm not sure what that means – it could be good, it could be bad. It doesn't matter. I know I can write, have always known it. And now I feel as if I've come out from under a great shadow.

I won't write under the name of Thornton either. I'll be Amelia Andrews.'

Just for a moment Brenda felt happy. Amelia Andrews had been such a lovely child. It was when that child had become Amy Andrews and then Amy Thornton that all the problems had started.

'That's good,' she said quietly, 'I like the name change.'

She stood and took the two mugs over to the sink. Amy picked up the tea towel and smiled at her mother.

'Do you approve?'

'It's not my place to approve or disapprove. I only ever wanted you to be happy. I presume Brian is responsible for this change in you?'

Amy nodded.

'I love him. Not in the same way I loved John. It's different. He's very caring, very considerate, treats me like I'm special.'

'Does he know about...?'

'Treverick?' Amy said the name quickly, almost spitting it out. 'Not yet. I'm telling him this weekend.'

She finished drying the mugs and put them away in the cupboard.

In disbelief, Brenda watched Amy perform the simple task of putting away the tea towel. She draped it over a hanger and walked away. No meticulous folding. Brenda felt a sense of relief flood through her and almost cried aloud with happiness.

This she had to report to Freda and as soon as possible.

'Of course we're going to take the book.' David smiled as he watched the tension ebb from Amy's face. 'You did an excellent job on it.'

'Well, I think I ought to tell you that it wasn't the intended ending. I didn't know until yesterday but apparently Mark knew John's plans for it and they're nothing like mine!'

'They wouldn't be.'

'I'll ignore that,' she said with a laugh. 'So – can I show you this?' She waved a sheaf of papers at him.

'What is it?'

'My next book.'

'Can you leave it with me?'

'Yes, it's all on disc. Mark saw to that.'

'Mark's back with you?'

'I needed him.' She said it while challenging him with her eyes. 'I can't work computers and what's more, I don't want to. He can.'

David shook his head from side to side.

'You never cease to amaze me, Amy Thornton. You humiliate him in the worst way possible, lose him his job, lose him his girlfriend and still he comes back to you.'

She stood and picked up her briefcase.

'You'll let me know what you think of that synopsis?'

'Within twenty-four hours.'

'Good. And just think about this, you sanctimonious schweinhund. I might have humiliated Mark and done the things you've accused me of but on that night, for a few seconds he was the happiest man alive. See you, David.'

She walked out of his office with a casual swing of her hips. Pausing in the doorway, she turned and blew him a kiss.

'Bitch,' he said and they laughed together.

'Love to Pat and the kids,' she called taking the sunshine out of his office with her when she went.

Ken knew he was drunk. Go down to the pub for an hour she had said. Freda's coming over and we can't have a proper natter if you're there. Go and take Malcolm for a pint.

But Malcolm had left at nine o'clock, not wanting to be away from his family. With Maria expecting their third child any day he wanted to be at home.

And so Ken had stayed in the Nail Makers pub, reflecting on how his life had changed; the plans he had made were all reaching fruition. The cake icing was a loving and happy marriage. So why did he feel like drinking himself to oblivion?

Amy.

Brenda had been excited when she had returned from seeing her daughter. He was unable to accept that there could ever be a new Amy. His dreams still occasionally featured the sight of her long legs, the pubic mound exquisitely outlined against the white silk panties when she raised her skirt to him in the glass house; the goading as she had offered herself to him on the dirt floor.

He couldn't believe that any woman could do that and then suddenly become an angel in disguise.

He downed the last of his beer and left the pub. He staggered slightly as he lurched against the doorframe and then tried to pull himself together.

'Straight line, owd duck,' he said to himself aloud. He couldn't walk in a straight line if he'd had parallel bars to guide him.

He made it to the bottom of the lane without falling over and then looked across the fields towards Amy's house. Without consciously knowing why, he set off towards it.

He stopped at the gates and moved into the shadow

of a huge laurel at the bottom of the drive. Suddenly the downstairs light went off and then he saw the bedroom light come on.

Amy's bedroom, where she had made love to Mark.

She stood in the window looking out for several moments. Then she reached up and closed the curtains, stretching the thin fabric of her blouse tautly across her breasts.

'Bitch, bitch, bitch,' he cursed, then unzipped his trousers and masturbated into the laurel bush.

CHAPTER FIFTY-THREE

May 1992

Amy sipped constantly at her brandy as she told Brian of her childhood. She watched his face carefully, searching for signs of revulsion. She saw no change in his expression.

He said nothing until she finished speaking.

'And that's what you've spent this week worrying about?'

She nodded and dropped her head. She wasn't sure she could look him in the eye.

'Why? Didn't you think I would understand? None of it was your fault, Amy. None of it.'

'But it was. I was alone on that field. We drill it into children never to speak to strangers, to scream and what did I do?'

'But it wasn't like that in... what, 1952? Nobody worried about such stuff back then. That's why it was so easy for Treverick to get to you. It wasn't your fault and it wasn't your mum or dad's fault. You were just in the wrong place at the wrong time. It could have been any little girl.'

'No.' She shook her head. 'No, it was always me. He told the police that he'd had me marked out because I was so beau... pretty.'

'Come here.' He held out his arms and she sat by him. 'Well,' he said with a smile, 'now that you've told me all that, at least we can sit together.'

'I couldn't sit next to you. I had to be able to see your face.'

'And?'

'And you didn't show a damn thing. Didn't you feel

anything?' she asked.

'Anger. A very deep anger. He was an animal and should have been treated as such. Prison was too good for him. It has changed my feelings towards you though.' He felt her stiffen and he pulled her closer to him. 'Now I not only love you, I feel more protective towards you. I don't want to leave you. I don't want to go back to London and leave you here. But I don't want to ask you to move to London to be with me. You'd be stifled there.'

'I couldn't live anywhere but here,' she said simply.

'I know. We'll work something out. I'm here until Tuesday if that's okay with you.'

'You know it is. Kiss me, Brian.'

He bent his head and traced the outline of her lips with his index finger before placing his lips on hers.

They separated and she moaned.

'I love you,' she whispered. 'For the first time in my life I feel – oh, I don't know – feelings.'

He held her away from him and looked at her.

'But you were married to John for all those years. Are you trying to tell me you didn't love him?'

She shook her head.

'No, it wasn't like that. I couldn't love him. It was totally unfair of me; I married him knowing I could never give myself fully. I was too twisted. But somehow you've released me. I don't understand it. I'm not even sure I want to understand it. You're a very different sort of person to John – he gave in to me. You'll never do that. Perhaps that's been the key all along.'

He kissed her once more, very gently.

'Go to bed, my love. You look drained. Tomorrow we'll start our lives. Yours and mine. Come on.' He stood and then pulled her to her feet.

'We could start our lives tonight,' she whispered. 'Will you come with me? To bed?'

He held her slightly away from him and looked at her, running his eyes from the top of her head to her feet. She felt a tingling, erotic sensation wash over her.

'That depends on the answer to my next question,' he said huskily.

'Will you marry me?'

Amy gasped and nodded. 'Yes.'

Without speaking he pulled her to him. Holding her tightly to his body she could feel his erection; she knew he wanted her as badly as she wanted him.

His next words surprised her and made her pull away from him.

'Then I thank you for the wonderful offer but no, I won't go to bed with you. I ache for you, Amy, always have, but our marriage is the most important thing that's ever happened to me. I want to wait for our wedding night to hold you properly, to make love to you. And,' he said with a grin, 'I think that's the most difficult thing I've ever done in my life.'

She laughed as she moved away.

'Then I'll not stand too close. You know, Brian, Brenda is going to be shocked. I think she and Freda decided some time ago that you had gay tendencies.'

He rubbed the front of his trousers, a rueful expression on his face.

'I think you can reassure them on that point. Now go to bed, Amy, before I change my mind.'

'So you can't be tempted?' A wicked gleam was in her eyes.

'Yes, I can. That's why I'm saying go to bed. I'll bring you a hot chocolate if you like. I'll stand in the doorway and throw it to you.'

'Okay,' she said and slowly began to unbutton her blouse, one button at a time. She climbed the stairs knowing he was watching every movement. At the top it fell from her shoulders and she heard him groan. She turned around and snapped open the front fastening of her bra. From that distance she heard the sharp intake of his breath.

'Hot chocolate,' she called with a laugh. 'Put bromide in yours.'

'So what do you really think?'

Freda shook her head.

'I don't know. I mean, I do like Brian but I thought you said he was gay.'

'If he's marrying Amy, he can't be gay, can he?' Brenda looked puzzled.

'You two sound like a pair of old hens,' Ken said with a chuckle from his armchair.

'Well, clever clogs, do you think he's gay?'

'When I lived in Rotherham, I knew a couple of gays. We called 'em queers, not gays. But no, I don't think Brian Lazenby's got a homosexual bone in his body. Just because he's quiet and well-mannered, and he's not been married before, none of that means anything. That's probably what's appealed to Amy.'

Freda looked at her sister-in-law's husband with interest.

'You sound as if you approve of this marriage.'

He put down his newspaper.

'I'm part of this conversation whether I like it or not, aren't I? Yes, I approve. If it keeps Amy off Bren's back, I approve.'

'Ken!' Brenda looked at her husband, surprise etched on her face.

'Sorry, love, but she's been a burden for all the years I've known you. She's a middle-aged woman now, Bren, and you should let go. Let Brian have her. Maybe John was wrong for her. Brian does seem very different – he's older for a start. I think they'll be fine. Now, can I read my paper?'

Freda and Brenda looked at each other.

'Shall we shut up?' Brenda asked, and Freda nodded.

'There's not much point in our saying anything. Have they set a date for the wedding?'

'She didn't say but I got the impression it won't be long. She seems to love him very much.' Brenda spoke with a touch of awe in her voice. 'Oh, I do hope that she'll finally find some peace in her life.'

Pat and David were witnesses at the marriage of Amy Thornton and Brian Lazenby. No one else was there.

They had decided to keep it simple, quiet and had sworn Pat and David to secrecy.

'If we didn't need witnesses, you two wouldn't be going either,' Amy joked.

'Well, I think it's a bit naff,' Pat had responded. 'We thought we'd have a good old knees up and here you are not even telling your mum and Ken. Sure you can't just get married over the phone?'

'If we could, we would. No, just be there at eleven o'clock, on the 15th.'

The sun had shone gloriously. Amy looked at Brian, immaculately dressed in a pale grey suit, his blonde streaked hair hanging low over his forehead feeling a surge of love for him. He had turned her life around and she knew that mixed in with the love was a sense of gratitude.

Amy had never looked more beautiful. The years hadn't detracted from her appearance. Her pale blue dress and her blonde hair sparkled. Brian felt true pride as he escorted her down the steps of the Registry Office.

'Well, Mrs Lazenby,' he said, kissing her for the second time as his wife, 'how do you feel?'

'Happy,' she said. 'Very, very happy.' The confetti fell over them in a cascade.

'Oy – pack it in! Didn't I say I wanted a quiet affair?'

'Confetti doesn't make much noise,' Pat said, smiling at her friend. She could hardly believe the difference; Amy had changed so much. It was ironic that it had happened when John was no longer around.

'What are your plans now?' Pat asked.

'We're going home.'

'Oh no, you're not.' Pat was adamant. 'We've booked a table at the Marquis and it's on us. Come on; don't let the champagne get warm.'

They climbed into the new BMW David had decided he couldn't live without and drove to the restaurant.

'Drink as much as you like, you three. David's allowing me to drive. Good of him, isn't it?' she said drily.

They were still laughing two hours later as they left the restaurant.

Pat dropped them off at home. Finally they were left to themselves.

'Mrs Lazenby, I love you.'

'And I love you, Mr. Lazenby. Thank you for a wonderful day.'

'You look beautiful,' he was rewarded with a smile of such love he felt warmed by it. 'Now, we have to tell people.'

She nodded, reluctantly.

'I know. I'll ring Ken and Brenda. Will you go through into the study and tell Mark?'

She lifted the receiver and dialed. Brenda answered. Amy hesitated briefly before speaking.

'I've got something to tell you...Mum.' Brenda felt the tears come into her eyes. It had been years since Amy had called her anything other than Brenda. 'I've changed my name.'

'You've... oh!'

'We're married. Very quietly, no fuss, with Pat and David as witnesses.'

And now Brenda really did want to cry.

'You're wicked, Amy Thornton,' she chided gently.

'Amy Lazenby now.'

'Are you happy?'

Amy looked at Brian, now standing with Mark at his side.

'Couldn't be happier.'

'Well, we're absolutely delighted for you both but we can't let today go unmarked. Will you come over for dinner?'

'I'll just check with Brian. Can you make it a light supper? We've just had a huge meal at the Marquis.' Brian got the gist and nodded. 'We'll come over in a bit. What time are we eating?'

'About seven. I'll get out the champagne.'

'Half a glass for me. My head hurts already. See you later then.'

She replaced the receiver and turned to Brian and Mark. Mark spoke before she could say anything.

'Many congratulations, Amy. And you, Brian. Now I'm going home. I'll catch up tomorrow. You need time on your own.'

He kissed Amy on the cheek and shook Brian's hand before returning to the study. Once inside he leaned his back against the door and closed his eyes. He tried to stop the tear but it rolled down his cheek anyway.

'Be happy, Amy, be happy,' he whispered.

Amy moved towards Brian.

'We're going over to Stonebrook later. What shall we do until then?' She put her arms around his waist and laid her head against his chest.

'Oh no, you don't, young lady. I've waited for my wedding night for all this time and it will be a wedding night, not a wedding afternoon.'

'Don't know if I'm sober enough anyway.' She giggled. 'Shall I get changed and we can go for a walk? It'll sober us up before we start drinking again at Mum's.'

'Good idea. We'll go round by the woods and end up at Stonebrook. How does that sound?'

'It sounds fine. We couldn't have taken the car anyway – I'm not sure either of us could point it in a straight line.'

The sun was glaringly hot as they followed the line of the stream. They behaved like teenagers sharing kisses behind trees.

Brenda spotted them walking down the lane from the direction of the woods and went out to meet them, dragging Ken away from re-potting cabbage plants.

'Many, many congratulations,' she said and kissed them both.

Ken held out his hand to Brian.

'Hope you know what you've taken on, pal,' he said. 'She's her mother's daughter, you know.'

They laughed and went into Stonebrook.

'You don't look much like a bride,' Brenda said,

casting a critical eye over her daughter's grass-stained jeans.

'She did this morning,' Brian said, a smile on his face. 'She looked beautiful. And still does now,' he added.

'Come and sit down,' Brenda said leading them into the lounge. 'Ken? The drinks?'

'Coming up,' he said and handed round the champagne.

They told Ken and Brenda about the service and their walk in the woods – about their day, about their happiness.

At eleven o'clock, the newlyweds left. It was a dark, moonless night. Amy shivered and moved closer to Brian.

'You're not cold, are you?'

She shook her head.

'No, it's just so dark. Hold me, Brian.'

'Willingly,' he laughed. 'I think I'd better hold onto you tightly, you're a bit wobbly.'

'Too much champagne. This walk will sober me up.'

'Think you can climb the wall?'

'Why on earth would I want to climb the wall?'

'Humour me, Amy. I want to show you something.'

'Kiss me first.'

He bent his head and pressed his lips firmly against hers.

'Wow!' she said, coming up for air. 'I think I can jump the wall now.'

He helped her over the wall and they began to walk across the playing fields.

'What are you showing me?'

'My wedding gift to you.'

She thought for a moment.

'You've bought some land...'

He smiled at her.

'No guessing. All will become clear.'

She stumbled a little and blinked to clear her vision. She had drunk too much champagne.

The blow to her back knocked her to the ground, winding her. She gasped and then felt her jeans being savagely pulled away from her.

'Brian!' she screamed trying to fight him off. Her fingers locked into the hair falling forward on to his forehead and she briefly felt the scar of an old bullet wound. The silk panties cut into her as he ripped them away and she could feel his huge penis on her leg.

'Brian, stop it,' she moaned, 'stop…'

The penetration was swift and painful. He clamped a hand over her mouth and she tasted the rankness of cigarettes; she was six years old again.

This time she fought back. The six-year-old little girl had grown up. She pulled on his hair and the pain of the punch to her face almost made her give up. She struggled to move away from him but he held her tightly, forcing her down and rendering her incapable of movement. She screamed as he gathered her hair in his hands and pulled her head to the ground once more. His hands went around her throat and he constricted and squeezed her perfect, beautiful neck until she felt the world darken then blacken. He bent his head and savagely bit her breasts but she knew nothing. He rammed into her so hard he felt her body move. Her lifeless body. Over and over again he took her. And he spoke…

'Beautiful, beautiful, beautiful…'

Brenda pushed home the bolt on the door and turned to Ken.

'Well, I think she's finally found the right man,' she said with a smile. 'They're a beautiful couple, aren't they?'

EPILOGUE

In the summer of 1992, Amy was buried with John; the name on the headstone was Amy Thornton.

Ronald Treverick disappeared again. Again, the family was assured he wouldn't come back. He had done what he came to do and they need not fear. Meanwhile they would keep looking for him until they found him.

He had taken Amy. But not Lauren…

THE END

WWW.BLOODHOUNDBOOKS.COM